MICHAEL K. TUCKER

For Lorraine May all your endings be Peaceful Michael

PEACEFUL ENDINGS

THE NOPOSAM PROJECT

Outskirts Press, Inc.
Denver, Colorado

This is a work of fiction. The events and characters described herein are imaginary and are not intended to refer to specific places or living persons. The opinions expressed in this manuscript are solely the opinions of the author and do not represent the opinions or thoughts of the publisher.

Peaceful Endings
The NOPOSAM Project

v3.0

Outskirts Press, Inc.
http://www.outskirtspress.com

ISBN: 978-1-4327-2739-0 - Paperback
ISBN: 978-1-4327-2765-9 - Hardback

PRINTED IN THE UNITED STATES OF AMERICA

… # ACKNOWLEDGEMENTS

There are many people who helped in the making of my first book.

David Howard, my first editor whose great suggestions at the beginning, guided me in the right direction. Ellen Taylor, who kept my writing straight so I sounded intelligent. My writing group, *The Writer's Circle*, whose excellent suggestions for Chapter 20 worked out nicely. Renee Bergstrom, a friend of many years, who boosts my ego. And special friend, Pat Cabrol, who still advocated finishing the book, even after reading just a rough copy.

Thanks to all of you. I really do appreciate all the advice, support, and suggestions. You helped me take my idea for a novel, and make it into a work that I can be proud to say is mine.

My last thank you goes to my sister, Marilynn *Two N's* Tucker, for all the invaluable help she gave me. Even though I pestered her with lots and lots of questions, she still found the time to help me during her busy schedule, and never complained once: or at least not in my presence. Thanks again, Marilynn. You get the first copy. Autographed, of course. But don't think I'm going to die, just to make it valuable!

* * *

This book is dedicated to my mother, Mary Tucker, who passed before she got to see Peaceful Endings completed. As a copy editor and reporter for a local Rhode Island newspaper for many years, she could never read any piece of work I gave her without editing and critiquing it. It was part of her very fabric to do that. It always drove me nuts that she couldn't just read it for the pleasure and value of it, although I did appreciate the guidance from someone with more experience than I. And I know that were she alive today, she would send my novel back to me with sticky notes on the pages she felt needed attention.

* * *

Author note: When reading *Peaceful Endings*, you will notice my sense of humor sprinkled throughout. I wrote this book to entertain you, and hopefully take you on a journey that at the end you will say, "WOW!". Turn the page, to start that journey.

Lindsey Palmer stood at Cassandra's side; tears flowed freely from her bloodshot eyes. Father Donnavan, from St. Mary's Church up the street, was also at the sick girl's bedside, administering last rites. It was quick and sloppy. He had many others to administer to at the hospital and his mind wasn't functioning as acutely as usual. His hand had rubbed away sweat from his brow many times before he had finished the ritual.

He drew a fatigued breath as he turned to face her. "Bless you child. Go in peace." Lindsey wasn't Catholic, but she still crossed herself. The priest, bent shoulders sagging from his heavy burden, walked out of the room, trying to suppress a nasty cough, while swiping beads of moisture from his forehead. He would be dead, like many others that day, before he finished the next one.

PROLOGUE

July 21, 1969
B.J. Stockton Military Base
Virginia

Captain Thomas Uxbridge followed a powerfully built Sergeant down a narrow brightly lit corridor with shiny floors. The clacking of their shoes echoed up and down the corridor, whose walls were covered with discolored photos from the forties and fifties, when the base functioned as a training site.

Some of the yellowing pictures were of young men marching on open grass fields, while others were pilots waving from cockpits of single-engine planes waiting on newly paved tarmacs to take off. But the majority of pictures were of soldiers, either taking target practice or running obstacle courses.

After rounding a sharp corner the tall, meticulously dressed Uxbridge glanced side to side, peering into rooms as he passed. What he saw were men in lab jackets doing various tests on male subjects.

"What goes on here now?" he asked.

The Sergeant did not respond, instead walking steadfastly with eyes forward, intent only in leading them to their destination. As they rounded a second corner Captain Uxbridge noticed more of the same rooms with diverse testing. From what he could see, both civilian and army personnel were being given injections by men in white coats, while others conducted reflex tests and jotted notes on clipboards.

When they reached the end of the corridor the Sergeant stopped at the door leading into conference room 201. "Your seat is the one in the middle, Sir," he said in a raspy voice that hinted at years of smoking. Opening the door he ushered the officer inside. "The meeting will convene shortly."

Captain Uxbridge walked across the room till the floor came to a step down. Pausing at the edge, he guessed the drop to be about eight inches. His seat, a wooden stool, had been strategically placed inside a rectangle of ten black high-back leather chairs dead center of the room. From behind, came the soft clicking of a shutting door. He turned his head back. The burly Sergeant was gone. He drew a deep breath and stepped down, then walked to his chair. Only after sitting did he realize that the chairs above him had been built on a wooden riser, putting them substantially higher.

He sat rigid on the stool with a palm placed on either thigh over perfectly creased pants, and scanned the room with untrusting eyes, especially making note of the more recent pictures on the walls. These were photos of soldiers dressed in suits much like what astronauts wear, while others wore what appeared to be odd-looking aluminum foil suits.

The ticking of a clock with bold numbers, akin to the ones used in public schools in the fifties, resonated loudly around the room and in his head. With each passing tick the officer grew more apprehensive. Not just because he didn't know why he'd been summoned from his base in Kentucky, but because he had the uneasy feeling he was being watched.

His gaze wandered out through a wide window directly in his line of sight, settling on a silver cylindrical object that lay on the ground some twenty feet away. It was about thirty feet in length, five feet high and four feet wide, with six-inch round windows located at opposite ends. There was no visible door, so he assumed it was on the other side.

He wondered what it was used for. Storage container? Possible, but not probable. Some type of fuel tank? But why would there be windows? Leaning forward, he studied it with eyes that desperately wanted to see inside.

The doorknob turned and his focus snapped back inside. Entering the room was a mixture of suits and highly decorated military officers of numerous ranks.

He watched the men choose chairs in an order that appeared to be by design. Even at six foot four, Captain Uxbridge found that the encircling chairs placed him in a disadvantaged position of looking up about a foot. He remained rigid in his chair, facing forward with unblinking eyes.

The gathering ignored the officer sitting in the middle of the circle, instead breaking into conversations in groups of twos and threes, and continuing for several minutes until a man in a dark navy suit sitting in front of the captain cleared his throat several times.

When there was silence, he spoke to the faces looking back at him: "Thank you for coming, gentlemen." Glancing left and then right he continued, "I know that it was short notice and that many of you were inconvenienced. However, if this situation plays out the way I think it will, then we will all be in agreement that it was worth it."

There was a splattering of *you're welcomes* and a few *my pleasures*.

The captain remained facing forward.

"Relax, Captain," said the man in the Blue Suit, who had spoken first.

Uxbridge put his hands together in his lap.

"At ease, Captain Uxbridge," said an older general on Blue Suit's left.

The captain's shoulders relaxed and he crossed his ankles.

"You just needed to use the right lingo, Myers," said the general, winking.

"Thank you, John," said Myers, a man with rich black

hair and a round tanned face. Again he cleared his throat, then said, "You're wondering why you've been summoned here, Captain?"

"Yes, Sir," said Uxbridge.

"You know the meaning of covert, Captain?" asked the general, who had a face and red nose that suggested lots of drinking.

"Certainly, Sir."

"Then you understand that what is said here, stays here."

"Understood."

"Before we begin, know that I have high hopes for you, Captain. Don't disappoint."

"I won't, Sir," said the confident officer, despite not knowing what he was answering for.

"We're going to ask some questions," said Myers. "Please be honest. We want to know your true feelings."

Looking up at Myers from his compromised viewpoint, the captain replied soberly, "I always speak the truth, Sir."

"Always?" asked the general known as John. "Even when a situation calls for lying."

"I don't understand, Sir."

"Suppose you're in a situation where if you tell the truth innocent bystanders could get seriously hurt, maybe even die," said a husky voice from behind. "Would you still tell the truth?"

Spinning around to face the questioner, Uxbridge said, "My duty is to follow standard procedure. Whatever happens, happens. I will not deviate."

"What if a close relative or friend were involved," said a Suit with black rimmed glasses and a high voice several seats to his left. "Wouldn't you make an exception for them?"

Uxbridge stared deeply into the man's eyes. Quickly unnerved, the man shifted uneasily in his seat. In a straight face the Captain said flatly, "There are no exceptions in my world, Sir."

"Do you have family, Captain?" asked a monotone Blue Suit from behind.

"No, Sir, I don't," said Uxbridge, twisting his body around to see behind. "I was an orphan. Never knew my parents. They died in a plane crash when I was an infant. Later I shifted from foster home to foster home, but never got attached to anyone."

"Do you love your country, Captain?" asked Myers.

"Yes, Sir."

"Would you take a bullet for the president?"

"Everyone should be willing to take a bullet for his president or his country," he answered squarely.

"Suppose the people in this room had the power to make you a General, Captain," asked the alcoholic general.

Uxbridge locked eyes with the high-ranking officer. They each held their gaze.

"But it had to be a unanimous vote," continued the general. "And suppose you found out on the day your promotion was to take place that one of us was an undercover agent for a foreign country and that if you turned us in, the loss of our vote would cost you your promotion. What would you do?"

"I'd look him square in the eyes and smile, then with a firm handshake I'd thank him for his vote of confidence in me and let him know that I'd do the rank justice. I would try to put his mind at ease."

"Nicely said," said a firm voice from behind and several seats to his right.

"You misunderstand," said Uxbridge.

"What do you mean?" asked Myers.

"That night I would have him killed."

A murmur swept around the circle from one seat to the next like a wave of falling dominoes.

"Are you a career man?" asked Myers.

"I can't see myself working in the private sector, Sir."

"Why not?" asked the general.

"There's no discipline. Especially, when you have unions protecting weak and lazy workers, when they should be weeded out instead. There's no true discipline in the private industry like there is in the Army."

"*General* Uxbridge," said a high-ranking official sitting far to his right.

Silence engulfed the room. A minute went by, then two. It was so quiet the sounds of swallowing and heavy breathing could be heard.

Taking his time and speaking deliberately, he corrected himself. "Excuse me, *Captain* Uxbridge."

Uxbridge never blinked.

"What do you think about power and money?" continued the officer.

"Some say money *is* power," said Uxbridge. "I'd rather have power, because power can exploit the people with money."

"Do you need a lot of friends, Captain?" asked Myers.

"I have associates," answered Uxbridge dryly. "I find that friends don't recognize or respect the uniform or the power associated with it."

Another murmur swept the circle.

When the whispering died, Myers asked discreetly, "You'd really take a bullet for the President?"

Directing his answer to everyone in the room Uxbridge said, "If asking me whether I want an assignment to guard the President is why you brought me here, Sirs, I would be honored. Saving the country and the President is what I live for."

He got out of his seat and stood tall and straight. In a voice that seemed to have deepened in the short time he had been there, he said, "Yes! I would take a bullet. But the shooter better make it a good shot, because if he doesn't kill me, I'll be sure to kill him!"

"Have you heard of the SIA, Captain?" asked the general.

"No, Sir."

"It's a newly formed agency," said Myers.

"Do the letters stand for covert?" asked Uxbridge.

"Yes they do, *General*," answered Myers.

Myers didn't correct himself. Uxbridge hadn't disappointed.

CHAPTER 1

June 12th
Present Day
Providence, Rhode Island

News videographer Doug Talbot stood beside a white van marked WJAM, TV-16, in large black lettering, locking his camera onto its tripod. He scratched his full scalp of midnight hair briskly several times, then looked through the viewfinder.

"Be with you in a minute," said a female reporter from inside the van. "Need to retouch my makeup. With my light complexion, this sun is going to create quite a glare on my face."

Doug panned the camera till it faced the opposite direction of the van, finally settling on the outdoor food court across the street. The fluid motion of the turn told him the rotation friction was just right.

"Not a problem," said Doug, still looking through the viewfinder. "This is it for me anyway. After I microwave this back to the station, I'm done for the day."

"Lucky you," said the voice inside the van. "I've got another story to do over at the zoo. Something about a newborn giraffe."

"Ahhh! Still doing those hard hitting news features."

"Sure, rub it in," said the reporter. "I think Shoemaker hates me; that's why he gives me all these fluff pieces."

"The man's an idiot!" said Doug. "He wouldn't know talent if it came up and bit him on the ass."

Testing the camera's zoom, he zeroed in on two army men sitting at a table who appeared to be having a heated discussion.

"Got any plans after we're done?" asked the reporter.

"I'm going across the street for lunch," he said, glancing up when the back door of the van swung open.

A young, shorthaired blonde stepped out next to him. He towered over her. Straightening her gray skirt, she said, "Ummmm! I love their mushroom burgers."

"Me too," he said, looking back into the camera at the two white military men across the street. "I'll be sure to have one for the both of us."

"Give me a second to set up," said the reporter, grabbing her microphone and stepping back to frame herself against the backdrop of the grand opening banner for the new Priced Right store.

Doug hit the record button. The two men's conversation had picked up in intensity. "Never know where you'll find news," he whispered to himself. He zoomed in far enough so that he could read the nametag on one of the men: General Thomas Uxbridge.

Suddenly, he squinted from a bright mirror-like reflection from a car parked near the restaurant. Its driver's window went up and the car rolled away.

"All set!" called the reporter.

Still recording, he zoomed slightly out from the men and realized that the glare of the sun had made the man on the left appear white. He stopped recording and swiveled his camera back around to face the reporter. He framed her in a close-up shot and said, "I'll start tight on you, then zoom out to show the store behind you."

"Fine," she said, staring down at her notes. She read her opening line in a low voice for practice.

"You're right about the glare," he said. "It already played tricks on my eyes."

The reporter repeated her opening one more time and then said, "Let's do it."

Doug hit the record button and the red tally light above the camera lens started blinking. He raised his hand out and counted her silently down from five to one by closing one finger at a time. When his thumb closed she said excitedly, "Thanks, Walter and Mary. I'm here at the grand opening of the downtown Priced Right store and as you can see, the place is packed with shoppers" – she paused and said, "This is where the editor can insert the b-roll video. I already did the voice over back at the station." Counting herself back in she said, "Three, two, one... Priced Right, and its everyday low prices, plans to open at least ten more stores throughout the state. This should create even more happy shoppers, more happy workers with new jobs, and hopefully happier days for the state's economy. Throwing it back to the station, this is Beverly Newton.

"That's done," said the suddenly relieved reporter.

"Not a minute too soon," said Doug, as another JAM news van rolled up beside them.

"Ah, my new ride," said Beverly.

Doug and the driver exchanged waves. It wasn't anyone he knew.

Beverly reached inside Doug's van and grabbed her pocketbook. Stepping towards the new van she said, "Are you microwaving it back now or after lunch?"

"Now. That way I can go right home after I eat. I'd like to be there when my daughter Cassandra gets home from school."

He stepped inside the back of the van, leaving the two doors wide open, hoping to get some air on an otherwise breezeless hot day. After hitting the start button to raise the microwave mast, he shot a wave towards the other van containing the reporter as it left to cover the story of the baby giraffe. When the van moved out of sight he dialed the station and began transmitting the news video. The car across the street with the shiny reflection swung over and rolled to a silent stop several feet away. The driver's window opened and six quick, successive pictures from a digital camera were snapped of him, sitting inside the back of the van.

* * *

General Uxbridge leaned towards Major Edwards. "It's too late to back out now," he said in a low, intensely angry voice. The much older officer watched the man sitting across the table from him in the food court squirm in his seat and swallow hard.

"But Sir," said the visibly shaken young black officer, swiping his hand over his cropped military-style black hair. "I don't want anything to do with your scheme anymore. It goes against everything I believe in. The very reason I signed to serve in the Army."

The General glared hard at Edwards, as if trying to bore a hole through him.

"Don't force me to make a decision."

"Innocent people could get hurt," said the Major in a low voice.

The General shrugged. "Innocent people already have."

"Suppose I tell someone?"

"Don't be an idiot. You'd never make it."

Edwards shifted uneasily. "What do you mean?" he whispered. "They'd kill me?"

"Not a problem for them."

"After all I've done - for them - for you?"

"Doesn't matter. They won't let you jeopardize the project."

The Major grabbed his scotch and water and downed it with a single swig.

The General snatched his own drink, a straight up double whiskey, and swallowed quickly. "Just take the money. Set your family and yourself up for an easy life."

"Why do you still hate Professor Woodsen after all these years?" asked Edwards, changing the subject.

The General's face flushed. "That bastard!" he growled like a pit bull. "You had to bring up his name and ruin my lunch."

"How did he jeopardize national security?"

"Because of that son of a bitch, we couldn't develop the chip right away. The base in Virginia didn't take off until seventy-eight, well after we were out of Nam."

"He did invent it," said Major Edwards.

"For Chrissake! He wanted it for the good of mankind!"

"So you took care of him?"

"Let's just say he was removed. He still had a few friends in high places. I found a place for him to live, well out of our way.

The Major's face took on the same look of confusion as a kid about to take a surprise test when he hasn't even opened the book yet.

"It was the only fucking way we could get the rights to the chip!" answered the General to the unasked question.

The Major stabbed a two-inch piece of blackened barbecued beef with his fork and swept it into his mouth with one quick motion. "Who's getting the specs on the new chip?" he said between chews.

"Can't say."

"Can't or won't?"

"The less you know, Edwards, the better off you'll be. Knowing too much can be a liability."

The Major breathed deeply and exhaled slowly. "Why do *they* want the chip?"

"Don't know!" snapped Uxbridge. "And it's none of our business." Waving to get a waitress he said, "Look, as long as they're giving me lots of money, I could give a good crap how they use it."

The Major sighed deeply. "What about allegiance to your country?"

The General laughed loudly. "Take the damn money and do as you're told, and everything will work out."

* * *

Doug Talbot walked out into the open-air food court, surveying the lay of the land for a table. As he did a panoramic scan, he found all the tables except one full. A woman wearing what looked like a white lab coat sat facing the street reading a book at a table for two covered by a red and white striped umbrella, near the end of the food court.

He made his way over.

"Excuse me," he said, shading his eyes from the bright sun with a free hand, while holding a plate with his meal. "Would you mind if I joined you? There are no other seats."

Without looking up from her book, the woman said, "Help yourself."

"Thanks," he said, sitting. "Whatcha reading?"

The young woman was about thirty, with long curly hair. When she looked up Doug saw for the first time how pretty she was. She had blue eyes that twinkled like newborn stars, a radiant facial glow that could only belong to a goddess, and an amazingly beautiful smile that he focussed on when her lightly shaded red lips moved.

"Patricia Cornwell's *Trace*. She's a favorite of mine. Do you like her work?"

"I don't read much. Mostly the sports pages. Why do you like Cornwell?"

The sandy-haired woman pulled back the flap of her jacket, revealing her nametag: Dr. Marilynn Harwell. "I have a vested interest in medicine and I like the way she writes from the perspective of a Medical Examiner."

"You work at Coventry General," said Doug.

"Very perceptive," said the Doctor.

"I recognize the logo on the lapel."

"Have you been there often?"

"I have a seven year old daughter who's accident prone. And her mother's no better. Been to the emergency room with them at least a half dozen times just in the past year." He opened his coffee and locked back the plastic tab. "My name's Doug," he said after taking a big gulp.

She played with her salad, then pulled to her mouth a

large bite of lettuce, tomato and a smattering of shredded cheese, saying in a muffled mouthful, "Nice to meet you, Doug. I hope your family was treated well by the staff the times you visited."

"Thanks, we were. You must be really hungry?"

She wiped her mouth with a napkin. "Have to eat fast. Never know when I could be paged for an emergency."

Across the yard a man in a dark navy suit wearing even darker sunglasses handed General Uxbridge something shiny.

"What's this?" said the General, accepting the chrome digital camera..

"We thought you'd want to see this," said the man, taking off his sunglasses.

The General's face turned scarlet when he looked at the four-inch TV screen and saw someone with a video camera taping him talking to the Major.

"What the fuck?" he shouted.

"One of our nearby undercover agents observed a news videographer recording you and Major Edwards."

"Look at this," said the General sliding the camera across the table to the Major."

Picking it up the Major said, "Damn! What the hell's going on?"

"What was this shmuck doing there in the first place?" snapped the General.

"He appeared to be shooting a news story about the grand opening of a grocery store across the street," answered the man in the navy suit.

"I want that tape!"

"Not a problem Sir, but...."

"But what?"

"It appears he microwaved *all* the raw footage back to Channel 16. We couldn't intercept it in time. That could present a problem."

"I'll make a call," said the General. "You go to this TV station and get that tape! It'll be waiting at the front door by the time you get there."

"What about the feed he sent back, Sir?"

"My call will take care of that too! Where's the guy who shot this?"

"You're not going to believe this Sir, but see the man across the yard sitting with a woman in a white doctor's coat?"

With unprotected eyes, Uxbridge squinted through the brilliant sunlight. "Yeah. What about him?"

"That's your man."

"Son of a bitch. He's right under our noses. Who's the broad?"

"Her name's Dr. Marilynn Harwell. She works at Coventry General Hospital."

"It may be harmless, but we can't take any chances. Find out everything you can about them."

"Already working on it Sir."

The General nodded.

* * *

Doctor Harwell got up from the table.

"It was nice to meet you, Doug. I have to get back to the hospital."

She turned and started to walk away and stopped. Turning around she said, " Don't take this personally, but I hope we never meet again."

"Ouch! That hurts," he laughed.

"But that would mean you didn't have to bring your wife or daughter back to the hospital."

They both laughed.

The doctor made her way across the food court, unaware her identity was being accessed from a governmental database. Doug sat gulping down his oversized mushroom burger, not cognizant that his was also being processed.

PEACEFUL ENDINGS

September 9th
Three months later
20 Water Street
10:03pm

Dr. Marilynn Harwell woke suddenly to Bruce Springsteen's unplugged version of *Born in the USA*. Pulling the bedcovers over her head she shouted, "Damn! It's time to get up already."

Jennie Sprague, her perky twenty-five year old redhead roommate pounced on top of her. "Come on, sleepy head. Time to get up. Coventry General needs its top Trauma doctor."

"Let me sleep another couple of minutes," cried Marilynn.

"Aren't you on call?" asked Jennie.

"No," said Marilynn. "I'm going in for a few hours to do some paperwork so I can have my weekend free. I have that convention in Boston on Monday. I told you about that."

Jennie snatched the covers back, revealing Marilynn's fully clothed body. "What's this? You didn't even have time to change into pajamas?"

"It's not what you think," answered Marilynn, rubbing her eyes vigorously.

Jennie lay down beside her with her hands cupped under her head. "Tell me all about your dream date with Ron," she said. Both stared at the ceiling.

"Some dream date," lamented Marilynn.

Jennie sat up yoga style. "Okay. What went wrong?"

Marilynn plopped a pillow over her face. "His idea of dinner was to take me to a burger joint," she said in half muffled words. "And then he took me to a bar to watch an exhibition football game! It wasn't even a real game."

"Jeez, Marilynn, that really sucks. Are you going out with him again?"

Marilynn pulled the pillow from her face and tossed it at Jennie, who ducked in time. "Are you crazy? Didn't you hear what I said? The guys a ten-year-old boy in a man's body. It'll be another twenty years before his mind catches up to his age. Damn!" she cried, flopping back. "By that time, I'll be fifty-one." Lifting her head off the bed she leaned on her elbow. "Is it too much to ask that I find someone nice so I can settle down and have a family?"

"No, it isn't," answered Jennie sympathetically.

Marilynn flopped back on the bed. "What the hell am I doing wrong?" she cried.

"Sit up," commanded Jennie, raising Marilynn by the hands. "Now turn around, so I can get to work."

Marilynn sat with her back to Jennie. Skilled and thorough hands kneaded her shoulders from behind.

"Relax," said Jennie softly. "Take slow, deep breaths. Release all that tension. Remember, you've got to work tonight." Jennie had taken several massage courses and was pretty good at massage therapy.

"The guy's a Dork!" said Marilynn, between sporadic breaths. "You'd think a full partner in a big time law firm would have an IQ higher than a doorknob. Men! You can't live with them and you can't live without them."

Jennie had worked her way down Marilynn's shoulder blades and was manipulating the lower back.

"That's nice," sighed Marilynn. "Don't stop."

"You know how I feel on the subject," said Jennie. "You *don't* need men to have a good time."

Jennie had slowly worked her hands and arms around to the front of Marilynn's lower stomach. Each hand pressed or stroked in a circular motion. Marilynn's breathing changed to short, heavy gasps. "I... I still ....like .....men," she said in a forced whisper.

Jennie's hands continued caressing, delicate cream-colored skin, working upward till settling on full, soft supple breasts. Marilynn pulled suddenly from her grasp. Jennie fell back, laughing.

"Sorry, Jennie. Nothing personal. I just don't feel the way you do."

Reverting back to a yoga position, Jennie began doing side-to-side stretches.

"I like men," continued Marilynn. "I know that some day the right guy will sweep me off my feet."

Jennie stopped her stretching. Marilynn could tell by the bewildered look on the girl's face that she didn't understand, so she left the room.

"Suit yourself," laughed Jennie, "But that's why you call him *your dream guy*! Because you only see him in your dreams!"

"What's on your agenda tomorrow?" called Marilynn from the bathroom.

"I thought I'd work from home!" said Jennie loudly, competing with the hissing of the shower. "Insap defense systems is having trouble accessing its new remote security servers and sub-servers."

Marilynn tilted her head down so that her long curly hair flowed under the shower's steady stream. As she lathered her hair she called through a steam-filled room, "Can I borrow your car? Mine's in the shop! It needs some work to pass inspection!"

"Yeah!" said Jennie, standing in the bathroom doorway. "I filled it with gas yesterday."

"Sticking her head back under the water to rinse Marilynn said, "I'm going to be late getting back. I may meet some friends for breakfast around eight o'clock tomorrow morning. Are you going to be okay without a car till I get home?"

"I've got plenty to do here. Plus, I'll probably go for a run. I won't need it."

"Make sure to put the alarm on," said Marilynn, doing a three sixty spin under the stream of hot water. "Even if you only go out for a walk. But I guess I don't have to tell you that. It's your system."

"Yes, mother!" snapped Jennie, retreating to her own room.

Her hair and body fully rinsed, Dr. Harwell stepped out onto eight-inch pink and white porcelain tiles. Her hand squeaked as it wiped the fogged mirror with several circular swipes. "Very funny, young lady!" she called, rubbing her body with a giant purple bath towel. "But I'm only old enough to be your big sister."

No counter-argument came from the other room.

Marilynn tossed the damp towel to the floor and methodically slipped on unexciting underwear. After spraying underarm deodorant, she dressed in white pants and a green top with the Coventry General Hospital logo. Both were hospital issued.

She blow-dried her sandy hair, then stepped back to look at herself in the mirror. Sticking her tongue out she sighed, "Hope the world is ready for me?" then headed for Jennie's room. Her roommate was sitting yoga position on the bed, but now she was deep in meditation. Her face looked peaceful and serene.

Marilynn liked kidding Jennie about her deep meditation, calling it *mindless drifting*. That always peeved Jennie. There weren't many things she took seriously, but meditation and her job were two of them.

Marilynn shook her head. There were times when she would call Jennie's name for at least five minutes before the girl would snap out of one of those deep trances. *God! I wish my life was that carefree,* thought the doctor side of her.

She stuffed her stethoscope into her pocketbook and grabbed her white doctor's jacket, then headed out the front door to Coventry General Hospital, leaving Jennie to her *mindless drifting*.

16 Lake Shore Drive
10:37pm

A seven-year old girl named Cassandra lay silently on her bed, tears trickling down her cheeks. Dressed in a short, black leather skirt and painted in way too much makeup, her forty something, shoulder length frizzy blonde mother shouted, "You were supposed to be here over an hour ago!"

Doug Talbot tensed with anger. "I overslept!" he shouted back. "Did you forget that I worked the overnight shift at the station this week and that I had to sleep during the day? What about that don't you understand?"

Standing in four-inch, fire-red spiked heels, his ex-wife screamed, "My date's waiting for me!"

"I don't give a damn about your precious little boy-friend!"

"You're just jealous!" shrieked the woman.

"I know you want me to drop everything whenever you need a baby-sitter for our daughter!" yelled Doug, "but who's going to baby-sit your twenty-year old boy-friend?"

Talbot's head swung violently to the side from the force of his ex's cracking slap. "How dare you?" she screamed hysterically.

The little girl lay quite still, tears glistening in the glow of an amber night-light.

"I need someone who can please me and keep up with me," replied the bitter woman. "Not someone who falls asleep in his recliner by eight o'clock."

"You're an ungrateful bitch!" swore Talbot. "I gave you everything!"

"Like what, mister cameraman at a small time TV station?"

"I paid for this house, which *you* own. We had a beautiful child together, and you had the luxury of being a stay-at-home mom."

"Screw you!" shouted the ungrateful mother. "I'm outta here!"

"You look ridiculous!" yelled Talbot, after she had left.

The little girl lay quite still.

MICHAEL K. TUCKER

Live Beat Lounge
Downtown
The Dance Floor
11:48pm

Jive Talkin, a local rock band, blasted out the words to their final song of the night. A gathering of 20, thirty-somethings gyrated up and down.

Holding the microphone to his mouth the lead singer screamed the words to the song *Over My Dead Body*. The drummer, with sweat pouring from his forehead, erupted into a solo, slamming his sticks and swinging his dirty scraggy long hair side-to-side. The crowd erupted, clapping wildly at this unplanned stage show.

After striking the bass, snare, and tom drums several times, the drummer ended his dramatic solo by slamming the symbols twenty-five times to the rhythmic clapping of the musically intoxicated crowd. On impulse, he stood and slammed his head into the symbols, sending the crowd into a wild frenzy.

The drummer flipped his sticks into the crowd and fell backwards to the floor. It would be ten minutes before anyone realized he was dead.

CHAPTER 2

Day One
September 10th
Coventry General Hospital
Graveyard shift
12:15am

Dr. Marilynn Harwell stepped through the front doors of Coventry General and stopped to take in the view. She filled her lungs with the hospital's fresh smelling antiseptic air, the result of a concentrated antibacterial, germicidal, and sterilization attack.

Exhaling the wholesome air sharply, she shifted her sight towards the scene in the front lobby. A nurse talking to an orderly and another on a computer entering data manned the nurses' station. Off to the right, occupying chairs that lined the wall on the left side of the emergency room waiting area sat a young couple just outside the double doors leading into ER. Sitting in the middle of the room on metal chairs that would look suitable at a card table sat three young men watching *ESPN*'s Sports Center on a TV that hung from the ceiling. A middle-aged man with early graying hair dressed in gray coveralls and green plaid shirt, bobbed his head while listening to music through a headset that was attached to a portable CD player as he rhythmically pushed a buffer in short semi-circles over a recently waxed floor at the opposite end of the corridor.

Nothing out of the ordinary. It was normally quiet at this

time of night. On occasion it would get hectic, but even on the busiest nights it would calm down by two AM. On slow nights like tonight and even when there were a lot of patients admitted, nurses could complete rounds in about two hours. That included giving patients their Meds and making them comfortable. The rest of the night, or morning as it were, could be dedicated to catching up on paperwork and getting down a hearty meal and plenty of coffee. Interns and residents would try to snatch a couple hours of sleep when possible, to break up long shifts of up to thirty-six straight hours.

Elyse McFarland, the nurse working on the computer, looked up and saw Dr. Harwell. Reaching down, she picked up a pink sticky note and waved it. Doctor Harwell feigned a smile and made her way over. "This can't be good," she said under her breath.

"Morning, Doctor," smiled the young nurse.

"Good morning, Elyse. How are things?"

"There are a couple of patients waiting to be seen, but they're minor cases and should be taken care of shortly. Dr. Koenig is the attending physician. It's been the usual steady night, but nothing we haven't been able to handle. Dr. Shoenfeld helped out for a while till it slowed down."

"That's good news?" said Dr. Harwell. "We need a night like this once in a while to make up for the bad ones."

Nurse McFarland chuckled and said, "Boy, you've got that right!"

"You have something for me?" asked Dr. Harwell.

"Oh! I almost forgot," said the nurse, handing her the pink note. "It's from Dr. Chang."

Dr. Harwell took the message and read it to herself. "Tricky case in 311 – have a question about my diagnosis – can I see you for consultation?" When she looked up she saw a young woman leading a stressed elderly man gingerly through the front doors and watched them make their way slowly across the floor to the emergency room

Looking back at the nurse she said, "I'm actually not on tonight, Elyse. I'm here to catch up on paperwork. I'm off to Boston on Monday for a medical convention so I'm trying to free up my weekend."

She turned and started towards the elevator. Nurse McFarland called after her, "Got it, Doctor. You're not here. Your secret's safe with me."

The door was open when she got to the ancient hospital elevator, so she stepped inside and pressed the green '3' button. Before it closed, she observed a middle aged woman leading a teenage boy and girl by the hands through the front doors. The last she saw of them as the doors whooshed closed was the woman dragging the teenage kids to ER. She thought it was a little odd, because the kids appeared to be about sixteen to seventeen.

She shrugged it off after the doors slammed shut, because she hated the banging sound the elevator made, especially late at night when she was alone in it. To her, it was usually a painful ritualistic start of a long night.

The decrepit elevator rumbled upward. Overhead, the sound of metal cables and grinding gears drowned out soft elevator music. *God, I hate the graveyard shift*, she thought, even though she wasn't scheduled to work. It was not the first time she had felt that way.

The elevator stopped with a sudden shudder, sending a resounding bang echoing back down the shaft. Coventry General and its ancient elevator was over thirty years old and in need of a major facelift inside and out. Unfortunately, most state funds went to Providence Hospital of Rhode Island, because it was located in the heart of the capital city, and also the state's major celebrities and politicians went there.

Dr. Harwell was recognized as the states best trauma doctor. Even competing hospitals would consult her in extreme trauma cases. She was even rumored to be up for a newly-created position of *Director of Trauma Program* for the state of Rhode Island, which would position her over all the doctors in that field. But despite her newly found status, and the hospitals' reputation of excellence, needed funds would not be allocated to Coventry General Hospital in the near future.

She waited as the gray metal doors rattled open, then stepped out onto West 3. Seated at the front desk reading a magazine was Lindsey Palmer, a pretty young blonde with a perfectly round face and body to match, fresh out of nursing school. With piercing blue eyes and playful personality, first impression seemed she was more suited for cheerleading rather than nursing. Harwell liked Palmer, but also was a little envious of her. *There should be a law against being that pretty and that young*, she had sometimes thought.

She kept her feelings to herself, though. It wouldn't look good for a doctor to be jealous of a staff nurse. Besides, she only got feelings and thoughts like this when she was depressed. And that was only after bad dates.

Leaning against the desk, she said, "Hi, Lindsey! What's going on?"

The young nurse put the magazine down. "Morning Doctor Harwell. You know how it is. Sometimes it gets pretty boring up here at night. They didn't teach us how to deal with that at Barrington Nursing School. Are you with us tonight?"

"Dr. Burns is covering. I'm only here to do some paperwork."

"That's good," said the nurse. "I know how you hate overnights. Me, I'm stuck on this shift till I can earn seniority."

"Hang in there, Lindsey. It won't be long before you're on days."

Dr. Harwell didn't like lying. She knew the poor girl was probably going to be stuck on the graveyard shift for a long time. A major cut in staffing would make sure of that.

"I'm sorry, Doctor, did you say Dr. Burns was covering tonight?"

"Yes. Why?"

"Well, it's just that he hasn't shown up yet. That's why when I saw you, I figured you were working."

"Probably overslept," said Dr. Harwell. "Give him a call

and remind him he's supposed to be here. Since I'm here, why don't you give me the patient log. I'll cover till he gets here so Dr. Chang can go home."

Lindsey handed her a clipboard. "It should be an easy night. There are only two patients. Because it's so slow, Dr. Chang assigned the rest of the West 3 staff to either surgery recovery or ICU."

"Good move," said the doctor. "More than likely, we won't even need them tonight."

"Margie left you a note, too" said Lindsey. "She must've thought you were working."

Attached to the clipboard was a handwritten note in doctor scrawl on hospital stationery, but before she could read it her pager beeped. She pulled it from her waistband and read the number. It was ER. She grabbed the phone off the counter and dialed emergency. It rang twice before someone picked up.

"Dr. Koenig!"

"David. This is Dr. Harwell. Did you page me?"

"Marilynn. Do you have any open beds up there? It's getting a little serious down here, and I'm going to have to admit a few patients."

"Let me see," she said glancing down at the clipboard. The patient list read:

John Crawford – RM 301
(Evaluation)
Darlene Little – RM 305
(Recovery)

"Plenty of available beds, David," she said into the phone. After a short response on the other end, she said goodbye to Dr. Koenig and handed the phone over to Lindsey. As the young nurse made transfer arrangements, she read Margie's note to herself:

> Hi Marilyn! How are you? We need to get together for a couple of drinks - or more.

Should be an easy night. There are only two patients. Crawford in 301 is there for evaluation. He had minor valve surgery this morning. He should sleep most of the night with the meds he's on.

You know Darlene in 305. We had so many empty rooms, I decided to put her there to sleep off her night of boozing. She's going to have one hell of a headache in the morning.

Like I said, it should be an easy night.
See ya in the funnies,
Margie

"I like Margie," thought Dr. Harwell out loud. "But after five years, you'd think she could spell my name right. It's Marilynn - with two N's!"

Something touched her shoulder and she jumped and gasped loudly. Spinning around she saw Dr. Chang, a thin middle-aged man with jet-black hair. Even though he knew no English when he moved here from overseas seven years ago, he spoke perfect English now.

"Sorry," said Dr. Chang, lightly touching her forearm. "I didn't mean to scare you."

She caught her breath and smiled. "Not a problem, Doctor. I got your note. How can I help?"

"I've got the damnedest case," said Dr. Chang. "A sixteen-year-old girl stopped by the ER about two hours ago complaining of a stomach ache, shortness of breath, and light-headedness."

Dr. Harwell asked, "What did your examination reveal?"

"Her vitals are very unstable. Her blood pressure is low, her heartbeat irregular, and she's sweating around the forehead."

"Did she have any bruises or trauma that you could tell?"

"None that I could see. However, she did keep complaining about being thirsty."

"Did you do any other tests?"

"I'm waiting results of a CAT scan."

"When was the last time you checked on her?"

Glancing at his watch Dr. Chang answered, "Maybe five minutes ago."

"Where is she now?"

"I just had her transferred up here to 311. The paperwork hasn't even come up yet."

"Let's go take a look at her," said Dr. Harwell.

CGH's top trauma doc turned away, leaving the pretty young nurse to her magazine. Two heavily padded doors leading deeper into West 3 burst inward as Dr. Marilynn (two N's) Harwell and Dr. Chang pushed through towards 311.

When both doctors entered the young patient's room they saw her lying calmly on the bed. Her head was angled slightly towards the door and her eyes were wide open. Two IV's dripped slowly into either arm and an oxygen mask covered her face, but it was all for nothing. The girl was dead.

State Medical Building
Coroner's Department
Downtown
1:43am

Dressed in black hip boots and a full-length red stained white lab jacket, Dr. Paul Crawford, the state's Chief Medical Examiner stood at the lower-level receiving door puffing on a cigarette stub.

"Christ!" he bellowed. "It looks like Christmas out here with all these flashing lights." Lined up waiting to make drops were an assortment of five ambulances and rescues. "What the hell's going on?" he yelled at an EMT who was opening the back of his truck.

"Dammed if I know," answered the irritated driver. "But I've got three bodies in here for you, and calls for two more pick-ups once I'm done dropping off."

"Weren't you here a couple of hours ago?"

"That's right. I dropped off an old man and woman. They were husband and wife."

"Was there some major catastrophe I didn't hear about?" asked Crawford, scratching the back of a full head of white hair.

The muscular EMT, about fifty years old and dressed in navy colored pants and matching shirt with Rescue One – Dave embroidered on the pocket, pulled a stretcher with a black body bag out the back with the help of another burly EMT.

"Not that I'm aware of!" he answered gruffly. "It's been nonstop."

"What happened to these three?" asked the coroner.

The ambulance driver released a lever and the stretcher raised like an accordion to waist level. "You'll never guess in a million years," said the second EMT, a man in his mid twenties.

"Don't keep me in suspense," growled the Medical Examiner, who was now in a foul mood. "What's their story?"

"These three college boys got caught being peeping Toms on a ladder outside a girls' sorority house," said Dave.

Leaning against the back of the truck, the second EMT said, "A group of girls saw what they were doing, so they threw water balloons from the floor above them. After getting hit a few times the boys ran off. Several hours later they were found dead in their dorm room by some of the girls who had thrown the balloons."

"I've never heard of anyone dying from being hit with a water balloon," snarled Dr. Crawford. "There must be something else to it."

"That's the whole story," said the younger EMT. "When we left the dorm, the police were finishing up taking statements from everyone involved and they seemed pretty satisfied with the girls stories."

"Where do you want them?" asked Dave.

"Bring them to storage room three!" barked Crawford, as he watched the flashing lights of another approaching rescue coming in from the highway.

Moments later the two EMT's returned to their vehicle after making the third and final trip.

"They're all yours," said the driver, jumping back into the driver's seat. "We'll be back in no time with another drop."

The rescue's engine roared to life and the emergency lights flashed ominously as it pulled out, forewarning of things to come.

Paul Crawford scratched his head with vigor. "I still think there must be something else to it!" he yelled as the rescue sped off with its siren screaming. He flicked his cigarette, nothing more than a stub now to the pavement, and ground it with a scuffed and blood stained boot. "Why the hell did I give Mendez the night off?" he muttered to no one. "I'll never be able to handle all these by myself."

Another rescue truck beeped as it backed up to unload, taking the place of the departed one. A white uniformed female EMT driver jumped out and opened up the back of her truck, then turned towards Dr. Crawford.

"You'll never guess in a million years how this dude died," she said.

WJAM-TV
Studio Control
4am News Cut-in

Ed Manning, the director for the five-minute news cut-ins every half-hour at WJAM-TV picked up his headset. Speaking into his microphone he said, "Okay people, two minutes to air." He then went on to tell them about a last-second change in format: a breaking news story about a fire.

Doug Talbot stood in front of the anchor desk adjusting the tilt drag on camera three, which was positioned directly in front of the talent. He would be responsible for the opening camera shot, a slow zoom in to a medium close-up of the anchor and meteorologist. He adjusted focus, then did a practice zoom. After fifteen years it was second nature.

"Okay people, thirty seconds to air. Remember everyone; stick around after we're done. Doug's treating us all to coffee and doughnuts."

"Thanks for being so easy with my money," laughed Talbot.

"Standby!" commanded the director. "In five, four, three, two, one. Master Control - switch us live."

Nothing happened. Studio control was filled with black-screened TV monitors.

"Wake up master control!" screamed the director. "Switch us live!"

Still nothing happened. Video black and static audio were going out over the air.

"Somebody run in there and wake the bastard up!" screamed the director, his face bright red. "We need to get on the fucking air!"

Doug locked down his camera and rushed to Master Control, on the other side of the soundproof studio door. He bolted in and found Joe Brooks, the engineering operator, slumped over the control board. Talbot pressed the red studio control button putting the news out over the airwaves. In his headset, he could hear the anchor offering apologies for the technical difficulties.

Talbot grabbed Brooks by the shoulder and shook him. "Brooks!" he yelled. "Wake up!" There was no response. He continued shaking. "Wake up Joe!" Brooks' head fell backwards and Talbot understood.

The engineer was dead. It appeared the last thing he did was spill coffee on his lap.

Coventry General Hospital
Dr.'s Lounge
6:00am

Sitting back in a plush leather chair, Dr. Harwell opened

up the daily newspaper and glanced at the day's headlines. Stock market was down and gasoline prices were up. "Same old stories," she sighed.

Sipping from a Styrofoam cup of fresh brewed coffee, she thought back to Margie's note and how the nurse predicted it would be a boring night. This was the first time she could recall Margie ever being wrong. Dr. Burns had never showed up and no one had able to contact him, so she had to cover West Three all night. It had been a fairly busy night, and this coffee break was the first real rest she'd had since coming in last night. Besides, she was really using the quiet time to try and figure out what was going on with all the patients. She never did get to her paperwork.

Thank God for nurse Betty, she was a blessing. Between the two of them, they had handled most of the shift, because the rest of the staff were elsewhere helping out. There had been a major influx of patients on the other floors and the hospital was overfilled, and more active than any daytime period.

Betty was what you'd call - to put it politely - plump. But that didn't stop Dr. Harwell from thinking of her as one of the best damn nurses the hospital had ever seen. Other than Margie, there wasn't another nurse she'd rather work with in a stressful situation.

Twelve people had been admitted during the overnight, all with varying degrees of pain. Oddly enough, they all were unusually thirsty and sweated freely around the forehead. Along with Dr. Chang's patient, three more had died and all of the others were in extremely bad shape.

Dr. Harwell didn't like to think of Betty this way, but one of the woman's attributes was that she was extremely strong, which was beneficial when bodies had to be removed or patients had to be lifted into beds.

"What I wouldn't do for the last few hours to go by faster and quieter," she said to herself, turning the page to the funnies. On cue, the direct line to emergency admitting started buzzing and flashing.

"Dr. Marilynn Harwell!" she said, reluctantly picking it up.

"This is Baxter in Emergency!" shouted an overly excited young male voice. "We need help down here!"

"I'm working West Three," said Dr. Harwell. She yawned into the phone and immediately felt embarrassed.

"But we need help!" snapped a flustered voice.

"Where's the Attending on duty?" she asked.

"He's busy right now and things are quickly getting out of control," said the voice, punctuated with urgency. "We really need some help here."

"Page Dr. Koenig," she said, hanging up.

The phone buzzed again. She snatched it up. "I'm doing everything I can," was all she heard before there was dead silence. Her fingers immediately hit 222 – emergency admitting. The phone rang many times. No one picked up.

Something wasn't right. She didn't need the sudden pang in her stomach to tell her that. She swore as she ran to the elevator and pressed the button for the first floor. Her eyes shifted towards the door for the stairs. Should she run the three flights down, or wait for the elevator. Her decision was made when the elevator finally arrived. She jumped inside and the doors slammed with a bang. She hit the button for floor one and the elevator shuddered noisily downward.

"What hell am I going to?" she wondered.

WJAM-TV
Live Special Report
6:02am

It was only two hours since losing one of their own and a troublesome anguish hung over the TV station. Everyone felt it. They spoke little as they went about their business preparing for the day's newscast, writing scripts, formulating weather forecasts and editing news video. Life had to go on.

The overnight news director called the staff together in the studio for a breaking news *special report*. The morning anchor, a twenty-something female with long brown hair and sporting a gray blazer, settled quickly into her seat as a male intern frantically shoved a script in front of her. "These are questions the producer wants you to ask," he said, before racing back to the control room.

A hush went over the set and the director counted backwards from ten seconds. At the count of one, he called for Master Control to make the switch and this time the anchor was switched live on the air when the red tally light lit up on camera three.

"Good morning, my name is Katrina Walker," said the anchor. "We interrupt regularly scheduled programming for important breaking news. A rash of strange deaths has swept the state this morning, flooding the Coroner's office at the state medical building with an unusual amount of bodies. We have a reporter on the scene. Let's go there live. Can you hear me, Sean Carpenter?"

The television screen was split in two, showing the field reporter on the right side and the anchor on the left. "I hear you, Katrina," said the reporter, staring into the face of the camera. A bright spotlight illuminated his already pale face penetrating the predawn.

"What can you tell us about the unusual amount of deaths this morning?" asked the anchor.

The young reporter, cutting his teeth with early morning assignments, stood wearing a brown two-piece suit and spoke straight-faced into the camera. "Well, Katrina, I'm standing at the receiving area of the state medical building and since I got here at five thirty, a little over a half hour ago, four ambulances and rescues have made drops with a total of seven new bodies." Waving someone over, the reporter continued, "At this time I want to bring in Chief Medical Examiner, Dr. Paul Crawford."

Portable lighting lit up Dr. Crawford, making his thick white hair look even whiter as he stepped into the camera shot next to the reporter. Their backdrop was the black Morgue Van with *State Medical Examiner* in large white lettering.

"Dr. Crawford, isn't this quite an unusual number of deaths for this short amount of time?"

The Medical Examiner stared into the camera and answered, "Yes, it is. It's an unusual amount for six months, never mind a twelve hour period."

"You mean you've been getting bodies in since six o'clock yesterday?"

"That's right."

"Is there any common ground with all of them? By that I mean do you think they are linked in any way?"

"Of course there's a common ground," said Crawford. "They're all dead!"

The reporter caught a whiff of alcohol from Crawford's breath and inwardly shook his head. "Dr. Crawford, what is it you and your staff are looking for when you check each one?"

"First of all, my staff consists of me and an assistant. The job usually doesn't warrant more help than that. I've had to call in five medical doctors from area hospitals to help out. To answer your question, we're just trying to give the poor bastards - I'm sorry can I say that on TV?"

"Well, no," said the reporter, "but there's nothing we can do. You already said it."

"Sorry," said Dr. Crawford, staring into the camera. "I'm just a little stressed and tired after going nonstop all night with the extra workload, plus my assistant wasn't here to help. Anyway, getting back to your question, we're looking closely at each case to verify the exact cause of death."

"What are some of the causes?" asked the reporter.

"There was the case of a woman falling out of bed, and another incident of a man cutting himself shaving, then there were the teenage boys who got their ears pierced."

"Are you saying these people died from minor, and I stress extremely minor injuries?"

"That's exactly what I'm saying."

"But how's that possible?" asked the wide-eyed reporter.

"That's yet to be determined. As soon as we figure something out, though, we will certainly release a statement to the media."

"Sean!" interrupted the anchor; "can you ask Dr. Crawford what the total body count is?"

The reporter listened to the anchor ask her question in his IFB earpiece, which fed him the station's direct line of audio into his ear. Relaying her question he said, "Dr. Crawford, our news anchor Katrina Walker would like to know if you have a total body count?"

The Medical Examiner directed his words into the microphone the reporter held in his hand. "So far we have received seventy-eight bodies in a twelve hour period."

The anchor then asked, "Sean, can you ask Dr. Crawford about area hospitals and how they've been affected?"

"Dr. Crawford, do you know how local hospitals have been affected?"

"I haven't had a lot of spare time to call around, but I know that, just from speaking to Providence Hospital, they've seen a tremendous increase in the number of people they normally see overnight. I think it would be safe to say that all the other hospitals have been adversely affected too."

As the two men stood there, three more rescues backed up to the receiving area behind them. Looking back at the trucks, Dr. Crawford sighed noticeably, "Seventy-eight. But that's about to change. If you'll excuse me, I have to get back to my work."

The state's Chief Medical Examiner walked off to greet the new arrivals and the reporter turned his attention back to the camera. "There you have it, Katrina: a total of seventy-eight deaths in twelve hours and more on the way. This is Sean Carpenter for WJAM news." The camera zoomed off the reporter to a shot of the rescue trucks. Two additional trucks had arrived and were parked, waiting their turn to drop off.

A now solemn looking anchor looked into the studio camera and said somberly, "This has been a live WJAM news special report. We now return you to regularly scheduled programming,"

CHAPTER 3

Coventry General Hospital
Emergency Room
6:05am

The elevator doors slid open and Dr. Harwell stepped out into chaos and hesitated. A boisterous and overly excited crowd blocked her path. Off to the side she saw a nurse attending to a crying woman sitting on the floor. At the nurse's station a stressed nurse stood taking information from an animated young couple. Three other nurses were doing their best to assist patients when several more nurses rushed in and started to help out. Other people were moving here and there trying to get someone to listen to them. Even on an abnormally busy overnight shift in the emergency room, it was never like this. The tail end of this shift was overcrowded with frustrated and angry patients.

"Who's Baxter?" yelled Dr. Harwell over the uproar.

"I'm over here!" shouted a tall intern with a buzz cut hairdo. His jacket was off and he was standing between a man and a woman who were ready to square off.

Putting her hands together to form a makeshift megaphone in front of her mouth, Dr. Harwell screamed, "What's going on?"

Baxter never answered. Someone had whacked him from behind with a chair and he fell forward in slow motion like a felled tree. Some of the crowd turned its attention towards the doctor, who was rushing to reach him.

They clutched and grabbed, tearing a side pocket off her jacket. She struggled for several moments, but managed to free herself and race to Baxter's side. Lifting his head gently, she saw deep brown eyes looking up. "They came in all at once," he whispered. "There was nothing I could do."

Gently lifting his head to inspect the back of it she said, "Don't worry, you're going to be okay. There's no bleeding and you don't have a concussion." She placed his head gently on the floor. As he closed his eyes, she noticed that his forehead was leaking sweat freely.

"OWWW!" she screamed, when her own head was suddenly jerked back. A large pot-bellied guy had her by the hair and was dragging her backward, caveman style. She squirmed and kicked but he was too powerful as he pinned her arms in a tight bear hug. Before she knew it, he had lifted her off the floor and was carrying her away.

"You're coming home with me, Doc, my family's sick."

A rough unshaven face scratched against hers. The stench of stale beer breath made her gag and she almost threw up. Trying to speak she squeaked out, "Let me go. I can't help you if you don't let go of me."

The stethoscope around her neck unexpectedly yanked sideways, choking her.

"Give her to me," yelled a short thin guy in a green suit. "I need the Doctor for my sick wife."

The burly guy placed Dr. Harwell on the floor. She was too weak to stand or flee. Beer breath then turned and flattened the short guy with a single punch to the stomach "Find your own doctor. This one's mine," he said, reaching down and picking her up in another bear hug.

The emergency room grew quiet. Three nurses stepped forward and were about to try and help her but beer breath snarled, "Stay back or I'll hurt her!" The nurses backed away, because he looked crazy enough to follow through with his promise.

Beer breath started for the exit doors with the doctor firmly entrenched in his grasp. They were almost there when the doors swung open and a tall man with coal black hair stepped out carrying a little girl, who lay limply across his arms.

"What the hell's going on?" he asked, his face contorted in surprise.

"Get your own freakin' doctor, buddy!" yelled beer breath.

"Put the lady down!" commanded the new guy, noticing Harwell's eyes were rolling and that she appeared ready to pass out.

"Screw you!" said beer breath, and he spit on him.

The new man placed the little girl on the floor off to the side, then stepped forward and smacked beer breath square on the chin. He staggered back several steps, let go of the doctor and fell to the floor. Harwell herself stumbled forward and almost fell down, but was caught in the arms of the new man. His sweet scent was a lot nicer to her nose. The room became a whirlwind as hospital security rushed in and began restoring order to Emergency Room East.

Standing in the arms of this new man, Dr. Harwell felt strong secure hands around her waist. She inhaled long, then released slowly. Her face flushed. She was embarrassed by the sensation she was feeling right there in the middle of the ER. Her mind went blank. She struggled to find words to say. Any words.

Finally, she bit her lower lip, causing a sharp, excruciating pain. This brought her out of whatever trance she was in and she said in a controlled voice, "You can let go of me now."

"Are you sure?" he said, still holding her in a firm but comfortable grasp. "Your eyes still look glazed."

Even though she felt secure in his arms, she said, "I really am fine. I've got my feet under me."

Reluctantly, the man released his grip and went over and picked up the little girl with the long straight auburn hair. Holding her in his arms like you would a large baby, he brought her to the doctor.

"This is my daughter, Doc. I don't know what's wrong with her."

Dr. Harwell studied the little girl's face. Tiny beads of sweat covered her forehead and she appeared to be half-asleep. "Has she complained of any stomach or head pain?"

"Not that I'm aware of," said the man.

"Have you noticed any other symptoms?"

"She says she's thirsty, no matter how much liquid I give her. And her forehead is always drenched with sweat."

Dr. Harwell felt the little girl's wet brow. "She doesn't seem to have a fever. Let's bring her to a private room so I can examine her." She grabbed his free hand and shook it, saying, "My name is Doctor Marilynn Harwell. I'm the head of the Trauma department. Thanks for saving me from that maniac."

"Doug Talbot," replied her hero. "And this is my daughter, Cassandra."

"Nice to meet you Mister Talbot. And you too, Cassandra," she said, flicking hair out of the little girl's eyes. "There's room on the third floor. We'll get away from all this distraction and your daughter can have a room to herself."

She straightened her clothes, then reached down and picked up her stethoscope. "Wait for me by the elevator, Mr. Talbot. I'll be right over." She turned and walked over to the nurse's station, picked up a house telephone and dialed 300. After a couple of rings, Lindsey Palmer picked up.

"Third floor West, Palmer!" shouted the nurse over crowd noise.

"What's going on up there?" asked Dr. Harwell, in a voice that didn't mask her concern.

"They all just showed up at once," cried Lindsey.

"Who showed up?" asked the doctor.

"A bunch of people, and it's just me and two other nurses! Someone told me it's like this all over the hospital!"

"Hang in there Lindsey!" said Dr. Harwell. "I'll get everyone back. When you have a chance, call Providence

Hospital and see if they have any extra help they can spare us. I'm on my way up."

She hung up the phone then hit the all page button. "May I have your attention please," she said over the intercom. "This is Dr. Marilynn Harwell. I would like all West Three staff to return to their stations immediately. West three staff report back."

She replaced the phone on its cradle and scanned the room. It was still overcrowded, but was at least a little more under control. Propped against the wall to the left sat beer guy rubbing his multiple chins. Satisfied, she zig zagged her way over to the elevator where Doug Talbot stood waiting patiently. The elevator doors were open so she stepped inside. Talbot followed behind carrying his semi-conscious daughter. The elevator lurched upward just like it always did, and a suddenly exhausted Doctor Harwell leaned against the elevator's side rail.

"Jeez!" she said, tilting her head back and shaking her hair. "What the heck was that all about?"

"Don't you know what's going on?" asked Talbot.

Dr. Harwell shrugged. "No! What?"

Coventry General Hospital
Front Desk
6:32am

RN Nancy Beakerman looked up from her computer. Standing in front of her were three teenage girls. They looked like typical teenagers: blue jeans with the ripped knees; tube tops; long blonde, brown, and strawberry hair; and assorted nose, tongue and navel rings.

"May I help you ladies?" asked Beakerman.

"She dropped a hair brush on her foot," said the Blonde, chomping on gum.

"Who dropped a hair brush?" asked the confused nurse.

"Brittany did!" snapped the Blonde, who, with the help

of the brown haired girl supported the redhead. Sweat poured from her forehead.

"Did you hear me?" yelled the blonde. "She like, dropped a freakin' hair brush on her foot! That's all she like, freakin' did."

Nurse Beakerman clicked on the intercom and yelled, "Code blue to the front desk... *stat*! I repeat, code blue to the front desk ...*stat*!"

"I'm so thirsty," said the redhead. It was the last thing she said, as she fell to the floor. She was dead before she hit.

Third Floor
West 3
6:35am

Dr. Harwell and Doug Talbot stood looking out at the same chaotic mess as downstairs. He followed her as she stepped over a group of nuns praying on the floor and then pushed past a middle-aged couple, who were shrieking something in her ear about their son and loud music.

When they reached the middle of the room Dr. Harwell stopped. "Where did all these people come from?" she asked over the clamor.

Doug shrugged.

They pushed forward again and, with great effort, finally reached the nurses' station. Lindsey Palmer stood waving her arms and shouting into a phone. Dr. Harwell grabbed Palmer's wrist and shouted, "Did you ever get Providence Hospital?"

"I'm on the phone with them now," Palmer shouted. Turning back to the phone she begged, "Can't you spare anyone? We're swamped!"

Lindsey's mouth dropped open. "That's not a nice thing to say!" she yelled.

Taking hold of the phone Dr. Harwell said, "Let me talk to them."

"Spare you help!" snapped a female on the other end. "Are you fucking crazy? We have people sitting on floors in every room! They're lined up and down the corridors! Packed like sardines! Hell, we've even got some sitting in the bathrooms! Sixteen people died since I came on duty at midnight and you want us to spare *you* fucking help!"

Dr. Harwell slammed the phone down. It had already gone dead. She pushed it back towards Lindsey. "Call Margie at home and tell her to come in. Tell her I realize she doesn't start till three, but we need her to come in *now*! After that, start calling the entire second shift and tell them to come in. And no excuses!"

She turned to Doug. "What the hell's going on? Was there a full moon last night?"

"I haven't had a chance to tell you what I know," said Doug. "The reason it's so crazy is....." But he couldn't finish. Dr. Harwell had been jerked around by the couple with the son that had loud music.

Grabbing the doctor's jacket in a clenching grip, the hysterical woman shouted, "Please help us!"

"What's wrong with your son?" asked Dr. Harwell, yanking the woman's hands off her lapel and pushing her out of her face.

Unfazed, the woman cried, "We don't know. They brought him into the operating room over two hours ago and we haven't gotten any information."

"Our son had headsets on and was his listening to his CD player at home," said the father in a monotone voice, with one arm embracing his wife's shoulder.

"I warned him about playing it too loud," said the mother. "I told him he would hurt his eardrums."

The man said, "That's right. She did warn him. When we didn't see or hear from him for a couple of hours, I stuck my head in to check on him and he was just lying there, shaking. I went to his bedside and saw that he was sweating out of his forehead. I asked him how he felt and he whispered so low that I had to bend down to hear him say that he was thirsty."

"Did you bring him here or did the rescue?" asked Dr. Harwell.

"As soon as we saw how bad he was we dialed 9-1-1, isn't that what you're supposed to do?" asked the woman, holding her worried face between her hands.

"Yes it is," said Dr. Harwell picking up a phone. "What's his name? I'll see if I can find out what's going on."

"Patrick Adams Junior," said the father. "He's only twelve years old and he must be really scared in there by himself."

Dialing admitting Dr. Harwell said, "Don't worry, your son's in good hands here." After several rings a frantic female voice answered. "Hendricks – admitting – hold!"

Soft instrumental music filled her left ear. She seized the moment to glance around the room and noticed that most of the West 3 staff had returned to help out. She breathed a sigh of relief. At the end of the pan she saw Doug Talbot standing calmly several feet away with his daughter slung over his shoulder, slowly stroking her long hair. A thin smile broke the tight crevices of her mouth.

"I apologize, Mr. Talbot," she said. "I'll only be a minute."

Doug smiled and nodded.

Lindsey Palmer handed her a second phone. "It's Margie, she wants to speak with you."

"Hey, Margie!" said Harwell, putting the phone to her free ear. "Why aren't you on your way in?"

"Sorry, Doc. My baby's sick."

"What's wrong with him?"

"I don't know. He's been throwing up all morning and he has diarrhea."

"Does he have any other symptoms?"

"Yeah. It's kind of weird though. He started sweating profusely from the forehead and no matter how much water I give him, he still seems thirsty. Of course, he's only six months. He didn't actually tell me that."

"Sorry to hear that, Margie, but all hell's broken loose here. We really needed you an hour ago."

"I was thinking of calling in sick, Doc, so I could stay home with my baby. I don't want to stick my mother with a sick kid to watch."

"Tell you what, Margie. Bring your baby. What's his name?"

"Darius Crandell, the 2nd."

"Bring Darius Crandell the Second with you and I'll check him out personally. That way you can still be near him and he'll get the best care available."

"Okay, Doc, you sold me. I'm on my way."

Dr. Harwell handed the phone back to Palmer and turned her attention to the one in her other hand. There was a soft click and Hendricks came back on the line.

"Oh!" she said in a startled voice. "You're still there."

"This is Dr. Harwell. I'm sorry to bother you. I know things must be crazy there."

"You don't know the half of it, Doctor. What can I do for you?"

"I'm trying to locate a twelve year old boy named Patrick Adams. He came in two hours ago. The parents say he went into surgery and they haven't heard anything since."

"I don't see his name on my current list, Dr. Harwell. Hold on a second and I'll check my computer."

A minute went by before Hendricks came back on the line.

"Found him, Doc."

Doctor Harwell smiled and raised her thumb towards the parents.

"Patrick Adams, twelve years old, was brought in by rescue two hours ago and was pronounced DOA. He was actually signed off by his parents."

Shaking her head she said, "Thanks."

After hanging up the phone she turned to the couple and said, "Mr. and Mrs. Adams, I'm sorry, but your son is dead. You both signed off on him."

"No! No!" shouted the frantic mother and father. "That can't be right!"

"Please call again," begged the father. "His name is Patrick Adams Junior, you asked for Patrick Adams."

"Go home Mr. Adams. There's nothing more you can do for your son."

The husband put his arm around his wife's waist and started leading the sobbing woman towards the elevators. Just before they stepped onto the elevator the wife said, "We did the right thing, didn't we? We dialed 9-1-1."

Dr. Harwell felt deep pity for them and stood there for a long moment after they'd left. Finally she turned and stepped right into a pregnant woman who towered about five inches above her.

"Can you help me?" asked the young lady politely. "I think something's wrong with me and my baby. I'm so thirsty and I think I must have a fever, because I can't stop sweating from my forehead."

Several more of the West 3 staff had returned. Dr. Harwell pointed towards one of them and said, "Tell your situation to that nurse and she'll help you."

Doug grabbed her arm. His eyes were narrow and his face muscles were so tense they twitched. "I don't know what it means Doc, but I told you my daughter complained of being thirsty and she's been sweating nonstop from her forehead?"

CHAPTER 4

Washington, DC
Defense Department
Special Intelligence Agency
Room 204
7:49am

Sitting straight in his chair, muscular and graying Four Star General Thomas Uxbridge turned to Robert Baker, the President's press secretary. "Where does the president stand?"

Baker, a meticulously dressed older man in a dark striped Ralph Lauren suit, looked around the table at the assembled group of high-ranking military officials, shifted thoughtfully in his seat, then picked up a metal pitcher of water. After filling a glass with ice water he took a quick swig and cleared his throat. The pause was intentional. Speaking slowly and articulately, he said: "The president feels you should do whatever is necessary and within your means to contain this. We don't want a national panic."

The general leaned forward. "When does he plan to issue a statement?"

"As soon as you come up with a strategy, General, he'll go on television and alert the nation. But he must have something concrete to present to the country. And it must be believable. It's important to have the public's confidence."

General Uxbridge scanned the faces of the others

seated at the table as if polling them. He turned suddenly to the man sitting next to him and whispered in his ear.

The man, much lesser in age and stature than the assembled gathering, listened intently. When the General finished, the young man thought intently for a couple of long moments, then whispered a brief response.

General Uxbridge nodded to the secretary. "Tell the president that we'll have a plan by the noon news."

The press secretary stared at the faces of the men huddled around the table. "Have no doubts gentlemen – should your game plan go askew, the president will deny any knowledge or involvement. Plausible denial: that's standard protocol. The president needs to stand tall and look good to the rest of the world. It wouldn't look good if he couldn't take care of his own country, while trying to dictate foreign policy to the rest of the world."

A one-star general leaned back in his chair. "Just what is he expecting us to do?"

"That's what you're all assembled here to decide," said the press secretary. "Please don't tell me this is over your heads? Do I need to go to other agencies, General Uxbridge?"

The general made a discerning face and let out a loud *hurrumph*. "There's no problem, Bob," he said, staring down the other general with the look of a madman.

A high-ranking official at the opposite end of the table stood. "I want you all to know the National Guard stands ready to assist in any way needed. With a call, I can have on average two hundred troops available from every state and, in some select ones, twice that."

"The Navy is ready to go into standby," said an admiral sitting in the middle of the elongated, dark cherry table. "We'll supply our usual strong air and water support. Half the fleet will be at your disposal."

"How about the Marines?" asked the press secretary.

A well-decorated official answered in a deep voice, "Gentlemen! The Marines will supply the usual myriad of air and land support. And we'll do the dirty work that no one else wants to do."

"Good," said the secretary. "Sounds like you've got things under control here, General Uxbridge. Now all you have to do is come up with a viable plan for the president to stand behind."

"Why don't we say that it's mad cow disease?" asked a low ranking officer.

"Don't be an idiot!" snapped General Uxbridge.

The officer slumped back in his chair.

"We could blame it on Russia!" shouted another.

"Can't do that," said Uxbridge. "We haven't been able to blame them for anything for years now, or at least since that plane incident. Besides, the president wants them as allies. That way we can keep an eye on them and constantly know what they're up to."

Despondence swept instantly over the room. It was as if they had been given the unfortunate news of a close friend dying. Everyone sat staring at their hands or the table in front of them.

General Uxbridge leaned back in his chair, lit a cigar, puffed out several wisps of smoke and said in a curious tone, "What do you think, Carl?"

The young man he had just spoken to fidgeted in his seat, then cleared his throat several times. The cavernous conference room added to his uneasiness at being around much higher-ranking officials.

"Gentleman," said Uxbridge, "for those of you who don't know him, this is Major Carl Edwards. He's my right-hand man. I never go anywhere without him. Whatever he lacks in maturity and tenure is made up for by being one of the best damn strategists and intelligence people working at the SIA."

Major Edwards, an average-sized man with his black hair in the usual military cut, blushed. Sensing that his hesitancy was perceived as a sign of weakness, he cleared his throat one last time and said in a deep and confident voice, "Tell the president we have our top scientists working on a solution and that we'll take care of everything on this end."

The press secretary walked to the door. Hesitating, he turned back and in a parting word said, "I like that. Our top scientists are feverishly working on the cause and solution. That's something tangible I can give the president. But that only buys you short time. I trust we'll be hearing from you later today."

After Baker left, the group stood around the room for several minutes mulling over the task set before them. They took turns weighing in with their own ideas for what should be done.

General Uxbridge, being the highest-ranking officer and head of the SIA, was highly regarded when it came to security measures. Calling everyone's attention he addressed the group after there was quiet.

"Men, we are about to enter into territory this country hasn't faced since nine-eleven." The room took on a silence, which could only be rivaled by a black hole in space. Continuing he said, "I have been in constant contact with Intelligence all morning and what they've told me so far sickens me. In a short time they will submit their final analysis to me, at which point I'll contact each of you through the *Bypass Alert System*. Meanwhile, put all available troops on standby. When this comes down, we need to be ready to act."

The group's mood turned somber. They each took turns shaking the general's hand or simply patting him on the back as they made their way out of the conference room. Everyone disbanded quickly – except one.

"That was good work, Major," said the general.

The major straightened proudly. "Thank you, Sir. Is their anything else I can do?"

"Actually, there is. Talk to Central Control and find out how many of our own men are available and put them on high alert."

"Right away," said Edwards. "How is everything going at the other end?"

"No delivery yet."

"Are you anticipating a problem?"

"Sometimes these things go slow then all of a sudden they accelerate and it gets crazy. Don't worry. Everything will be fine. Now go check on those men."

"Yes, Sir," said Edwards, snapping off a salute before heading out the door.

The General returned the salute, then spun his chair out of view of the door and pulled a cell phone from his inside front pocket. He hit the pound key three times. It rang twice before someone with a deep British accent said, "Reid!"

"Noposam is in trouble," said the General. "What do I tell the president?"

There was a lengthy disquieting pause, interrupted only by heavy breathing.

"There's been a biological attack against the United States by an unidentified terrorist group," said the Englishman.

Corner of Elm and Jefferson
Downtown Providence
Minor traffic accident
7:54am

Officer Charles Dennigan sat in his patrol car doing the last thing he wanted to do before his shift ended: filling out an accident report.

"I can't believe this old goat called the police for a minor bumper tap," thought the portly police sergeant out loud. "Now I'll be late getting home for dinner."

All at once there was rapid tapping on his window. Jim Silvia, the young man whose car tapped bumpers with the old goat's car, stood frowning. Dennigan cracked his window open.

"This jerk Johnson wants us to call an ambulance!" shouted Silvia, jumping up and down. "He says he doesn't feel good. You know this is just a gimmick so he can sue the pants off me. Man, I barely touched his car. You can't even see a freakin' scratch on his bumper."

Officer Dennigan shook his head and rolled his eyes. Glancing over at the pristine green 64' Oldsmobile where Johnson sat behind the wheel he said, "Looks okay to me."

"Go over and talk to him," pleaded Silvia.

Dennigan sighed deeply as he got out of his cruiser. "Let me see what I can do," he said, adjusting his gun in his squeaking leather holster.

The sergeant ambled over to the Oldsmobile and tapped on the window. Old man Johnson made no response. He had a firm grip on the steering wheel and stared straight ahead.

The sergeant rapped on the window a second time, but still the elderly man didn't look up.

"Hey! Johnson!" yelled the officer. "Look at me."

The old man remained frozen. The irritated officer yanked the door open and started to reach in but suddenly pulled back. Sweat poured from the man's forehead and he was pale white. The old man looked up at the patrolman with eyes that looked far away. "I'm so thirsty," he said weakly.

"Hang in there, Mr. Johnson, help's on the way!" yelled the officer, bolting towards his cruiser. Johnson was dead before the officer finished dialing 9-1-1.

Coventry General Hospital
Third floor
Room 310
8:00am

Dr. Harwell jotted a few notes on Cassandra Talbot's chart. The seven-year-old already had signs of early morning hair, as she lay staring up with unblinking blue eyes. Her father was fidgety standing beside her bed.

"How do you feel, Cassandra? Did that glass of water help any?"

"I'm so thirsty," she moaned. "Can I have another?"

"Sure you can, honey," said her father, gently rubbing her arm.

Dr. Harwell scribbled a few more notes on the child's chart, while her father filled a paper cup with water from a plastic pitcher.

"Mr. Talbot, has Cassandra suffered any type of trauma recently?"

"How recently?"

"Within the past month or two."

"Not that I'm aware of. Why"

"Sometimes injuries take a while to surface. Not that long ago, I had a patient who was experiencing severe back pain, but couldn't recall doing anything that could have caused it. It turned out he had been knocked down by a jogger while out for a walk, but didn't realize until three months later that he had pinched a nerve."

Doug considered her question. Glancing out the window, he stared past the foot traffic coming and going up the front walk of the hospital, and was unaware of the moving vehicles going up and down the street.

"I don't know if this means anything," he said, "but about two months ago Cassandra had an accident during gymnastics practice."

"What kind of accident?"

"She was trying to learn the balance beam and she slipped off and fell hard on the floor mat."

"How badly was she hurt?"

"Mostly bruises to her arms and shoulders. Problem was, she landed awkwardly on her neck. The school nurse suggested she get an MRI done just in case."

"Did you?"

"Two days later Cassandra complained of a stiff neck, so I had her mom call the family doctor. After checking her, he said it wouldn't be a bad idea to go ahead with an MRI, just to make sure there was no hidden damage."

"Where did you go for the tests?"

"The doctor's office set her up at an open MRI facility downtown. But it didn't go well," said Talbot, shaking his head. "Poor Cassandra's claustrophobic. Even though it's an open MRI, she was stressed out so much that she was sweating like crazy, just like she is now. About five minutes into the test I went in and sat with her, thinking that if she had company, she'd get through it. They restarted, but she just couldn't handle it, so it was canceled."

"Did the sweating stop?"

"She was back to normal about two hours after I got her home. At the time I figured she was just really nervous."

"Does your family or your wife's family have any history of diabetes?"

"My ex-wife," said Talbot. "I'm divorced."

"I'm sorry. I didn't know. Are you aware of any existing diabetes on her side of the family, or of anyone in yours?"

"Not that I know of, Doc."

Doctor Harwell turned to Cassandra. "This won't hurt a bit," she said, placing her stethoscope under the girl's shirt. "I just want to listen to your heart."

The little girl forced a thin smile. "I know what that's for," she said quietly. "The school nurse showed us at the beginning of school last year."

"That's great," said Dr. Harwell. "Did she show you how to take a person's pulse rate?"

"I don't think so," she whispered.

The doctor took the girl's wrist in hers and started timing on her watch. "By counting how many beats your heart goes per minute, I can tell how fast your heart is going."

"That's pretty neat," said Cassandra. "I think I want to be a doctor when I grow up, so I can help sick people too."

When the doctor was finished, she placed the girl's hand gently back on the bed and wrote more notes on her chart. Looking down at the girl she said, "After you finish school, Cassandra, I want you to come back here and you and I can help sick people together."

"That would be fun," said Cassandra in a whisper. "I like you. You're really nice." The girl curled up into a ball and quickly slipped into an uneasy sleep. Her father tucked her in.

Dr. Harwell motioned to go out into the hallway, and they tiptoed out, trying not to wake Cassandra.

"I'm concerned about your daughter, Mr. Talbot."

"First of all, call me Doug. No more of this Mister Talbot stuff. It makes me feel old, okay, To-ens?"

Dr. Harwell blinked several times, and hesitated before continuing. "As I was saying, I'm concerned about your daughter."

"In what way, To-ens?"

The doctor's mouth dropped open and she stopped talking.

"What's the matter, Doc? Something wrong?"

Dr. Harwell glanced away at the floor, then turned back and met Doug's eyes. Under the bright light of the hallway, it was the first time she noticed how they seemed to see right through to her mind. She struggled to keep from blushing.

"Doctor, is there something wrong?"

"I'm curious why you keep calling me To-ens?" she asked.

"Marilynn - with two N's, right?"

"Yes, but what does that have to do with it?"

"Most people spell it with one 'N'. So it's *Two N's or To-ens,*" he said, shrugging.

Dr. Harwell couldn't stop herself from laughing out loud.

"If it bothers you, Doc, I won't say it."

"No......it's okay. It's kind of cute. You can call me that, I don't mind. Finally, someone who actually pays attention to my name."

Waving the clipboard, she went on, "On a more serious note, Mr. Talbot, I mean Doug, I'm worried about your daughter. She has the classic symptoms of acute diabetes. I want to run a couple of blood tests on her and I'm going to set her up an IV. Her blood sugar level may be so elevated that she risks going into a seizure. Trust me Doug, you don't want that to happen, because it could be fatal."

Al's Bowling Alley
St. Mary's third grade
Field trip
9:30am

Al's Bowling Alley was alive with the sound of kids' chatter, rolling bowling balls and crashing pins. Mrs. Bannister's third grade class formed teams according to best friends and quiet kids who didn't have any.

Amber Prior found herself on one of the latter teams. She wanted to have fun, but none of her teammates talked other than to say, "You're up!"

By the third frame, Amber was doing poorly. She had only knocked down seven pins in four throws. A boy who had just narrowly missed a spare walked back to the players' bench and pointed at Amber. "You're up," he said stoically.

He sat down, crossed his arms and said nothing else. Amber stepped up to get her ball, full of hope that she would knock down some pins. First she waved her hands over the air blower, drying the dampness off her palms. Next, she picked up a black, five-pound bowling ball and walked to the starting line, standing dead center. Raising the ball to eye level, she scrutinized the front pin at the other end of the alley.

She walked several steps and lobbed her ball. It picked up speed as it raced down the alley, striking the lead pin and continuing through until all ten pins fell down.

"A strike!" she screamed, jumping up and down. "I got a strike!"

But Amber had failed to hear the buzzer that had gone off. Her throw didn't count because she had stepped over the foul line.

"That's okay," said Mrs. Bannister. "You get a second throw."

Dejected, the girl picked up a random ball, stepped forward without even lining up her shot, tripped over her foot and stumbled around till she fell backwards onto her butt.

She stayed on the floor as jeers and taunts came at her from all directions. Even the boy who told her it was her turn pointed and laughed. Mrs. Bannister placed a hand over her mouth, concealing a sliver of a smile from the children.

Amber reached up and brushed away perspiration that was beginning to form on her forehead.

* * *

Doug Talbot and the doctor remained talking outside Cassandra's room. "As I said Mr. Talbot, her condition could get serious. Maybe even fatal."

"Straight from the hip, To-ens. You don't mince words."

"Not when it comes to human life, especially a precious child."

"Whatever you need from me, Doc, you've got it."

"I do need to know one important piece of information."

"What's that?"

"Do you have custody of your daughter or does your ex-wife?"

"She does. Why?"

"I need her consent on the admittance form."

"Damn!" shouted Talbot.

"What's the matter?" she asked.

"She's probably sleeping off a night of boozing with her twenty year old boyfriend."

"There's a phone inside your daughter's room. You can call her from there."

They eased back inside and Dr. Harwell said, "While you're here it won't hurt to check you out too. I'd like to satisfy my concern about any family history on your side.

Take off your shirt and I'll check out your heart, or should I say, check to see if you have one."

"Ouch! That hurts. Where'd that shot come from?"

"Gee! I don't know. Maybe the To-ens remark."

"I thought you liked that?" said Talbot, dialing his ex's phone number.

Marilynn smiled to herself.

He let it ring about a dozen times before giving up. "She's probably passed out drunk," he said shaking his head.

"The shirt!" she said, pointing at him.

He unbuttoned his denim shirt, pulled each arm out till it was free and tossed it on the floor.

"To-ens – Doc – are you okay?"

Dr. Harwell stood still as a statue, staring at his bare taut, slightly hairy chest.

"I'm sorry," she said. "My mind was someplace else."

Feeling her face flush she turned away, pretending to adjust a few instruments on a table. Talbot's pager started beeping. He ignored it.

"You know, Doc, you look familiar," he said, sitting on a stool. "Have we met before?"

Composed, she placed her stethoscope over Doug's heart. "Sorry, I don't remember you. Hundreds of people come through the hospital every day. If you were one of them, I don't remember."

"Damn! That's cold!"

"Don't be such a wimp. Your daughter didn't complain?"

"It's a known fact kids are stronger at pain tolerance than adults."

"Bull," she said. "Now keep quiet so I can listen."

His heartbeat was steady and strong and she found herself strangely focused on each subsequent beat to the point where shots of electricity tingled through her body. The hypnotic steady rhythm of his heart was overwhelming and she became aware of her own heartbeat going faster.

Embarrassed by this overwhelming affect he had over her, her face flushed again. Luckily, Doug was looking down at the floor and didn't notice.

"Anything there, Doc?"

Clearing her throat, she stepped behind him. "Just barely," she answered, placing the stethoscope on his bare back. "Take deep breaths."

He inhaled several full breaths and she felt herself breathing in cadence with him.

"Lungs seem fine. We're almost done," she said, placing a pressure wrap over his upper arm. "I just need to take your blood pressure." She inflated the gauge to maximum pressure, then turned the release valve open.

"One forty over ninety. Your blood pressure is a little high," she said, unwrapping the cuff. "You seem to be in pretty good shape, so maybe the high number can be attributed to being nervous and apprehensive because of Cassandra."

"I don't get nervous," he said. "And I am in good shape."

"Nevertheless," she went on, "your heart rate was a little fast and your blood pressure was slightly

high. I suggest we retest tomorrow, just as a precaution."

"Fine," said Doug. "And I promise I won't complain if the stethoscope's too cold."

"Very brave of you," she said. "I just wish I had a lollipop for you for being so brave!"

"Guess I had that coming."

"Ya think," she said, chuckling. "Also, be ready to do some blood tests. There may be something there that's been dormant or overlooked in your past physicals. I would like to rule out any inherent sign of diabetes."

"But I feel as fit as a racehorse, To-ens. Besides, I haven't needed a physical since I played high school sports."

"I'm setting you up for some tests right now," she said, her face and tone serious. "You shouldn't have gone that long without even having a basic physical."

Doug's pager beeped three loud chirps. "Damn! The station's paging me."

"What do you mean station? Like a fire or police station?"

"I work for WJAM-TV, and I've ignored their pages for so long they probably filed a missing person's report. There's probably some big breaking news story."

"Look, Doug. There isn't much you can do for your daughter right now. Why don't you go check in at the station and that'll give us time to run tests on Cassandra. The sooner we diagnose what's wrong, the sooner we can start treatment."

"If you're sure that's a good idea, then let me give you my cell phone number," he said, scribbling on a napkin from a food cart. "Call any time, if you have any concerns or questions about my daughter."

She folded the napkin in two, then stuck it in her front pocket. "Trust me. I won't hesitate."

"Great!" said Doug, putting his shirt back on.

As he started for the door she called, "Don't forget, I still need your wife to sign the consent form!"

He opened the door halfway and stopped. "I'll give her a call from work. If she gives me any trouble, I'll drive to her house and physically carry her here on my back."

"That'd be pretty funny, Daddy," whispered Cassandra.

Doug flew to his daughter's bedside. "You rest up and get better, munchkin. And do what the doctor tells you to do. She wants you to feel good again, just as much as I do. Now promise me you'll do whatever she asks."

Cassandra looked up with strained, sunken eyes. Sweat gleamed on her forehead. "I promise, Daddy," she said, her voice trailing off.

Doug knew his daughter had used every bit of strength she had to answer. He felt the pain all the way down to his toes as he stroked her hair soothingly and then kissed her on the side of her face.

"I've got to go," he mouthed to Dr. Harwell. She nodded and smiled, flashing him the okay sign.

Doug stepped out of the room and suddenly felt the weight of the world on his shoulders. The elevator ride to the first floor gave him no reprieve and he had no interest in reading any of the love hearts on the walls. When the doors swung open he stepped out onto a congested floor, but it was a much calmer atmosphere than earlier. A young nurse sat typing on a computer as a man offered information about his son.

"Excuse me, nurse," he interrupted. "What happened to the guy I smacked earlier?"

The nurse looked up from her computer, her face expressionless and her eyes empty and colorless. "He died a short time ago," she said in a flat voice.

Doug's jaw dropped. "How can that be? I didn't hit him that hard. He seemed okay when I left here."

"Shortly after you hit him, he complained of being thirsty and said his forehead wouldn't stop sweating," explained the nurse. "We didn't pay any attention to him at first, because we figured he was just being a pain in the butt after all that'd happened. When we realized he wasn't faking I started to do vitals on him, when he suddenly died in my arms. Nine other people have died that way this morning."

The other man grabbed the nurse's arm. "My boy is complaining of being thirsty, and he's sweating from the forehead. Is he going to die?"

Doug didn't wait to hear her answer, instead abruptly turning away and making for the automatic doors. He never heard the young nurse say, "We'll do all we can to help your son Mr. Roberts. I promise."

Stepping out onto a red speckled walkway, he pulled out his cell phone and dialed the station.

"WJAM-TV, news desk. Jeff Page speaking."

"Jeff! It's Talbot. What's going on?"

"Dude, where've you been? All hell's breaking loose."

"My daughter's sick. I've been at the hospital all morning."

"Don't you check your messages, dude? We've been

paging you for two hours and Shoemaker is pissed you're not here."

"I'm on my way, and tell Shoemaker to stick it! It's not my week to be on call."

"Hey, it's your ass dude, not mine! Just wanted to warn you. Gotta go. My other line's ringing. The freakin' phones haven't stopped since I got here. Get here as fast as you can."

The connection went dead. Doug jumped into the station's gray SUV with WJAM, TV-16 in large white letters stenciled on the doors and headed back towards the station. He really didn't care what breaking stories were going on in the world right now. His biggest concern was his daughter.

Driving ten miles over the posted 45 miles-an-hour speed limit, he began a conversation with himself as he sped down the two-lane blacktop highway. "What did the nurse say? The guy I hit died just like nine other people and he complained of thirst and was sweating from the forehead."

He thought about it for a long moment. Suddenly his midsection felt a violent jolt. It was as if someone had dive-bombed a fist into his stomach.

"Jesus! That's exactly what's wrong with Cassandra!" he shouted.

His thoughts were not on driving as he stared off into space, rethinking everything that had happened that morning. The crying mothers and frantic fathers - all the chaos and confusion. What was happening?

A loud thump shook the right side of the car as it hit dirt and grass, sending debris flying high in the air. A passing car on the opposite side blasted its horn as it passed. He snapped out of his brief lapse of concentration and spun the wheel several times to the left, then back to right. The car fought him and he struggled to get it under control for about fifty feet, but he finally got the tires rolling once again over blacktop.

"Son of a bitch!" was the last thing Talbot said as he turned into WJAM-TV's parking lot.

Coventry General Hospital
Emergency room
Front Desk
10:38am

Charge nurse Nancy Beakerman looked up from her seat behind the counter of the nurses' station.

Mrs. Bannister, Saint Mary's third grade teacher stood holding the lifeless body of nine-year-old Amber Prior. Bannister's blue eyes were cracked with jagged rivers of red.

"I didn't mean to laugh," she cried. "I didn't mean to laugh."

Meanwhile, several miles away a rescue truck follows closely behind an ambulance, weaving along a rural two-lane highway. They approach an intersection with shrieking sirens and flashing lights, adjusting speed to allow cars and trucks ample opportunity to move out of their way so they can proceed through the fast approaching red light.

After getting through the intersection, it's a short distance to the entrance for 95 North – which will lead them to Coventry General Hospital. Once on the highway it's two miles of driving to exit seven, a sharp winding curve leading them south on route one. The ambulance negotiates the curve at a brisk speed, but the rescue truck needs to slow down in order to round the corner. Traffic on the four lane highway parts as if Moses himself had raised his staff and instructed them to, and both rescue vehicles throttle up to make the two minute drive to the hospital in only one.

A large blue sign marked *Coventry General Hospital – Emergency Vehicles Only*, was marked by a white arrow pointing inward. The ambulance and the fire-engine-red rescue turned up a circular driveway to the side emergency admitting entrance. The truck had barely come to a halt when the EMT driver burst out and headed to the back door. Another technician released it from inside, sending the door flying open.

"I've got this end of the stretcher," said the driver."

"Got it!" yelled the inside technician. "Go!"

The stretcher flew out the back. The patient had an IV attached to his right arm and an oxygen mask covered his face. A light perspiration glistened on his forehead.

With a skill honed from many other similar missions, they placed the stretcher on the ground, raised it to hip level and raced towards the automatic opening doors. The doors magically slid open with precision as they approached and the EMT's burst into the hospital.

They immediately met resistance as they tried to get to the front desk. Inching their way forward, they tried pushing through a hallway jammed with patients standing and milling around. The noise was louder than a church social. Their progress was slow as they swerved to avoid hitting patients who had their own IV's hung from rolling portable stands. They excused themselves to get by patients sitting on the floor, while others stood leaning against the hallway walls or sitting in wheelchairs. Finally, they had to stop and physically move a group of five senior citizens that stood blocking the way.

Reaching the front desk, the driver called out, "This is Tony Scarnekia. Where do you want him?"

A middle-aged nurse talking frantically on the phone turned his way and said, "There are no rooms. Find a place against the wall. As soon one opens up we'll take him in." She returned to her spirited phone conversation.

"Hey!" said a man in a dark suit and sunglasses, who'd followed the stretcher in. "Didn't you hear the guy? This is Tony Scarnekia from *The Hill*. Where da ya want him?"

The harried nurse put the phone against her chest and looked directly at the man in the dark suit. Speaking just above the bedlam she said, "I told you to find a place against the wall! Are you blind? Can't you see how hectic it is? We don't have any rooms or doctors available!"

The man in the dark suit reached to his midsection, unbuttoned his jacket and pulled it slightly open to reveal a black shoulder-holstered gun. "Maybe you didn't understand me, lady. Where can we bring my boss?"

Unperturbed, the nurse replied, "I know who your boss is, Sir, but as you can plainly see, we are a little overwhelmed. Please take your employer off to the side and I'll see what I can do after I finish with this call."

The man re-closed his jacket and buttoned it. "That would be greatly appreciated," he said stone-faced.

State Medical Building
Coroner's Office
Downtown
10:52am

Dr. Paul Crawford, Chief Medical Examiner at Providence Medical Morgue, pulled his buried head from his hands, startled by a ringing phone. He glanced at the *Jack Daniels* bottle on the table in front of him and cursed. It was empty.

The ringing phone persisted. "I'm fucking coming!" he yelled at the inanimate object.

At sixty, Crawford had seen it all. Suicides, fire casualties, gun and knife victims, car accident fatalities, but worst of all, abused babies. The years and tragedies had taken their toll on his nerves. Drinking was the only sanity he knew now.

The phone had rung countless times by the time he shuffled his short rotund body across the room. He never rushed to answer anymore. It was always death and grief for some poor unsuspecting family.

Snatching the phone he answered, "Medical Examiner's office, Crawford!"

"Paul," said a soft voice on the other end.

"Hey, Marilynn," he answered shakily. He needed a drink bad.

"Are you okay?" she asked with concern.

"Not really. I've gotten sixty-eight bodies in the last twenty hours. The walk-in refrigerator is bursting at the seams and all six tables in the autopsy suite are filled. I had to call in extra help."

"Where's your assistant?" asked Marilynn. "What's his name?"

"Mendez," he answered with great effort. "Would you believe it? I gave him the night off to go to a freakin' play at the Arts Center."

"I guess you've got your hands full."

"Yeah," he answered despondently, burying his head between his hands again. "Just another day at the office. Now, what can I do for you?"

"I wanted to know if you've noticed anything unusual about all these victims?"

"Yeah! They're all dead!"

"I'm serious, Paul. Is there anything about them that....."

"Not that I've noticed," he interrupted. "As a matter of fact, I just finished working on someone named *Jack Daniels*."

"You're drunk, aren't you?"

"Look, Marilynn. I only drink to excess."

"Paul, I need you to do me a big favor and you need to be sober."

"Okay! Okay!" he said, lifting his head out. "I'll put on a fresh pot of coffee as soon as I hang up. So what's the big favor?"

"You know I wouldn't ask if it wasn't important."

"Even drunk I know that."

"I need you to match all the causes of death."

"And just what am I looking for?"

"I'm not sure. Look for a pattern of anything odd or strange."

"Got it! Make note of anything strange or odd."

"This is important, Paul. Can I depend on you?"

"How long have we known each other, Marilynn? Have I ever let you down before?"

"Thanks. I knew I could count on you."

"Give me some time before you call me back. I'll see what I can dig up. Bad pun."

"And Paul."

"Yeah?"

"Don't forget."

"Forget what?"

"That pot of coffee."

There was a soft click, then a dial tone.

SIA Headquarters
Bypass Alert System
Conference call
11:00am

General Thomas Uxbridge waited till he got the okay sign from his assistant that all high-ranking military personnel were on the line. Engaging the talk button on the six inch by six inch black *BASS* box, the *Bypass Alert System* communicator, he said in his deep and powerful voice, "Good morning once again gentlemen."

After a few responses, he went on: "I've called you all together because we have a serious and lethal situation. Intelligence has confirmed that there was a biological attack against the United States yesterday at approximately six PM by an unidentified terrorist group."

"What the hell's going on, Tom?" said a voice belonging to another general. "Why didn't we hear about this sooner?"

Uxbridge formed a thin smile. It was a cunning one, which supported the fact he knew more than he was about to give up, and he knew the right words to say. "The attack was so subtle that no one knew it had even happened. Only after hospitals reported an unusual amount of abnormal deaths did it come to light."

"How the fuck was it started?" asked a younger voice.

"I don't have all the specifics yet, but I expect to have them by day's end. What I do know, and I've passed this on to the president, is that a slow-acting chemical that affects the immune system was released. Unfortunately, a lot of people have died in the past seventeen hours and more are expected."

"Son of a bitch!" shouted an irritated voice on the system.

"As of this moment," continued Uxbridge, "the United States is on high alert. The security and stability of our country is in serious jeopardy. While Washington's top scientists and doctors work to find an antidote, it's up to us to secure the nation and make sure that mass hysteria doesn't take hold."

An eerie silence engulfed the alert system.

"What are your orders General?" asked a serious, but understanding voice.

"We're starting at level six, the maximum alert level," boomed the general. "You should all receive your orders from *Intercom* shortly." Uxbridge drew a slow and noticeable breath and exhaled sharply. "Make no mistake gentlemen. Those plans are to be followed to the letter. Any deviations from this strategy and your asses will be on the line. You *will* be held accountable!"

After a short pause he continued. "Our main focus is to secure our waterways and shipping ports, bridges, airports, railways and subways. But it should be done with as little fanfare as possible."

He hesitated a moment to catch his breath, and also so everyone had a chance to catch theirs.

"Also," he continued, "as further intelligence comes in, forces will be needed to track and arrest suspects. As of ten o'clock this morning the president has issued a directive to close our borders. Plans are currently in place for him to address the nation in about an hour. I fear that we have a potentially dangerous situation once that information gets out to the public. Should that happen, I will ask the president to execute martial law.

You all now know the seriousness of our situation. But this is what you have been trained for and I expect nothing less than full execution of your orders. Gentlemen, it's time for all forces to come together in a united stand to save our country. Can I count on your cooperation?"

"We understand, General," came a monotone reply.

CHAPTER 5

98 Lake Shore Drive
11:07am

Doug Talbot had changed his mind at the last minute. Instead of going into the station he performed an illegal U-turn and was weaving his way down Main Avenue. It took all of his twenty-six years of driving skill to avoid the wandering people in the street. Most of the pedestrians he was dodging seemed disoriented and lost, with no clear idea of where they wanted to go. He swerved at the last second, avoiding a young woman and her two children, then quickly turned the wheel the other way to keep from hitting a parked car.

He was speeding and the tires were squealing when he rounded the corner of Main onto Lake Shore Drive, and headed towards his ex-wife's house.

"Jesus!" he yelled, as his car struck a man and threw him onto the windshield. The man's face was pinned against the glass. What caught his attention when he pulled the car to a screeching stop was that the man was dressed only in his underwear.

Doug scrutinized the distorted face staring in at him. He was shocked and surprised, because he recognized it. It was his ex-wife's date! *The Kid,* as Doug called him, had wide eyes and fear stretching his youthful face.

"Are you okay?" yelled Talbot through the glass.

The kid was shaking and shivering and sweat was oozing from his forehead as he stared back in horror. "You okay?" repeated Doug. The boy's mouth opened, but no words came out. He scrunched his eyes and slid off the hood, then ran away down the street with arms flailing.

"Damn!" shouted Doug. "That's as crazy as it gets. Thank God he didn't crack the windshield. Shoemaker would be pissed." It had just been replaced last month.

Looking back over his shoulder at the fleeing young man, he said, "And thank God I didn't hurt *The Kid*. He'd have been pissed at that too."

Nearing the one story gray Ranch, he felt a few fond memories stir inside him. Before his ex-wife had turned weird, they had worked hard to scrounge enough for a down payment on the cute three bedroom home on the waterfront in hopes of starting a family. Everything had been great for the first five years, before she turned back into an adolescent. He shook his head. Too bad she ended up with the house!

The tires crunched on gravel as he pulled into the driveway and parked next to Christine's white Ford Mustang convertible. It was a car that was way too powerful for her, something he had reminded her of on many occasions, only to have her tell him, "Mind your own freakin' business!"

Leaping up the three stone steps to the back kitchen door, he pounded several times and waited for the usual groggy response. It wasn't etched in stone that she'd be awake after sleeping off her night of boozing.

He inspected his former house while he waited. It needed a paint job and some of the moldings were coming off the windows. "I guess boy toy isn't a carpenter," said Doug to no one. His ex always dated people she could use. When she needed work done on her bathroom, she'd date a plumber. When she needed her car fixed, she'd go out with a mechanic. He once told her she was prostituting herself doing that, whereupon she'd called him names he'd never heard before.

When she didn't respond to his initial knocks he

pounded three solid times on the door yelling, "Christine, open up! It's me, Doug!" He heard no stirring inside. "Come on, Christine, get your ass out of bed!"

He waited several minutes, then called, "That's it! I'm coming in whether you're up or not." Lifting the worn rubber welcome mat lying at his feet, which had only faint traces of the letters C and E left, he snatched up a spare key. She hid it there so he could get in on days she couldn't pick up their daughter from school, which, lately, had happened often due to her promiscuousness. After letting himself inside, he had to step over countless empty beer cans and a few wine bottles strewn over the floor.

"Damn it, Christine!" his voice echoed. "Don't you ever clean in here?" He stepped tentatively over the debris as he made his way across the kitchen to the hallway, which led to her bedroom. On the way, he stepped over clothing that was lying haphazardly on the floor.

He stopped at the doorway and knocked one last time before entering. "Christine! It's me, Doug. I'm coming in." The door was unlocked and pushed in easily. He stepped over the threshold, the same one he had carried her across the night they got married, and went to her bedside. She was lying on top of the bed wearing just a shiny velvet bra and matching panties. Even though her eyes were closed, he knew she wasn't asleep – he had seen that same look on Joe Brooks' face that fateful day in Master Control.

He reached down and felt the pillow under her head. It was soaking wet from the moisture that had leaked from her forehead.

Coventry General Hospital
Nurses Station
Third Floor, West Three
11:23am

"Look who I've got!" shouted Margie Crandell to Lindsey and Dr. Harwell, who stood behind the nurses' station with their backs to her. Crandell saw tired eyes and troubled faces when the Doctor and young Nurse turned her way. "Where's the funeral?" asked Crandell playfully.

"Put your baby in 305," said Dr. Harwell in a deadpan voice.

"But Darlene is in 305."

Palmer stared at the floor. Her eyes were watery and she struggled to speak between sniffles. "She.... didn't make it."

"What do you mean?" asked Crandell.

"She died sometime during the night," said Dr. Harwell.

Crandell's mouth dropped open. "She was just sleeping off a night of boozing."

"We don't really know what happened," said Dr. Harwell solemnly. "The autopsy report should shed some light."

Laying her hand gently on Margie's arm, she continued, "Rooms are at a premium. Take your baby to 305 and I'll be in to check him out as soon as I can. Then I need you to go down to emergency and give them a hand. They're overloaded."

"I noticed that on my way in. What the hell's going on, and who are all these people up here?"

Scanning the crowded room Lindsey said, "This is how it's pretty much been for the past five hours."

"The hallways are jammed," said Margie. "People are even sitting on the floor. I had to come up the back way."

Dr. Harwell leaned forward till her body rested against the countertop. "I wasn't kidding when I told you we needed you as soon as possible."

"I can see that," said Crandell, shaking her head. "I guess I'll catch up with you guys later after I get my baby settled in."

"Nonsense," said Dr. Harwell. "I'll join you in a couple of minutes to check Darius Junior. Then you *have* to get to ER."

"Gotcha!" said Crandell, waving her hand behind her

head as she walked away. No one noticed her swiping a thin film of glistening perspiration off her forehead.

Dr. Harwell handed Lindsey the wrinkled paper that Doug had scribbled his phone number on.

"This is Doug Talbot's phone number. He works at WJAM-TV."

"You want me to call a television station?" asked Lindsey.

"This is his personal cell phone number. Let me know if he's gotten his ex-wife's consent for his daughter's admittance. Things may be crazy and hectic around here, but we're still going to do things the right way."

"I'll page you as soon as I get hold of him, Doctor."

Dr. Harwell left to join Margie and her baby in 305. When she got there she found Crandell singing to her baby, who was lying in an oversized crib.

"How's he doing? Has he stopped throwing up or is he still the same?"

Margie glanced up. "He seems a lot better, and he hasn't been sick since I got off the phone with you."

"That's good news," said the doctor, trying to sound optimistic.

"But it's the damnedest thing," she said. "He's still sweating a lot and no matter how much water I give him, he still wants more. I took his temperature. It's normal."

"Why don't you go down to emergency and give them a hand while I take a good look at him," smiled Harwell. "I'll let you know if I find anything."

"Okay, Doc. I know I'm leaving him in good hands." She leaned down and pulled her baby to her chest. After giving him a big kiss on the forehead she said, "Promise you'll call me if you find anything?"

Dr. Harwell guided the nurse towards the door. "I promise," she pledged.

The door snapped shut behind Crandell and a worried look replaced the smile on the doctor's face. Darius Crandell the Second did not look good.

20 Water Street
11:37am

Dressed in a light purple sweatshirt, black shorts and black striped white running sneakers, Jennie Sprague turned up the radio on the coffee table till it was loud, on her way out the front door for her daily jog. After pulling it shut, she tested the doorknob to make sure it was locked.

Satisfied, she slid a pink headband over her long, curly strawberry hair and stepped quickly down the front slate walkway, turning left at the sidewalk. She pulled the head-set for her portable CD player over her ears and hit the play button. The passionate Heartland rock sounds of Melissa Etheridge's song *Like the Way I Do* filled her ears and she increased her gait to a light jog.

Unnoticed by her, a dark navy-blue sedan followed a safe three car lengths back. A second identical car pulled up in front of her house a short time later. Two tall men in gray suits wearing dark sunglasses went up the front steps. One of them pulled out an odd-looking key and unlocked the front door with no resistance. They slipped quietly inside.

Two minutes into her jog Jennie throttled up her stride to almost a full run. The dark sedan kept pace. A few random cars passed her from each direction, and an elderly couple out for a walk with their dog smiled and said hello. The early September sun felt warm and comforting on her back.

Meanwhile, back at the house, two strangers were nosing around inside. They quickly found Dr. Harwell's and Jennie's address and phone books. One of the men pulled out a mini digital camera and snapped pictures of the books' contents. The other man went room to room taking note of anything of suspected value, until he found Jennie's computer. These men were good at what they were doing. Undercover work was something they reveled in.

Jennie increased her speed to the max and her tail

sped up just enough to keep her in sight. Her red hair blew straight out in her wake, until finally she peaked and started to slow her pace by half. Her hair quickly fell back against her shoulders. During this time, one of the intruders was dumping file information from her computer onto blank discs. He had already filled two.

It was fifteen minutes into Jennie's run when she came to the end of the last street before turning back onto Water Street. The car that had been tailing her sped up and passed her. Inside, the driver pulled out a cell phone and dialed up the two house intruders. Moments later, they exited the house with five discs of data. They had removed the dark sunglasses and looked right at home leaving the house. Passersby would never have suspected they had just stolen someone's personal computer files.

Jennie walked slowly up the front walk, her chest heaving like a ship on a rough sea. When she got to the door she reached into the front pocket of her shorts and extracted a key on a plain key ring. Pushing it into the doorknob and turning it part way, she discovered the door was already unlocked.

"I swear I locked this," she thought out loud. Pushing the door slightly inward, she peeked inside. Everything seemed to be in its place. Feeling confident, she stepped into the front hallway and took a moment to make one last quick scan. "Maybe I didn't lock it," she said under her breath. "If someone did break in, they were pretty bad thieves, because nothing seems to be missing."

Coventry General Hospital
West Three
Room 312
11:58am

Lindsey Palmer bolted into room 312. "There's breaking news on all the TV stations!" she shouted, her voice quivering. "The president's about to speak."

Dr. Harwell and Nurse Crandell had just finished giving examinations to thirteen patients in various degrees of decline who were crammed into the room. "I wonder how much money he wants from us now?" cracked Crandell.

"The reporter on the television said to call friends and relatives and alert them about an important special report by the president," said Lindsey. He's says it's very serious and that it will affect *everyone*."

All at once, a message came over the Hospital paging system instructing the staff to turn on all available televisions for an important presidential announcement.

"Put on Channel 16," said Dr. Harwell to Nurse Crandell. "That's the station Doug - I mean Mister Talbot -works at."

Crandell reached up and turned on the television to Channel 16. The call letters WJAM-TV Providence, were faintly displayed in the left-hand corner out of the way of the president's face.

The three women stood motionless. Strained eyes focused on the twenty-inch television suspended above them, watching the President standing at a dais in front of a collection of television cameras set up on tripods, waiting for his cue to speak.

President Newman was the most popular and respected president of all time, having received three quarters of the electoral vote and seventy percent of the popular vote. When he spoke, people listened and believed in what he said. After several minutes, a young woman in a smoke-gray suit walked out and whispered into the president's ear.

The president stepped to the podium. Surrounded by five FBI agents wearing the usual dark sunglasses and suits, he leaned forward and spoke into the nest of entangled microphones. "It is with grave news that I come before you today," he opened. "Your country, our country, has come under attack by an unidentified foreign terrorist group."

The president paused, waiting for the words to sink in. The medical staff in room 312 exchanged anxious glances and collective sighs. Some of the patients groaned.

"This blatant attack on the United States," he continued, in a louder and more grim tone, "is so vulgar, so underhanded and cowardly that it makes me sick to my stomach to have to stand here and tell you!"

Again he paused, scanning the room of reporters, giving his profile to the horde of flashing cameras located on either side of him. He waited a little extra time before continuing in a slower monotone voice: "At twelve PM on the ninth day of September, the United States was attacked with an invisible biological virus called *B-Thrax*. This virus attacks the immune system, causing death quickly, usually within the first twenty-four hours."

A loud gasp and screams of *Oh my God!* escaped the mouths of the three medical personnel in 312, and just about everywhere else where televisions were being watched.

The President stood composed. "I want the citizens of the United States to know that our top scientists in Washington have been working on this reprehensible situation. They have assured me that they have an antidote in the form of a vaccination and spray, to counteract this invisible biological invader."

He took a deep breath and continued: "Very shortly, you will be seeing our brave servicemen and women dressed in contamination suits spraying in your neighborhoods and inside public buildings. Airplanes will be flying over watersheds and out-of-the-way places dropping the spray."

He hesitated several long, agonizing moments while staring directly at the camera facing him. His face was sad, his voice subdued. "Unfortunately, some people will die before we can distribute the vaccination shots or spray every contaminated area. I'm sorry to bring you this unfortunate news. It disheartens me deeply that innocent people will die. Remember! That's the root of terrorism!"

He moved back a step, breathed deeply, then stepped up to the microphones again. "I realize this is a disturbing reality." Shaking his head he said in a voice that trailed sadly off, "We just won't be able to cover the whole country in time....."

The conference room was still and the air was thick with anger. Pointing emphatically at the cameras he said in a strong tone, "As your president, I make you this promise: We will go after these animals that masterminded this egregious and unforgivable act and we will make them pay!" The president's expression grew more serious and strained as he paused to regain his breath. He glanced side to side several times, making it a point to look into each television camera.

"Let there be no mistake!" he said, his voice rising with each word. "We will make the United States, your country, our country, safe once again!" He dropped his voice, tried to sound encouraging. "General Thomas Uxbridge, our top SIA official, has assured me that he has the country under control. All he asks is that you remain calm and cooperate with his soldiers. Please do not interfere with them as they do their job. This will ensure everyone's safety being restored as quickly as possible. I fully support the general in this. He and I agree that anyone caught hindering the completion of this effort will be regarded as a traitor and will be prosecuted to the fullest.

God bless the citizens of this great nation. We will get through this together. And I promise you, we will find the terrorist thugs that were responsible and we will bring them to justice."

The president stepped away from the podium and retreated with his security entourage out a side entrance. The three women in room 312 felt as if they had been jabbed in the gut with a knife, and all the air inside of them had suddenly fizzed out.

Nurse Palmer wrapped her arms around herself and squeezed hard. "Jeez!" she said in a shivering voice.

Margie Crandell went to the door and paused. "I need to check on my baby," she said with trepidation in her voice. The others nodded. Again they didn't notice the nurse swipe a stream of sweat off her forehead as she exited the room.

"Dr. Marilynn Harwell, please call extension 333," came a page over the hospital system. The doctor picked up a wall-mounted phone by the door and dialed the extension to West Three.

"This is Doctor Harwell," she said to a nurse named Saunders on the other end.

"Doctor, I have a Miss Sprague on the line for you."

"Send it to 312," she said. There was a short silence as the call was forwarded.

"Marilynn," said Jennie, "do you have a second?"

"Sure, what's up?"

"I hate to bother you at work, it's probably nothing, but I thought I should call you, and like I said, I don't want to bother you, because it's probably nothing anyway."

"Jennie, you're not making any sense. What's the matter?"

"Well, like I said, it's probably nothing, but after I came back from my run a short time ago, I found the front door unlocked. And I'm sure that I locked it before I left."

"Did you notice anything missing or disturbed?"

"Not that I could tell. I mean, everything that's worth anything is where it should be. If someone had broken in, they surely would have taken the computer setup and the entertainment center. Heck, you even have four rolls of quarters on your bureau and they're still there. What do you think?"

"I wouldn't worry," said Marilynn. "Maybe you thought you locked the door, but when you pulled it closed, the lock was only halfway turned and it snapped back open."

"Yeah, that's got to be it," said Jennie, much relieved.

"Things are really hectic here, Jennie. More than likely I'm going to get home a lot later than I thought. Maybe even late tonight. Will you be okay without a car for a little while longer?"

"Yeah. Keep it for as long as you need to. I don't think I'll need it for a couple more days."

"Thanks," said Marilynn. "I owe you one."

"You owe me more than one," laughed Jennie.

"By the way, Jennie, how do you feel? You don't feel overly thirsty or have any unusual sweating around the forehead, do you?"

"I'm fine, why?"

"There's something going around and I just wanted to make sure you're okay."

"Thanks for asking, mom, but I feel great!"

"Hey! I told you. I'm your big sister," laughed Marilynn. "I've got to get back to work. Is there anything else you need?"

"Nah," said Jennie. That's all I called......"

She stopped in mid-sentence.

"What's the matter?" asked Marilynn, concerned now.

"The radio!"

"What about it?"

"I'm positive it was on when I left."

Marilynn was sure it was on too. "Call the police," she said.

CHAPTER 6

Washington, DC
SIA Headquarters
Data Control Room
12:53pm

General Uxbridge stepped into SIA Data Control. Two mammoth army soldiers followed, fully armed and brandishing, posted just inside the doorway. "Do you have the information I asked for?" barked the general.

The busy room was filled with fifty cubicles each set up with a computer, printer and a direct line to SIA Central. There were no outside lines for personal calls, and no internet for needless web surfing. This place was all business. The men and women manning each sterile chamber stopped what they were doing and stood peering over their walls to see what the commotion was about.

A tall middle-aged woman with short black hair, dressed in a white lab coat, raced to the general's side. Holding a clipboard out towards him she said proudly, "We've fed the data Major Edwards provided us into our extensive database network and we should have the results shortly. If you'd like, we can wait over by the terminal where the information will print out."

"Let's go!" snapped the General. "Time's at a premium."

Uxbridge followed the woman across the well-lit, cool computer room to a workstation at the far end of the room. The computer terminal was occupied by a young man in a white short-sleeve shirt and black tie, which was standard uniform for males. Standing behind the man with arms folded he asked, "Well?"

"Any moment, Sir," answered the woman, becoming flustered.

"I don't care what kind of pressure your people are working under, Margaret. I need that information. The nation's security depends on my getting that intelligence in my hands now!"

Swallowing hard, Margaret said, "Yes, Sir."

"It's coming out!" shouted the young man at the computer.

They watched a 8½ x11 color picture of Doug Talbot ease out of a giant laser printer. The computer whiz handed the picture to the general as a second, one-page bio slid out. Talbot's full name was printed across the top. He handed it to the general while a picture of Dr. Marilynn Harwell started inching out, also followed by a one-page bio. The technician handed both to Uxbridge.

After quickly scanning them, Uxbridge smiled widely. Waving them high in the air as he walked away he shouted, "Perfect! Freakin' perfect!" He left without a thank you or acknowledgment.

He went back to his office one floor up for a staff meeting he'd called only an hour earlier. He handed the bios to Major Edwards and threw the pictures on the table.

"Gentleman," he said to the seven men sitting there, "these are the two I told you about." He was all smiles.

A one-star general grabbed the pictures and said, "They don't look very dangerous to me."

Another officer snatched up the pictures and, after eyeing them briefly, said, "This woman looks as if she's in the medical field and he looks like an average Joe. Are you telling me these people are dangerous?"

"After intensive surveillance, our intelligence people tell us these two are engaging in covert terrorist activity. It's quite possible they may have been the catalyst in the recent virus attack on the United States, or at the very least, responsible for what happened on the eastern seaboard."

"Are you sure your intelligence is accurate? They don't seem to fit the profile."

"Don't be naïve, General! Criminals come in all shapes and sizes. That's why they can pass under the radar. We've actually had these two under observation for quite some time, but only recently did we get the break we needed."

"That's good enough for me," said a high-ranking officer sitting at the far end of the table.

Another sitting to the generals right asked, "Can you give us more on their background?"

Uxbridge sat down and pulled a large cigar out of his side pocket, then produced a fancy silver lighter in the shape of a rifle from the opposite one. A blue and yellow flame torched the tip of the cigar, and the General puffed hard several times until it caught.

Sitting back in his chair, he pushed out three puffs of white smoke that smelled like old oily rags, and said in a cocky voice to the man on his right, "What do ya have for us, Major?"

"I've read through the intelligence reports," said Major Edwards, "and have noticed some interesting facts." Holding up the doctor's stat sheet, he continued. "The female is Dr. Marilynn Harwell, Chief of Trauma at Coventry General Hospital. She's approximately 31 years old, stands five foot seven and weights approximately 125 pounds."

The General leaned back in his chair, smiling inside and thinking how well his plan was beginning to take hold. His chest stuck out as far as the billowy smoke he eagerly pushed out of his mouth. Suddenly he was pulled back by Edwards's voice.

"She's single," said Edwards, "with no immediate plans of getting married. Recently we assigned an agent to tap her phone. Some strange conversations in an odd code were made to one Jennie Sprague, who resides in her home. Harwell was last seen working the overnight shift at the hospital, but then disappeared.

"His name is Doug Talbot. He stands six foot three, weights about 190 pounds and is thirty-nine. He's recently divorced with his ex-wife getting custody of their seven-year old daughter after an ugly court battle. His occupation is that of a camera operator at WJAM-TV."

Uxbridge eyed Edwards blankly, listening with unnoticeable disdain. He was extremely prejudiced against African Americans and never would have placed the man onto his staff, especially one of high regard and stature, except he tolerated Edwards because he was the best at his position. Uxbridge beamed widely. He knew that he'd eventually discard Edwards onto a scrap pile once he'd outlived his usefulness, just like all the others that had been used over the years.

"They have become fast friends and spend a lot of time together at the hospital," continued Edwards. "Wire taps have caught them discussing areas that are secured subjects, which only classified personnel should be familiar with. Keep in mind he has access to satellite uplinks. He can send and receive messages encoded in video feeds to and from the station and no one would be the wiser."

"Okay, Major," said Uxbridge, "I'll take it from there." He stood so that everyone had to look up to him, heightening his perception of power. "Our psychologists say Talbot is an emotional mess from a bad divorce. Hell, his wife left him for a younger man and she got custody of the kid. His manhood has been stripped away." The General started walking slowly around the table. "So he feels a deeply embedded anger and grudge against life," he continued, "and an outlet like terrorism offers him a release valve and a way to reinforce that manhood. Recently he slugged a man in the emergency room and that man ultimately died, and when confronted, he showed no remorse."

At the quarter mark around the table he said, "Psychologists also say that Miss Harwell has a firmly embedded depression. She hates working at Coventry General Hospital and tends to take it out on the staff. When we first had suspicions about her, we assigned a field agent to follow her. The agent found a wrinkled note on hospital stationery in a wastebasket from a nurse named Margie Crandle suggesting they meet at their usual place for heavy drinking and drugs. Crandle has a long file indicating her involvement with underground groups and she has been linked to violent protests outside of Washington."

Uxbridge stopped at the opposite side of Major Edwards and puffed hard on his cigar several times, then pushed out an impressive white cloud of smoke. All eyes stayed trained on him. No one made a sound. Even their breathing was silent.

"Harwell lives with a woman by the name of Jennie Sprague," he went on, continuing his walk at a brisker pace, "with whom she is having a lesbian affair. Miss Sprague is a Systems Analyst and Harwell depends heavily on Sprague's ability to hack into most secured systems to get her information."

The General waited for everyone to absorb what he'd said, then started talking again. "Gentleman, these people have lots of anger and hatred, which is being taken out on the poor unsuspecting American public by helping a foreign terrorist group with the release of the deadly *B-Thrax* virus." He came to a stop in front of his own empty chair and placed his free hand on top of it.

A one star general across from him said in a low, deep voice, "Okay, Tom, you've got our attention. What do you want from us?"

"I need you to find them before they can do more reprehensible harm. Capturing them is vital, so put all your efforts and resources into searching possible escape routes. The public deserves no less from us. They must be stopped!

"And one other thing: because they are dangerous, I'm authorizing you to empower your men to shoot to kill if capturing them is not an option. I promise there will be no repercussions should that happen."

The meeting broke up quickly and General Uxbridge was left to his own. He reached into his inside front pocket, pulled out his cell phone and hit the pound key three times. A familiar British voice answered, "Reid!"

"It's done," said Uxbridge.

"Good!" said the Englishman. "Everything fits perfectly. While everyone targets them, we can figure out a solution to this mess."

"I just hope they don't kill them too quickly!" said the General.

* * *

Fear gripped Doug Talbot as he peeled out of his dead ex-wife's driveway, leaving the rescue workers to attend to her body. It wasn't fear for himself that tormented him. It was the disturbing phone call he'd gotten from Coventry General Hospital about his daughter, Cassandra. Speeding back down Route Two towards the hospital, he pulled out his cell phone and checked his messages. There were three calls listed in his voice mail: two from the station and one anonymous.

He hit the message button and a soft, sensual female voice said, "*Message One: Jeff Page – WJAM-TV – 7:50am.*" He hit the button again and a second later Jeff's voice popped in: "Dude, call the news desk. Shoemaker wants you to come in as soon as you can! Later, dude!" The message ended with a loud beep and an end of message prompt on the phone's viewfinder was followed by "*End Of Message*" by the female voice.

"That's old," he said out loud.

"*Message Two,*" said the voice. "*Jeff Page – WJAM-TV – 8:15am.*" He chuckled nervously as Page's voice came up again: "Dude, where the hell are you? Don't you check your messages? Shoemaker's freakin' out. He wants you here NOW! Bring doughnuts. Later, dude!"

"Later, dude!" he said back.

"*Message Three,*" said the female voice. "Damn," thought Talbot, "I love that voice." "*Anonymous*

Call," continued the voice – "*10:30am.*"

"Jesus!" he shouted, yanking the phone from his ear, startled by loud static and crackling. He pressed the phone close for short intervals, and could distinguish a few intelligible words mixed in occasionally, struggling to filter them out of the static.

"What the!...." he shouted. It was suddenly nothing but gibberish on the other end.

He pulled into the hospital's parking lot and drove into a parking space reserved for the media. The phone message was still going and he was about to hang up when he distinctly heard a man's deep voice say, "Mind your own business or you'll end up like your wife."

Doug sat in his seat listening to static for more than a minute. A loud beep startled him and he shifted in his seat.

"End of Message," said the soothing voice. *"There are no more messages."*

Leaving his car, he hit the END button on his cell phone and stuck it in his front pocket. By entering through the side door of the hospital he circumvented the main entrance and avoided any contact with patients. It was a trick a doctor once told him about when he was shooting video of a staff strike at the hospital several years ago. Once inside, he found the service elevator and hit the UP button. He paced back and forth, waiting for its arrival. Overhead, sounds of excited voices and shuffling footsteps reminded him of the turmoil he'd seen earlier in the day.

A loud bang and grinding cables told him the elevator was on its way down. Moments later, it boomed as if it had slammed the bottom when it reached the basement and the doors slid open. As echoes died away, he stepped inside and hit the button for the third floor. The elevator shuddered, then started upward, sending him sideways. Grasping a railing with both hands to keep from falling down, he wondered if anyone had heard the elevator noise or even cared if they did.

Service elevators are not known to be people friendly. They are mostly for transporting equipment. There was no music, so he took to reading the graffiti. There were lots of hearts engraved with lovers' names. He chuckled at the "Marty loves Barry" heart. But the message that struck him most was *Mona was here 7/11/63*. "Christ," he mumbled. "How old is this thing?"

The elevator squealed like a car with bad brakes as metal ground on metal until the elevator trembled to a stop. The gliding doors opened with a loud swoosh that normally would have been heard all the way down the hallway, except it was lost over the chaos on West '3'. Pausing momentarily, he studied the scene unfolding before him, finally stepping out into an overcrowded corridor. Some people sat in the middle of the floor improvising for the lack of chairs, silently waiting their turn. Others stood leaning against walls, their eyes giving the impression that their minds were in faraway places. One man darted here, then there, without a destination or purpose to his movements. But what struck him as the most odd, was how the staff looked lost in this mass of humanity.

He didn't even excuse himself as he bumped his way over, around, and between people. They were all in varying degrees of pain and anguish and it wouldn't have registered with them anyway. After a five-minute struggle to go about a hundred feet, he stood in front of the nurses' station. An older nurse was arguing with a middle-aged man.

"I told you sir, we don't have the B-thrax vaccination yet! When it does come, you'll have to wait your turn at number seventy-eight. Please find a place to sit or stand and wait for your number to be called."

"Do you know who I am?" he snapped.

"Yes I do," she snapped back. "But being a city councilman does not give you any more rights than anyone else. Now go sit down and wait your turn!"

"Why you black bitch!" he shouted, grabbing her by the collar with both hands and pulling her to within an inch of his face. "Get me fucking in first for my shot or I'll kick your big black ass!"

The guy barely had the words out of his mouth when

Doug grabbed him from behind and flung him into the wall to the right. After the stunned councilman slid to the floor, he walked over and leaned down with a threatening finger and said, "Don't go near the nurse until she calls your name, or I'll throw you out of the hospital – from the third floor!"

The councilman crawled away on all fours and retreated into the corner of a doorway.

"Thanks, man," said the harried nurse. "You saved my *big black butt*."

"No problem. Where the heck is security?"

"They're all sick, missing, or dead," answered the nurse, shaking her head despondently.

"That sucks," said Doug. "I mean what I said. If he gives you any more trouble let me know and I'll throw him out, and not necessarily from the first floor."

"I don't think *mister big deal* will be a problem again. Now is there something I can do for you?"

"My name's Doug Talbot. To-ens, I mean Dr. Harwell is expecting me."

"I think I know where she is. Hold on, I'll give her a call."

The nurse stepped away to a phone on the opposite side of the nurses' station and dialed a three-digit number. She returned after talking to someone for a short time.

"Dr. Harwell is waiting for you in room 310 – take the corridor to your right and follow it until it splits. Follow the left corridor and 310 is five doors down on the left side The floor is color coded with yellow and blue lines so if you get lost, just follow the lines until the blue one splits to the left, although you might have trouble seeing them, with all these people milling around."

"Thanks, but I've been here before." He winked and said, "Remember what I said. He gives you any grief let me know."

The nurse smiled, gave him a thumbs up, then went back to helping another patient.

Doug glanced down the crammed hallways to his right. It would take a gargantuan effort to get through. It was so thick with people that the white coats of the few doctors and the pale blue uniforms of the nurses were lost in the blur of colors. Suddenly, to the complaints of many, he tramped down the corridor, pushing through like a giant ship that breaks through ice to open up shipping lanes.

As he stepped over the multitude of humanity he noticed the hospital's usual hygienic smell had become more pungent, like that acrid odor people give off when they haven't bathed for a while. He wondered how long it had been since normal housekeeping had taken place. His nose twitched and he wanted to sneeze, but somehow managed to hold it in.

He was exhausted when he walked into 310 and found Cassandra lying quietly on a bed with tubes sticking out of her arms and one in her nose. Dr. Harwell was standing over her, watching several green screened monitors. With a heavy heart, he made his way over to Cassandra's side. Seeing her like this sent stabbing pain shooting across his stomach. It was as if someone was punching him there over and over.

"She looks worse," he gasped. "What's wrong?"

"I don't know, Mr. Talbot, and I'm really worried. Her vitals are steadily dropping. I do know that we can rule out diabetes, though."

He tried to check his emotions, but couldn't keep from choking up. "You've got to save my daughter. She's all I've got."

"I'm trying, Mr. Talbot – Doug," she whispered. "But I can't treat something that I can't diagnose."

Doug sighed deeply and lowered his head to his chest. Dr. Harwell felt overwhelming compassion at the sudden loss of strength from the man standing next to her. She put her arm on his shoulder and said softly, "You need to stay strong for Cassandra. She needs to be able to lean on *you* for support until we can find a solution. Can you do that for her?"

He stiffened. Determination and conviction shaped his face and voice. "What do you need from me?"

"There's nothing you can do for her right now except support and love her. Unfortunately, your daughter has the same symptoms as all the people who have died. She's always thirsty and has extreme sweating around the forehead."

"What are you saying?"

"Did Cassandra receive any trauma that you can think of?"

"Like what?"

"Did she bang her head, fall down, or get shaken up in any way?"

"Not that I'm aware of."

"That's consistent with our preliminary physical. There are no bruises on her body. I'm going to take her for x-rays and an MRI, if I can get through that mess of mankind out there."

"Wait a minute," said Doug, "now that I think of it, Cassandra did overhear my wife and me have a blowout fight. It was about two hours later that I discovered her in the condition she's in."

Dr. Harwell perked up. "That could be significant. Maybe it's not a physical trauma, but an emotional one that she's suffering."

"Is that any better or worse than physical trauma?"

"Studies have shown that deep seated emotional problems can cause severe physical complications to the human body. We won't know for sure till we finish the normal examination. But I'll definitely keep an open mind at this point."

She faced him straight on. "I'm not going to sugar coat it, Doug. Your daughter is in serious trouble. A lot of people have died in the past few hours who shouldn't have, with no logical explanation. Many were much physically stronger than she is."

"I'm grateful for everything you've done for my daughter, Doc. I realize you have a whole hospital depending on you, and a lot of other people to worry about."

"Not a problem, Doug. As far as treatment, I hope to

be able to give her a shot of the vaccine when we get it. It's supposed to counteract that virus the President warned us about. It's more of a preventative measure at this point, though. It's a shame we didn't get it earlier. It might have helped all those people who have already died.

"On the plus side, your daughter's pretty resilient. That can't be said of a lot of people."

"She's a tough little girl," said Doug proudly.

"I suspect she takes after her father," said Dr. Harwell. "Did you speak to your wife?"

"I meant to tell you about her. She's dead."

"What happened!"

"The nearest I can tell is she went to bed drunk and never woke up."

Cassandra suddenly started shifting in her bed and her breathing came in short, quick gasps. Doug reached down and stroked her hair, then bent down and whispered in her ear. She relaxed and went back to breathing normally.

"What'd you say to her?"

"I just told her daddy was here to take care of her and that she wasn't getting out of doing her homework that easily. School started a week ago."

"Not bad," she said, patting him on the back. "I have to go see what's going on out there in that zoo, but I'll be back to check on Cassandra and take her to x-ray. You can stay as long as you want. Just let me know if you intend to leave."

"How can I get in touch with you?"

"Pick up any phone and dial zero. The operator will find me." She placed her hand gently on his shoulder and said, "Hang in there, Doug. I'm doing everything I can to find out what's going on. It's possible that whatever she's suffering from may be linked to what's bothering everyone else. I've made a few phone calls to some specialists I know. Maybe they can give me some answers. If it's not the biological virus that's bothering her, then there has to be another logical reason.

"That's not exactly encouraging," said Doug, his face

and voice etched in despair. "A lot of that type of people are dying."

Coventry General Hospital
Third Floor, West 3 Room 305
1:13pm

Nurse Margie Crandell made her way towards room 305. She was franticly waving her arms and mumbling to herself, because she was slowed by hoards of people in her path as she followed the blue lines on the hallway floor. Getting to her baby was her only mission. Along the way she thought about the President's speech and it troubled her. Things like this always happen in other countries, not in the United States. The situation seemed surreal and it strained her nerves and heightened her concern. She swiped a steady sweat off her brow.

She quickly forgot about that when she reached the door to her baby's room and went in. Her only thoughts were on her bundle of joy lying in the oversized crib. Looking down at him brought a broad smile to her face. He appeared peaceful and restful, something he hadn't been for the past few days.

She reached and stroked her baby's hair. The smile quickly faded from her face. Room 305 filled with a loud wailing, "NOOOOOOO!!!!"

Darius Junior was dead.

The streets of
Downtown Providence
1:20pm

Several helicopters turned inland after hugging the coastline of Narragansett Bay, pushing straight towards the heart of the city. The beat of their rotating propellers and roar of their engines magnified as the sound ricocheted off tall buildings after they descended to 100 feet to begin their mission of releasing onboard *B-Thrax* spray over the panic-stricken city.

Scattered soldiers dressed heavily in camouflaged anti-contamination suits were walking the streets with spray canisters, spraying the same liquid into dark and reclusive corners. A man on a bullhorn walked along yelling out instructions for people to stay indoors so the military could do its job of releasing the serum to start the process of making the city safe. Many other soldiers walked the same streets in full combat gear, including gas masks, with rifles held in firing position. Military Jeeps and Hummers patrolled the side streets, stopping occasional passing cars and ordering them to leave the area.

Seven miles away, the pneumatic front doors of Coventry General Hospital swept open and an entourage of highly armed military personnel entered carrying several locked silver metal lab containers marked *Secured Military Biological - To be opened by authorized personnel only.* Over at Providence Hospital of Rhode Island a similar group entered carrying identical boxes.

The soldiers pushed through Coventry Generals' packed hallways. Eight burly soldiers made no attempt at politeness, shoving the sick and dying aside as if they were insignificant outdoor waste. Even though there was not enough space for them, they somehow squeezed up to the front desk.

"Hey!" screamed charge nurse Nancy Beakerman. "What the hell are you doing? Don't treat those patients like that!"

Silence engulfed the room and hallways as rumor that help was on the way swept around the building. A young lieutenant stepped forward. "Ma'am! We are here on official military orders. It is against United States law to interfere in government matters!"

"I don't give a damn what your business is!" snapped Beakerman. "You have no right to mistreat people like that!"

"Martial law, which was recently issued by the president, gives me that right," snapped the Lieutenant. "And that right is to do as we see fit to execute our mission. Should anyone interfere with our objective, we will be forced to use whatever means necessary to eradicate that interference. And whom might you be, Ma'am?"

"I might be the person to come over and slap some manners into you!" uttered the nurse.

Two soldiers instantly pointed rifles at the suddenly stunned nurse. "That wouldn't be wise," said the soldier. "I assure you. You'd be dropped before you even took a step."

He waved the two gunmen to lower their rifles. "Look, Ma'am," he went on, "we're dealing with a very serious matter here. It's not an idle threat when I say that we will blow away anyone who gets in our way."

A loud murmur swept around the room. Nurse Beakerman felt as if she'd just been kicked in the stomach, but she kept a façade of calmness. Looking him dead in the eyes she asked in a serious and methodical voice, "What is it you need, *young man*?"

Taken aback and angered by the insult the soldier's head snapped back and his face flushed. He wasn't used to subordinates testing his authority. Unflinching from the staring contest with the nurse and keeping his composure as best he could, he snapped his fingers and another soldier reached out a key.

Grabbing it, he opened up one of the metal containers and pulled out a small vile of clear liquid.

"This is the vaccination serum for the *B-Thrax* virus that the president promised. You are to give it only to those who are not currently affected. It is unproductive to give it to anyone who is afflicted with the virus, and would be a waste of valuable serum. It is best used by giving it to healthy people to prevent the spread of the virus."

"Are you telling me I can't give any of this to the people who need it the most?" asked the dumbfounded nurse.

"That's exactly what I'm saying," answered the soldier

in an edgy voice. "These sentries will stay to make sure you follow my orders. The rest of my men are going to start spraying the serum throughout the building, beginning with this floor and working up to the top. Do you need me to instruct you again? I realize old people like yourself have short attention spans."

"No!" snapped the nurse. "I have two little boys at home like you and I understand exactly what they want when they play their MIND games."

The lieutenant snapped off a salute. "I'll be taking my leave now, Ma'am," he said, turning and heading back towards the exit. Before leaving, he turned back and said, "Make sure not to bother my men!" He then disappeared out the door.

The room erupted into chaos and panic as people grabbed for the boxes of serum. The remaining soldiers snatched the boxes and rushed behind the nurses' station where they stacked them on the floor. A semiautomatic gun suddenly went off, spraying the ceiling with a short burst of bullets. Patients jumped backwards or fell to the floor covering their ears. "Stay back!" shouted one of the burly soldiers, "or next time I start aiming."

The agitated crowd remained at bay. Nurse Beakerman was left wondering what rules to follow when administering the serum. How was she going to play God? How was she to determine who lives and who dies?

Third Floor, West 3
Employee's Bathroom
1:47pm

Dr. Harwell, Lindsey Palmer, and seven other staff members huddled together in the employees' bathroom to discuss a plan of action. It was the only secluded room left in the hospital.

"I know it's been hectic, but everyone needs to keep their wits about them," started the doctor. "It's beyond crazy out there, but we still need to try and keep some semblance of order and sanity about us. If we can show control to these people, it may have a calming effect on them. Even if only some act like human beings that will make our job that much easier. Remember, most of them are just scared and it's up to us to give them reassurance that help is coming."

"Who's going to give us reassurance?" said a nervous voice.

"I am," said Dr. Harwell. "Let me start by commending everyone for the valiant effort given today under such adverse conditions. And I want you to know that no one has the right to touch you or get physical with you in any way. I am authorizing all staff members to do whatever is necessary to protect themselves, within reason of course. Please pass this information on to other staff members.

And just so you know," she said, "I have been in contact with the Director of the hospital. Due to unfortunate family matters, he has not been able to get himself here. In the meantime he has conveyed to several other doctors and myself that we should try to conduct business as best as we can. I and the other doctors agree with him."

"What about the assistant director?" asked one of the nurses.

"Repeated calls to her have gone unanswered."

Softening her voice, she continued: "An unofficial count of dead so far is forty-nine." The cramped room seemed to turn into a vacuum, all the air sucked out of it. The strain showed on everyone's faces.

"I realize that news is overwhelming, especially since we're in the business of helping people. Know that it's not a reflection on you or your ability." After sighing loudly, Dr. Harwell continued gently, "Sometimes things happen that are not within our control. Life deals us a hand that just isn't winnable." There was another short pause and she finished sadly, "I feel the same pain you do."

She paused to let everyone catch their breath, then went on, "I know that a lot of you have worked straight through your regular shifts and are now working a second one with no sleep and that you're working on fumes. Trust me, I know how you feel. You've all shown true character and professionalism, and I promise you will all be recognized when this is over. You can pass that on to the rest of the staff too."

She scanned the faces that stared back, but couldn't tell if she was getting through to them.

"Just so you know," she continued, "we're working on getting more staff in here to either relieve you, or at the very least give you a break to get some rest. I have also ordered the kitchen to not charge for food so everyone can eat. Now let's get back out there and continue servicing the patients as best as possible and start administering the vaccine shots."

The group disbanded. Dr. Harwell intercepted Lindsey at the door. "Have you seen Margie?"

"Not since she went off to check on her baby."

"What room did we put Darius in?"

"Three oh five," answered the nurse.

"Before you go, Lindsey, I want you to know that you've done a great job working under these crazy conditions. You've been as good as any seasoned veteran and should be very proud of yourself."

"Thanks, Dr. Harwell, that means a lot to me coming from you. I've always looked up to you and try to pattern myself after the way you conduct yourself."

Smiling and patting Lindsey on the back, Dr. Harwell said, "Okay, let's not get mushy."

Thinking back to last night she suddenly felt guilty about envying the girl's youth and looks. It seemed trivial now.

"Kind of makes you wish it was still a boring night, doesn't it?" laughed Lindsey, walking out the door.

Following her out, the Dr. replied, "I'll never complain again."

* * *

Dr. Harwell walked the same route down the corridor that Margie had followed. She turned the corner and passed 301 and 303 on her right, then reached 305. She opened the door and stepped inside. Wedged into a back corner of the room sat Nurse Crandell cradling her dead baby in her lap, singing and rocking back and forth. Tears cascaded down her cheeks and sweat flowed freely from her forehead.

Dr. Harwell reached down and felt the baby's pulse, but it was a waste of time. "I'm sorry, Margie. Darius Junior deserved a lot more time with his mother than this."

Margie kept rocking back and forth singing the words to *Rock a Bye Baby*. She didn't look up. She just kept rocking and singing.

"I'm concerned about you, Margie. Why don't you come with me to the emergency room, so we can take care of you?"

Margie didn't respond. Dr. Harwell reached to take the baby, so she could help the tormented woman to her feet. Margie reacted violently, pulling away and clutching the baby to her chest.

"Please, Margie! Let me help you."

Margie's voice grew weaker. She struggled to sing the words. "Rock a bye.... Rock a baby....Rock a rock."

Dr. Harwell's eyes misted over. "Please, Margie," she cried. "Let me help you."

Margie never spoke. She had drawn her last breath. There would be no more song and no more rocking. Marilynn stared down at the nurse holding her baby in her arms and she thought how beautiful they looked together as a family for one last time. Uncontrollable tears streamed from the doctor's eyes as she wept the loss of this dear, close friend. Road rage anger gripped her and she called through clenched teeth, "This has to stop! And I'm going to do whatever I can to make it stop!"

West 1
2:03pm

Second-shift nurse Molly Stoneman looked up from the chair where she sat entering patients' personal data into a computer. Six military men stood on the other side of her desk with guns and rifles. Hands-free headsets hung from their ears with mouthpieces that wrapped around their jaws to their mouths. They looked ready for combat.

"We're looking for Dr. Harwell and Mr. Talbot!" called out one of the soldiers, showing her 9x10 color glossies of the two.

Getting up from her chair, the mature nurse ran a hand through her short black hair and asked, "And you are?"

"I'm Sergeant Carpenter, here on official government business. We'd appreciate your cooperation, Ma'am."

Something about his tone scared the nurse, but she stayed assertive. "What kind of business do you want the doctor for?" she asked calmly, without the slightest change in her voice.

The Sergeant leaned over the counter and whispered so only Molly could hear. The nurse fell back into her chair. Her face turned a deathly pale. A vampire couldn't have sucked the blood out of her face faster.

"I think... she's ....off until next week.....," stammered the flustered nurse. "And I don't know any Mr. Talbot."

"Just to satisfy my own curiosity, Molly, we will be performing a room to room search of the hospital. I can not express any more plainly that we are not to be interrupted. The Government appreciates your cooperation!" said the Sergeant, snapping off a salute. Leaving Doug's picture on the counter, he continued, "By the way, should the doctor or Mr. Talbot happen to come by here, notify us. I promise, it's only for routine questioning."

Molly remained in her seat. She reached out and picked up her water bottle for a drink, but her hands shook so much she couldn't get the water out of the bottle and into her mouth without spilling it all over her face.

The sergeant turned to his men. "Peterson, come with me! The rest of you start at the other end of this floor and work your way back here. If you don't see me here by then, go to the next floor and start searching." The stunned nurse watched the soldiers start down the left end of the hallway, which was still a little crowded, and Carpenter and Peterson disappear around the corner towards the other end.

Saint James Church
Downtown
2:30pm

Doug Talbot hadn't gone back to the station, but instead had stopped off at a church to say a prayer. Kneeling in the third pew from the altar he watched an elderly couple off to the side struggling to light a votive candle. It was the man who held a wooden stick over the candle, which he had lit from the flame of another one. But his hands were unsteady and he couldn't make contact with the unlit wick. Doug watched him try several times, then finally got up and made his way over to them.

Whispering, he asked, "May I help you?" They answered in a language he didn't understand. Doug picked up another stick, lit the end and motioned towards the couple's unlit candle. They smiled and nodded their approval.

Doug swiped the flame over the wick several times and it caught. He then stuck his lit stick into a cup of sand to extinguish it. The elderly woman took his right hand and kissed it and the elderly man shook his other hand. Embarrassed, Doug shouted, "You're welcome!" as if shouting would make them understand *his* language.

But they did understand somehow, and they smiled and waved as they shuffled to the middle of the church arm-in-arm, where they genuflected with difficulty. After finishing, they ambled out of the church using a side door.

Doug felt warm inside. On a day when things were going in strange directions, he was able to make a difference. He returned to his pew, crossed himself as he knelt, then began a little prayer. "Lord, I understand that you haven't seen me much lately. Heck, it's actually been since I got married in here eight years ago. And you know how that turned out." He paused for a moment. A lump had formed in his throat and his eyes misted. Finding it difficult to continue, he swallowed hard, took two big breaths, then continued: "I realize I'm beyond saving, but it's not for me that I'm here. It's my daughter, Cassandra. She's pretty sick, but you already know that."

Doug sniffled, then looked up at the large crucifix hanging in the middle of the altar. Staring into the sad eyes of Jesus, he cried, "Lord, she's just a kid! She doesn't deserve to go through all this suffering. She's had enough misery in her life the last few years, with me and Christine fighting all the time. I'm sure you heard the yelling, even way up where you are." Staring at his hands he mumbled, "Please. Cassandra hasn't even experienced the joy of going to high school where she could meet and make new friends. If you take...." he choked, "if you take her away from me now, she won't even experience the joy of meeting her first boyfriend or the thrill of her first kiss. Although, you'll have to forgive me Lord, this boy would have to get by me first before trying that kiss. I'm sure even you would back me up on that."

He slid back in the pew and sat slouched forward with his hands in his lap. After gathering his thoughts he said softly, "Anyway, I guess what I'm asking is for you to please help my little girl. I know you must get a lot of requests like this and each one is special in it's own way, but this girl is really extraordinary. I'll even make you this promise if you let her get better. I, Doug Talbot, do swear before you in this sacred place, that it won't take me getting married again to visit church."

Tears cascaded down his cheeks. "Cassandra's all I've got," he cried. "If you take her away from me, you might as well take me too, because I won't have a heart left to keep me going."

Doug sniffled and wiped the tears away with the palms of his hands, stood and re-crossed himself, then went to the middle aisle and genuflected. He left the church using the same side door the elderly couple had used. He trusted that he had made a favorable impression.

He started his car and pulled out in front of an oncoming pickup, cutting it off. The male driver blasted his horn and shook his middle finger vehemently at him. Doug smiled and waved at the driver, then finished making the U-turn and sped back towards the hospital. He wanted to see Cassandra. The station could do without him today, he thought, as he pulled back into the media's reserved parking area at the hospital a short time later.

Bolting through the entrance doors he went directly to the front desk. "Do you know where Dr. Harwell is?" he asked.

"And you are?" asked Molly Stoneman.

"Doug Talbot. My daughter is a patient of hers."

"Oh!" shouted the nurse, covering her mouth with her hand and falling back into a chair. "You're Talbot!"

"Have we met?" he asked.

The nurse's hands were shaking and she avoided making eye contact when she said, "A Sergeant Carpenter and a group of armed soldiers were here a short time ago asking about you and the doctor. They even had pictures of both of you."

"Did he say what he wanted?"

"Only that you were wanted for questioning. Frankly, I don't believe him," she said, looking up at Doug. "I believe there's more to it than that."

"What did you tell him?"

"I didn't tell him anything. I have no idea where Dr. Harwell is. She's supposed to be off duty. I tried calling her at home, but there was no answer. As for you, I don't know who you are."

"But Dr. Harwell *is* here. She's working up on the third floor."

Doug anxiously tapped his fingers on the countertop. "I don't like the sound of this," he said, before sprinting off to the elevator.

Molly grabbed the phone and dialed West Three. Lindsey Palmer answered on the second ring, then forwarded the call to Dr. Harwell. Composed again, the nurse said, "Good evening, Dr. Harwell. Something has happened at the hospital that you should know about."

"What's up, Molly?"

"A Sergeant Carpenter stopped at the desk a short while ago and showed me a picture of you and Mr. Talbot. He said you're wanted for questioning."

"A police sergeant?"

"No, military."

"Did you tell him anything?"

"I told him you were off for the weekend," responded the nurse. "I didn't know that you were working."

"That was a good answer, Molly. I came in last night to work on papers because I was going to Boston Monday, when all hell broke loose. I've been here ever since. I'm curious. How did you find me?"

"I just spoke with Mr. Talbot and he told me you were here," said the nurse.

"So he's back."

"Are you okay, Doctor?" asked Molly. "You sound as if you've been crying."

"I just received some sad news."

"Well, whatever it is, I'm sorry," said Molly in an affectionate tone.

"Thanks, Molly. I have to go. If you need to get in touch with me call my cell phone. The number's 555-6789. And if those soldiers come back, don't give them any information."

"Don't worry, Doctor," said Molly. "You can depend on me. If that nosy sergeant comes back, I won't tell him you and Mr. Talbot are here."

The two exchanged good-byes, then the nurse hung

up the phone. She turned to go back to her computer and stepped right into Sergeant Carpenter.

Sal's Auto Sales
Uptown
2:53pm

Price Slashin' Sal sat back in his oversized black leather chair behind his desk, puffing on a long, smelly cigar. "Look folks," he said to a young couple with a baby. "I can offer that sweet little model to you for only ten thousand dollars. Just so you know, I'm not gonna make any money on this deal.

The husband and wife exchanged dubious glances.

"I know you must think I'm crazy, cause I'm selling that car so cheap, but I have a soft spot in my heart for a young couple like you just startin' out. It wasn't long ago, that me and the missus were in the same boat as you, with a baby too, trying to afford a new car. I just wish someone had been there for me when I needed help."

The husband and wife nodded to each other, then said in unison, "We'll take the car, Price Slashin' Sal."

"That's great," the car dealer said with a sly grin. "I'll even throw in a free gas fill-up for you. You just need to fill out these forms." He slid a packet of papers across his desk, and the packet's end caught on the edge of a book, running a sharp tip over the end of Sal's finger. "OWWW, he howled, as blood spurted from a paper cut.

The couple began filling out the registration forms, while Sal sat back puffing on his cigar and pressing a tissue to his finger. Sweat instantly formed on his forehead, and after a couple of minutes he started smacking his lips from thirst. The young couple looked up from their writing just in time to see the cigar drop from the car dealer's lips and his head slam down onto the desk.

The woman screamed.

Price Slashin' Sal was dead.

* * *

Doug reached the third floor and found it less chaotic. There was no resemblance to the craziness of earlier, although he still had to evade a few stragglers here and there before entering Cassandra's room, where he found her in a restless sleep. The tube in her nose had been removed. The ones in her arms remained.

He caressed her hair with long sweeping strokes. He hadn't been there long when the door opened and Dr. Harwell came in and joined him. He noticed that her eyes were red and swollen. He knew instantly that she'd been crying. The Dr. reached down and began stroking Cassandra's hair.

"She's so beautiful," she said, almost choking up. "She must take after her mother."

She couldn't suppress tears any longer and suddenly leaned into Doug's chest, sobbing. Instinctively, he wrapped his arms around her, engulfing her with a comforting hug.

"What happened?" he whispered.

"I lost a dear friend," she cried into his chest.

Doug held her in his arms, but didn't speak. He knew she needed this little respite in time, where the world didn't seem to exist. He had come to feel that this was a woman who was usually strong and never needed anyone's help. Only needless death got to her, cruelly sapping away her strength, leaving her devastated, much like Superman and Kryptonite. He knew she would speak when the time was right.

They remained entwined in each other's arms for several minutes, when Cassandra stirred and asked for a drink of water. If there was one thing that could bring Marilynn back, it was a cherished life. Using both hands to wipe the water from her eyes she smiled at the little girl and said, "Of course you can have a drink. Your daddy would be glad to get it for you."

A smile instantly appeared on Doug's face. "Hey,

munchkin," he said softly taking the little girl's hand and gently squeezing it. "One cup of cool water for my honey, coming up."

As her father poured a cup of water from a plastic pitcher, Cassandra asked Dr. Harwell in a weak voice, "Have you been crying?"

"I'm just a little sad right now," said Marilynn, this time using her shirt sleeve to wipe her eyes.

Cassandra drew a big breath. "Whenever I feel sad I try to do something that makes feel me better."

"Like what?" asked the Doctor. "Maybe I can try it." She knew the girl was mustering her strength to talk.

"Sometimes I put on a favorite CD and sing along."

"I don't think that would work," said Marilynn softly, rubbing away tears with her hands and sniffling several times. "I'm not a very good singer."

Doug used his free hand to gently lift his daughter's head, while placing a pink plastic cup against her lips. The girl sipped several times and refused the rest, so he lowered her head lightly back onto her pillow.

Cassandra stared at the ceiling, trying to recall something else from memory that she could suggest. Finally, she turned back to face the doctor and said, "Sometimes I'll draw what made me sad and paint it with cheery colors."

"I can't draw very good," said the doctor. "Everything I draw looks like stick figures."

The girl smiled and then giggled weakly. Looking deep into the Doctor's eyes she said, " Most times, I talk to my dad and he always makes me feel better about sad things by explaining why they happen."

"That sounds like great advice," said Marilynn, glancing at Doug and smiling a wide grin at Cassandra.

"Why don't you talk to my dad? I'm sure he could help you?"

"You know what, Cassandra? I feel better all ready, just talking to you."

The girl forced a return smile, then rolled over on her right side and fell into an uneasy sleep.

"You have a very bright daughter, Mr. Talbot."

"She didn't get *that* from her mother!" said Doug.

Turning serious, Marilynn said, "I want to do something to stop all this needless death."

"Like what?" he asked, plopping down into a chair next to his daughter.

Marilynn pulled another chair next to him and sat face to face. "I haven't figured that out yet, but I know that whatever it is, it's got to be soon. Too many people are dying from extremely insignificant injuries."

"How about that serum they're giving out? Isn't that helping?"

"That's the strange thing. It doesn't seem to be doing any good. They all have the same symptoms and the serum has no affect. People are still dying."

"Please don't tell me the symptoms are what I think they are."

"Sorry, but they're still the same. Profuse sweating from the forehead, and an unquenchable thirst. The weird part is that people with minor injuries, like falling down or dropping a hair brush on their foot, are dying."

"What are you saying? That the serum is ineffective?"

"I don't know what I'm saying. It wouldn't be right to jump to conclusions, without knowing what the serum is made of and what it's designed to actually do. Without a sample I can't make an educated decision."

"If that's all it's going to take, then why don't you get a sample of the stuff?"

"How do I do that?"

"Aren't they giving you the stuff?"

"Do you mean the serum?"

"Yeah. That stuff."

"Yes, but it's guarded by military personnel and they won't let you take it unless you administer the shots in front of them."

"What would you do with the sample if you had it?"

"I'd run some lab tests to see what it's made of, then I'd have a better understanding of what it can do."

"Then let's get a sample."

"How?"

"We need to get our hands on one of those canisters they're using to spray everywhere."

"Funny you should say that," said Marilynn. "There are a few soldiers spraying inside the hospital right now and I think they're working on this floor as we speak."

Doug stood and kissed Cassandra on the cheek. "Let's get your sample," he said, heading for the door.

The doctor's cell phone rang. She pulled it out of her side pocket and tried to answer, but it stopped ringing. "That's strange," she said, turning to Doug. "I wonder if that was Molly?"

"Molly Stoneman?" asked Doug.

"Yeah."

"I met her a couple of minutes ago on my way up here. She told me the strangest thing."

Marilynn touched his arm. "She called a short time ago and told me some soldiers came around showing pictures of us and asking if we were here."

"That's what I got from her too," said Doug.

"What the hell is that all about?" said Marilynn.

"I'm not sure. Maybe we should start being more cautious till we figure out what's going on."

Marilynn still had the phone in her hand when it rang again.

"Hello!" she said after the first ring, before whoever was on the other end had a chance to hang up.

"Molly, slow down. I can't understand what you're saying." She looked to Doug and with wide eyes and tight lips shook her head. After listening for a few moments she said, "I understand, Molly. Don't worry, you did the right thing. It's not your fault."

Marilynn closed her cell phone and placed it back into her jacket. "They know we're here and they're coming up to get us."

Doug stared at the doorknob. When it didn't turn he

said, "I don't like the sound of this. What the hell could they want with us?"

Standing with hands on hips Marilynn said, "I don't know. What could we have possibly done to cause the United States Army to want to seek us out?"

"Damned if I know. The fact that they're showing pictures of us tells me they're serious, though. Until we find out what's going on, we need to avoid them."

"You had an idea about getting a sample. Let's go get it," she said, leaving the room.

Doug followed her down the hallway. As they passed mostly closed doors she asked, "Do you know where you want to go?"

"I need to find one of those canisters."

"What are you going to do, walk up and spray yourself a cup of the stuff?"

"That's the general idea," he said. "I just don't know where to find it."

There was no one in sight and their footsteps echoed as they rounded a corner and Marilynn said, "By the way, why did you leave a message with the operator that you needed to speak with me right away?"

Doug stopped. "I didn't leave any message for you," he said, with a concerned look. "Why did you leave a message on my phone telling me it was urgent that I rush back to the hospital?"

Marilynn cringed. Grabbing his arm, she said, "I never did any such thing."

"I have a bad feeling abut this," said Doug. "If I didn't know any better, I'd think someone wanted us both here."

Back around the corner from where they had just come was the sound of elevator doors opening. "Start checking every room," barked a man's deep voice.

Marilynn took Doug's hand and walked off, pulling him with her. "I have an idea," she whispered. "Come with me, I know where we can start."

CHAPTER 7

Fourth Floor
Lab 'B'
3:38pm

Doug and Marilynn squatted together in the farthest dark corner of Research Laboratory 'B'. On this floor, there were no patient rooms, just labs where all the testing was done. Neither had spoken for several minutes.

"So this is your plan?" he whispered. "To wait in the dark until they come in and spray, then soak the liquid up off the floor?"

"At least it's a plan," she said softly.

"Okay. I'll give you it's a plan. But I'm not going to wait here hoping someone sprays enough for us to get a sample."

"Do you have a better idea?"

"I'm going out to see what I can find."

"Why can't you wait here with me?"

"This will give us two chances to get something."

Touching his forearm she said, "Watch yourself."

"Don't worry about me. I'm a TV cameraman. I'm used to slinking around unseen getting video of people."

Releasing his arm she asked, "Did you disable the light switch so it won't switch on?"

"Don't you trust me, To-ens?"

"Believe me, trust has noting to do with it. If I'm going to be here by myself in the pitch dark, I want to know that it won't flip on."

"Go try it if you're concerned."

"If you say you did, then that's good enough for me. Do you think I'll be safe hiding in here?"

"I'm not sure about anything but this: we have to try and find a way to get some of that liquid they're spraying everywhere, so you can check it out."

"Hey! I'm not a chemist. I only had a few semesters of chemistry in college and that was ten years ago."

"Chemistry's like riding a bike. Once you learn it, you never forget it."

"I haven't been on a bike in a long time either."

"We have to try," he whispered. "Do the best you can."

Marilynn squeezed his hand. Speaking hardly above a whisper she said, "Promise me you'll come back for me."

"Oh, I'll be back. You're not getting rid of me that easily."

She reached out and pulled him into a hug. "Be careful," she said softly in his ear. "I have enough people to save."

Getting to his feet Doug said, "Don't worry, I won't be one of them."

Shivering, Marilynn embraced herself and asked, "What do you want me to do while you're gone?"

"Just stay put. I think you'll be safe staying right here in this corner out of the way. It's dark enough to keep you hidden."

"Suppose it's a while before you come back. How long should I stay here?"

"Use your judgment. If you feel it's been too long or that it's unsafe, head back to the cafeteria and I'll meet you there."

"Good luck," said Marilynn. "Don't try to do too much or take unnecessary chances."

"I guess you don't know me very well," he said, as he groped in the dark till he located a workbench. Fumbling over the countertop he found a large adjustable wrench, then stumbled back to Marilynn and placed it in her hands.

"Don't be afraid to use this on anybody who comes through that door that you don't recognize."

"How do you aim it?" teased Marilynn in a low voice. "I've never shot one of these before."

Doug smiled and marveled that she could still have a sense of humor in a time of extreme stress: What a woman!

"A full shot to the back of the head should do nicely," he answered. Although it was dark as pitch, he knew she was trying it out. The jingling noise gave it away. "It's show time," he said, making for the pale sliver of light under the exit door.

"Shit!" he shouted, after a couple of steps.

"What's the matter?" she whispered into the darkness.

"I walked into a freakin' stool," he snapped.

"I told you to be careful."

"Why didn't I think of that?' he mumbled to himself.

He shuffled along taking baby steps and after a painstakingly long time made it to the door without further incident. Pressing his ear against the steel door, he heard muffled noises. Were those footsteps down the hall? He pressed his ear harder, thinking that would magnify the sound. The beating of his heart seemed loud, and each nasal breath reverberated around his head. Could anyone else hear this racket his body was making? Random thoughts raced through his brain faster than an *Indy 500* racecar.

He fumbled for the doorknob, but restrained from turning it. Instinctively he looked back to check on Marilynn. With straining eyes he peered through the darkness to where he guessed to be the back corner of the room. He couldn't be sure she was still there.

He had come to realize that Coventry General Hospital's top trauma doctor was very capable of taking care of herself. That disturbed him. He liked women who depended on him and needed him. Yet he was strangely attracted to her and her independence.

Suddenly, nearby voices snapped him back to reality. He cracked the door enough to see two soldiers dressed in full anti-contamination suits. Each carried a spray canister.

"I need to take a dump," said a muffled voice through

a gas mask. "Why don't you go on without me. I'll catch up when I can."

Doug shut the door with a soft click. Footsteps and a slamming door somewhere down another corridor echoed back down the hallway. He waited until there was quiet, then cracked the laboratory door a second time, his shoulder muscles tense.

He listened attentively.

Silence.

Nothing but silence.

"Okay, now it's really show time," he whispered to himself. He took several deep breaths, then on the last exhale stepped out into hallway in the farthest point of West '4'. He shot quick glances to the left and right.

He saw no one.

A sudden burst of adrenaline shot through his body. Three doors down sat a spray canister on the floor, probably outside the bathroom the soldier was in.

"I've got to get a sample of this stuff," thought Talbot. "To-ens can run a lab test to see just what it is they're spraying, then we'll know exactly what we're up against."

He stepped cautiously, following the parallel blue and yellow lines on the floor. But by the time he got to the canister he realized he had nothing to put the sample in. He didn't have time to go back and search for something in the lightless laboratory. Looking both directions revealed an empty hallway.

He decided to follow the corridor to the right, for no other reason than to follow the blue line. It went fifty feet before coming to a perpendicular hallway. The yellow line veered left and the blue line broke right. Again he favored the blue line and went right in hopes of finding a container.

Rounding another corner he spied a pushcart about twenty feet up on the right side. Hustling over, he stood before it with hands on hips shaking his head. It was a food cart, with nothing but half-empty plastic lunch trays.

Suddenly, he snapped to attention. It was muffled by distance, but the unmistakable sound of a flushing toilet resonated through the vacant hallways. A tingling chill shot up the back of his neck. The busy soldier would soon be coming back out.

Searching feverishly, he scanned the food cart from top to bottom, then bottom to top. Now he was frantic, hunting through the bottom shelf of the two-tiered cart and flipping over empty trays. He was frustrated and wanted to yell. There was nothing he could use.

A door slammed and he froze in mid reach. It was the soldier's bathroom door. He was desperate. What was he going to use to take a sample, if he wasn't already too late? But then it came to him. He grabbed a used gelatin cup and bolted back towards the canister.

When he got to the bathroom, he was surprised to find it still lying where the soldier had left it. He bit his lower lip, as piercing pain shot across his stomach. Panic-stricken, he suddenly realized it hadn't been the soldier's bathroom door he'd heard after all.

It was Laboratory 'B'.

* * *

Crouching in the dark forsaken corner, Marilynn watched Doug close the lab door behind him, leaving her with nothing but her thoughts and the adjustable wrench. She was alone and scared: something she wasn't used to. She wanted to pray, but could only remember *Now I lay me down to sleep*. It had been a long time since she'd been to church.

Doug wasn't gone very long when the lab door re-opened. Marilynn got to her feet and was about to yell, *What did you forget?* but the words stayed in her mouth. A dark figure stood in the doorway. But it wasn't tall enough to be Doug.

She ducked back down as fast as she could, making little noise. The light switch flicked up and down several times. No lights came on. She was sure her heart skipped a beat.

"Fuck!" shouted an angry voice.

The door slammed shut. Doug had done his job.

A flashlight snapped on and a steady stream of light started searching the far corner of the room. She squatted low, but still felt vulnerable. Only darkness concealed her.

The light methodically searched behind cabinets and across walls then quickly changed course, darting here and there over the floor. Marilynn knew it was just a matter of time before she'd be found. Feeling helpless and hopeless, she waited for the inevitable.

Both her head and stomach hurt and she found herself breathing in quick shallow gasps. She closed her eyes tight, as if that would make it go away. But the footsteps drew nearer and she was compelled to look. Judging with eyes as big as silver dollars, she guessed the distance to be ten feet. She tightened her grip on the wrench.

Watching the stalking beam's circular motion was hypnotic. Her thoughts drifted to Jennie and her meditation trances. Why had she always teased her, calling it mindless drifting? Her face flushed, a product of the deep and painful feeling of guilt that overwhelmed her.

"Fucking stool!" cursed the tracker, banging into the same stool Doug had. Startled back to reality, she watched the swath of light focus on the stool. Two hands snatched it up and flung it against the wall where it shattered into shivers. The probing light pushed forward, searching behind a tall filing cabinet off to the left.

It was only several feet away and would soon be searching *her* corner. A swallow stuck in her throat. After a short struggle, she forced it painfully down. She wondered if the prowler had heard it.

Satisfied nothing was behind the cabinet, the intruder and his hunting light started towards her corner. Tracking slowly across the floor it hit directly at her hiding place.

It was empty.

Marilynn had crawled to the opposite wall and was scrambling along the shadowed baseboard, just like a cockroach would do when discovered in a dark corner.

Disappointed, the hunter with his investigative searchlight changed directions and methodically inspected the same wall.

Crawling on all fours, Marilynn had finally reached the other end of the room. A mouse would have been proud of the way she had maneuvered her way through the dark maze. Crouching as low as possible, she slithered behind a three-foot high wooden storage cabinet. Had she been followed? There was only one way to know and she knew what she had to do. It was getting up the courage to do it that was the problem. As she knelt there pondering her fateful move, visions of her and her Dad, tiny snippets of time gone by, flashed through her mind.

There was a quick image of her tenth birthday when he'd surprised her with a pony. Then a brief flash of the day he showed up at her first Saturday softball game, after pretending to be sick and leaving work, which for him was monumental, because he hadn't missed a day of work in seventeen years.

Then a brilliant thought, full of color and chaos, which transformed into the night they had lost their home and everything in it to a chimney fire. But suddenly, the next flash was interrupted by something touching her hand. She couldn't see it, but she could feel it. It had lots of legs and she knew it was somewhat furry by the slight rubbing of its underbelly on her skin. It crawled over her hand and stopped at the base of the big knuckle of her middle finger, perhaps to rest after a long journey, or pausing to decide which direction to travel next.

A new lump formed in her throat. She wanted to stand and shake her hand violently in the air, freeing herself of whatever sat using her hand as a refuge. But approaching footsteps reminded her that it wasn't a good idea.

The unseen creature began walking again, this time retreating up her arm towards her face. Then all at once she lost contact with it. It had left the traceable confines of her hand and forearm, for the unknown territory of her shirtsleeve. "Where the hell is it?" she wondered.

Problem number one recaptured her attention. The footsteps had reached her corner and the probing light was swirling all around the walls and floor surrounding her hiding place. Whoever it was, was a mere three feet away.

Problem two, however, won back her focus. The unknown thing was on her neck, crawling towards her face. Her breathing quickened. Only the fact that she couldn't see what it was kept her from screaming. It walked slowly up her neck till it reached the underside of her chin, where it took another break. After a short rest, it marched onward on its myriad of legs, gripping and propelling itself upward, working it's way towards the face of Mount Marilynn-more.

When it finally reached her cheek, she puffed wisps of air towards *creepy crawly* out of the corner of her mouth. As silently as she could, she tried to blow it off. First once then twice, she tried unsuccessfully. The slight breeze seemed to heighten the bug's curiosity and it started towards her mouth. There was only so much she could take and she was reaching the breaking point. Again she puffed and puffed and then on the fifth try, she felt it drop off.

Whoever brandished the light had turned his back to her and had started to recheck the far wall. She drew several quiet deep breaths, then stood slowly for a look. But she was clumsy and brushed against a coat rack, sending it toppling forward. Struggling to grab hold, she grappled with it, but it slipped through her hands and fell with a soft clank on the floor.

The flashlight swung towards her head, but she managed to duck in time. Hurried footsteps moved towards her new hiding place. In no time the light began searching around the doorway and the wall behind her.

Marilynn lay face flat on the floor breathing through her mouth, cognizant that the nose can make all sorts of noises. She could feel her heart pounding against the hard vinyl flooring. Sweat formed on her forehead.

Her face felt dirty from the dust on the floor. She was allergic to dust. Would she sneeze? In her mind, she sure as hell didn't feel anything like Coventry General's best trauma doctor.

From where she lay, she could see the stream of light darting frantically around her. She stared so hard through the darkness that her eyes ached. Slowly the light inched its way down the wall behind her and stopped. A partial silhouette of her head reflected back on the wall behind her. She wondered if *creepy crawly* was also visible.

It's funny the things that go through one's mind during stressful times. This time her thoughts turned to Doug. She smiled. She wasn't sure why, but a warm rush swept over her and suddenly she felt a sudden surge of renewed strength and energy. A strong urge to survive swelled through her like no feeling she had ever felt before.

Now she was angry and somebody was going to pay. I'm not going down without a fight, she pledged to herself. Her grip on the wrench grew tighter. If there had been light, she would have seen that her knuckles were white hot.

She played out in her mind the scenario of how she would jump up and swing her weapon at the unsuspecting intruder. Striking fast and first was her only chance. She would only get one shot.

The probing light drew closer. She raised the wrench. The time to strike was now.

West One
3:47pm

After leaving Dr. Harwell, poor Lindsey was commandeered by another doctor to help administer *B-Thrax* shots to the throng of people that at the time stood waiting in line for their shots. It had taken several hours before things quieted down, as a few more doctors and nurses had joined the overworked night staff. The crowds thinned to only a few stragglers coming in off the streets. Now the nurses and doctors were left to caring for the sick and dying. Every room in the hospital was bulging with patients.

Nurse Beakerman looked up from her station in the emergency room and saw an older unshaven man in tattered clothes standing there. Twirling his hat in his hands the smallish man said sheepishly, "Excuse me, Ma'am. I was wondering if I could get one of those shots they're giving out for the virus that the president said is going around? I don't have any money to pay for it though."

"Of course you can," answered the nurse with a smile. "They're free. The government's paying for them."

"I knew there was a reason I would have voted for the president," said the man, smiling through a mouth missing most of its teeth.

20 Water Street
3:56pm

Jennie Sprague came out of the bathroom to answer the front door after the doorbell rang three successive times. She pulled it open and a Providence police officer stood there.

"Mrs. Sprague?" he asked politely, taking off his police cap.

"Miss Sprague," she said politely back, "but you can call me Jennie."

"Jennie, my name is Officer Devin Graham. Did you call the police about a possible break-in?"

Jennie looked at the man standing before her. He was a couple of inches over six feet tall, had sandy hair and gray-blue eyes, the kind that Marilynn called *Bedroom Eyes*. She could tell he was serious about working out. His uniform was filled with broad shoulders and muscular arms.

"Yes, ...I did," answered Jennie, her voice slightly hesitant.

"You sound like you're still a little shook up. Are you okay?"

Not knowing why she had spoken that way, Jennie answered, "I'm fine, really."

"Would you like me to come in and take a look around?" asked the policeman.

"Yes please, Mister officer," said Jennie.

The policeman stepped over the threshold and glanced around the living room. He was even more impressive standing only inches away.

"Please, call me Devin, if that makes you feel more at ease."

Jennie felt her brain go blank and then her face go flush. "Okay, Devin it is."

"Mind if I go into the back rooms to take a look?"

Jennie stood in a full-face grin with her hands together as if in prayer. "I'd appreciate that. It's down that hallway," she said, pointing to her left.

Officer Devin smiled big pearly whites and headed off towards the rear of the house.

Jennie's face was a contortion of confusion. She shook her head as if she had just gotten up and was trying to shake the cobwebs out. Softly she said to herself, '"Yes please, mister officer? I'd like that.'" Why the hell am I babbling?" She left the living room and went immediately to the bathroom. She could hear Officer Graham checking out her computer station. She looked into the mirror, stuck out her tongue and sighed deeply. She was still wearing her jogging outfit and her hair was a mess. She grabbed a hairbrush and frantically tried to brush out the tangled mess her little jaunt had created. She heard footsteps coming back down the hallway, so she straightened out her clothes as best as she could, then walked out and rejoined the policeman in the living room. He smiled. She felt giddy.

"Everything seems okay," he said. "If someone had broken in, they would have surely taken your computer and all its hardware. Judging by what you have there, you've obviously spent some money on that setup. Plus, I noticed your entertainment center appears untouched."

"I noticed the same thing," said Jennie. "I really thought I locked the door before I went out for my jog, though."

"You like to run?" asked Devin.

"I try to run about thirty minutes a day," said Jennie proudly.

"Me too," said the officer in a soothing voice. "I usually go to the gym and lift weights for another half-an-hour.

Jennie shifted uneasily. She was confused at the queasiness she felt. She smiled a foolish grin. "You look good," she said. "I'm mean, your muscles look like you work out."

"That's a pretty nice set-up you have in there," said the officer. "Are you a computer expert or something?"

Jennie felt mesmerized staring into his soft gray-blue eyes.. "Yes," she said shyly. "I'm a Systems Analyst. I work from home, servicing companies that have problems with their security systems. Sometimes I reprogram their servers and subservers.

"Wow!" said the policeman, smiling wide to reveal his bright polished teeth. Waving his hand over his head he continued, "That flew right over. I've been thinking about taking computer lessons, but haven't found a place that teaches basic courses to computer dummies like me."

"I'm a pretty good teacher," said Jennie, standing with her knees leaning against the end of the sofa. "I'd be glad to teach you the basics."

"Maybe some night after work I can come over and you can teach me a thing or two," said Devin.

"That'd be great!" said Jennie excitedly.

"I'm off duty tomorrow," said Devin. "Would that be too soon?"

"No," she said eagerly. "Say, six o'clock."

"I'll even bring pizza and beer," winked the officer.

"My favorite meal," smiled Jennie.

"Great!" said Officer Devin reaching for the door. "Then it's a date!" Before shutting the door behind, he smiled one last time.

Jennie smiled back, then closed the door. Standing with her back against it, she suddenly realized she had a date with a man and she was excited about it. What the hell was that all about? she wondered.

After walking down the front walkway, Officer Devin Graham turned right and headed up the street. A few houses back, on the left, an unmarked blue sedan's engine roared to life and it followed two car lengths behind the policeman. When the officer turned the corner and stepped onto the next street, the sedan pulled up bedside him and stopped. The windows on the car were so dark, he couldn't see who was inside. The front passenger window rolled down slowly and a large man in a dark gray suit said, "Get in!" His eyes were hidden behind sunglasses.

The back door popped open and Devin Graham walked over and slid inside. The man in the dark glasses turned his head around and, pulling them off, said, "Well?"

Officer Graham smiled. "Everything's set."

Jennie never noticed that there had been no police car out front.

* * *

Doug Talbot had a tough decision to make. Help Marilynn or get the sample. Time was running short and he needed to act fast.

Having made up his mind, he lifted the canister's nozzle and sprayed clear liquid into the gelatin cup. From inside the bathroom came the sound of an electric hand dryer. He dropped the hose and nozzle and started tip-toeing away. He was almost out of sight when he heard an angry voice shout, "Hey! You! What the fuck are you doing?"

The sound of a rifle cocking froze him in his tracks. He stood with his back to the stranger.

"I asked you!" shouted the irritated voice. "What the fuck are you doing?"

Doug turned around slowly and came face to face with a middle-aged, ruddy-faced soldier with a dark handlebar mustache. He could see the soldier's face because he hadn't put his gas mask back on yet.

"You look familiar," said the soldier, eyeing him up and down. "Do I know you?"

"Do you work at the hospital?" asked Talbot, "because I'm here a lot getting tests done."

The soldier's eyes narrowed. Doug could see he was running his face through memory banks, trying to figure where he had seen it before.

"What's *that* in your hands?" asked the soldier, pointing the rifle at the cup he held.

Doug shrugged sheepishly. "What, this?"

The soldier pointed the gun at his face. "Yeah! That!" he snapped.

Doug held the cup to eye level and said, "It's a specimen cup of urine. They're testing me for AIDS." He pushed the cup out towards the soldier. "Do you want to smell it to make sure?"

The soldier scrunched up his nose in disgust. "NO!" he shouted. "I don't want to smell your freakin' pee!" He stepped back and picked up his canister, then jogged off in search of his partner.

Doug pulled the cup close to his face and sniffed. Thank God it had been lemon gelatin in the cup. It had turned the clear liquid yellow.

* * *

Dr. Harwell's heart raced as she knelt in striking position behind the metal cabinet with her trusty wrench. Her hands shook at the thought of the vulgar act of hitting someone to cause bodily harm, because she was torn between self preservation and her self imposed humanistic approach to life. The searchlight was only a couple of feet away, fixed on the wall to her right. She started counting backwards. Three – two – one, but the doorway suddenly burst inward, filling the room with brilliant light from the hallway.

"Come on, Peterson," said a muffled voice behind a gas mask. "Captain Adelade wants us to meet back on the first floor. We have new orders."

"But Sir, I may have found something in here."

"Now!" shouted his superior. "Let's go! Double time!

You know how Adelade can be when you're late to his damn meetings. And I'm not peeling any freakin' potatoes because of you."

"Okay! Okay!" snapped the intruder. "I guess I imagined the whole thing."

Marilynn heard the lab door slam shut and the room morphed into darkness. She lay still for what seemed an eternity, then decided to chance standing. It was time to head back to the cafeteria. But at that moment, the door opened slightly, pushing a sliver of hallway light inside. The door pushed all the way in and soft footsteps moved into the doorway and stopped. A long dark shadow of a man stretched across the floor.

So they've come back, she thought. I may not get the last shot in, but I will get the first and they'll remember it. She drew in a deep soundless breath, filling her lungs to capacity. Silently counting backwards she jumped into the doorway swinging the wrench forward, yelling, "Aiiiyyy!"

"Whoa!" shouted Doug, ducking the wild swing and spilling half of the cup's contents as the wrench narrowly missed his head.

"Oh! God!" cried Marilynn. "I'm so sorry."

Doug got to his feet and embraced her. Her shivering body vibrated into his arms and chest. She looked deeply into his eyes. "I could have killed you," she babbled.

"No, you wouldn't have," he whispered, pulling her head to within several inches of his. "You might have rearranged my face a little, though." She released a nervous laugh. They stood frozen in time, searching each other's eyes wondering what the other was thinking.

Suddenly their bodies pressed together and Marilynn felt Doug's steady heartbeat against hers. She was very aware of her own quickening.

They kissed.

Danger was all around them, but they didn't care because it felt right. Moments later, they walked back into the lab hand in hand. There was work to do. They now had a sample of the vaccine.

They located other light switches in the room for alternate lighting and turned them on. Marilynn got out all the necessary equipment and began mixing different chemicals with the serum, trying to see what kind of reaction they would have. She assigned Doug the task of writing down her results on a log.

When his job became tedious and he had nothing to do but watch, he said, "You can handle this. I'm going exploring. I'll be back in a while."

Without looking up from her microscope, she warned, "Be careful. You don't know how safe it is out there."

"Yes, mother!" he said sarcastically.

"You're the second person to call me that," she said, focusing on her specimen.

Before stepping out the door Doug looked back and said, "Don't worry! I'll take chances and I won't be careful." Marilynn was busy studying the sample and didn't respond. Doug chuckled to himself.

Sticking his head halfway out the doorway, he was quickly satisfied the corridor was empty. He stepped the rest of the way out and noticed a lit red neon sign with white lettering about fifteen feet to the right that said EXIT – STAIRS. An arrow pointed to the right.

Figuring it was safer to take the stairs and avoid the elevator so as not to attract unnecessary attention, he made his way to the metal door that led into the stairwell. He listened for signs of activity, but heard nothing.

The door opened outward and he took several steps into the stairway leaving West Four behind. He let go of the door as softly as possible, but it snapped shut. The acoustics were such that the loud noise resonated downward towards the other three levels.

Irritated, he snapped, "Damn it!" His heart was in his mouth as he waited near the top of the descending stairs. A protective guardrail attached to the wall behind him wound its way around to the top of the stairwell. He leaned over the rail and peered down at empty concrete stairs leading down several floors, hearing nothing but the fading echoes created by the slamming of his door. He relaxed and his shoulders slumped.

Confident it was safe, he stepped cautiously down the stairs, deliberately putting one foot after the other. When he reached the third level he found another metal door marked West Three in five-inch black stenciled lettering. He put his ear close to the door, but heard nothing.

He continued downward until he reached the next concrete landing: West Two. He placed his head against the cool steel door. All was quiet. Assured, he pulled the door inward and walked out into a brightly lit hallway. Looking to his left, he saw an unmanned nurses' station about fifty feet away. Glancing up, he saw four signs on the wall in front of him that resembled green and white street signs. Three signs marked Primary Care, Pediatrics and Obstetrics & Gynecology, pointed left towards the nurses' station. Another sign marked Clerical pointed straight ahead.

Suddenly, there were voices and footsteps coming from the stairwell. Doug considered his options. If he went in the direction of the nurses' station, there was no telling who or what he would encounter there. If he went straight it was a dead end, putting him in a position of entrapment. The voices sounded as if they were near the bottom of the stairs. Doug went straight. He walked briskly down the short hallway and found doors marked Records One, Records Two, and Records Three. Behind him, the stairwell door opened, so he slid into room Three. It was small, about twelve by twelve, and had gray metal filing cabinets that filled the surrounding walls up to six feet high. Sitting in the middle of the room was a small wooden desk with a computer and monitor that was lit by a small green office lamp.

He slid behind the desk and turned the lamp off. Standing in the dark, he could hear voices mumbling words he couldn't understand. The door to room One opened and slammed shut. Moments after, Records Two opened, then slammed closed, sending a shock wave through the floor that he felt through his shoes and up his legs.

The voices and the nameless faces behind them stood outside Records Three. The doorknob turned. Doug ducked to the floor as the door swung open. He watched a white beam sweep over the wall to his left, then the wall to his right, then directly behind him.

"There's no one here," said a deep voice, which belonged to Sergeant Carpenter.

"Do you think they're still in the hospital, Sarge, or do you think they've bolted out of here?" asked a young voice.

"What do you think, Peterson?" snapped Carpenter. "You heard what that nurse said. They're here somewhere and we're going to find them and bring them in!"

"What do you think they'll do to them?"

"That's not our concern," said the sergeant. "Our orders are to find them. The rest is up to the big shots."

"So where do we look next?" asked Peterson.

Carpenter answered, "Let's finish the rest of this floor and if they don't turn up, we'll meet the guys back on the first floor." The door slammed shut, sending shudders through Doug's entire body.

West 4,
Lab 'B'
4:47pm

Sitting on a stool and leaning over a microscope, Dr. Harwell added a drop of the anti-virus spray to the smear she was studying. Behind her came the soft click of a doorknob.

"What'd you forget, Doug?" she called, as she focussed on the specimen.

"I need to talk to you, Marilynn," said Doug in a deadpan voice.

"I'm kind of busy. What do you need?"

His voice expressionless he said, "Marilynn, I really do need to talk to you."

Grotesquely hunched over the microscope, she said excitedly, "Hold on a minute! I think I've found something!"

"Please turn around, *Marilynn*!"

"What's this with the Marilynn stuff?" she asked, spinning around on the stool. The barrel of a semi-automatic rifle pointed two inches from her nose.

Standing with arms raised in surrender Doug said, "Sorry, To-ens."

"You're forgiven this time," said Marilynn, her eyes focused on the point of the rifle barrel. "Don't let it happen again, though."

"Don't move or I'll blow you away," commanded a young voice, muffled somewhat by his gas mask.

"I promise," said Dr. Harwell calmly. "I won't move. But, do you think you could lower your gun out of my face?"

The soldier pulled the rifle to his hip, where it wasn't any less threatening. Standing in full anti-contamination gear he said, "I knew there was someone in here."

Dr. Harwell locked onto the brown eyes of the soldier behind the mask. "I don't know what they've told you about what's going on," she said, "but things are not entirely what they seem. We're trying to figure out what the vaccinations are made of so we can understand why they aren't working."

"My orders are to search for a Dr. Marilynn Harwell and a Doug Talbot and detain them. I think you're them!" snapped the young soldier.

"Don't you get it?" shouted Talbot. "We're only checking the virus spray to determine what it is. We're concerned because it doesn't seem to have any effect on anyone! Do you understand? Its effectiveness is questionable!"

Doug crumpled to the floor, victim of a rifle butt slammed into his stomach.

"Doug!" screamed Marilynn, reaching down.

"Stop!" shouted the soldier, shoving the gun in front of her face. "Move and I shoot!"

She froze in mid reach. The weapon was inches from her temple.

"I need to see if he's okay," she said stiffly.

"Ma'am! Don't even breathe loud," commanded the young soldier. His arms shook, as if he had Parkinson's.

Marilynn turned slowly and made eye contact with him. His goggles were foggy and he appeared confused and wobbly.

"You don't look so good," she said. "What's wrong?"

"Nothing!" answered the soldier through clenched teeth. "Duh, Don't tr-try to confuse me."

Struggling to regain his breath, Doug staggered off the floor. "She's right, you don't look too good," he said, rubbing his stomach gingerly. "Take off your suit and let the Doc take a look at you."

"Sss, sstop, trrr, trrrying to to confuse meeeee," stammered the soldier. "I – I, ta ta told youuuu, not ta ta, move."

"We're not," said Doug.

The suited soldier swayed side to side, then crashed to the floor in a heap. Doug snatched the gun. Marilynn pulled the rubber mask over the soldier's head. Blank eyes stared up and sweat was already forming on his forehead.

"I'm so thirsty," gasped the soldier.

"What's your name?" asked Marilynn in a soothing voice.

"Donald Peterson, Ma'am," he mouthed in a soft whisper.

"Hold on, Donald," she said. "We'll get you something to drink."

Doug went to a water cooler in the back of the room.

Marilynn asked, "Did anything strange happen to you today?"

In a whisper the soldier said, "I was cleaning my rifle this morning, Ma'am, and accidentally poked myself in the eye with a cleaning rod." Grabbing Dr. Harwell's arm, he clamped an unexpected vice grip. "Am I going to die?" he gasped with wide eyes.

"Here's the water," said Doug reaching a paper cup down.

Marilynn's head dropped to her chest.

"He's gone," she said, her voice deflated like a popped balloon.

She unclenched the dead soldier's hand and reached down and gently closed his eyelids.

"God!" she shouted. "He was just a kid."

Doug rubbed her shoulders with short tender strokes in an effort to ease her torment. One thing he'd learned about her in the short time he'd known her was that she hated losing to death. It was a constant personal battle that she waged against the Grim Reaper. To her, death was nothing more than a premature taker of life and she would do everything in her power to delay its mission.

"There's nothing we can do for him, Marilynn."

She shook her head and sighed heavily.

"We need to get out of here before someone else comes," he said, staring towards the doorway.

After she placed Peterson's hands together on his chest, he helped her to her feet.

"What do we do now?" he asked softly.

Picking up the half-full cup of liquid he'd brought her, she said, "I think I know what the spray is." She put the cup to her mouth and poured it in and swallowed. Talbot's eyes grew wide.

"It's okay," she said in answer to his unasked question. "It's water. Nothing more than a placebo."

"Geez, To-ens! You scared the hell out of me!"

"Sorry. I was just trying to prove a point."

"Well, I got it!" he said, still trying to rub away the remains of the earlier shot to the stomach.

Seeing him wincing she asked, "How are you feeling? Do you need me to check you out?"

"I'm fine," he said. "I just lost my breath."

She studied him closely, watching for any sudden signs of the new, robber of life, trauma.

"That's good," she said. "I'd hate to have to do this by myself, because you couldn't go on."

"What, and miss out on all the fun," he said, pacing

back and forth like an expectant father. "Anyway, shouldn't we tell someone or do something?"

"I know just the person to call," said Marilynn. "My friend at the Coroners office. I need to find out what he knows."

She turned her back to him as she reached into her pocketbook for her cell phone, missing his quick hand swipe of a couple of glistening drops of sweat off his forehead. Looking back at the water cooler where he'd gotten the drink for Peterson, he wondered if she would think it odd that he suddenly needed a drink.

CHAPTER 8

State Medical Building
Coroner's Department
Downtown
5:05pm

"Crawford - Coroner's office," said a tired voice on the other end of the line.

"Paul, it's Marilynn. Do you have anything for me?"

"Where the hell have you been?" said Crawford in a low voice. "I've been waiting for your call."

"I've been a little busy. What's wrong?"

"They ripped this place apart, that's all."

"Who did?"

"The SIA! They were here for over an hour checking out my lab. They said they received a tip that I had access to a deadly biological virus that's supposedly been unleashed on the United States."

There was a long pause.

"I could be in a lot of trouble, Marilynn," he said shakily. "That's considered a national security breach."

"What could they want from you? You don't know anything."

"That's not entirely true."

"What's going on, Paul. Did they actually find something?"

"No. They didn't find any of what they said they were looking for."

"They must have had a good reason for showing up uninvited."

"It all started when I called a friend of mine in Washington. He's a medical examiner I went to school with many moons ago. Now he's a big time medical expert on television for one of the large networks. His name is Dr. Jason Parker, you may have heard of him."

Doug tapped Marilynn's shoulder to get her attention. When she looked up he said, "I'm going out for a few minutes. I want to see what's going on. I'll be back."

"Hold on a second, Paul," she said, cuffing the phone with her free hand. "Meet me at the cafeteria in a little while," she said.

"Where's that?" he asked.

"On the other side of this floor."

"See you in a bit," he said, waving his hand over his head as he left the room.

"Sorry, Paul, name doesn't ring a bell. Why did you need to call him?"

"You asked me to look for any odd patterns. Well, it took me a while and it sure wasn't easy, but I finally found something."

"What?"

Crawford suddenly became defensive. "Just remember, I waited and waited for your call, but it didn't come. That gave me time to think things over and it just seemed too big to keep to myself, especially with this supposed deadly germ going around. That's when I made the call to Parker."

"What are you trying to say?"

"Ten minutes after I called my friend, I got a call from a General Uxbridge of the SIA, and he's all excited and starts asking me all sorts of questions."

"Like what?"

"He wanted to know what I knew, and whether I had shared that information with anyone. Trust me. He was very serious during that conversation and it scared the hell out of me."

"What did you tell him?"

"Sorry, Marilynn. I told him all about you and how you were interested in finding what all the deaths had in common. I explained that if it weren't for you, I never would have made the discovery. Believe me, the only reason I mentioned your name was because I wanted you to share in the glory and honors."

There was a long, exaggerated silent pause.

"What the hell did you tell this Uxbridge?"

"I told him what I found on all the bodies."

"What?" shouted Marilynn, suddenly losing her composure.

"Don't yell, Marilynn. I'm still upset after what's happened in the past few hours."

"Sorry. I've been pretty stressed out myself. I guess my patience is a little thin."

"You're forgiven," said Crawford, drawing a deep breath. "Anyway, it wasn't noticeable at first and I almost didn't catch it. As a matter of fact, if I hadn't slipped and spilled some booze on the shoulder of the body I was working on, I probably would have overlooked it altogether."

"I guess your drinking was helpful after all," she said, trying to make him a little less apprehensive.

"I never did get to that pot of coffee."

"Not to change the subject, but what happened to all the help you called in?"

"They left before I made my discovery. I couldn't blame them. They only wanted to get back to their families. Anyway, I reached down to wipe the shoulder clean and noticed a tiny little red mark just above the vaccination scar. I figured it must be either an insect bite or possibly some type of trauma induced during transport."

"That's the similarity you found?"

"I started checking above the vaccination scars on other bodies and sure enough, each one had the same little red mark."

"Anything else?"

"Only that it was not indigenous to anyone in particular."

"What do you mean?"

"It wasn't preferential to race, size, or gender."

"I guess no one is immune to it," said Marilynn.

"A couple could have been a coincidence, but twenty-seven?"

"I'd say that's a hell of a pattern," she said. "What'd you do next?"

"I performed a skin graft and checked it under a microscope. What do you think I found?"

"Have no idea?"

"It was the damnedest thing. The last thing I would have thought and definitely not anything I had ever encountered before."

"Damn it, Paul! What was it?"

"Are you sitting down?"

She wasn't, but she said yes anyway. He would have waited till she was if she didn't placate him.

"A computer chip!" shouted Crawford.

"A computer chip. Are you sure?"

"Positive. It was about the size of a pinhead, but very thin layered and strategically placed just under the skin. If you feel just above your smallpox vaccination Doctor, you should feel a slightly raised area."

He waited for her to feel the described area.

"It's very slight," she said, sounding perplexed, "but I do feel something! It's funny, but I never noticed that before."

"I guess no one else has either. You and I may be the only ones to know about this."

"The questions we need to be asking," said Marilynn, "are what are they, what purpose do they serve and more importantly, who put them there? But I guess that's hard to know since it doesn't come with a set of instructions."

"That's not entirely true," said Dr. Crawford.

"What do you mean?"

"I had to increase the magnification to maximum, but

there was no mistaking what I saw. There were words inscribed on them."

"I'm almost afraid to ask, but what did it say?"

"There were two lines. The top line had GOV-69, and the bottom one had the word NOPOSAM."

"Noposam?" uttered Marilynn. "What the hell is that?"

"Damned if I know," shot back Crawford. "But my guess is that GOV-69 could represent Government 69. The number 69 could be anything though: maybe even a year. Once I saw that, I phoned my friend in Washington to see if he knew what it was. He was baffled too, but said he would pass it on to a friend of his in one of the investigative agencies."

"That would be one General Uxbridge," said Marilynn. "That's when you told him what you found?"

"Not everything. I didn't tell him the second line of the code on the chips. Funny thing, though. His tone changed suddenly to serious and menacing. It was almost like he knew that I was suppressing information. That's when he threatened me."

"Why would he feel the need to threaten you?"

"I don't know, but it became real obvious after he said he was sending over a team of high level security investigators from the SIA to see what I was doing. He told me that withholding information that could be tied to the terrorist's biological attack on the United States would be construed as me being a terrorist conspirator. He also said I would suffer extreme consequences, because I would be classified a *National Security Threat,* which is punishable by life in prison or possibly even death."

"Don't worry, Paul. I'll vouch for your integrity. And I know at least ten other doctors who would be willing to go to bat for you."

"Thanks, Marilynn. That makes me feel a whole lot better. I've been so shook up that I haven't had a drop to drink since that phone call."

"Who the hell are the SIA?" asked Marilynn. "I've never heard of them."

"The SIA is the Special Intelligence Agency. They're pretty tough guys from what I hear. They get all the cases the FBI, CIA, Navy Seals, Green Berets, and any other special forces you can think of don't want, because of being too dangerous or next to impossible to carry out."

"That's some pretty serious stuff."

"No kidding. That's when I knew I was on to something."

"Until we get to the bottom of this, I don't want you to stay there by yourself. Mendez is at least there with you, isn't he?"

There was a long quiet pause, then a grievous sigh from Crawford.

"Mendez was brought in this afternoon," he said sadly. "After the play ended last night, he and a female friend were leaving the Arts Center through the lobby's front revolving doors. He mistimed his step going in and got caught in between. His girlfriend told me they were both laughing and joking because it seemed pretty funny at the time. But it wasn't funny after all, because twelve hours later, he died at home."

"I'm sorry, Paul. I know he was like a son to you."

"He just turned thirty last week. I was grooming him to be my replacement for when I retired in a couple of years. You know, I even paid for him to go to college."

Suddenly, there was a loud crash. Marilynn switched the phone to her other ear.

"Who the hell are you?" she heard Crawford shout.

"Paul!" she yelled into the phone. "What's going on?"

"Get out of here!" yelled Crawford, "or I'll call the cops. I mean it! My phone line is tied directly into police headquarters."

"Paul! What's happening?"

In the background came the sounds of crashing furniture and breaking glass so loud that she had to pull the phone from her ears.

There was a long silence and she suddenly felt nauseous.

"Paul!" she cried. But there was no return answer, only loud thunder.

She knew the sound of a 344 Magnum. She'd heard it the day she was invited to a marksmen exhibition at the Providence police firing range. Stunned, she held the phone tightly to her ear, hoping Paul would come back on the line.

There was an unsettling silence and then footsteps. Footsteps crunching on broken glass, and footsteps kicking away wood debris. Mixed in were soft voices, but she couldn't tell what they were saying.

She listened hard, her heartbeat pounding inside her head. And then the phone suddenly had dial tone. Someone had hung up the other end.

* * *

Doug walked into the third-floor cafeteria and found Marilynn sipping a cup of coffee at a table in the middle of the room, which was otherwise empty.

"I snuck around the third floor but didn't see anyone of interest," he said excitedly. "What's going on?"

"You know what?" she said matter-of-factly, "I hate old coffee. It always tastes bitter." Looking up with swollen red eyes, she asked, "How do you feel on the subject?"

"I like ice coffee," he answered blankly.

Marilynn drew in a long, slow, slurping sip. "It's not only bitter, but it's freakin' cold!" she snapped.

Doug's eyebrows pushed upward. "Are you okay? he asked. "Did something happen while I was gone?"

Perturbed, she answered, "Oh yeah!"

"Do you want to talk about it?"

"Nope!"

"You can't kid a kidder. What's wrong?"

Marilynn glanced slowly up with tear-filled eyes and cried, "I just lost a good friend and it was my fault."

"Something happened to Dr. Crawford?"

"He was shot as I was talking to him on the phone," she answered through clenched teeth.

"Who shot him?"

"My guess is the SIA!"

"Are you telling me you think the SIA murdered your friend?"

"Yup!"

"How do you know that?"

"Just before he died, Paul told me that he'd spoken to a General Thomas Uxbridge. This General told him that he was sending over a team of investigators from the SIA, because they had intelligence that he was withholding information that tied him to the terrorist's biological attack on the United States. He was being classified as a national security threat."

"So you think *that* was enough for them to kill Crawford?"

"Yes – maybe - I don't know! I'm so confused." She buried her forehead in her hands. Gathering a breath she said in a low voice, "What I do know is he found the something I asked him to look for and now he's dead!"

"This doesn't make any sense," said Doug, shaking his arms above his head. "The United States government is not in the practice of killing people just because they suspect them of something illegal."

Marilynn sat upright and crossed her arms. "How do you know that!"

"That's not the rule of thumb."

"Maybe this is an exception to that rule."

Not convinced, Doug shook his head. "I have a friend who's a captain in the army reserves. I'll call him. Maybe he can find out what's going on."

"I'm going to call the police and see what they have to say," said Marilynn, drying her eyes with her shirtsleeves. She sniffled a couple of times, then went on, "I spoke to 9-1-1 when I called in the shooting and a short time later a female police officer called me back to confirm that he was dead. She didn't have any other details."

Doug reached across the table next to them for a napkin and handed it to her. She blew into it several times then rolled it up into a ball and tossed it on the floor.

Doug slid a chair next to hers and sat with his hand under his chin, mulling over everything she'd told him, using all his reasoning and rationalization to make sense if it. After a couple of moments he said, "Even if he was murdered like you think, you believe it's your fault?"

"Ohhhh yeah!" she said, her eyes trained on the cup she was rotating in her hands.

He placed his hand gingerly on hers, blocking the cup from spinning. "Okay Marilynn, I need to know more. Tell me everything that happened."

"Uh, oh!" she said. "You really mean business now. You called me Marilynn."

Sighing deeply, Doug shook his head. He knew getting her through this was not going to be easy.

"Before we get into this, where is everyone? I figured this place would be packed with nurses and doctors filling their faces."

"The cafeteria's closed," she mumbled.

He looked around the empty room, and at the vacant serving area. "I don't understand."

"What's to understand? They ran out of food because there haven't been any deliveries. No sense in staying open if they don't have any food to serve."

"Damn. I was looking forward to a nice cup of hot coffee."

"Do what I did," she said, stifling a laugh. "Help yourself to a nice cup of stale cold coffee."

Doug rubbed his chin thoughtfully, then locked his hands together in his lap and said, "Tell me what happened."

She proceeded to tell him about her conversation with Dr. Crawford. Specifically, how he found the chip in all of the bodies. Also, how Paul had called his friend in Washington, and then about the threatening call he received from General Uxbridge. She finished up by telling the part where she heard the fatal gunshot.

Doug slumped in his chair, as if he were in a recliner, weighing everything he'd just heard. Five silent minutes passed, because he wanted to choose his words carefully, knowing full well she was teetering on the edge of a precipice with a deep drop.

Sitting up straight, he spoke soothingly, "First of all, Marilynn, it's not your fault. Do you want to know why?"

She looked up with strained eyes and said in a bitter tone, "Why isn't causing death my fault?"

"Because you are a doctor, and as a doctor you took an oath to help the sick and dying. If during the course of making tough decisions someone innocent dies due to an unfortunate event, it's not your fault. It's life simply following its destined course and no matter what you think, it's totally out of your control."

"I'm supposed to save people's lives, not cost them!" she snapped. "If he wasn't checking those bodies for me, he never finds the chip, then he doesn't make that call to Washington." Her head lowered and she pulled in a deep breath and pushed it out quickly. In a downhearted voice she said, "And he'd still be alive!"

"Are you saying you should stop being a good doctor, because there are risks involved?"

"I'm saying that it's my fault he's dead, because I could have done more."

"Christ, Marilynn, you're not Superwoman. You can't be responsible for everyone, and you can't save everyone."

She buried her head in her hands and sobbed freely.

He moved behind her and started rubbing her shoulders with gentle squeezes and rubs. "Sometimes in life, things happen for a reason," he said softly, "and neither you nor anyone else can change that."

Looking up with a face and voice full of hate and resentment she said, "That sucks!"

"No, that's life," he said.

After letting her cool off a little, he continued. "Would Dr. Crawford want you to sit here feeling sorry or would he want you to use the information he gave you, which he died for by the way, and put it to good use?"

Marilynn flung her coffee cup, spraying coffee across the table and floor. "That's easy for you to say, nothing bothers you!" she shot back.

"That's not true. There are lots of things that bother me."

She screwed her face into a deep scowl and glared. "Like what?"

"Like waiting in the express line at the grocery store for some yahoo to use their debit card for the first time. Then the cashier has to take time to explain how to use the damn thing."

"Don't be a freakin' idiot!" she snapped. "That's not the same thing!"

"You know what else bothers me?"

"No," she said dryly, with scrunched up eyes that would freeze the devil. "But I'm sure you're going to tell me."

"When someone tells me, 'Have a nice day', when my day's already in the toilet."

"Jesus Christ! Now you're mocking me! Be serious and come up with something that's germane to my situation!"

"I'm not mocking you," he said calmly.

He stared down at his shoes. Finally he said, "Here's another one. How about getting home with a takeout order, only to find it's wrong."

"That's just stupid! God, you are an idiot."

"You know what bothers me most, though?"

"What?" she asked sarcastically, her eyes and nose scrunched.

"When someone tells me, *nothing bothers me*."

Marilynn's face softened. She sighed deeply as her head settled on her chest. "What's your point."

"My point is, it bothers me to see you torturing yourself all the time because of circumstances that are out of your control. Damn it, Marilynn! Don't cheapen Paul's memory by not utilizing his contribution."

"What do you mean?" she asked, using her sleeves again to dry her eyes.

"Let's figure out what the chip is and what it does. Then we'll go from there."

"*That's* your plan?" she snapped. "To go from there."

"Hey! It's a starting point. Tell me more about this chip Crawford found."

Marilynn rubbed her eyes and sniffled several times, then stood and removed her white jacket. After rolling up the green shirtsleeve of her hospital-issued top, she pointed to an area just above her vaccination and said, "Right about here is where Dr. Crawford said each of the bodies had the same red mark. When he did a skin graft, he found a computer chip that was very thin and about the size of a pinhead. Feel this spot right here."

He lightly rubbed her shoulder up and down. "Son of a gun, there's something there! It's tiny, but I do feel it." Examining the area carefully he said, "But I don't see any red mark on your shoulder."

"I know," she said. "Roll up your shirt and let's see if you have one."

He unbuttoned his denim shirt and slipped out of it, revealing his shoulder. She rubbed the area above his smallpox vaccination.

"Identical to mine," she said shaking her head. "And I don't see any red mark on yours either."

Sticking his hands in his pockets he asked, "What do you think that means?"

"According to Dr. Crawford, it's not indigenous to a select group. He examined a cross section of people and the result was the same. They were young and old; black and white; short and tall; fit and stout. Each one had the same red mark and computer chip."

"But they all had one thing in common that we don't," said Doug.

"What's that?" she asked.

"They're all dead."

"Good point."

"So what do we do next?" asked Doug.

"There's only one thing we can do," she answered. "One of us needs to be a guinea pig, while the other removes a skin graft."

"Are you insane?" snapped Doug. "You want to remove a perfectly good piece of skin off my shoulder?"

"Who said we were going to take it from you?"

"Well, I'm the man here, aren't I?"

Marilynn chuckled loudly. "That's about as sexist as it gets!" she said, standing with hands on hips.

Doug couldn't hide his reddening face. "I just assumed," he said.

"Well you assumed wrongly."

"You are the doctor here."

"You couldn't even handle a cold stethoscope on your chest," she said laughing. "Besides, the reason I want to take it from my shoulder is because if there is something there, I want to give it to my roommate Jennie. She's a computer whiz and all my vital statistics are in her computer's database, so she'll have something to cross reference."

"Why don't we both do it?" he asked.

"What if Jennie finds something? We'll need another chip to present to the State Medical Board and that's when we'll need yours."

"I guess that makes sense. But how are we going to get a skin graft from your shoulder?"

"Follow me," said Marilynn heading for the doorway. "We need to go down the hall to one of the operating rooms."

"Isn't there surgery going on?" he asked.

"Hold on a second," she said. She made her way over to a wall phone and had a conversation for only a few seconds. After returning, she said, "Because of the crazy day we've had, everything's been cancelled. Besides, there are no surgeons available."

"I guess there's no excuse then," he said.

"Nope," she said. "So let's go."

He scrambled after her and in no time they were standing inside a fully functional operating room. Marilynn went over to a portable table that held a silver tray with assorted scalpels arranged by size. She studied each of them before selecting a short and very sharp looking instrument.

"This will do," she said, handing it to him.

"This will do what?" he asked, his face contorted in surprise.

"This will be good enough for you to remove a piece of my skin."

"Say what?" he shouted.

"I want you to use this scalpel," she said in a serious and commanding tone. "It's sharp enough so that you won't have to apply much pressure. It'll almost do the job for you."

"Now I know you're crazy!" he said. "You actually think I'm going to cut your shoulder with this?"

"It'll be quick and painless," she answered. "Where's that macho sexist man from a couple of minutes ago?"

Doug fidgeted with his watch. "I think he left the building."

Rolling the knife around in his hands to get a feel for it he said, "Okay! I love a challenge just as much as the next guy."

"Quick and painless," she reiterated, sitting on a wooden stool. "All you have to do is press the scalpel lightly against the skin slightly below my vaccination, then quickly push up and out. It's almost like a flick of the wrist."

Doug lay the knife exactly where she instructed him. She inhaled deeply and closed her eyes.

Room 305
5:33pm

Lindsey Palmer stood at Cassandra's bedside checking the readings on the monitors and writing them onto the girl's chart. Cross-referencing them with the previous ones taken an hour earlier revealed most were in the same general range, fluctuating only slightly higher or lower.

Cassandra stirred and shifted around to face Lindsey. Her eyes were mere slits. Forcing a smile, she said in a hoarse voice, "Is my daddy here?"

Lindsey reached down and brushed the girl's hair out of her face. "He's with Dr. Harwell. He told me to tell you that he would come by to check on you as soon as he was finished doing something important."

"I miss Daddy and Dr. Harwell."

In a soft voice Lindsey said, "Me too."

Cassandra's face drooped. "I'm really thirsty," she said in a sad voice.

The nurse filled a six-ounce plastic cup with ice water from a metal pitcher and handed it to her. Cassandra drank it all in one big gulp and said, "I'm still thirsty, can I have another one?"

The nurse poured a second cup and handed it to her. As the girl drank that one more slowly, the nurse wiped tiny beads of sweat off the girl's forehead.

CHAPTER 9

West three
Operating room one
5:35pm

Doug pulled the knife away from Marilynn's shoulder. She opened her eyes and said, "Don't be a wimp, Talbot. I told you it'll be quick and painless. All you have to do is press the scalpel lightly against the skin just above my vaccination, then push up and out."

Doug hesitated and wiped his sweaty forehead.

"You're sweating. Are you okay?"

"I'm sweating because I'm nervous."

"You told me you never get nervous. You're not hiding anything, are you?"

"I'm fine," he said, leaving out the fact that he was also thirsty.

Again he laid the knife exactly where she had instructed him. Marilynn drew a second deep breath and held it, then closed her eyes.

"Hey! Don't close your eyes," he said. "One of us should have our eyes open when we do this."

She exhaled a burst of air, coughing several times. "Very funny," she said. "Come on. The patient's ready."

They both inhaled deeply. After exhaling he said, "On the count of three."

"One!

"Two!"

Suddenly the scalpel flicked the Doctor's shoulder. She winced but didn't cry out.

"What happened to *three*?" she snapped.

"I figured it would be best to just do it because I might have too much time to think about it and mess up," he said. "Does this make me an honorary surgeon?"

Marilynn examined her shoulder. A couple of drops of blood appeared on the surface where a small slice of skin had been removed.

"Just as good as I could have done it," she said, dabbing the wound with a cotton swab. "Now prove how good you really are and put this Band-Aid over it as well as a nurse would."

He stretched the Band-Aid over the wound. "Tah Dah!"

"Not bad," she said, approving his work.

"And I didn't have to spend thousands of dollars on medical school to get this good."

"Ten years later and I'm still paying for my Ivy League education," she kidded. "Go figure."

Leaning in so he could get a better look at the piece of skin in her hand, he asked, "What are you going to do with this thing?"

"I'd like to check it out under a microscope so I can see what Paul was talking about. Then I'm going to bring it to Jennie and let her work her magic. Maybe she can find some information on the code that's stamped on it."

"You know, there's one important thing about Paul Crawford that worries me," said Doug.

"What's that?"

"Why he was killed. Of all people, why was he singled out?"

Marilynn shrugged. "I don't know," she answered. "It doesn't add up."

"Think about it," he said. "It might give us a clue or, at the very least, a hint as to what's going on."

"Maybe they thought he knew too much?"

"But what?" asked Doug, rubbing his chin. "There's

something about these chips that struck a nerve in some very important people."

Marilynn started pacing. "Now I really want to get it to Jennie," she said. "It'll be interesting to see what she can find out! There are so many new places to get information on the Internet."

"While you're doing that I need to go back to the station. Are you going to be okay while I'm gone?"

"I'm fine. You were right about moving on. We need to find a solution to this mess and put a stop to the insanity. I'm sorry if I seem impatient at times. It's just that I want to find an answer as quickly as possible.

"No need to apologize," said Doug, his face softening. "I know how passionate you are in your work."

"You know," she continued, "I forgot to tell you Dr. Crawford mentioned my name to Uxbridge so I could share in the glory, that's how unselfish he was."

"What?" he asked, doing a double take.

"He mentioned my name and that I worked at the hospital."

"I don't like the sound of *that*," he said, his voice full of concern.

Sliding forward to the edge of her seat, Marilynn asked, "Do you think that's a problem?"

"He probably implicated you by saying that, which explains why there are military running around looking for you. I just don't know why they're looking for me. Anyway, we should leave. A good friend of yours was just murdered and we don't know the answers to the sixty-four thousand dollar questions of who did it and why. And there are still people running around looking for us."

"It's important that I check the chip out first, so I can explain it to Jennie. I promise I'll only be a few minutes, then I'll head home. When I get there I'll give the police a call."

"I'd feel safer if you left now, but I know you better. You're stubborn and you'll do it your own way."

"That's pretty good for only knowing me for a short time. What else do you know about me?"

"That's easy. You don't like to lose, especially when it comes to people and their well being. You take it personally."

"Not bad," she said chuckling. "Do you want to hear what I noticed about you?"

"Save it for another time. I'm going back to the station for a few things that I think will help us. What are you going to do after you give Jennie the chip?"

"I'm going to take a long hot shower and get a change of clothes. I've been in these for almost forty-eight hours."

"Yeah, I was going to mention that," said Doug.

"That's one of the things about you that I was going to mention," said Marilynn, playfully tapping his shoulder. "You like to divert attention away from yourself, by using sarcastic humor."

"Do you charge for therapy by the hour or by the day?" he said.

"See! There you go again."

"It's good to see you're feeling better," he said, kissing her on the top of the head, then starting for the doorway.

"What the heck was that?" she asked in surprise. "What am I, your daughter?"

"I don't like to start things I can't finish," he answered, without turning around." Looking skyward he said, "If you know what I mean?"

"Yeah, I know what you mean. You be careful. I've already lost one friend today. I don't want to lose another."

"So, we're *just* friends," he said, standing at the doorway and spinning around.

"Hey, there are friends and there are friends," she answered.

Shaking his head he said, "Women! They always leave you guessing what's inside their heads."

"What the hell does that mean?" she asked.

Doug walked back and stood in front of her. "Only that women expect men to know what they're thinking and what they're feeling at every moment. Men are not good at reading minds and we're pretty much dumb when it comes to understanding the female species."

"Now it's all coming out," she said with a biting laugh.

"I'm just being honest," he said. "We men pretty much give up and do whatever you women ask. That's the easy way out."

"Give me an example!" said Marilynn.

"My ex-wife once got mad at me because I didn't know why she was feeling a certain way after an argument. I didn't even know we had an argument, so how the hell could I know what feelings she was having?"

"So she got mad," said Marilynn, matter-of-factly.

"Yeah she got mad. I'm not psychic and I'm not a mind reader!"

Marilynn shook her head and laughed, "I think I understand why you're single again."

"Women!" he said. "You can't live with them and you can't live without them!"

Marilynn quickly thought back to when she said the same thing about men to Jennie. She didn't understand why, but her stomach suddenly felt queasy again.

"I'm going," said Doug, heading out the doorway. "I have to get to the station, so I can get back here for Cassandra. I'd feel safer if you'd take that wrench with you for protection. You seem to be pretty adept with it."

"Where are we going to meet?" she yelled, just as he disappeared.

"I'll meet you back here!" he shouted back, his voice an echo.

* * *

Marilynn stuffed her trusty wrench in her pocketbook. Not a bad idea she thought, stepping briskly down the well-lit narrow corridor to the lab. The hospital's microscopes were not as powerful as the coroner's, but she was hopeful it would provide enough magnification to make out markings on the computer chip.

Despite the horrifying event that took place in the first lab, she felt no trepidation bolting into lab 'C'. She was on a self proclaimed mission.

The room was set up much like 'B', except that it had another, smaller room off the back end with a washtub for cleaning and washing up, and it was twice the size. It was fitted with a half dozen microscopes of various sizes on small individual workbenches used by clinical technicians for doctor-ordered blood tests. The microscope furthest from the door was the one she chose. It was the most powerful one the hospital owned. Placing the specimen under it, she used a pair of tweezers to clear away a thin layer of her own epidermis to reveal the chip, then adjusted the magnification to maximum. To her pleasant surprise it went from blurry to finely focused, easily displaying the markings. Just as Paul Crawford had said, the top line was marked GOV- 69, and the bottom bore the letters NOPOSAM. She shook her head wondering what it meant.

She suddenly cringed. There was movement somewhere in the back of the washroom. "Who's there!" she called weakly, scanning the back. Her rapid surveillance revealed nothing unusual. "I'm a little wired from no sleep," she said to herself, sighing deeply. "My imagination's getting the best of me."

She went back to studying the sample under the microscope when the hair on the back of her neck stood and her arms popped many tiny goose bumps. There was definitely the distinctive sound of soft-approaching footsteps coming from the clean-up room. Grabbing the specimen out from under the microscope, she placed it in a blue plastic container used for biopsies and threw it into her handbag as she ran out the door and straight down the hallway to the elevator. She pressed the down arrow three times, then a fourth. The sound of slamming elevator doors reverberated back up the shaft. The light up above indicated it was at the basement, exactly where she needed to go.

Somewhere back up the corridor a door slammed shut.

Marilynn's stomach went queasy, because she knew it was the room she'd just left.

"Come on stupid!" she shouted at the closed elevator doors. The light showed it was at floor two. Her head swiveled right and she stared back up the hallway, but she couldn't see very far. Heavy padded footsteps were slowly making their way towards her. It sounded like an extremely large person that was not very mobile.

The steps came closer and she felt a threatening presence. Whoever it was would come into view at any moment. Her face betrayed her anxiousness.

The elevator shuddered to a stop and the doors slid open to the sound of a clanging bell. She jumped inside and held her finger on the green button marked basement. "Close!" she yelled in a panic. It paused for what seemed an eternity, then slowly began to shut. They were almost closed, when two giant hands reached in and tried to pry them open. The doors separated a couple of inches and Marilynn caught a quick glimpse of a large muscular man with brown hair. The gap widened a few more inches and he grunted and groaned as if he was in a weight lifting competition. Suddenly he stuck an arm through and grabbed Marilynn's collar.

The guy's face squeezed between the doors as they tried to close, pushing his mouth into a hideous looking fish mouth. "Please hold the elevator!" said a deep voice through a puckered mouth. She whacked downward on his arm with double fisted hands – two, three, then four times. He finally released his grip and the door slammed shut like a giant snapping turtle. It then began its usual unsteady journey downward. Fish-mouth cursed violently as the elevator rumbled away.

Reaching its destination it stopped with its usual shudder. The jingling overhead bell announced her arrival to the basement as the doors flung open. She froze. Was Fish-mouth waiting for her? Was anyone waiting for her? She wanted to step out, but her legs wouldn't move. The doors started to close, so she held the stop button.

Peering out, she heard quiet.

Unsettling quiet.

She stuck her head out and searched frantically in every direction. Her ears perked as she listened for encroaching footsteps.

She heard nothing and saw nothing.

Satisfied, she stepped out of the elevator. Going out through the basement level was a shortcut that would lead her quickly to Jennie's car. All she had to do was walk across the handicapped spaces, then go through a short garden walkway and she'd reach the doctors' parking lot.

She stepped confidently out into the sublevel parking garage, which was reserved for the higher-ups of the hospital. Her footsteps echoed throughout the mostly empty cement cavern and in no time she was standing outside in front of the brilliantly lit doctor's parking lot looking out at a handful of cars. Jennie's wasn't one of them.

"I know I parked here last night, or rather two nights ago," she thought out loud. But no matter how hard she searched the lot, the car was nowhere to be found.

"I am pretty tired," she said, again out loud. Still confused, she scanned one last time. "Maybe I parked in the patient's lot. It has been quite a while since I came to work. Another reason why I hate overnights," she muttered.

It wasn't far to Parking Lot 'P', the patients' lot. She knew another shortcut that a lot of the nurses used to save time and walking, especially in the winter. She only had to walk down a side street, go through a back passageway named blind man's alley, named for a blind man who stood there each day peddling newspapers, then go down a cement ramp. She stopped and looked back to see if she could see anyone. Only emptiness echoed into what was now near darkness. It was a void she was happy to have.

Satisfied the coast was clear, she headed off. Although the parking lot was well lit, the side street and alley wouldn't be. You never knew what could be out there waiting in dark shadows. Over the past five years, three nurses had had their pocketbooks ripped off.

It was twilight, the time of night where it's not completely dark, when outlines of objects have you questioning whether you really see what you think you see. It was that time just before the night creatures walked, crawled, or flew. Her senses adjusted quickly, becoming sensitive to sound and darkness. She trusted those sensations completely to guide her through the precarious territory as she walked down the side street. She stepped slowly but confidently. The soft padding of her footsteps, the product of thick rubber soled white shoes, was the only sound she heard. A street lamp about every twenty feet on the opposite side of the street slanted her shadow to the right.

She was almost to the alley, when she suddenly stopped.

There were footsteps behind her.

CHAPTER 10

Coventry General
Parking lot
6:32pm

Sitting in his SUV, Doug Talbot dialed his army buddy Bill Murphy.

"You've got to admit, Murph, something isn't on the up and up here."

"I've heard a few weird theories going around, but nothing as bizarre as what you suggest," said Murphy. "But that might not mean anything, because I've only been in meetings with lower brass. No one of any stature has come out and given us any details about what's going on."

Aggravated, Doug snapped the phone from his head and vigorously rubbed his forehead with the back of his hand. After a pause he put the phone to his ear.

"Fuck, Murph! I was hoping you could help!"

"Hey! I'm not saying what you told me isn't true. I just haven't heard anything to say differently. So what is it you need from me?"

"Put out some feelers. See what you can find out."

"Tell you what. I'll talk to my Captain and see what he thinks about it."

"I don't think Doc and I are overreacting, Murph."

"I trust your instincts," said Murphy, " and that really scares me, because if you're right, there's some serious shit going on."

"Just watch your back, Murph. A lot of strange things have been happening lately."

"Danger's my middle name."

"I thought it was Patrick."

Murphy chuckled. After a pause he said in a serious tone, "Don't speak about this to anyone else till you hear from me."

"I'll call you tomorrow," said Talbot.

They hung up simultaneously.

Doug stuck his cell phone inside his front pocket and started the car. Shifting it into drive, he sped out of the parking lot heading back towards WJAM. He encountered little traffic on the road and was making great time. As a matter of fact, it occurred to him as he entered the station's parking lot that he hadn't seen a car during the last ten minutes of his ride, only an occasional truck.

The security gate to the station's parking lot was open, so he drove in and pulled into the vehicle's appointed parking spot. As he got out, he had a feeling that it was safe to go inside. Most of the day shift would be gone because the six PM news had already aired. Walking to the security camera, he swiped his magnetic key card through the scanner. It buzzed - a nasty sounding noise - and released the locked door. He stepped through the back entrance with urgency and made his way down a narrow hallway, pausing briefly outside the closed glass door of master control. Glancing in, he saw Joe Brooks' replacement. He was a young man of about twenty, who sat slumped in a faux leather chair. Dread that another unfortunate accident had happened overwhelmed Doug and the urge to run in and check to see if the kid was okay was strong. All at once the young man sat up and started pushing buttons on the control board, switching commercials on the air with an on-line digital commercial server. Doug breathed again.

Looking through the window reminded him of all the times he had bailed Brooks out when he'd fallen asleep at the switch. His shoulders slumped, because he wished he could have bailed him out one last time on that fateful night. After all, he may not have liked Brooks, but he certainly didn't want to see him die. He reached up and wiped sweat off his forehead. Got to find a water cooler, he thought.

The young man finished running his commercial break and swiveled around in his chair. The new guy had bright red hair and a badly pimpled face. They exchanged waves, then Doug turned and walked away towards the newsroom. Again he wiped sweat from his brow.

When he entered the newsroom he saw a small crew already starting preliminary work on the eleven o'clock newscast. Most of them he knew at least by name. Several producers were busy checking the Internet news wire and writing fresh scripts, and a couple of interns were doing linear editing. Doug stopped at the assignment desk and picked up the work log to see what story they had assigned him. He was stunned to see it blank.

Jessica, a cute girl of about twenty-five manned the assignment desk.

"Hey, Jess!" he called, tossing the clipboard on the desk. "What the heck's going on? I don't see anything on the assignment log for me. Am I editing a vignette for the morning news tomorrow?"

The girl swiveled her chair towards him, sending her brunette ponytail swirling, and shot an embarrassed smile. "Jeez, Doug. You look like crap. When was the last time you slept?"

"Hey, I'm not the one in front of the camera. It doesn't matter what I look like. So what's going on?"

Shifting uneasily in the chair she looked at him through chocolate colored eyes. "Didn't Shoemaker call you?" she asked gently.

"No! What's up?"

The girl carefully thought about her next words.

"I'm sorry," she said, "but you've been suspended. And you're not allowed to take any company property, including the station SUV. I'm supposed to take your keys and give them to Fred, the freelancer."

Doug's face flushed as he succumbed to anger. "Nobody talked to me about this!"

"Sorry," said the girl sheepishly. "Please don't yell at me. I'm only the messenger."

Doug threw the keys on the desk. "I need to get a few things from my locker," he snapped, walking away to find the photog's room.

"No problem," replied Jessica. "Take your time." The girl slumped down in her chair.

Doug walked into the videographer's room and went directly to his locker. He meticulously turned the black wheel of the chrome *Yale* lock right, left, then right again and it popped open. He pulled the lock off and the metal door opened with a loud clang. He reached inside and pulled out a green gym bag and unzipped it. One by one he threw the contents back inside the locker. First it was white sneakers, then a gray WJAM sweatshirt. Finally he pulled out a pair of smelly white socks. "Whew!" he said to himself. "These could probably walk home by themselves."

With his empty bag in hand, he left the room in search of the news studio. The studio lights, placed strategically around the lighting grid to accent the faces of the talent, were dimmed. He headed in under the cover of faint light and stepped uninhibited across the room till he was behind the anchor's set. He found what he was looking for lying on the floor, just inside a walk-in closet: his portable digital video camera, plugged in and charging.

Placing the gym bag on the floor he picked up the camera and placed it gently inside the bag. "Damn!" he mumbled. "I need something soft to keep it from rolling around inside." He swiped his shirtsleeve across his nagging damp forehead.

After zipping the bag closed he stood up to see if anyone had noticed his covert act. Satisfied he was alone, he walked cautiously down the hallway to the station's satellite control room. The lights were off when he entered. It reminded him of an airplane cockpit, with the hum of machinery and all the different lit red and green buttons and knobs. He turned on the switch to a bank of florescent lights and the room was instantly veiled in bright light. He headed over to the cabinet marked 'Digital Video Tape' and took out five used sixty-minute tapes. One by one he placed the tapes in a degauss machine to demagnify them. This was a process that would scramble the video and audio tracks. The machine vibrated his arm, but Doug just shrugged it off. It had a short in it and always did this.

Because the tapes were one-tenth the size of most other formats, they would fit easily inside the bag next to the camera. He unzipped the bag and placed the tapes around the insides, forming a buffer for the camera. Even though he hadn't had time to get a drink, he suddenly felt as if he didn't need one at that moment, and thought how odd that he suddenly felt that way. He reached up and touched his forehead. It was dry. He thought that was odd, too.

He sneaked like a cat burglar back up the hallway towards the newsroom. If he could just get past Jessica he would be home free. The young overnight assignment producer was busy on the phone when he walked by the desk. Without stopping, he raised the bag towards her and whispered, "I emptied my locker. Mostly smelly clothes." He started towards the exit door.

"Wait a minute!" shouted the girl. "I've got Mr. Shoemaker on the line and he wants me to verify what you're leaving with."

Doug stopped short. "I told you, it's only smelly clothes. I want to take them home so I can wash them, for when they un-suspend me."

The girl hung up the phone and made her way over.

"Sorry," she said with her hands extended towards the bag. "Orders from the big guy."

Doug drew a deep breath and released it slowly. Shaking his head he said, "No problem. I know it's not your fault they're all idiots around here."

Jessica reached for the bag, but stopped short and suddenly ran back to the assignment desk. The police scanner was going crazy.

"Officer down!" yelled a policeman. "All hell's breaking loose! Send back-up and call 9-1-1!"

Doug took advantage of the distraction to sneak away. He ran down the carpeted hallway and shot out the back door and soon found himself standing safely out in the parking lot. He jogged over to his car, and threw the gym bag onto the back seat, then hopped into the driver's seat. Reaching into his pockets he felt for his keys. "Fuck!" he yelled, slamming the steering wheel with both hands.

Jessica had them.

Now he was frantic.

He jumped out of the car and began pacing back and forth, searching for an alternate ride. Realizing his plight, he stopped. Frustrated, he swallowed hard as he stood staring out at the waiting road.

How the hell was he going to get back to To-ens?

CHAPTER 11

6:40pm
Side street
Downtown

A brisk wind tossed a solitary, tattered newspaper page across Marilynn's path, and an empty diet something plastic bottle rolled ahead until hitting up against a building and settling on its side. Off in the distance a garbage can banged and rattled to the ground and a squealing cat cry resonated off the sides of buildings till it was quiet.

It was the second week of September and the temperature was close to eighty, but Marilynn still shrugged several times as a cold shiver tingled up and down her spine. Her head throbbed from a newly formed headache as she frantically searched each direction, swiveling her head like a submarine periscope searching for unseen enemies. Satisfied no one was there, she resumed walking towards the alley.

After a few steps she stopped. Her instincts told her to spin around. Peering back into the dimly lit street, her eyes shifted from the silhouette of a parking meter to a recognizable shape of a fire hydrant, then to a garbage barrel and hastily over to a telephone pole. She saw nothing. A warm wind blew at her back and yet another chill went up her spine.

She pulled her doctor's jacket together in front and

quickly buttoned three large buttons. But something caught her attention and she glanced up. She had heard footsteps, faint, and hardly noticeable, but undeniably there.

Staring hard for any sign of movement put undo stress on her eyes and that, coupled with her headache, made her head feel as though it would burst. She stared at the telephone pole, then back towards the fire hydrant. She could discern no movement. Her eyes shifted over to the parking meter and then a quick v-line to the garbage barrel, but there was still nothing. She had a bad feeling.

Her eyes moved frantically in circles and figure eights until settling back on the garbage barrel. Was there movement or was the dimness playing tricks on her eyes? It was hard to tell if the barrel was moving or only appeared to be because she was mesmerized by it. Was it the marooned person on a tropical island syndrome, where you hallucinate that the palm trees are moving, talking people?

She closed her eyes and rubbed them hard with the palms of her hands. When she reopened them the barrel seemed taller. Her heart sank faster than a rock tossed into water. Suddenly, she realized it was no barrel after all and it was coming steadily towards her. She turned and ran for the alley.

"Come on, Marilynn," she encouraged herself. "You can make the other side. Be strong, you can get through this."

With trepidation, she entered into blind man's alley. There were no lights to illuminate the way. Only the far reach of a distant lamppost on either end of the alley pushed a minute amount of light to navigate by. A lost ship in a blinding rainstorm guided only by a far away lighthouse would have better luck.

She was almost through the alley, when she stopped. She needed to look back. Turning quickly, she saw a dark figure standing at the entrance. The thin hairs on the back of her neck stood up. Ice-cold chills raced up and down her body and she shivered. She fingered the metal wrench inside her pocketbook.

"Who's there?" she said. Her voice was shrill and it didn't even sound like hers to her own ears.

The dark figure stood silent. Unwavering.

She shuddered. This had the feel of one of those bad grade 'B' movies you see late at night. The one where the hero or heroine is running from some unseen assailant, then predictably trips and falls to the ground hurting an ankle, while the aforementioned attacker closes in brandishing a very large ax.

Feeling a panic attack coming, she looked ahead and saw that it was only about thirty feet to the end. She stared back down the alley. The dark figure seemed to be moving. She turned and ran as fast as she could. *There will be no tripping*, she promised. Behind her was the soft patter of moving feet. *They must be wearing sneakers too*, she figured.

In no time she emerged out of the alley, but stubbornly stopped and looked back. She stood defiantly under a bright floodlight, fearful of seeing a maniacal freak. She listened intently. It was quiet. The footsteps had stopped. She felt rather than saw that the stalker was not far away.

She urged her body to move towards the cement ramp up ahead, which led to a gateway out. But it was like trying to run in a swimming pool. Her legs were moving, but she didn't seem to be going very fast. But she did pick up speed till she came face to face with the chain link doorway. Her heart sank to a new low. It was held fast by a flat crossbar that pushed into a metal clamp. She tried to pull the bar up, but it resisted. "Damn!" she cried out. She wasn't strong enough to lift it.

Peering through the chain link fence, she could see Jennie's car sitting under a tall parking lot light. "I don't remember parking there!" she said out loud. Fast approaching footsteps came up behind her. She pulled and grunted, but the bar wouldn't budge. She was trapped!

She reached into her handbag and pulled out the

large adjustable wrench. Throwing her handbag to the ground, she spun around screaming and brandished it with a threatening gesture in the face of a middle-aged man.

"Jesus, Hospital lady!" he yelled, backing away. "You trying to kill Benny?"

"That's the general idea," she said brandishing the wrench in his face. "Get away, or I'll bust your skull open!" Her eyes were as wide as her stance and she looked like a crazed wild animal.

"I saw you having trouble opening the gate so I came over to give you a hand," said the man who stood so close she could smell his foul breath. She looked into his eyes and saw tiny dark pupils that appeared cold and heartless. Inching forward and pointing a bony finger in her face he said, "Benny wasn't trying to hurt you!"

She swung the wrench several short, intimidating strokes as good as any *Jedi Knight*, and he backed up a step so the wrench missed him. Her pulse was racing and her face flushed with rage. Her adrenaline had kicked into high gear as she raised quivering arms high over head, and stood poised to strike her assailant with a blow that would at the very least knock the man off his feet, and at the very most do serious harm. He didn't flinch or move.

But she struggled with the thought of striking him down. Her aching arms wanted to hit hard and smash his ugly face to bits with the wrench, smash it so hard that it would become even uglier than it appeared now. But her mind opposed her. A voice deep inside her head said stop, this isn't right.

In that brief moment of teetering on the edge of violent anger, justified or not, she did a quick study of this man more closely, and inside she felt a tingle of mercy. All at once the anger exited her body too quickly and she lowered her arms, but they continued shaking even after they were again at her sides. She drew several full breaths and relaxed her muscles, particularly in the shoulder area. It was a therapeutic exercise that Jennie had taught her to calm this kind of trauma, but her anger had taken its toll, and she was exhausted.

The man appeared to be about fifty and he was dressed in worn shoes and filthy tattered clothes. She now saw that his hands were cupped with arthritis and he stood with a slightly stooped back. She had avoided a serious mistake. In no way did the man resemble fish face.

"Why did you follow me down the alley?" she asked abruptly.

"Benny not follow hospital lady. Benny was going through garbage barrels over there," he said, pointing to a couple of green city garbage barrels about fifteen feet away, "when he see hospital lady run up to gate and have trouble opening it."

"Weren't you just standing at the other end of the alley watching me?"

"Like Benny said, he was going through barrels over there when he see hospital lady having trouble with the gate."

She realized he would have a hard time walking, much less running.

Being that angry had taken a lot of energy out of her, and had done nothing to help her headache. She gathered what little strength she had and said, as nicely as she could, "I'm sorry for what just happened. I thought I was being followed down the ally by some crazy person and I became quite nervous and overreacted."

"Benny understands," said the man. "It's late and dark. You were frightened."

Tilting her head to one side, she appraised him with questioning eyes, like a parent confronting a teenager who has missed curfew. "What are you doing out this late at night?" she asked.

"This is the best time for Benny to shop. I find half-eaten sandwiches and bottles of soda that have only a few sips out of them. Benny also finds lots of money. Sometimes as much as two dollars."

"Sounds like you have quite an operation going on

here, Benny. But I hope you're cautious. There are a lot of crazy people out at this time of night and you can't be too careful." *I'm testament to that*, she thought.

"Benny knows how to take care of himself," he said, producing a small wood bat from inside his tattered jacket. "Can I help with the gate?"

"I can't seem to get it open."

"There's a trick to opening it," said Benny shuffling over. "Benny knows it."

He placed one arthritic hand under the bar, then whacked upwards, striking it from underneath with his other free mangled hand. The bar went flying upwards. She now had passage.

"There you go, hospital lady," said the street man.

Marilynn slipped the wrench back into her bag and at the same time pulled out her wallet. "Thank you for your help," she said, handing him a twenty-dollar bill.

"No need to thank Benny," he said. "Just trying to help."

"Nonsense, Benny. After the way I treated you, I insist you take something for your trouble."

"Okay, hospital lady." Waving the bill over his head, he turned and shuffled back towards the barrels. "You have a good night!" he yelled back when he reached them.

She watched Benny for a few moments as he became lost in rummaging for undiscovered treasures in his personal grocery store. Finally, she glanced back towards the alley, but saw no one. She turned and stepped through the gateway and started across the long parking lot towards Jennie's little blue car, which still sat under the towering parking lot light. It was easy to pick it out. There were no other cars within a hundred feet of it.

Halfway across the lot she heard the clank of the gate's metal bar. Stopping, she twisted round expecting to see Benny. No one was there. She ran the rest of the way to the car.

She paused at the front for a few moments, then approached the driver's side with caution. Before unlocking it, she peeked into the back to see if anyone was crouching low behind the seat. The light from the pole was dim where she stood, and she struggled to see through the gray tinted windows. She thought it looked empty. Satisfied, she unlocked the door and plopped down in the driver's seat. She tossed her pocketbook on the passenger's side and strapped on her seatbelt.

She looked in the rearview mirror just in time to see two hands coming over the top of her headrest, until settling tightly around her throat. She gasped loudly, and her body convulsed upwards several times. She tried to breathe, but couldn't. Her body shuddered and she slouched low; all her muscles quivered like gelatin.

She exhaled loudly and buried her head in her hands and cried softly. "Nothing like being paranoid," she said, her words muffled by her hands. Exhaustion was beginning to play mind tricks, but there was no time for rest. That would have to come later. She hit the electronic lock button and all four door locks snapped shut with a thud.

Trembling hands pushed the key towards the ignition, but it was upside down and refused to go in. "Shit!" she snapped, flipping the little plastic yoga doll key ring over and shoving it in the right way. The small engine whined and caught.

An unmarked black Suburban parked in the far shadows of the lot started about the same time. Moments later it drove out of the parking lot in pursuit of Jennie's car with the headlights off.

Marilynn sped down Route One, a fairly straight two-lane road, heading for the entrance to the freeway. Once on the highway it was only a short distance to her exit and then a two-minute jaunt to her house. She looked in the rearview mirror and saw no headlights behind her.

The dark truck with the clandestine occupants followed like a stealth plane keeping enough distance to stay just out of sight, but lurking close enough to keep tabs.

She pressed down on the gas and the car easily negotiated the short curve of the entrance to interstate 95 north.

The dark SUV kept time, putting its headlights on after getting on the freeway. It would be difficult maneuvering through the dark at speeds topping out at seventy miles an hour.

She turned the radio on and it took several station switches, but she finally found a song she liked. Usually she preferred top-forty music, but tonight she chose the soothing sounds of *Kenny G* to settle her nerves. She laughed when the DJ said the title was *By the Time This Night is Over.*

The music was definitely having a calming effect on her and she dropped her speed to sixty. She never noticed the black sedan that had pulled up to within a car length behind. It would be another mile before she paid attention to it.

"Three open lanes with no traffic and you've got to get right behind me," she said into the rearview mirror, after finally taking notice. With eyes focused on the mirror, she pressed gently down on the gas pedal and watched her car put distance between them. The Suburban stayed back, so she focused on the road and her driving. It wasn't long before she saw the sign for Exit 5. Slowing to take the exit, she rounded the sharp turn a little too fast and the car slid to the right side of the curb, rubbing its tires against a raised mound of tar. She tapped the breaks several times and easily got the car under control. Taking this exit was usually not a problem. It was one she took every day on the way home from work. She now had a second enemy to worry about: fatigue.

The streetlights had been on for a while when she left the exit ramp, so she had plenty of light to see by as she approached an intersection and a red traffic light. After the car rolled to a stop she was tempted to take a right on red even though it wasn't permitted there. But she figured that with the luck she was having tonight, a cop would be parked right around the corner. She fidgeted with the radio while waiting for the light to turn. After selecting her favorite top-forty station, the light changed to green and she drove right onto Water Street. The dark Suburban had stayed back at a safe distance, but moved up and made the same turn.

She pulled into the driveway and parked close to the back door. There was music blasting inside, a sure sign Jennie was home. Stepping in through the back door of the kitchen, she found the girl eating a giant salad.

"What kind?" she asked.

"Tofu and water chestnut," answered Jennie. "Want some?"

Scrunching up her nose Marilynn said, "I'll pass."

Jennie laughed. "What's up?"

"I've got something for you to look at."

Jennie followed her into the den where she watched Marilynn take something small out of a blue specimen container and put it under their microscope. After adjusting the focus, she turned to her roommate and said, "Check this out and tell me what you think."

Jennie stooped low and looked into the microscope's viewfinder. "What the heck is this?" she asked.

"I was hoping you could tell me," said Marilynn.

"I've never seen anything like it," said Jennie, fine tuning the focus. "It's some kind of microchip. What does NO-POS-AM mean?"

"Doug and I think it could be an acronym for something important."

"Doug and you?" said Jennie straightening up. "So who's Doug? A new boyfriend?"

"No! He's not my boyfriend!" protested Marilynn. "He's just someone I met at the hospital."

"Sure," teased Jennie. *"I believe you."*

"Okay, Miss Smarty-Pants, can you help me with this or not?"

"I don't know. Where did you get it?"

"It came out of my shoulder."

"Your shoulder!" shouted Jennie.

"I had Doug cut it out. I think everybody has them."

"Do I have one?"

"Check under your vaccination."

Jennie pulled her shirtsleeve up till she could see the area.

"Now what?" she asked, staring at it.

"Rub it gently," said Marilynn.

Jennie pressed her thumb against her skin and did soft circular motions.

"Damn!" she said. "There is something there. What the hell is it?"

"I don't know. They were initially discovered in bodies at the morgue, only theirs had red spots there."

"This is bizarre," said Jennie. "Do you think it's tied to all the recent deaths?"

"That's what we need to find out."

"What do you want me to do?"

Marilynn flicked her long curly hair back using both hands. "See if you can find out what NOPOSAM means or why GOV-69 is on them, and how they're related."

"I'll check with a couple of computer geek friends of mine that graduated top of their MIT class, especially Jack the Hack. He can break any code or system. I'm sure he can help. I promise, we'll scour the Internet till we find something."

"Thanks a bunch," said Marilynn, rubbing Jennie's shoulders. "I've got to meet Doug back at the hospital."

"So you're seeing your new boyfriend again?"

Marilynn tapped Jennie on the head and said, "Very funny, young lady." She left the room for a short time and returned tucking a pink short-sleeved tank top into a pair of black jeans.

"Okay. I'm leaving you to your task. I should be back in a few hours to check on what you've found," she said, pulling on a pair of black running shoes.

"See ya later," said Jennie, looking back through the microscope. "Say hi to Doug for me!"

CHAPTER 12

7:00pm

Marilynn reached into her pocketbook and pulled out her cell phone. She put the car in reverse, then backed Jennie's car out of the driveway and headed back towards the intersection with the traffic light. Unnoticed, the dark Suburban had pulled out from a hidden driveway and followed several car lengths behind.

Anxious to get a report on Dr. Crawford, she dialed the state police. As the phone rang on the other end, she drove through a green light and turned left heading back towards the entrance to 95 South. It would take her roughly ten minutes to get to the hospital. After five rings someone picked up and a stressed female voice said, "State police! How can I direct your call?"

"This is Dr. Marilynn Harwell of Coventry General Hospital. I called in the 9-1-1 for state medical examiner Dr. Paul Crawford. I was told I could call to find out what happened."

"Hold please," said the female in a monotone voice that said she was having a bad day. "I'll direct your call to the detective in charge of that case."

There was a soft click as her call was put on hold. Marilynn looked at her speedometer. She was going fifty-five, ten miles over the posted speed limit. She wasn't concerned, since she was the phone with the state police. Besides, it was less than two minutes to the highway entrance.

Her train of thought was interrupted, when a strong but soothing male voice said, "Dr. Harwell, this is Lieutenant Ron Shelton. How can I help you?"

"Lieutenant Shelton, I'm calling to inquire about Dr. Crawford. I was on the line with him when the shooting took place."

"You and Dr. Crawford were very good friends, weren't you, Doctor?"

"We were good friends professionally," she replied, "but what does that have to do with what happened?"

"I'm asking, because it seems he had a serious drinking problem. Are you aware of that?"

"Yes, I am. But he never let that affect the quality of his work. He was extremely good at what he did and was always professional. Besides, it was the strain of his work that made him drink."

"Dr. Harwell, Paul Crawford was not shot as you suggested in your 9-1-1 call." The professional and even-tempered voice continued, "When paramedics found him, he was on the floor in a pool of his own blood. It seems he had drunk too much and lost control of his wits. He actually fell to the floor and hit his head on a blunt object."

Marilynn was stunned. This didn't make any sense. She was irritated and subconsciously pressed the gas harder. The car sped up and the tires squealed as it rounded a curve and pulled back onto the highway.

"Are you suggesting that I didn't hear a gunshot or the place being torn apart?"

"I think what you probably heard," said the Lieutenant, "was Dr. Crawford staggering and falling to the floor, pulling instruments with him. He then stumbled getting up and knocked over a chair and a couple of workbenches and tables, which to you sounded like someone destroying the place. You know, Doctor, he actually bled to death. It's all in the autopsy report."

She glanced quickly at the green exit sign that appeared on the right side of the road. It would be another three miles to hers. Concentrating on the road and the conversation she was having with Detective Shelton was a tough balance, because she didn't want to miss her exit. The next one after that was five miles and it would take her well out of her way.

"Whose report would that be?" she asked.

"Doctor Harwell, you of all people know the State Police have access to any Medical Examiner in the country. Since Dr. Crawford was the Chief Medical Examiner of Rhode Island, we called in Dr. John Harvey, the Massachusetts Examiner.

"Can I get a copy of that report sent to Coventry General?" she asked.

A cold reply came from the other end. "Not a problem, Doctor." After a slight pause he said in a voice that bordered on patronizing, as if he was the parent and she was the child. "What was the purpose of your conversation with Dr. Crawford?"

"I wanted to know what his findings were. The hospital was sending too many cases over to the morgue, for what I deemed ridiculously minor reasons."

"Did Dr. Crawford say anything to you about the rationale for these unfortunate deaths that would link it to terrorist activity?"

There was a long pause as she tried to figure where Detective Shelton was going with his line of questioning.

"Dr. Crawford was just beginning to explain that there was a similar pattern to all of these tragic deaths, something every Medical Examiner does, Mr. Shelton. But I never got much of a chance to speak to him about it, because of his unfortunate murder."

Lieutenant Shelton's voice elevated. "Keep in mind the reason why the SIA was there in the first place, Dr. Harwell. They were there to ask him about the rumors that he had uncovered secret terrorist information and was withholding that intelligence. Conspiracy is a federal offense, even for a state Medical Examiner."

"I've known Paul Crawford for many years and I can

assure you, his intentions and allegiances are nothing but true to his profession, his state and his country!"

There was an even longer pause. "I'm sure that is how you want to remember him, Marilynn," said the lieutenant, his voice testy and irritated, no longer serene like when they first started their conversation.

She was irritated too, because of this sudden change. And she didn't like him addressing her by her first name.

Then he asked, "Did he mention anything about a chip?"

She almost drove off the road. She hadn't mentioned the chip. Instantly, she ran the list of people who did know through her mind. There was Paul himself, Jennie, Doug, and Crawford's friend in Washington.

"Are you a policeman?" she asked.

"I'm a member of the SIA." He waited a moment then said in a nauseating voice, "Does that scare you, *To-ens*?"

Suddenly, her back arched and she shivered hard. It was as if she'd been hit with icy water from a giant container, like when football players sneak up on their coach and douse him after a big win. She wanted to speak but nothing came out.

"What's the matter, Doctor, cat got your tongue?" said Shelton in a nasty voice. "You're never at a loss of words when you stick your nose in affairs that are none of your business!"

Regaining her composure, while driving with her left hand and holding the cell phone to her ear with the other, she asked, "Why was the SIA so concerned about Paul Crawford?"

"There are some people who know more than they should know and they're beginning to become national security threats. Amateurs like yourself and your friend Mr. Talbot should leave these things to the professionals."

Dr. Harwell gasped loudly into the phone.

"That's right, Doctor, we know all about your friend. Why don't you two come in to the State Police barracks and talk to us. We only want to brief you on what's going on."

"Tell me something, Lieutenant. Were you there when Paul was murdered or did someone else do the dirty work?"

"I told you, Doctor," said Shelton in a hard, cold voice. "Dr. Crawford's autopsy showed his death was an accident due to excessive drinking."

"Very convenient excuse you have there," she snapped. "By now, I'm sure you have everyone else believing it too."

"Remember what I told you, Doc. We only want to talk to you. Bring your friend in to headquarters, before you get into real trouble."

"Give me time to think about it," said Marilynn. In the back of her mind she was thinking, *No way, you bastard*!

"Let us know where you are and we'll even send a car to pick you up," said Shelton. "But know this, the invitation and the pleasantries won't last forever."

The phone went silent.

She braked, slowing the car enough to pull off the edge of the highway onto a grassy area big enough to fit Jennie's compact car. When the car rolled to a stop she inhaled deeply, held it for a moment then released it fast. She slipped the shift lever in park and turned the engine off. The disturbing conversation and harrowing day had exhausted her. She yawned deeply and unwittingly closed her eyes.

She was startled awake by successive, rapid knocks on the driver's side window. She sat forward and turned her head. A man's face was pressed right up against the window staring in at her. She gasped, and clutched her chest.

"Arrr ouuu okee aiddy," said a deep voice.

"What?" she asked, trying to get her wits back.

"Are - you - okay, lady," repeated the man. This time she understood the baritone voice.

He looked middle-aged with light brown hair, matching brown eyes and a pleasant enough face. But she felt herself breathing in quick gasps, as if she'd just finished a long jog. He was an imposing figure, standing taller than Doug and weighing in at about two hundred seventy or eighty pounds. And he was dressed in dark clothes. She noticed that even his undershirt was dark.

Feeling uncertain, she looked at the door lock - it was in the open position. She looked up and found him also staring at the lock.

The man quickly glanced at his watch, shook his head and said, "Come on, lady. I've got to get to work. Are you okay?"

She knew he could have opened the door at any time if he was some kind of maniac looking to harm her. She rolled her window down and said, "Yes, thank you. I'm fine. I was just resting my eyes for a bit."

"You should be more careful this time of night," he said, pointing at the door lock. "There are a lot of crazies out there. You're lucky it was me and not some homicidal nut who stopped to check on you."

"You're right," she said. "It was a mistake. I'll be more careful in the future. Thank you for your concern."

The man smiled, but it was a cunning smile, much like when someone knows something you don't know. "I believe you," he said. But then his face took on a more serious look. "You should leave here *now*. You never know what could happen if I were to leave you here by yourself."

Looking in her rearview mirror she blinked from the bright light of the man's car headlights. She couldn't tell what kind of vehicle it was, just that it was big.

"Are you military?" she said, turning her attention back to him.

"Used to be. I wear my army fatigues when I go hunting."

"You hunt at night?" she asked.

"Not usually, but I am tonight."

She noticed his face had an odd look to it when he said, *but I am tonight*.

She gripped the steering wheel tight. "I'll follow you out," she said.

"No!" he said sternly. "I'll follow you out to make sure you're okay."

The sudden change in tone and manner chilled her to the bone.

"I'll be fine," she said, trying not to sound distrustful or frightened. "Besides, I need to get myself together before I start driving again." Her next sentence really hurt to say. "You know how bad we women drivers are, even when we're wide awake."

She was pretty good at reading people's faces. She didn't like this one. "If looks could kill," she thought.

He crossed his arms and said with his nose slightly elevated, much like a school bully trying to intimidate another child, "It's late and it's dark, and I'd feel really bad in the morning if I read in the newspaper that something bad had happened to you. I'll follow YOU out!"

Now she really felt threatened. She definitely trusted her senses more than she trusted this guy. Even though she hadn't seen a single car go by during their conversation, which was strange for this time of day and stretch of road usually overflowing with traffic heading for Boston, she knew she should obey. Confrontation was not something she was prepared for in her fatigued stage. Besides, if something did happen, there would be no one around to help.

"You're right," said Marilynn smiling widely. "I wasn't thinking straight. I'll go first."

"That's a good girl," he said, slapping her side door.

His comment made her cringe inside, but she concealed her disgust well. Choosing her tone carefully, so as to not upset him, she said softly, "As soon as I see you get into your car, I'll pull back out onto the freeway."

"Good choice," he said gruffly. He reached inside the car and pushed down the door lock. "Stay safe."

He turned and headed back to his car.

"You too!" she yelled out the open window. Staring in her rearview mirror she watched him open the vehicle's door and the dome light switched on, bathing the inside.

She felt a sharp stabbing pain across her stomach, as if someone had pressed a sharp knife from one side to the other.

There was a man sitting in the passenger side holding a rifle.

The SUV's horn blasted and she jumped in her seat. Her hands shook as she fumbled with the keys, which were still in the ignition. She pulled her hand away, closed her eyes and drew a deep breath, exhaled slowly, then reached down and turned the car on. She glanced at the clock on the dash and realized that she'd fallen asleep for ten minutes. Another blast of the SUV's horn made her jump again.

The engine whined hard and it spun the wheels, peeling up grass and dirt that hit the parked car behind her. The tires finally caught, and the car slipped back out onto the deserted highway.

"Serves you right, jerk face!" she shouted, as the car began picking up speed. The speedometer already read forty-five in what was about ten seconds. She looked in the inside mirror. The SUV hadn't followed. It was still sitting in the same spot.

"So much for following me out," she mumbled. She relaxed her grip on the steering wheel and sighed lightly as her hand turned on the radio. After searching a few preset stations she settled on some light rock, and started humming along with Barry Manilow. Looking in the outside mirror she saw two headlights about a half mile back and wondered who they belonged to.

Exhaustion overwhelmed her again and she struggled to keep her eyes open. She reached down and switched the radio to a station playing hard rock. "This'll keep me awake," she said, yawning. Her little rest hadn't helped any and she needed all the help she could get to reach the hospital safely. Besides, her exit was fast approaching. Suddenly there was a blinding light in the rearview mirror.

"Jesus!" she screamed. The other vehicle was right up to her bumper. It was the SUV! She stepped hard on the gas, creating separation, but this time the tailgater did the same and pulled right up to the bumper again. "What the hell!" she screamed. "Get off my ass!"

She stepped hard on the accelerator and put her left blinker on, even though there were no other cars around. She quickly changed lanes. The Suburban pulled forward to about half a car length away in the slow lane. She was about to breathe a sigh, when it swung over and pulled behind her to within an inch of the back bumper.

The tailgater flashed its highbeams. "Just what I need!" she screamed. "A road rage nut!"

She looked into the rearview mirror and her own deep brown eyes stared back. Shifting her eyes for a better view, she thought she saw two figures sitting inside the car. Anger now gripped her. Her face flushed, and her hands gripped the steering wheel so hard they began to shake. She tried to swallow but couldn't. Remembering her breathing exercises, she inhaled and exhaled, but they were sporadic breaths. She gave up trying to relax.

Glancing ahead she saw the large green sign for the Hospital exit. If she didn't get over soon she'd miss it. She stepped hard on the gas and the car lurched forward. The engine whined as all four cylinders gave all they had to push the car faster. She looked in the rearview mirror again and saw the SUV closing in. She started to pull back into the exit lane, but the stalker's car was faster and it veered in and pulled up beside her. She yanked the wheel back the other way, barely avoiding the car. As they raced side by side at eighty-seven miles an hour, she felt the pounding of her heart right through her blouse. She half expected to see it come sticking out of her chest, like in the Road Runner cartoons. Sweat formed on her forehead.

"Oh shit!" she cried. "Don't even go there!" Then she remembered the chip had been removed.

Although Jennie's car was new, it was maxed out for speed. It was built for economy not quickness. There was no way she could get into the other lane ahead of this maniac. She watched her exit pass by and quickly felt the air go out of her like a balloon that's been punctured with a pin. She gritted her teeth and tried to see into the other car, but it was futile. All the windows were tinted dark.

An idea popped into her head. The next exit would be coming up in a few miles. She plotted her plan as they continued racing side by side, neither one moving beyond the other. She was content to bide her time, and parallel drive with the maniac for another couple of minutes.

Those minutes felt like hours, but the next exit's sign finally came into view. She pumped the gas pedal several times then held it all the way down, while shaking the steering wheel and pleading, "Come on, honey! Give me just a little more speed!"

The car responded and edged past the SUV, although the engine whined and sounded like it would explode at any moment. The speedometer read 93 miles an hour and she was a full length ahead. Seeing the opening, she started to slide into the other lane to take the exit, only a hundred feet down the road. The dark sedan reacted the way she knew it would, quickly pulling up to block her path.

This time she slammed both feet on the brake pedal, hoping the other car would pass her. The tires cried and squealed, burning rubber and smoke. But the other car sped up, cut in front of her and unexpectedly hit its brakes, and she was forced to turn the wheel to the right to avoid crashing into it. Her car fishtailed and she fought for control as it did a 360. Her pursuer continued up the highway spewing smoke from its squealing tires until coming to a stop a hundred yards further up.

The world was a blur as her car spun around a second time, like one of those amusement park rides that scrambles and rotates until you want to throw up, so she hit the gas and aimed the wheel to the right, attempting to force it up the exit ramp.

She almost managed the maneuver around the sharp turn, which would have made even Tom Gordon the *NASCAR* driver proud, but instead hit the road's edge. She fought the steering wheel hard and furiously, but the car jumped a two-inch tar berm and landed on a steep hill. The slope's sharp angle lifted the right front wheel off the ground, and she feared she was going to roll over.

Dirt and low-lying dead branches bounced off the hood and trunk, as it rolled and rattled downward. The front passenger wheel struck the ground with a thump, and the vehicle pushed through shrubbery and winding vines and struck something semi-solid. The car plummeted straight down the hill.

She pumped the brakes, but it didn't help. It was picking up speed and she couldn't stop it.

All at once, she let out a piercing scream: the car was headed towards a giant oak tree. She braced herself for the imminent crash.

Out of desperation, she pumped the brakes one last time when she reached the bottom of the hill and it slowed the car slightly before it slammed into the tree with startling force. The front air bag deployed within a nanosecond of impact, slamming just as hard. Marilynn's head recoiled back into the headrest.

"Ow!" she cried. "Son of a.... That hurt!"

The engine coughed and sputtered and the car convulsed for about thirty seconds, then stalled. Steam fizzed out the sides of the buckled hood. Marilynn didn't care, she just wondered why the side of her face felt warm as she reached down between the air bag and the door for the handle.

CHAPTER 13

7:11pm
20 Water Street

Jennie sat yoga style at her computer typing an e-mail to her friend Jack the Hack. Jack loved a challenge and prided himself on always being able to crack a code or secured system. Jennie knew how to play on that. The best way to get him to do something was to tell him he couldn't do it. She knew how to push his buttons.

She read aloud the e-mail she was sending:

Hey, Hack! Came across something interesting you might want to check out. I have no idea what it is or what it means, so I'm going on the Internet to see what I can find. I'd ask you to help me, but I think this is way out of your league. I know you've been able to crack a lot of codes in the past, but I don't think you would know where to look for this baby, so I'll do the best I can.

Anyway, my roommate Marilynn brings me this tiny disc with *GOV-69* inscribed on the top line and *NOPOSAM* on the bottom line. Trust me! This thing is small – it's so tiny you have to check it under a microscope.

The freaky thing about this chip is that it came

out of someone's shoulder. According to my roommate there are a lot of other people that had it in their shoulders too. I checked, I even have one.

Got to go, because I've got a few ideas I want to check out. Keep Hackin'!

Love – Yoga Girl.

She ended the message by adding a dozen tiny *smiley faces* jumping across the bottom, then clicked *Send* and waited for a response. It wouldn't take long. Hack was never away from his computer for any stretch of time, except to get food or go to the bathroom. Sometimes he even slept next to his computer. Plus, she knew this would get his goat and he would want to prove her wrong as usual.

Her idea worked. Within two minutes she received a return e-mail.

From: Jackthehack.com
To: YogaGirl.com

Hey, Yoga Girl! What's this nonsense you're throwing around about me not being able to help you! This is Jack the Hack you're talking to here! There's no code these eyes and fingers can't crack.

As a matter of fact, I'll bet you a pizza – extra large – topped with anything you like that I find out what it is before you!

Hey! NOPOSAM sounds like a road-kill.

Love ya back,
Jack the Hack
PS: I'll want lots of pepperoni on my pizza!
Spread across the bottom of the screen were a dozen

miniature animated blue hacksaws sawing up and down.

"Worked to perfection!" said Jennie.

A telephone rang in the living room. She uncrossed her legs and stood with her arms stretched to the heavens. "I'm coming, hold on to your horses," she scolded, after the phone rang about seven times. When she picked it up, there was nothing but loud static.

"OWWW!" she cried. She pulled the phone from her ear and slammed it down. She headed back to her computer and typed the letters NOPOSAM into the search engine INQUIRER. After a minute it came back with a *No matches found - check your spelling* message. She typed in GOV-69 and hit the enter button, but it came back with the same response. She got up from her chair and put the computer into sleep mode.

"I'll wait for the Hack to do his thing," she said, heading back to the kitchen to finish her tofu and water chestnut salad.

SIA Headquarters
Washington, DC
7:20pm

General Thomas Uxbridge sat swiveling his chair, reading an e-mail from a senior state senator, when his phone rang, interrupting his train of thought. Annoyed, the general grabbed the phone and snapped, "Uxbridge!"

"General, how are you today?" said a stately voice on the other end. "You sound a little upset. Is everything okay?"

Recognizing the voice, the general's tone softened. "Hello, Mr. President. I'm fine. I'm just frustrated that we haven't made as much headway in our situation as I'd like." Kissing some serious butt, the general continued, "I'm always glad to hear from you, Sir. You know that I'm one of your biggest fans. As a matter of fact, my wife asked me the other day when our families could get together again for one of those great barbecues of yours. You know how everyone loves your famous barbecued spare ribs!"

"Maybe after things calm down and we've gotten a hold on what's going on I'll have the First Lady give your wife a call and set something up. Enough socializing, General, fill me in on what's happening!"

"We've made a major breakthrough, Sir," said the General. "SIA intelligence has identified two suspects, a Mr. Doug Talbot and a Dr. Marilynn Harwell, in a place no one would ever suspect. Who would have ever thought that terrorist activity would take hold in Rhode Island, the smallest state?"

"Are you sure about this?" asked the President.

"Their bios fit perfectly, Mr. President. This is their dossier: Doug Talbot is recently divorced. He's unhappy because his ex has custody of their seven-year old daughter. He's employed at a television station as a camera operator, where he has unsupervised access to satellite uplinks. He has a violent temper. Upon entering a local hospital he punched out a patient, because he wanted the doctor that was treating the guy to look at his daughter. When the patient asked him to wait till the doctor finished, he slugged the patient. Unfortunately, that patient died.

Talbot also threatened to throw a city councilman out a third-story window because the councilman took exception to Talbot cutting ahead of seniors in line for anti-virus shots. We're currently following up on a possibility that he may have also killed his ex-wife."

The president cleared his throat and asked, "What about the woman?"

"She's single and is the top trauma doctor at a local area hospital. She's manic-depressive, she has a hard time relating to men, and has turned to a gay live-in lover. This woman who lives with her is a computer expert who works on security systems for big private companies, most of which are financial and business institutions with foreign interests."

"Hmmm," said the president.

After a pause to catch his breath, the general continued: "They've been seen together quite often, Sir, and we've recorded some strange conversations taking place between them at the hospital. We think they are speaking in some type of code. Our top decoders here in Washington are working on cracking those codes. Don't worry, Sir, we'll get them."

"You're right, General," said the president, "they certainly fit the profile."

"That's why I'm not taking any chances with these two," Uxbridge said. "I don't want to risk losing them, and any connection they may have with the mastermind behind this attack against the United States. I'm sure they can lead us to the ringleader, so I've authorized my people in the field to follow up on this as quickly as possible. Remember, this woman has access to any medical information she needs and could easily distribute the virus, and he has access to any microwave and satellite uplink he wants, and could send or receive concealed secret terrorist information."

"Sounds like you've got things under control, General," said the president, "so I won't hold you up anymore. It's important that we tie things up soon, so our citizens are safe. Do whatever you have to do to get it done. Hopefully, General, the next time I talk to you is around a barbecue pit."

The line went silent. A smile inched its way across the general's face as he pulled a cigar out of his pocket and lit it. Satisfied, he went back to his e-mail.

CHAPTER 14

7:24pm
WJAM-TV

Alone in WJAM's parking lot, Doug Talbot paced back and forth. Getting a cab this late would probably be impossible. The buses had already stopped running. He could thumb his way, but there were few cars on the road. Besides, you never know who was picking you up or whether they could be trusted. Just how the hell was he going to get back to Marilynn?

Suddenly, before he knew what had happened, two men wearing military gear ran up and grabbed him from the sides. "Come peacefully, Mr. Talbot," said the one on his right in a contemptuous tone, "and you won't get hurt."

"Who the hell are you and what do you want with me?"

"Like I said, don't give us any trouble and you won't get hurt," was the monotone reply.

"Okay, okay. I'm not resisting. Just answer my questions. Who are you and what do you want?"

"I guess it wouldn't hurt to tell him," said the second soldier. "Where he's going, it won't matter."

The first soldier began shaking Talbot by the collar. "Fine!" he shouted. "We were told to bring you in by some very important people at the SIA. They want to talk to you about a matter of national security."

"National security? What the hell's that got to do with me? I'm not a threat to anyone."

"Everything, smart ass," grumbled the first soldier, grabbing him lower on the front of his shirt. "They want to speak to you and your girlfriend!"

"I don't have a girlfriend. I'm recently divorced."

"We know all about your sweetheart, buddy. What's her name? Dr. Marilynn Harwell. Oh, I forgot. You like to call her To-ens!"

Doug tried to pull his arms free, but the soldier's grips tightened. Gritting his teeth, he said, "If anything happens to her, someone will have to answer to me!" Their hold got tighter.

"Don't get your panties in a knot!" yelled the first guy. "She's being picked up by field agents right now. You were warned to mind your own business, but you two just had to put your noses where they didn't belong. Now the both of you are looking at a long time in prison, buddy."

Adrenaline coursed through Doug's veins and he reacted by slamming his right foot into the instep of the guy in front of him, followed by a front ball kick to the stomach. The soldier cursed as he let go and dropped to his knees.

Doug lifted his right leg and kicked the other guy in the groin with a snapping right roundhouse kick and followed with a back-fisted punch to the guy's face, then finished him off with a jumping side-thrust kick. The soldier flew several feet into the air and fell writhing to the ground.

The first soldier rebounded and charged at him with flailing fists. Talbot did a spin around back kick to his face that stunned him, then sent him flying backwards into a Dumpster with another jumping side kick. Neither one of the attackers wanted any more. Thank God for all those karate classes at the Y.

Seeing an opening, Doug took off running down Route Two as fast as his legs would take him. It was five miles to the hospital and he would have to run all the way. The sky was clear and all the stars were visible despite the brightness of a three-quarter moon. It was warm, but not overbearing, and a slight breeze pushed at his back. It was a good night for a run.

Ten minutes and several quick stops later, he had gone about a mile, when he felt his cell phone vibrate inside his front pocket. He slowed to a stop, then reached inside for the phone. He was out of breath, huffing and puffing pretty hard. It had been a long time since he'd done this much running. "I guess I'm not in as good a shape as I thought I was," he said aloud, in between sporadic breaths. He pressed the menu button. The words *You have one new message* flashed across the screen.

He hit the start button and Marilynn's voice whispered, "Doug. I'm in trouble." There was lots of static and a garbled voice. It finally cleared and he heard, "I need your help!"

He scrolled the text back to the main menu. Marilynn's call had been recorded at 7:29pm. He lifted his wrist to see what time it was, but his watch was dead. "Damn!" he shouted. "That freakin degauss machine." It had accidentally drained his watch battery lifeless.

Meanwhile, back at the station, Fred the Freelancer walked out with a camera and jumped into Doug Talbot's car. He turned the ignition and the car exploded, sending car and body parts raining all over the parking lot.

* * *

Marilynn knew she needed to get out of the car and the area as quickly as possible, or she'd risk meeting up with the homicidal maniac who put her there in the first place. She felt lightheaded, but not disoriented.

"Now I know how icing wedged in the middle of an Oreo cookie feels," she thought, as she sat pinned between the airbag and the seat. Before attempting to get out, she decided to give herself an examination. She wiggled her toes and moved her ankles. She felt confident none of them were broken, although there was a throbbing in her left leg. She tried moving the fingers in her left hand and then her right, and they seemed fine. Other than the pressure of the airbag pushing against her chest and lungs, there was no excruciating pain in any of her bones, so early indications were nothing was broken. The location of the pain in her head was a possible sign that she'd suffered a concussion. There was also the threat of internal bleeding, but there would be other telltale signs if that was the case.

The possibility of a concussion is what worried her. If she had one, and didn't know the extent of the trauma she'd suffered without the benefit of an MRI, she would need to stay awake or risk not waking up. "If I make conversation with myself, that should do the trick," she said out loud.

After what seemed like a long time, but was actually only a minute, she found the door handle and popped the door open. Oddly enough, the dome light still worked, and she squeezed a look in the rearview mirror. It wasn't a pretty sight. Her face was slightly swollen and beginning to turn purple on the left side, her hair was a mess and blood trickled down her right temple.

"This isn't going to be easy," she said aloud. Because the impact had pushed the dashboard in, the air bag had her pinned against the seat pretty good and it would take every bit of remaining strength to squeeze out of the car. Sticking out her left arm and leg would be relatively easy. The rest of her would be a struggle.

She sat gathering her strength before trying to get out, using the time to run the events of the last few minutes through her mind. "Why didn't the guy do something to me when he found me parked on the side of the road in a compromising position?" she whispered. "And why did he wait till I was back on the road to make his move?"

Her head throbbed like no headache she'd ever had before and she found it difficult to reason. She was inhaling short quick breaths that made her head throb even harder, as she sat trying to figure it out.

"Think, Marilynn," she said out loud. "Why did he wait for you to get back onto the freeway? What would be the benefit?"

Suddenly it dawned on her. "If he drives me off the

road, it looks like an ordinary accident and no one's the wiser. The day's headline in the local paper would probably read, *Top trauma doctor dies after falling asleep at the wheel.*" She shook her throbbing head lightly and said, "Ain't gonna happen, homicidal maniac." Giving herself encouragement, she continued, "Okay, To-ens. You can do this."

She stuck her left arm and left leg out, then leaned to the left till her head was most of the way out of the car. She then wiggled her butt a little at a time till half her body was outside. Exerting that much effort exhausted her, so she stopped for a quick break. Getting out of the car was going to take more of an effort than she'd thought.

She fought hard to stay awake. After all, she knew a person's first impulse is to shut their eyes when experiencing deep pain. She also knew Jennie would say, "That's a response to clear the mind." After resting for a short time, she went back to the chore of getting out of the car, an activity that she would never again take for granted. She wiggled her butt some more, thus inching her way closer to freedom. This time she was able to get her right foot out. Now her left arm and leg, and most of her head and right foot, were all sticking out of the obstructed doorway. The air bag pressed hard against her stomach, making it difficult to breathe. She sounded like a person with a bad case of asthma as she tried filling her lungs. Feeling like a contortionist, she said to herself, "How the hell do those circus clowns packed inside a small car do it?"

After a brief rest, she put all her effort into one big push and slipped out from between the air bag and the seat, plopping onto the ground and rolling over onto her back. She grappled with getting up, falling down each time she tried to stand, like a newborn foal. Finally, she rolled over onto all fours and crouched, then got to her feet, swaying unsteadily side to side. After several agonizing moments she regained her balance and began brushing dirt off. Looking back up to where the car had started it's descent, she saw headlights creeping along the edge of the roadway.

She reached inside the car, pulled her cell phone out of her handbag, and clipped it to her waistband. She stared hard at the bag, then threw it back onto the seat. "Only slow me down," she said, as she shuffled off as best as she could. "Come on Marilynn, get the hell out of here!"

Moonlight filtered through a sparse forest of tall, thin layered oaks and scruffy pines, giving her plenty of light to see by. She stopped at the edge of the woods and searched both directions. Off to the right was a dirt path that led straight and deep into a waiting forest. She took a quick look back up the slope. Two flashlights were moving deliberately down the steep embankment.

She started into the woods. It was then she realized that she was moving with a slight limp. "Could this get any worse?" she mumbled. The hitch in her step did get worse as she ambled further along. Her leg was getting weaker with each painful step and it slowed her considerably to the point where it caused her foot to drag. She glanced back anxiously. The steady beams of two flashlights darted in short semi-circles like frantic fireflies. She knew they were searching Jennie's incapacitated car.

Despite her pain, she quickened her pace enough to move at a decent clip, shuffling and dragging her leg. It was a dumb mistake to stop and look back, but she did. Peering over her shoulder sent a chill down her spine, temporarily making her forget the pain in her leg. The searchlights were coming down the same path!

She considered her options. The fireflies were at least fifty feet away, but were closing in fast; there was no way she could outrun them in her condition. Desperate, she swiveled her head from left to right. She needed a place to hide but there were only the sparsely-layered oak and pine trees, thinned because they couldn't grow any bigger this far inside the forest. She moved forward a few steps and spotted a hiding place: two large rocks about fifteen feet off the beaten path.

She limped and dragged towards her sanctuary with

trepidation and slid behind the medium sized boulders. Peeking through the sliver of a crack between them, she gauged the flashlights were still some thirty feet away. Then an idea came to her. She pulled her cell phone from her belt. The last call she'd made was to Doug Talbot, so she hit the REDIAL button. It beeped and booped seven times then started to buzz on the other end.

"Damn!" she cried softly. "A busy signal!"

There was a click on the other end and a soft female voice said, *"Your call cannot be connected at this time. If you would like to leave a voice message, hit any key or hang up and try again later."*

She pressed her thumb against the pound key. After another click, Doug's voice came up. "This is Doug. When you hear the tone, leave your message and I'll get back to as soon as I can. Don't forget to leave your name and number. I'm not psychic."

A monotone beep was her cue to talk. "Doug. I'm in trouble," she whispered into the phone's mouthpiece. "My car was forced off the road and down an embankment just off exit eight. I'm in the woods and two people are chasing me! I need your help!"

After another bland beep the same soft female voice said, "Your voice message will be forwarded to......*Doug Talbot. Have a nice day.*"

"I've got your nice day," fumed Marilynn, hitting the END button.

Snapping twigs and crunching footsteps on dead leaves caught her attention. She peered out through the thin crevice between the boulders and her heart sank even further. The approaching lights were only a few feet away. Now voices accompanied them.

"She must have come this way," said a deep, older man's voice, as he scanned his flashlight's beam on the ground. "See where the dirt has been disturbed here?"

"Don't forget," said a lighter, much younger voice. "Our orders are to bring her in if possible. Don't shoot first, then ask questions later."

"Ahh! They take all the fun out of it!" said the older, deeper voice.

Deep voice searched the ground in concentric circles, each one wider than the previous. Younger voice got down on his knees for a closer look. "There will be plenty of time for fun later when they get interrogated," he said. "Don't forget, Johnson and Jonsen are doing the job that we wanted. What was that guy's name?"

"Talbot!" said deep voice. "I would have had some fun whacking *that* dude."

"Would you have let me in on the fun?"

"Nah! He would have been all mine!"

"Now you're taking all the fun out of it for me!" said lighter voice.

They laughed and snickered and she tried to get a good look at deep voice, but his back was to her. She was sure his name was *Homicidal Maniac*.

"Come on," said deep voice. "Let's go further up the path. She must have gone on ahead."

They trampled off, kicking away anything that got in their path and had advanced some feet, when Marilynn's cell phone started ringing.

"Shit!" she said, throwing it to the ground. She tried to muffle the sound by sitting on it.

"Did you hear that?" said the younger voice.

"Hear what?" said deep voice.

"I thought I heard a phone ringing."

Marilynn breathed silently. The cell phone stopped ringing.

"Are you sure?"

"I'm pretty sure I heard something."

"You'd better not be wasting my freaking time," said deep voice. "Let's double back and take a look."

Their steps crackled and popped over dried leaves and snapping sticks as they retraced their path towards her hiding place. They didn't try to move silently. Their lights were searching into the woods and deep voice asked, "About where do you think you heard it?"

"It's hard to tell," said light voice. "Sound travels at night."

She ducked just in time as one of the lights swept over the rocks.

"What about those boulders?" asked deep voice. "They look like a good place to hide. Check 'em out!"

CHAPTER 15

20 Water Street
7:39pm

Jennie Sprague had finished her salad and was filling the dishwasher with dirty dishes when she decided to check her e-mail. It had been a good hour since she'd e-mailed Jack the Hack and she half expected a reply.

Spinning the red plastic ball on the mouse woke the computer out of slumber. The monitor changed quickly from black to her desktop showing a dozen icons across the top. She clicked on the e-mail and a robotic man's voice said, "You - have - three - new - messages."

The first message was titled New Rates and was from a mortgage company. She deleted it. The second message titled *You Never Call* was from her mother. Reluctantly, she clicked it open and a three-page letter started out, "Why don't you ever call me? Sending e- mails is so impersonal. Aren't I important to you anymore? Better still, why don't you come by for a visit?"

Jennie couldn't take any more of her mother's badgering so she X'ed out of the e-mail. She just wasn't in the mood to listen to her rant and rave for another two and a half pages.

She clicked opened the third e-mail that was named BEWARE! It was Jack's e-mail and it was taking a long time for the message to download, so Jennie went back to the kitchen for a cup of herbal tea and returned just as it finished.

Sitting in front of the terminal she began reading the Hack's e-mail:

> Hey, Yoga Girl, this is some serious shit you've got yourself into. I've attached a couple of files for you to check out. Don't go to these sites. You might not be able to get out clean. I barely did and I'm a hundred times better than you.

She glanced casually up at the window to her right, her attention drawn to it by the closing of a car door outside, but quickly went back to reading her screen.

> Yoga, I did some serious hacking. I didn't know where I was till it was too late and discovered I was inside the SIA defense system. They've got some serious *hacker tracker* systems. I didn't even know I was inside until I found their insignia and name on an obscure file in a back page of a phony website. I know I've hacked some pretty famous sites in the past, but this is a scary place even for me. I was able to backtrack and get out before they found me, but it was extremely close. I sure as hell wouldn't want to get caught by them. It's rumored these guys kill just to stay in practice.
>
> By the way, you owe me a large pepperoni pizza from Mama Giavonni's. Feel free to send it any time tonight. I'm starving!
>
> Hope this is a help to you.
> PS. Be careful.
> Jack the Hack

Jennie opened up the first file named *Base*. It was taking a long time to download, so she figured it had to be a video file. She sat patiently and watched the animation of paper flying into a small in-box one sheet at a time. When it finally finished loading, the screen was filled with a black and white group photo of scientists. There was wording under it, which Jennie read aloud: "Professor John Woodsen and staff – July 21, 1969. B.J. Stockton Military Base, Virginia."

She paged down to a second black and white picture, another group shot. The caption under this photo read: Woodsen and Government replacements. June 12, 1970. B.J.Stockton Military Base, Virginia.

Her curiosity piqued, she sat forward on the edge of the seat. Again she paged down to another group photo. It was marked May 19, 1973. It was a completely different group of people and Woodsen was not among them. She scrolled down to yet another picture, this one in full color and dated August 30, 1980. This photo appeared to be of military personnel: they were dressed in Army fatigues.

She struck the Page Down key and the screen was blank. To make sure there were no other pictures she hit it again and a fifth picture popped up. The date was March 1, 2000. Inscribed under it was "General Thomas Uxbridge and staff, B.J. Stockton Military Base, Virginia."

Jennie saved the file to her hard drive, minimizing it in case she wanted to go back to it again. Then she opened a second file named *Noposam*. The screen immediately cleared and turned black. At first it looked like there was a downloading problem, but after a minute something threatening started to take shape on the screen.

"Holy shit!" shouted Jennie, standing up. "Jack! What *are* we into?"

The screen cleared to all white, then, starting from the top and working its way downward, a shape began forming. She was almost sure what it was, and as it got about halfway down, her fears became reality. She knew exactly what the large brown insignia represented - a very dangerous organization. She was suddenly afraid.

"Damn!" she shouted, jumping back a step after a loud knock at the front door.

Actually it was more like a slamming of a fist. A cold shiver shook her shoulders as she stared at the screen and its surreal content. Hugging herself, she yelled, "I'm coming!" even though she knew they couldn't hear her from the back room. She continued studying the monitor and its text for several seconds. Making a quick decision, she clicked on her web site address and saved everything Jack the Hack had e-mailed her.

The banging at the front door got louder. This time it was more pronounced and angry. She didn't bother to answer. Putting herself into hurry mode, she snatched a blank disc off her desk and opened the disc drive. Sliding it inside, she clicked save. A little orange light on the hard drive flashed, indicating *Noposam* was saving to the disc.

"Come on!" she urged. When it finally finished she maximized the *Base* file and saved that to the disc. She ejected it and clutched it to her chest, while searching the room for a hiding place. It had to be an unusual place where no one would ever think to look.

The knocking on the door sounded loud enough to break it down. All at once she thought of a hiding spot. Snatching a white protective sleeve off the desk and sliding the disc into it, she ran to the bathroom and opened the medicine cabinet. She reached in and pulled out a blue plastic package. It was just the right size so she stuffed the disc inside and put it back in the cabinet. Her heart was beating as fast as when she went on her daily runs.

She hurried back to the computer room and deleted everything Jack the Hack had sent. "Whew!" she sighed deeply and loudly, as she shut the computer down.

The pounding on the front door had changed to a single loud bang about every five seconds, when she unlocked the metal door and pulled it open shouting, "What?" Before she got an answer, a large dark figure rushed in.

* * *

Marilynn pressed her body against the ground in an effort to make herself invisible. She started sucking small amounts of undetectable breaths into her fully open mouth so as not to breathe too loud. It was a trick she learned as a child when she thought there were monsters under her bed at night and she didn't want them to hear her. She listened intently as Light Voice stepped haphazardly over dried leaves and dead branches trampling his way towards her. She wished she had her wrench.

Suddenly a cell phone went off. Her ears perked. Was it the one under her? Her head was spinning and she couldn't think straight. The phone rang again and still she wasn't sure. After a third time, she realized it belonged to Light Voice. Relieved, her body shuddered when she relaxed.

"Rossi!" said Light Voice, answering his phone. "Just a second, sir. It's for you, Betters!" he shouted back.

Betters was annoyed. "Well! Bring it to me!"

Rossi retraced his steps the same bumbling way and handed the cell phone to Betters.

"Christ! Don't you even know when your own phone's ringing?"

"I told you sound travels," snapped Rossi.

Betters grabbed the phone and answered, "Betters here. Yes, sir. We're hot on her tracks. We anticipate apprehending her shortly." After a short pause he continued, "I understand, sir. We'll see you as soon as we have her in custody. According to our map there's a farmhouse just up ahead and I suspect that's where she's headed."

There was a loud snap as he closed the flip style phone. "Let's get our asses going," said Betters. "We've lost a lot of time and she's probably way ahead of us."

She listened to the two stomp off arguing. When she could no longer hear any sign of them, she grabbed her cell phone off the ground and got to her feet. Warily, she limped slowly out from behind her hideaway and stood motionless – her ears tiny satellite dishes, listening for any sound of her personal trackers. Satisfied they weren't within earshot she doubled back to Jennie's car, shuffling as fast as possible. One look at it and dread swept over her. It was totaled and would never again be of any use, unless it was melted down and made into beer cans.

Hope rushed out of her faster than one-armed bandits take money in Vegas. She placed her throbbing head between both hands and said, "It's a wonder I walked away from this."

After retrieving her pocketbook, she looked back up the embankment where her car had left the road, and spied Better's and Rossie's car with the headlights still on. "There's a ride," she thought out loud as she started up the hill. The going was tough - shuffling up the slope caused stabbing pain in her leg. To amuse herself she said, chuckling, "They can borrow Jennie's car if they want."

By the time she reached the top and found a dark Suburban parked at the edge of the road, her leg was throbbing and she was winded. "Awfully sweet of you boys to let me borrow your car," she said, jumping into the driver's seat. "Ah! Even left me the keys!" She placed her cell phone and handbag on the passenger's seat, then turned the key in the ignition. The engine roared to life. She shifted into drive and the SUV peeled up dirt and pebbles after she floored it.

In seconds, she was doing eighty-five miles an hour. The engine purred and didn't even break a sweat, in contrast to Jennie's stressed car at that speed. She was feeling confident she had pulled the heist off when suddenly overhead, the beating blades of a helicopter stirred up dirt and dust around the perimeter of the car. She could barely see ahead, so she started lightly tapping the brakes to slow the car. The digital speedometer dropped gradually from eighty-nine to fifty-two.

A searchlight on the underbelly of the helicopter snapped on, illuminating her new ride. She mentally noted the mileage – 12,327. The helicopter stayed above her, matching her speed. She glanced at the odometer and the mileage was already up half a mile. Her breaths came in quick spurts, and she knew her heart rate was rushing too fast. "Jesus, it's a good thing there's no traffic on the road," she said, struggling to keep the car in her own lane. Mileage was now up a full mile.

The helicopter continued matching speed. Other than that and the probing light, they weren't attempting to stop her. At the two-mile mark the copter unexpectedly flew off, leaving her a clear view of the road. She sighed heavily and pushed the gas down till the car reached a speed of ninety.

"Don't know what the hell that was all about." she said, looking out the window and up at the sky. "Wonder how long before my buddies discover their car missing?"

Suddenly her cell phone rang, startling her. She stared at it on the passenger seat as it rang a second time. Reaching tentatively, she picked it up off the seat and said, "Doug?"

"Dr. Harwell, we want our fucking car back!" said deep voice.

"Shit!" she yelled, hitting the END button and throwing the phone back onto the passenger seat. She located the radio knob and turned it on. Rap music blared. "Freakin' figures!" she said, shaking her head.

She pushed the car to one hundred, then went back to concentrating on the road and her driving.

The phone rang.

She stared down at it.

It rang again.

She stared at the road, then down at the phone.

It rang a third time, then a fourth and fifth.

She snuck a peek at it then snatched it up and hit the answer button yelling, "How did you get my freakin' number, you asshole!"

"You gave it to this asshole!" said the voice on the other end.

It was Doug.

"Damn, am I glad to hear your voice! I crashed my car as I was being chased by two madmen who chased me into some woods but I escaped from them and took their car and was just chased by a helicopter and they know my number and called me and now I'm talking to you thank God!"

"Whoa!" said Doug, "Slow down. Take a deep breath. I didn't understand a word you said. Who's chasing you?"

She inhaled deeply and with slightly more composure spoke slowly and coherently.

"I don't know who the two of them were or why they were following me, or even why they ran me off the road, but I did notice they were definitely military. They wore army fatigues."

"They could be a couple of mentally challenged hunters," said Doug.

"I heard them talking on their cell phone. They kept saying Sir, and they were talking about bringing me in."

"I wonder if they're SIA?" said Doug. "That's what the guys who attacked me were."

Startled, she said, "What guys attacked you?"

"It's a long story. It'll have to wait"

"At least tell me if you're okay?"

"I'm fine."

"You're not just saying that, are you? You're really okay?"

"I'm fine. I promise. I can't say the same for them, though."

"Now I'm really concerned. Do you want me to meet you at the hospital?" she asked, racing along 95 north. "I'm one exit away from there."

"That would be a neat trick if I could pull it off," he said, laughing sarcastically.

"What do you mean?"

"Only that I'm walking, or I should say, running down Route Two towards the hospital."

"Where's your car?"

"The station suspended me and confiscated the keys. My own car's at home, so I had no ride."

"I can't be very far from you. I'll come pick you up."

Peering up the road he said, "You might as well meet me at the hospital, because by the time you get here, I'd be there anyway." Breathing in short gasps, he continued, "Although I'm not in as good as shape as I thought I was."

She could hear his breathing coming in loud and fast bursts. "You poor thing! I'll stay on the line with you till we meet."

"No! I'd rather hang up. I'm pretty winded and won't be able to speak for more much longer."

"All right, have it your way. Just hang in there till I see you in a few minutes."

Doug waited for the line to go silent but it remained open. "Are you still there?" he asked into the phone.

"I'm still here."

"Why didn't you hang up?"

"Why didn't you hang up?" she asked back.

"This is so high school," he said.

"So hang up," she threw back.

"You know what?" he said. "It's kind of nice. Let's stay on the line till we meet or our cell phone batteries..."

Doug stopped mid-sentence.

"What's the matter?' she asked.

"Shit!" he whispered. "Hold on. Don't say anything."

She pressed the phone hard against her ear. The sound of rustling brush and pounding feet running on leaves was all that she could hear. "Doug," she whispered softly. "What's going on? Doug."

There was no answer, only more rustling bushes and thumping feet on crackling leaves. She held her breath and tried to block out the jabbing pains in her head and leg. She could hear Doug's sporadic breathing. Only now it seemed more apprehensive than labored. A minute went by. To her it seemed longer.

Doug finally came back on the line.

"Don't say anything," he pleaded, his voice hardly audible.

* * *

Lying prone on dried leaves, hidden behind old dead brush and small bushes, he watched a dark SUV roll deliberately along the side of the road almost exactly across from his hiding place. A probing beam of light emerged from the front passenger window, stretching into the woods directly behind his head, dancing and darting in search of its prey.

The car came to a stop only fifteen feet from him. Voices emanated from inside.

"He can't be far from here," said one he recognized. It was the big mouth soldier that had grabbed him back at the station.

"Are you sure he came this way?" said a voice he didn't know.

"He had to," said big mouth, "if he's going back to the hospital!"

"Then why don't we just go to the hospital and wait to grab him when he shows up?"

"That's not a bad idea," said big mouth. "But he's all mine. I have a score to settle."

The cars tires squealed as they peeled out and the vehicle sped away, leaving Doug to himself.

"Don't know if you heard any of that," he said softly.

"A little," she said.

"I'm going to take you up on that offer to pick me up!"

"Where on Route Two are you?"

"I'm about halfway down, just past where Pendleton's Furniture used to be on the right side. I'm in the middle of a big section of pine and oak trees. You can't miss me."

"Hang in there! I'm on my way."

"Good!" he said. "I'll be the one hiding in the bushes."

Doug lay on his back bracing his head with his hands, staring up at the hot white glittering rocks in the clear, mystical sky. He was pretty sure it was the Big Dipper he was looking at, until he saw another group of stars to the right that looked like the Big Dipper. Focusing on that, his peripheral vision caught something moving off to the left and close to the horizon. Watching it glide across the sky, he figured it was a shooting star. But shooting stars go down when they cross the sky. This one was moving up as it moved out of the west and it was actually getting bigger.

"What the...?" he said, jumping to his feet. He studied the fast-approaching astral body as it continued to grow larger and closer. Now bewilderment was rapidly changing to fear. The approaching UFO, which was traveling at a high rate of speed, was nearly overhead. It had a red pulsing light on top and a wide search light dropped from its underbelly to the ground. He gauged the height at about thirty feet.

It was then that he heard a beating sound that reverberated through the trees and pounded inside his head as it got even closer. Was it a UFO on a mission to take him away to do unspeakable experiments on him? Straining his eyes upward, he watched the wide searchlight reach down into nearby trees.

It was very close and Doug finally recognized the beating engine. It wasn't an Unidentified Flying Object on a light year mission to study earthlings. It was a helicopter. Its whirling propellers and rotor blades whirred as it drew near. The searchlight angled in different directions, searching in a cylindrical motion. It closed within a few feet of where he stood.

That's when he understood that it was looking for him. He ducked to the ground and slid under thick bushes with pickers that bit into his unprotected bare arms like bees that attack when their nest is disturbed. The force of the copter's blades tossed dirt and dead dry leaves into the air as if the place were suddenly caught in the middle of *The Wizard of Oz*. The probing light passed right over his head and the bushes he was hiding under. Even though they couldn't hear him from inside the copter, he held his breath, so as not to make any noise.

The helicopter hovered above for what seemed an eternity, then made a couple of short passes over the street and back. He tried to see who was flying the machine, but it was impossible in the dark, from his vantage point. On a return pass, it hovered overhead like a dragonfly, aiming its probing light randomly over the ground. It darted herky jerky, with no true strategy, the sound of it's beating engine bouncing off the tumultuous terrain.

Unsuccessful, the helicopter began moving slowly away, searching other areas, but consistently heading in the direction of the hospital. Doug watched from his hiding spot until the flying machine was just another star in the sky.

Confident that they were gone, he slid out from under the bushes and stood facing the street. He lifted his arm to check his watch, gauging how much time had passed since he had talked to Marilynn.

"Fuck!" he shouted. "I forgot this thing's dead." He'd hardly gotten that out when he saw headlights approaching from behind him at a very slow pace, not more than twenty yards down the road. The maniacs had come back.

The SUV slowed almost to a stop as it rolled closer. He could see the front passenger window was lowered half way. It stopped almost perpendicular to where he stood.

He ducked back behind some bushes, trying to make no sound, and studied the vehicle from his knees. Even with help from the nearby street lamp, he could see very little.

Time passed, and the car just sat there. No one got out and he heard no voices.

Feeling a cramp in his leg, he squirmed from his kneeling position, stretching his leg out to unkink the knot. As he stared at the parked car, he was sure there was a pair of eyes looking directly at him, penetrating his thin layer of skin. When the pain in his leg became too much, he sat with his legs pointed forward and did a couple of toe touches.

Suddenly, the SUV began inching away.

He crouched, straining his neck trying to look over the top of the bushes that formed his sanctuary. The car rolled slowly down the road.

"That's it, ya jerk!" he whispered loudly. "Keep going – all the way to the hospital!"

But the car stopped. In fact it started backing up - the reverse lights were lit. It was going at a pretty good rate, its whining engine echoing in the air.

Had they seen him?

The engine wound down and stopped completely. The car was again almost directly across from him. He peered through the branches of the mostly dead bushes and cursed that he couldn't see better.

The driver's side door closed with a slam. A lone dark figure walked around the back of the car and stepped to the edge of the roadway. Stooping low, it searched the ground as good as any bloodhound.

He reached down and picked up a short, thick branch off the ground and gripped it tightly. "Look all you want, ya bastard" he said under his breath. "Doug's got a nice surprise waiting for you."

The searching menace was faceless, because the street light was at it's back..

"Came back to finish the job, did ya?" he mumbled in anger, shaking with anticipation.

But then there were words – unrecognizable words. He wondered what the hell the dark figure was saying. Probably trying to trick him into coming out? His mind and heart raced faster than a pubescent teenager madly in love.

Finally, the words began making sense. They were whispers – whispers in the clear, mild night air.

"Doug!" said the whisper. "Where the hell are you?"

He pushed out from behind the bushes and the figure immediately turned towards him. He dropped the stick to the ground with a nasty thump as he approached and called out in a steady voice, "You scared the hell out of me!"

They met and embraced in a long and passionate kiss with eager mouths. Teenagers used to call it, "sucking face." She squeezed him, and he squeezed her back.

"Why didn't you answer?" she asked, letting go.

"I didn't recognize the car. Whose is it?"

"It belongs to the jokers that were chasing me. They

were kind enough to let me borrow it. Didn't you recognize my voice?"

"Not at first. I thought you were one of those guys that attacked me earlier."

"Any other situation I'd consider being called *one of those guys* an insult. Can we get out of here and get back to the hospital?" she said, pulling him towards the car.

Sitting in the passenger's seat, Doug pulled his cell phone from his front pocket and said, "Before we go I want you to listen to this message someone left on my phone."

He scrolled back to a previous message and hit the start button.

Doug Talbot, mind your own business or you'll end up like your wife, said a deep voice.

"We need to be real careful, To-ens, these clowns mean business."

"I've heard that voice before," she said. "It belongs to one of the creeps that chased me."

"I don't think it's a good idea to go back to the hospital right now," he said. "That's where they were heading."

"I have a suggestion," she said. "How about getting something to eat in a quiet, out of the way place, where we can think things out? Neither of us has had a good meal in a while."

"Sure, as long as you buy. You're the rich doctor."

She slipped the car into drive, did a quick U-turn in the middle of the road, and drove off fast. She was enjoying the new found power of the car.

"I know a place not far from here called the Country Kitchen, that serves breakfast twenty-four hours."

"Sounds good," he said, settling back in his seat. As she pushed the car faster he said, "Tell me about these bimbos that chased you."

"Not much to tell. A couple of maniacs named Betters and Rossi followed me from the hospital, kept me from taking my exit, then forced me off the road and down an embankment."

"That's when you called me and left a message?"

"Yeah," she said. "It got pretty hairy for a while, but I hid, then took their car after they went on ahead looking for me."

They were in a small area of the city and traffic had picked up. Vendors were back on the road, making their usual milk, bread, and chip deliveries. After following a couple of cars for a few blocks, she turned right at a green light, then pulled immediately into the parking lot of the Country Kitchen restaurant. There were two cars parked further down the lot so she drove forward and pulled up into the first parking spot, inches from the front door.

Before getting out Doug turned to her and asked, "Did you get a good look at their faces? Do you think you could recognize them if you saw them again?"

"I didn't get much of a look at them from where I was hiding. It was a fair distance away and I had a somewhat obstructed view. But I'd recognize their voices. That's why I'm sure the voice on your phone was the one named Betters."

They got out of their stolen transportation and went inside. Fifties style maroon leatherette booths with lots of chrome were placed strategically through the room, so that you had to walk past each one to get to an empty one.

They walked by a teenage couple sitting in the second booth holding hands and making eyes at each other as they waited for their order. They passed a cab driver with white hair that suggested he was working past retirement, who was busily digging his fork into an order of pancakes. Finally, they walked by two older women, who briefly stopped eating their eggs and home fries to smile at them.

Doug and Marilynn were too tired to return the smile, so they made their way to the last secluded booth in the corner, which happened to be closest to the kitchen. A short time after sitting down, a waitress came over and put place settings in front of them.

"My name is Dottie, and I'll be your waitress," said the older woman in a yellow dress and white apron. In a tired voice she asked, "Would you both like coffee?"

"I'll have a cup, please," said Marilynn, unrolling her napkin to reveal a fork, spoon and knife.

"I'll have two cups," said Doug.

The waitress laughed. "Tough night, huh," she said, reaching for a pot of coffee sitting on a hot plate on a nearby portable table.

"You don't know the half of it," said Doug, rubbing his eyes.

The waitress poured both of them a steaming cup of Java. "Well, Honey, maybe some breakfast will make everything better," she said, sliding an order pad out of her front pocket and pulling a pencil from behind her ear. "You need a menu?"

"Thanks, but we know what we want," said Doug. "I'll have something with lots of bacon and eggs."

"I'll have French Toast with strawberries and cream," said Marilynn.

"Great choices!" said the waitress. "I'll be back shortly with your orders."

The woman disappeared and Doug got up and turned on a television that hung over the booth next to them. After switching it to Channel 16, he slid back down on the leather seat. Stretching his hands high over his head he said, yawning, "Might as well see what's going on in the world." The television came to life in the middle of a commercial for one of those medications that has about fifteen weird side effects, delivered rapid-fire so you can't understand what they're talking about.

"Damn it!" said Doug, banging his head with the palm of his hand, then using it to get his cell phone out. "I haven't checked on Cassandra for a long time."

"Give me the phone," said Marilynn, taking it out of his hand. "I can get through faster than you using a back door number. And don't beat yourself up. So much has happened, you couldn't have called." She stroked his hand lovingly. "You're a great father."

All at once he noticed the side of her face. "You okay?' he asked. "The side of your face is a light shade of purple.

Putting her hand gently to her face she said, "It stings a little right now, but it's going to hurt like hell in the morning."

He grabbed four packets of sugar and emptied them into his cup of coffee, then poured milk from a metal creamer till it was a weak shade of brown.

"What are you making, coffee milk?" she asked while dialing a secret number only staff members knew.

"What can I say, I like my coffee light."

The phone rang six times before someone answered.

"Lindsey Palmer, how can I help you?"

"Lindsey, this is Dr. Harwell. Why haven't you gone home?'

"Hi, Doc. Things have finally quieted down, so I'm about to head out. What can I do for you?"

Doug was half-listening to the conversation and half-listening to the TV. Overhead, a repeat of the six o'clock news was showing video of some of the craziness that had gone on during the past couple of days. There were shots of people in three different hospitals getting vaccinations, and video clips of military personnel walking the streets, spraying neighborhoods. He could hear the young male anchor saying the government had made a formal announcement that the situation was now under control.

He reverted back to eavesdropping on Marilynn's conversation with Lindsey.

"Is she still stable?" she asked.

He could see by the expression on her face that she was engrossed in the nurse's answer. Looking back up at the TV, his eyes grew wide. Photos of him and Marilynn stared down at him.

"In other related news," said the anchor, "these two people are wanted for questioning relating to possible terrorist involvement. Her name is Dr. Marilynn Harwell, a prominent doctor at Coventry General Hospital. His name is Douglas Talbot, and he's a camera operator here at Channel Sixteen. They are reportedly on the run from military officials."

Doug reached over and grabbed Marilynn's arm, shaking it vigorously to get her attention.

"What?" she said, pushing his hand away.

He nodded up at the TV several times. Getting the hint, she looked up. Her mouth dropped open.

"Police say they are only wanted for questioning and that no formal charges have been made at this time," the anchor said excitedly. "If you have any information about these people, you are asked to call your local police department. Do not try to detain them. They are considered extremely dangerous."

Marilynn went back to her phone conversation: "Go home Lindsey! Get some rest! Just go home!" she said, hanging up.

"We have to get out of here," whispered Doug.

They got up and started to leave, when the waitress came back carrying two plates with their orders. Standing at their booth, she asked. "Don't you want your food?"

"You eat it," said Doug, throwing a twenty-dollar bill on the table. They rushed towards the front exit, but stopped short of going out.

"You have change coming!" shouted the waitress.

Parked next to their stolen car was a police cruiser. Standing between the two cars was a policeman speaking to the cab driver from the restaurant. A second officer sat inside the police car talking on a cell phone.

They watched intently as the cop showed the cab driver a couple of pictures. He instantly waved towards the restaurant. It was easy to read the policeman's lips saying, "Are you sure."

They didn't wait for the answer, turning abruptly and heading towards the back of Country Kitchen, where Dot met them.

Holding a pot of coffee, she asked, "Changed your minds?"

"We need to get out of here fast," said Marilynn anxiously. "Is there another way out?"

The waitress shot a quick glance towards the front

door, catching a glimpse of the two policemen. "Are you in some kind of trouble, Honey?"

"No," said Doug in a low voice, so as not to attract attention from the remaining four customers. "We just want to avoid a misunderstanding."

"That's really all it is," said Marilynn, backing his explanation.

"Follow me," said Dot, grabbing Marilynn by the wrist and dragging her towards the kitchen. With Doug right on her tail, they rushed past a surprised cook in a full-length white apron and avoided walking into old dented aluminum pots and pans that hung on hooks from the ceiling. The smell of bacon and eggs frying on a grill taunted their nostrils and empty stomachs.

When they reached the back screen door, they found it propped open with a broken wooden stool to ventilate the heat out of the kitchen.

"We kind of lost our transportation. Is there a bus that runs by here?" asked Marilynn.

The waitress reached into a side pocket and pulled out a set of keys on a plain circular key ring. "Here," she said, "take these. They go to that beat up red junk over there by the Dumpster."

"We can't take your car," said Marilynn, gently pushing the woman's hand away.

They quickly became aware of commotion going on out in the front of the restaurant. Doug grabbed the keys, saying, "Yes we can. We need to go. Now!"

"Take it!" said the waitress. "All I ask is that you leave it in some store's parking lot when you're done with it and call me to let me know where it is. She ripped a piece of paper from her order pad, scribbled her phone number and handed it to Marilynn.

"Thanks, Dot," smiled Marilynn, pulling the woman into a hug.

"Gotta go," urged Doug.

Marilynn released her hug and went out the propped open door. The waitress turned to Doug and said, "Follow that winding road to the left and it will bring you back out to the main road, but much further down."

He pulled out his wallet and took out two twenty dollar bills and handed them to her. "Here," he said, "this will pay for the gas we use."

"I can't take money for being nice," she said.

He stuck the bills into the woman's front pocket and kissed her on the forehead. "We'd feel better if you did, Dot. Thanks for your help!"

"Hey, Dotty!" boomed a voice from inside the dining room. "Get out here! The cops want to talk to you!"

"Go!" said the waitress.

Doug shot out the door and jumped in the dilapidated 1989 Chevy. He turned the key and the car started after laboring for a few agonizing seconds. He shoved the automatic shift on the floor into drive, and the two fugitives drove down the winding road with a trail of white smoke coming out the back.

"Where do we go now?" asked Doug, looking back over his shoulder to see if they were being followed.

"Let's go see what Jennie has for us."

* * *

Back inside the restaurant, Dot stepped through the kitchen doors and was greeted by the policeman who had spoken to the cabby. "Were these two just in here eating?" asked the cop, showing her the two pictures.

"They don't look familiar," lied the waitress.

"That's what I told them," said her boss, the cook from the kitchen.

"Are you sure?" asked the second cop, who had joined the group.

"We get so many people, I can't remember all the faces," said Dot.

"Yeah, I can tell from all the empty seats," said the first cop.

CHAPTER 16

8:59pm
20 Water Street

Doug pulled Dot's beat-up car to a stop in front of Marilynn's home, an old Victorian house. The two fugitives studied it thoughtfully, their faces basking in the green glow from the lit dashboard.

"The lights are out," said Marilynn.

Doug sensed an edge of tension in her voice.

"So?"

"Something's not right," she whispered.

Leaning over to get a better look, he whispered back, "Seems pretty quiet inside."

Marilynn placed her hand on Doug's forearm. "That's what's wrong. Jennie and I have a simple alarm system for when we're not home."

"Like what?"

"The last one to leave the house turns the radio up loud so that it sounds like voices inside, and we leave lots of lights on. Even if we're home, we still leave lots of lights on. Inside and out."

Doug shrugged. "Maybe she forgot."

"Shhhh," she interrupted.

"Aren't you overreacting?"

"Keep your voice down," she whispered. "I have a bad feeling about this. This system is Jennie's idea. She lectures me every time I forget!"

A deep silence enveloped the car for several long moments.

"No," sighed Marilynn. "Jennie would never forget."

"Maybe she went to bed," said Doug.

"She still would have left the lights on for me."

"We can't stay out here all night," he said in a hushed voice. "I'll go in and check the place. Wait here."

Their eyes met in the dim light and he saw the concern on her face. "We'll go together," he said.

"Good," she said. "I don't want to hang out here by myself."

"It's probably best we stay together," he said, turning the engine off.

They got out of the car and shut the doors softly. The clicks were barely noticeable. The creaking floorboards ominously forewarned of their coming as they made their way across the open front porch. Marilynn pushed her key into the doorknob and unlocked the door.

"Let me go in first," said Doug firmly.

"I'll be the one right behind you," she whispered.

He turned the doorknob to the left and pushed the door open slightly. It was, to use his vernacular, *Show Time*.

"Ready?" he whispered. In the pitch black darkness, he thought he saw her nod.

He pushed the door all the way open, revealing even darker shadows inside. He was concentrating on trying to identify the approaching dark forms when he was startled by a tug on the back of his shirt.

She had a vise grip on it.

"There's a light switch on your left side," she whispered in his ear.

He felt along the wall until his hand touched a switch. He flipped it on with a disturbingly loud snap. After being in darkness for so long, both had to throw their hands up to block the sudden piercing bright light from their blinking eyes.

Marilynn gasped loudly. The living room had been ransacked. Her dinette set and couch lay upside down. Books were torn and strewn everywhere. Place settings lay smashed into tiny pieces and Jennie's computer, pulled from the back room, was mangled into twisted pieces of metal. Everything she and Jennie owned was trashed.

"What the hell happened here?" she said.

Movement came from the back of the house. Doug grabbed her arm.

"Someone's here," he whispered.

"That came from Jennie's room." said Marilynn. "Jennie!" she called out. "Are you okay?"

"Maybe it's not her," he said in a low voice. "Let's be cautious."

"What if she needs help?"

Doug reached down and picked up a splintered leg broken off a dinette chair and held it above his head, ready for combat.

"Stay behind me," he whispered.

They took several steps to the edge of the hallway and stopped. A low groan came from the back bedroom.

"Jennie!" shouted Marilynn, charging down the corridor before Doug could stop her.

"Stop!" he yelled, charging down the hallway after her. He didn't know the layout of the house, so he stopped to look in each room along the way.

A shrill scream directed him to the right one.

When he rushed in the doorway he was knocked to the floor by a burly guy coming out. Struggling to get up, he fell back down. Brandishing his stick he shouted, "Stop, or I'll shoot."

But the assailant had already reached the front door, slamming it behind him as he left. Doug lay gasping, struggling to regain his breath. Marilynn sat on the edge of Jennie's bed, cradling her roommate's head.

"I'm here, Jennie" she whispered, fighting back tears.

On his feet again, Doug found a light switch and flipped it. He made his way over to the bed and immediately saw that Jennie was in a bad way. Her eyes were crimson, gruesome from many broken vessels. Blood seeped from the side of her head and her mouth was moving but no sound came.

"Don't try to talk," whispered Marilynn. "Just hold on. I've called 9-1-1, and they'll be here any minute."

Doug felt helpless standing by Marilynn's side.

Jennie opened bloodshot eyes and choked out, "Sorry, mom. I mean - big sister. I... I .... should havvvvve ..... put ...the alarm on......."

"There's nothing to be sorry about," stammered Marilynn. "You're going to be okay. I'll make sure of it. Just hold on a little longer."

"So, this must be Doug," she whispered.

Marilynn nodded and said sweetly, "Yes. This is Doug."

Jennie closed her eyes and said through dry lips, "Two words, Dream Guy."

Marilynn couldn't speak, she just kept stroking the girl's hair as tears rolled down her cheeks.

"The chip – I..... found information......"

"That can wait," said Marilynn, stroking off sweat that had formed on Jennie's forehead.

Jennie's voice was fading. She gathered in a big breath and said clearly, "I saved it to disc and hid it in a place no one would think of. Oh yeah. I also saved it to my website. It's some pretty scary stuff."

She coughed up some blood and her eyes rolled in her head. She breathed in several sporadic breaths, before looking up and forcing a flat smile. Marilynn forced a smile back through tightly clenched lips. Tears streamed down her cheeks.

"Don't forget what I told you," said Jennie in a barely audible voice.

"What's that?" whispered Marilynn, stroking the girl's hair.

"You don't always need men," she laughed in her final breath.

"Noooooo!" screamed Marilynn, pulling Jennie's bloodied head to her chest.

Doug placed his arm gently on Marilynn's shoulder and

held her firmly against his body. He knew it was little consolation.

They stayed like this for several minutes until finally she looked up and their eyes met.

"What good did it do?" she cried.

Doug looked at her with deep compassion, fighting back his own tears. "What good did what do?" he asked softly.

"I'm one of the top trauma doctors in the state. What freakin good did it do?"

He had no answer.

Marilynn rocked back and forth, clutching Jennie's lifeless body. Off in the distance, the wailing sirens of Rescue One screamed as it rushed towards 20 Water Street, not realizing it would be just another dead body for the morgue.

* * *

They stood at the front door, with Doug's arm wrapped around Marilynn's shoulder, watching the rescue truck drive away until it disappeared into the night on its way to complete its grim mission.

Marilynn's tear filled eyes met Doug's.

"The side of your face," said Doug. "It's bleeding. Are you okay?"

"I'm fine," she answered. "I struggled with the killer when I ran into Jennie's room and I fell and hit my face on the bedpost."

"If I ever get my hands on that guy, he'll wish he never was born," said Doug, through gritted teeth.

Marilynn put her arms around his waist and pulled him tight against her shivering body. "I'd hate to be him, then," she said, her head buried deep in his chest.

"I don't want to pressure you in such an emotional time," said Doug, "but we should get out of here before somebody comes back looking for us."

"You're right," Marilynn sniffled, wiping away tears. "But

first we need to find the disc Jennie hid. It contains all the information she found."

"She didn't tell you where it is, did she?"

"No. She died before she could," said Marilynn, rubbing her nose on her shirtsleeve. She sniffled twice and said, "She said she hid it somewhere no one would think to look. And to use her words, *it's some pretty scary stuff.*"

"If we can find it, my ex-wife has a computer we can download it to. It's also connected to the Internet in case we need to go to any web sites. It's really my computer, but she got it in the divorce settlement. I don't think she'll mind if we use it."

"I don't care if you hate your ex-wife, Doug. Have a little respect for the dead."

"Hey, that's how I feel."

Marilynn shook her head.

"I don't give a crap how she felt about me, but she was never there for our daughter."

Marilynn's eyes had the look of disappointment and Doug immediately felt guilty.

"Okay, I'm sorry she's dead. And I won't talk bad about her, at least until more time passes. After that I can't promise anything."

"If you ever want closure," said Marilynn, "you need to forgive her."

She headed for the back bedroom, but stopped and turned around. "Not for her sake, but for you and Cassandra so you can move on with your lives."

"I see your point," said Doug. "I'll give it a shot. It's just going to take some time."

"Do the best you can," said Marilynn. "Now let's go find the disc. Time's wasting."

She headed off to search Jennie's bedroom. He went to the living room and started rummaging through the mess on the floor. He knew it was probably fruitless, but he checked the mangled computer to see if it was still inside the disc drive.

It wasn't.

After ten futile minutes, he went to find Marilynn in the back bedroom. It was obviously Jennie's, because it was designed with bright cheery colors with curtains that were yellow and green striped. The floor was covered with a maroon shag rug and the walls were covered with pictures of therapists instructing the proper way to give massages. On the bureau were several bottles of assorted massage oils with exotic names.

Marilynn was busy searching through dresser drawers when he stepped beside her. "This is like looking for a needle in a haystack! There has to be a better way."

"I need to think about this for a minute," she said, sitting down on the edge of the bed. "Jennie said she put it in a place no one would think to look."

"Then you need to think like Jennie," he said, "if you want to find the disc. What would be a strange or weird hiding spot in her mind?"

Marilynn buried her chin in the palm of her right hand. Leaving her in deep thought, Doug went to the kitchen to see about finding something to eat, as he knew they were both starved. He found the room unharmed. Grabbing a half loaf of wheat bread off the sideboard, he opened the refrigerator. He scanned the contents of the top shelf: half a can of tuna; an unopened bottle of mayonnaise; a quart carton of soymilk; a head of lettuce, a bag of carrots and a package of sliced mushrooms. The bottom shelf had an assortment of apples and a couple of kiwis, plus an unopened package of ground turkey and six cups of various fruit flavored yogurt.

"I'd starve to death living here," moaned Doug, sliding open the drawer of the deli tray. "This is more like it!" he said, reaching in and pulling out a package of sliced American cheese and a deli pack of smoked ham. Before closing the refrigerator door, he took out the head of lettuce and bottle of mayonnaise. Placing all the contents on the kitchen countertop, he began to make four ham and cheese sandwiches. He was just about finished when he heard Marilynn yell.

"I know where it is!" she shouted.

Doug put down his knife and raced back to find her waiting for him at the bathroom doorway. "I know where she put it!" she said excitedly.

"Where?" said Doug.

She opened the medicine cabinet, then reached inside and pulled out a blue box labeled Twelve Hour Protection Tampons on the side. She opened the top flap and reached her fingers inside. After maneuvering them a little, she pulled out a square white paper cover. Tilting it sideways, she slid out a shiny silver disc.

"Not bad," said Doug, "and not surprising either."

"Now we have to get to your house so we can use the computer."

Doug took her by the hand. "Come with me first," he said, dragging her off to the kitchen, where he proudly showcased his main course.

"I'm impressed!" she said. "What if someone comes?"

"I'm starving," he said. "I think we can chance a minute."

They moved their feast to the kitchen table and sat on wooden stools, where they quickly started devouring their sandwiches. "Hold on!" said Marilynn getting up from the table and walking off towards a back pantry. "I've got just the right drink!"

Swiping a couple of drops of sweat off his forehead, Doug said under his breath, "I'll bet it's carrot juice or some awful tasteless fruit drink." He felt a little winded and leaned on the table to catch his breath.

"Tah Dah!" said Marilynn, reappearing with a couple of Budweisers.

Doug's eyes lit up. "Now that's more like it! I'm so thirsty!"

CHAPTER 17

9:49pm
Lake Shore Drive

It took only fifteen minutes to get to the silent, uninhabited house on Lake Shore Drive.

"There's a spare key," said Doug reaching under the welcome mat. "I know, not very imaginative." He unlocked the side door and pushed it inward and the smell of death greeted their nostrils. It was many times worse than a rotting refrigerator.

Stepping inside, he flipped a switch and a ceiling fan with three frosted glass shades instantly bathed the room in soft florescent glow. After Marilynn was inside, he closed the door and locked it. Stepping over beer cans, wine bottles and various clothes that were still strewn on the floor, they made their way down a narrow corridor. He opened a wooden door and stepped through, and she followed him up the stairs to the second floor.

When they reached the top he said, "Follow me. The computer room's down the hall."

"This is not a bad house," said Marilynn.

"Thanks," he said, leading her down the hallway.

"I really like the tower that goes up the side. You should seriously think about keeping this place. But I'd hire a cleaning service first."

Stopping just outside a doorway, he turned to her. "That was my first thought. It's a great place to live, especially since it's close to the waterfront. Hey! My ex-wife may have been a dingbat, but she knew a fantastic house when she saw it."

Marilynn shook her head at the mention of dingbat.

They entered a room with eggshell colored walls. The only decorations were pictures of snowy mountains with snowcapped pine trees. In the far corner was a black, contemporary, two-tiered computer desk with several drawers. Sitting on the top shelf were the monitor and printer. A gray tower containing the hard drives sat on the floor, out of the way. The keyboard and a phone sat on the main desk top. Nothing about the room suggested it was a converted bedroom.

Doug stepped in front of the computer and rolled out a high-back maroon leather chair. "Ahhhh!" he sighed, sitting back. "This is a great chair. I can't tell you how many times I'd fall asleep while I was working or playing on the computer." He closed his eyes and whispered, "I'd forgotten how much I missed it!"

"Another time," she said, shaking his shoulder.

He sat up and switched the computer on. After it downloaded all its settings he placed Jennie's silver disc in the drive and it instantly began humming as the information started to download.

"Your turn," he said, getting up.

Marilynn sat back in the leather chair and immediately groaned with pleasure. "You're right," she said. "This is a great chair. I could fall asleep in this in about ten seconds."

"Well you can't," he said. "Your agenda's a little full right now."

"Right," she said, clicking on the d-drive, which showed that there were two files. Suddenly the screen cleared, then turned to all white as the computer worked feverishly inside. "I don't know what's going on," she said, "but whatever it is, it's big." After several minutes the screen changed to one sentence in a font that filled the entire screen. "*WATCH YOUR BACK, YOGA GIRL!*" The screen cleared again and brief instructions came up: There are two files for you to open – *Base and Noposam*. Click on the one you wish to open.

She chose Base.

"This should be interesting," said Doug.

They watched the screen change and flicker various times for about thirty seconds, spewing an assortment of hues in a wavy pattern across the monitor until the file was open. What they saw on the screen was an old black and white photo. Marilynn read, "Scientist John Woodsen and staff – July 21, 1969, B.J. Stockton Military Base, Virginia."

"Who the heck are they?" he said.

"I don't know," she said. "Let's see what else is there." She hit the Page Down button and a second black and white picture popped up on the screen. It was another group of scientists in suits and its caption read, "Scientist Woodsen and replacements." The date on the photo was June 12,1970. B.J. Stockton Military Base, Virginia.

"Pretty much the same stuff," he said. "Can't be that important."

"Why was the original group suddenly replaced with these guys?" she said.

"Great question," he said, leaning forward with both hands on the desk. "Let's see if there are any other pictures that can offer us a clue."

She paged down again and another group photo was revealed. The date under it was May 19, 1973, at the same military base. This one was another completely different group of people.

"Interesting," he said, removing his hands off the desk and straightening up.

"What?" she asked.

"Woodsen's not in this picture."

"Wonder why?" she said, rubbing her chin.

He put his hands in his pockets. "Let's see if there are any answers to this new riddle."

Excited, Marilynn struck the Down key with the type of force needed to push down a key on an old typewriter.

"Whoa!" said Doug. "A color photo."

"August 30th, 1980," she read. "There's no other information, but there's no mistaking they're all military."

"These guys look pretty intense," he said.

"I wonder if they're scientists."

"They look more like eggheads than fighters. What else have you got?"

She shrugged, then hit the Down button. There was nothing there but black.

"I guess that's it," she said, leisurely striking it a second time. Suddenly, a full-page photo filled the screen.

"Damn!" she cried. "Look at the inscription. General Thomas Uxbridge and staff. B.J. Stockton Military Base, Virginia, March 1, 2000."

Doug placed his hand on her shoulder. "So that's our buddy Uxbridge?"

"That's the *scumbag*," she said, with emphasis on scumbag.

"At least you can now put a face to the scumbag."

"I'd like to put more than a face to him," she said fiercely.

Doug rubbed her shoulders a few times. "Easy, To-ens, I think a time will present itself for you to speak your mind. Are there any other pictures?"

She punched the Down key five more times, but the screen stayed blank. "That's all that's in this file."

"This guy Woodsen must have been pretty important," said Doug. "My gut feeling tells me we're not through with him yet."

"One way to find out," said Marilynn, closing up Base then clicking open the *Noposam* file.

Again the screen went black, then the computer's hard drive flashed and hummed as it pulled the file up.

The screen flashed white several times. At first it looked like there was a downloading problem, but after a minute, large ominous words materialized on the screen:

YOU HAVE ACCESSED A SECURED GOVERNMENT AREA. LEAVE IMMEDIATELY! IT IS A FEDERAL CRIME TO ENTER THIS GOVERNMENT DOMAIN AND IS PUNISHABLE BY THIRTY

YEARS TO LIFE IN PRISON AND OR FINE OF UP TO $500,000. THIS IS YOUR LAST WARNING TO LEAVE THIS CLASSIFIED SITE!

"Holy shit!" said Doug, pulling a chair next to hers. "What the hell have you got here?"

"I don't know."

The screen went black again. They sat speechless, staring at the blank screen. Finally, they watched as brown and white pixels worked their way painstakingly downward from the top. At first it wasn't recognizable, but as it got about halfway down, they knew exactly what it was.

"Jesus!" he said. "This is unbelievable!"

What they saw on the monitor when it had fully downloaded was a full screen insignia for the SIA: The Special Intelligence Agency. Located in every corner was a small American flag. Written across the bottom was the slogan: "*The last line of defense when all others quit!*"

"Fuck!" yelled Doug, standing up and sliding his chair out of the way. Stepping back several steps from the computer he said, "Close it up before they catch us!"

Looking back over her shoulder, Marilynn said calmly, "Relax. This is only a copy of Jennie's e-mail file. They can't trace it here."

"They know where it originated and it won't take them long to figure out places to look!"

"That's probably true," she said. "But I owe it to Jennie and all the innocent people who are dying to find out what I can. If this jeopardizes my safety, then I'm willing to take that chance. If you have a problem with that, then leave and I'll go it alone!"

"Don't get me wrong. I'm not afraid of finding out the truth. Why do you think I work in the TV news business? I just think we need to use caution. These guys play hard ball."

"Understood," she said. "Especially since we've seen their work firsthand."

"This is overwhelming," he said. "Hold on a minute, I need another beer."

After he left the room, he wiped his forehead free of a few blotches of dampness. He needed the beer to quench the unquenchable thirst he had recently acquired. When he reached the kitchen, he leaned up against the refrigerator to catch his breath. After a brief respite, he grabbed a couple of generic beers out of a mostly empty pantry and returned to the den before suspicion was aroused.

"Thanks!" she said, taking one of the bottles. "Ready?"

He nodded. "Okay To-ens, let's go get 'em."

She struck the Down key. A small picture popped on the screen. The caption read, "Scientist John Woodsen and Captain Thomas Uxbridge."

"Uxbridge was only a captain when this was taken," she said, striking the Page Down key.

This time, the heading *The NOPOSAM Project* filled the screen.

"Jackpot!" said Doug, tapping his bottle with a clank against hers. "This is the break we've been looking for."

"Yeah," she said, but her voice was filled with anxiety. Her hand shook noticeably as she struck the Down key, barely making contact. The screen went blank for what seemed an eternity, but was really only several seconds. A new heading called *Gov-69* appeared. More information under that began scrolling downward, filling the screen with text.

They glanced over the copy, mostly in computer code or military terminology, much of which they didn't understand.

"What the hell does all this mean?" said Marilynn, throwing her arms in the air.

Equally frustrated, Doug answered, "I don't know, scroll ahead, there must be something we can understand here."

She hit the Escape key several times and the scrolling stopped. What appeared on the screen caused them to take notice.

"Son of a bitch!" said Doug.

Marilynn began reading out loud: "Professor John Woodsen, founder – NOPOSAM Project, April 10, 1969."

Born December 10, 1929.

Chelsea, Massachusetts
Married: June 23, 1952
Delores Pinto
Providence, Rhode Island
Scientist, EDC
Experimental Development Company
Pittsfield, Massachusetts
1965 - 1969

Professor, MIT
Massachusetts Institute of Technology.
1969 - 1973
Status: retired
Block Island, R.I.

Access Code (Eradicated)
Current status: (Not Available)
Confidence Level: High.

Project NOPOSAM – Original design: Mini computer chip placed internally under the skin, intended to help extreme trauma or terminally ill patients. Method: Humane death, by putting patient peacefully to sleep.

Government altered chip design: Termination by superficial trauma, for military weapon application only.

Warning: NOT INTENDED FOR PUBLIC USE.

Marilynn slumped deep in her chair. Her arms fell limp at her sides. She sat open mouthed. It was as if she'd seen her best friend of many years, someone she'd known as a meek and pious person, suddenly arrested for a vile crime.

Doug paced in a short circle, vigorously rubbing his head. Suddenly he stopped short. "What the hell is this?"

"It's nothing like I expected," answered Marilynn, sitting up.

Neither moved or said anything. The room was quieter than a wake. Outside, the night noises grew louder. It was as if the house was in the middle of the deepest jungle of

Africa. The ticking of a wall clock bounced from wall to wall, like the cracks and pops of a long ping pong volley. Marilynn put her hands together in her lap, as if in prayer. Doug bit on his thumbnail with vigor.

Spitting a piece of nail away he walked over and tapped her on the shoulder. "We need to get to Block Island. We have to find Woodsen."

Glancing back over her shoulder, she said, "How? By swimming?"

Looking at the clock on the wall he said, "It's ten fifteen. Let's find out when the next ferry leaves. More than likely, it's early tomorrow morning."

"Do you know the number?"

"No, but I know where to find it," he said pulling out his ex-wife's personal phone book from the bottom drawer of the desk. He thumbed through a couple of pages. "Here it is, under 'B' for Block."

Using the phone on the desk, he dialed the number. After several rings a deep male voice answered.

"Hello," said Doug. "I realize it's late, but when is the next scheduled ferry to the Island?" He turned towards Marilynn and repeated, "The last ferry leaves in about forty-five minutes? Thanks! We'll be there before it leaves."

Hanging up the phone, he said, "There's a special ferry leaving for the island carrying a few rich people. I guess they paid a lot of money for the extra late run."

"Do you think we can make it in time?"

"We'll have to fly, but if we leave now, we should be able to catch it."

"And if we don't catch it?"

Doug stroked his forehead and said, "How good a swimmer are you?"

There was a disturbance out in the front yard. With eyes wide, Marilynn whispered, "Did you hear that?"

Doug nodded.

Pounding suddenly rocked the front door.

"Company!" he said. "Grab the disc. I know a secret way out."

She hit the eject button and the disc drive popped open. She snatched the silver DVD and slid it back into its protective sleeve, then put back it inside the Tampon box.

Doug looked at her quizzically.

"Makes a great hiding place."

"Good point," he said, grabbing her by the wrist. "Come on."

"Wait!" she said, yanking free. "I've got to close out the computer! We can't leave it for them to find."

There was more pounding.

"Make it fast. That door isn't going to hold out much longer."

She closed the file, then opened the *My Computer* icon. Doug watched her drag the Base and NOPOSAM files into the Recycle Bin and emptied it to the sound effect of breaking glass. She then did a crash shutdown by yanking the plug out.

"Finished?" he asked.

This time, she nodded.

The floor shook from a violent crash downstairs.

"They're inside!" he said. Grabbing her hand he dragged her towards the back of the house, following a narrow hallway to its end.

He released her hand and whispered, "This is where we get out." He jumped up and hit the ceiling above his head and a thirty-four by thirty-six inch wooden tile pushed away leaving a hole. "Give me your foot, and I'll boost you up."

The urgency in his voice told her to hurry, so she stuck her right foot into his cupped hands and grabbed hold of his shoulders for balance.

"Ready?" he whispered. She tapped him on the right shoulder and he lifted her up with little effort. She grabbed hold of the wooden opening and she pulled herself until the ceiling swallowed her. With a flick of his hand he motioned her away from the hole, then quickly leapt to the edges of the hole and pulled himself up, chin-up style. He worked his elbows through and braced himself for a big push. Marilynn got behind him and grabbed hold of his shoulders.

Neither moved.

They heard footsteps coming down the hallway. Doug turned his head around towards Marilynn and mouthed the word, "Now". He pushed while she pulled and he finagled his butt onto the ceiling pulling up one leg and then the other, just as someone wearing a contamination suit and carrying a rifle appeared below them. The soldier searched the left bedroom, as they stared down through the opening in the ceiling.

Doug grabbed the free tile and with as little noise as possible, started sliding it over the hole. He stopped when he had it halfway. The soldier turned 180 degrees and walked to the threshold of the right bedroom, where he stood checking it out.

Doug nodded towards the hole and she caught his drift. Taking hold of the other side of the tile, they lifted it softly and nestled it back into position.

Not a moment too soon. The soldier suddenly looked up.

They sat in semi-darkness in what was an undersized attic. Besides lots of dust, there were small boxes strewn randomly about the room. "This way," said Doug, crawling toward a gleam of light in the middle of the wall twenty feet ahead. Guided by this beacon, they crawled in darkness on all fours across bare plywood flooring. The unsanded floor was rough on their hands and knees, but neither whimpered or complained as they navigated around a few boxes that blocked their path. When they had covered a safe distance from the hole they stood. Because the ceiling was low, they were slightly bent over as they walked the rest of the way to the window. When they stood looking out through an illuminated glass pane, they realized the source of light was a nearby streetlight.

Marilynn whispered, "So how do we get out of here?"

"Through here," answered Doug even softer.

Standing with hands on hips she whispered tersely. "I can't fit through there."

"Through where?' he whispered back.

"This window?" she said.

"We're not going out the window," he said, shaking his head and smiling.

"Where then?"

Waving her to follow, he said, "Come on."

They went to the right, where the plywood ended. Stepping lightly on six inch support beams as if they were on a balance beam, they found there was just enough head room where the roof peaked and the going was easy. When they reached the far wall they found a small wooden door, about five feet by three.

"This door leads to the tower that goes up the side of the house. It actually extends up another floor above the house.

"So what's the problem?"

"Before we go out, I need you to understand that there could be someone on the other side. You willing to take a chance?"

Marilynn smiled a tight-lipped smile. "You need to ask that after all we've been through?"

Before he could answer, she grabbed his lapel and pulled him close. He had heard the same muffled banging sound she had.

"They're at the escape tile," he said.

"What do we do?" she asked, nestled against his chest

Turning the doorknob slowly he said under his breath, "*Show time*."

Ducking low, he stepped through the doorway with Marilynn following close behind. The same streetlight pushed its filtered light in through a large window on the far wall, which was half covered by a dark green curtain. They stood in a room that was about 12 foot square, with wooden stairs on the opposite side leading either up to the floor above, or down to the one below.

Doug motioned for her to wait. He stepped cautiously

over to the stairway and leaned over the guardrail. There were two sentries, one at the base of the floor below and another at the base of the first floor.

Turning back towards her, he shook his head.

There was a commotion. He looked back down to the second floor and his eyes made contact with the sentry, who had now been joined by a second one. A shot rang out and a wood chip from the railing flew past his head.

"Come on!" he yelled, running for the stairs.

Marilynn was right on his tail.

Several more shots rang out, striking the walls around them. Marilynn stumbled and fell with a shout, banging her knees on the wooden steps.

Doug was many stairs ahead when he looked behind and realized she wasn't following. He started back down so fast that he almost tripped, but caught himself from taking a header by grabbing hold of a side railing. As his foot reached the bottom, another round flew past his ear, hitting the wall behind him and sending shards of wood chips flying.

"Fuck!" he shouted, wrapping arms and hands over his head and ducking. "Come on!" he yelled, reaching out and helping Marilynn to her feet. He dragged her unceremoniously up the stairs, their destination being the flat above. When they made the next level, he went to the east wall and gripped a metal grate insert that protected a large rectangular window. With both hands, he yanked it free so they could see outside.

Three plain cars were parked randomly in front and an official looking black SUV with Government plates was half on the lawn and half in the street. The engines were running and the headlights were on, as if waiting for quick getaways.

The window was held shut by a simple turn screw that worked like a dead bolt. Doug twisted the screw counterclockwise and the window popped outward. A burst of warm air rushed into their faces.

"Follow me," he whispered. Pushing both arms through,

he was able to wriggle his body most of the way out the two-and-a-half-foot wide window, before diving the rest of the way onto a small roof that jutted out towards the front yard. He peeked back through the hole.

"You can do it," he said softly.

"I'm not a contortionist like you," she whispered.

"Come on," he said, his voice strained with urgency. "We don't have much time!"

Being smaller in stature, she was able to make it through the portal easier and faster than he had. Holding on to his arm for balance, she said, "What next?"

"We climb down that tree," he said, pointing to a giant oak which grew close to the house, still green, because it was too early to be touched by Mother Nature's kaleidoscopic fall foliage show.

Shots rang out and they ducked, then squatted.

"Did you grow up in a circus?" she asked, throwing her hands up.

"I used to do this all the time when I had to paint the house. It saved me getting up on a ladder."

"So how do we get down the tree?" she said, rubbing her chin.

"Listen!" said Doug, looking back towards the hole they had just climbed out. There was no mistaking what they heard.

Voices!

* * *

Doug had shimmied his way down the tree and stood waiting on the ground, waving her to follow. Marilynn had jumped to a branch ten feet above his head and was planning her next move when shots rang out, just missing her and striking the branch she stood on, splitting the bark.

Holding onto the limb above her head with both hands, she started to lose her balance as more shots were fired. Her foot almost slipped out from under her and she struggled with her balance, but caught it in time. Then her left hand slipped off, leaving only one hand to grip with.

"Jump!" shouted Doug, as she bobbed forwards and backwards like a drunk at a New Year's Eve party.

"What?" she yelled back.

More shots splintered around her.

"I'll catch you," he said, holding his arms out.

She leaped into his arms and they fell to the ground in a heap. She rolled off him and got to her feet. "Are you okay?" she asked, helping him up.

"I'm fine. The ground broke my fall."

Gunshots from the window they'd left sent an unrelenting rain of bullets all around them. The looks they each saw in the other's eyes said, "We're lucky to be alive."

Not needing to urge each other on, they sprinted hand in hand towards their car. The pop, pop, pop of rapid gunfire was at their backs, and bullets riddled the dirt and grass around their churning feet.

"Better the ground than us," she said, trying to catch her breath.

Dull thumps and pings sprayed the side of the beat-up red jalopy, just after they jumped in. The shooters were closing in on their marks.

Marilynn shrieked a long, piercing scream.

Doug yelled too, as he stepped hard on the gas and they sped off.

After a few moments, he looked back over his shoulder and said, "They'll be on us in no time."

"What're you saying?" she asked.

"I'm saying, we can't outrun them in this junk. We need something with more balls!"

White smoke poured out the back, as the car struggled to give its all.

"We promised Dot we'd leave her car somewhere where she could find it and that I'd notify her where it is."

"I really don't want to stop, but this car is no help."

"Up ahead!" she shouted. "There's a shopping plaza."

He slowed the car as he drove into a brightly illuminated mini-mall entrance almost on two wheels. They passed by six small mom and pop stores and had covered about five hundred feet searching for the right place to park, when Marilynn grabbed his arm. "Pull in there!"

He drove forward into a space directly in front of a closed barbershop.

Marilynn pulled out her cell phone.

What are you going to do?" asked Doug.

"I'm going to call Dot, to let her know where her car is."

"I don't know if that's wise," said Doug. "It could be tapped by now."

"Then give me yours."

"We can't take a chance with mine either. They could both be tapped."

"Then how the hell do I let her know the car is here?"

"Look!" said Doug, pointing to the right side of the barbershop.

"Excellent idea," said Marilynn, jumping out of the car and jogging over to an old-style phone booth. She slipped inside and the accordion door snapped shut with a loud thump briefly startling her. Reaching into her pants pocket, she fished out a quarter, a dime, and a nickel, and slid them one at a time into a coin slot. After the last chime when the final coin hit the coin box inside, and she had dial tone, she dialed the number scrawled on the wrinkled piece of paper.

After several rings a voice she recognized as Dot's answered, "Hello?"

"Dot, this is the woman you loaned your car to."

"I'm glad you called, Honey," said Dot, barely controlling herself. "The police forced it out of me. I had to tell them you had my car. You guys need to ditch it, because they're on to you."

"They already found us!" shouted Marilynn. "We're leaving your car in a small shopping center." Scanning the parking lot she said, "It's the one with the AM/PM Mart, a video store, Calvin's Car Parts, and the Shop-n-Go Supermarket!"

"I know where that is," said Dot. "It's over on Route 27. You get yourselves out of there as fast as you can!"

"Thanks for everything," said Marilynn. "We'll never forget what you did for us."

"No need to thank me," said the waitress. "I'm sure you have a good reason for what you're doing. Good luck to you and your husband."

Chuckling to herself, she said, "Thanks," then hung up the phone. She couldn't wait to tell Doug that one. Scanning the parking lot, she spied him two rows back on the right sitting behind the wheel of a fairly new silver Toyota Camry. She raced over and jumped into the passenger's seat.

Doug's head was ducked under the dashboard and he was feverishly crossing a red wire with a blue one.

Looking down at him she said, "The police forced Dot to talk. They know we have her car."

"That explains how they found us," he said, stopping to look up at her.

He went back to playing with the wires. "If I can get this thing going, we can borrow this one," he snapped, now in a foul mood.

"You'd better hurry!" she said. "They're probably close by!"

Frustrated, he yelled, "Don't push me! I'm going as fast as I can! I've only done this once before, and that was my uncle's farm tractor."

"Are you telling me you can't hotwire this thing?"

"Car theft is not my regular job!" he snapped.

"That's no way to talk to your wife," she snickered.

"What?" he said, his eyes and face screwed up like the winner of an Ugly Face contest.

"I'll explain later," she said, looking back over her shoulder.

Their new car's engine whined and labored and valiantly tried to start.

"Damn!" he shouted, banging his head on the dash as he turned himself around and sat up. "Almost had it!"

"You didn't try very hard," she said.

Stunned, he said nothing.

Looking out the back window for signs of the police, she said in a calmer voice, "I don't mean to pressure or stress you out, but please try again. I have a very bad feeling."

Suddenly, there was a tap on the windshield. When they looked out, a short stocky man in worn denim coveralls stood pointing a shotgun. Doug opened the door enough to poke his head out. "Whoa, buddy!" he said. "What the hell are you doing with that thing!"

"Don't move!" said a mouth missing most of its teeth. "I know this ain't yer car. Yer tryin' to steal it."

"It's not what you think," said Marilynn. "We have a car just like this one and accidentally got into the wrong one."

"Ma'am, I ain't stupid!" said the middle-aged vagrant. "I seen yer pictures on the TV, and I already called the po - lice."

She stared into his eyes and said, "I don't know who you think we are, but we're just a married couple out buying groceries."

"If that's so, lady" said the man, raising the rifle eye-level, "then where's yer shoppin' bags?"

She had no answer for him.

Lowering his rifle, the man reached behind and pulled from his back pocket a copy of the daily newspaper and threw it inside the car.

"Tell me this ain't you," he said, holding the rifle over his shoulder, pointing away.

Doug reached down and picked the newspaper off his lap. Reading the top headline out loud he said, "*Fugitive couple wanted for questioning in death of Dr. Paul Crawford.* Government officials are anxious to question Dr. Marilynn Harwell of Coventry General Hospital and Doug Talbot, an employee of WJAM-TV, in the brutal murder of State Chief Medical Examiner, Dr. Paul Crawford."

"That's bullshit!" snapped Marilynn. "The State Police tried to tell me that his death was accidental, a result of his drinking, and that my 911 call was inaccurate."

Doug said, "Well, that's not what they're saying now."

"What are you sayin'?" asked the almost toothless man.

"I'm saying that the State Police lied to me. Detective Shelton of the SIA told me the agency found Dr. Crawford dead when they entered the morgue. I know differently, and I'll testify to that. My gut feeling is that *they* were instrumental in his death."

"That's pretty strong accusin'," said the man, still pointing the gun. "I heard they're offerin' a reward."

"Look buddy," said Doug. "I'll make a deal with you. Let us go, and I'll give you three hundred bucks in cash."

The man's eyes narrowed and his head tilted. "Let's see the money."

Off in the distance the sound of fast approaching sirens interrupted their conversation and all three glanced in that direction. Since the sun had set five hours ago, the temperature had dropped a few degrees. It wasn't cold enough to be chilly, but their predicament was.

They returned to their discussion.

"I'm going to reach into my back pocket for my wallet," said Doug, not wanting to make any sudden movements. Pulling it out of his pants, he slid out three bills, which he held up and fanned.

"See? Three one hundred dollar bills."

The sirens were so close they seemed to be just around the corner.

"We don't have much time. Do you want the money in exchange for letting us go or not?"

The man lowered his rifle and rubbed his chin thoughtfully. After agonizing over it he said, "Deal!"

Doug handed him the money through the open door.

"Hey!" the guy shouted. "This is only three dollars!"

"Really," said Doug. "Let me see," he said, suddenly slamming the door into the man's side.

The man yelled and dropped his rifle, which clanked on the ground. Jumping out of the car Doug snatched the rifle and jabbed it into the back of the guy's head, knocking him senseless. He was not accustomed to dishing out violence like this, but recent past events had hardened his usually good nature.

Suddenly, there were screeching tires at the entrance to the mini-mall.

"They're here!" shouted Marilynn.

Doug dragged the unconscious man to the sidewalk and propped him up against the side of the telephone booth so it appeared he was sleeping, then ran back and jumped inside the car.

They locked eyes and Marilynn said, "It would be nice right about now, if you could start this thing."

"Second time's a charm," said Doug, ducking back under the dashboard.

He re-crossed the wires and the engine miraculously caught. "Hey!" he shouted, sitting up. The two slapped high fives, then quickly ducked on the seat as the rear window imploded into tiny bits across the back seat. A ricocheting bullet lodged somewhere inside the back passenger door.

"Stay down!" Doug yelled, as another round of fire struck the side of the car.

"Floor it!" screamed Marilynn, from a squatting position. "Go! Go!"

"Wish I'd thought of that!" he yelled, shoving the shift into drive and slamming the gas pedal to the floor. Squealing tires spun in place, then finally gripped pavement, sending the Camry fishtailing. He fought the steering wheel hard and eventually gained control, just avoiding parked cars. Steering straight, he sped the car out of the opposite side of the parking lot and down a dark two-lane road.

He glanced in the rearview mirror. "I don't see any headlights."

"Give'em time," said Marilynn, staring up from her hiding spot. "They're tenacious."

Moments later, Doug said, "Still no one. I think you can get up."

She climbed back in her seat and pulled the seat belt across her chest, locking it in place.

"You okay?" he asked "You weren't hit anywhere?"

"I don't feel anything," she answered, "other than the usual aches and pains."

"That makes two of us," he said.

"Do you think we can still make the ferry to Block Island?"

Doug looked at the speedometer as they approached a four-way intersection; 87 mph. He pushed harder on the gas pedal as he glanced at her and smiled. "Gonna try like hell. We've got a long ways still to go."

Marilynn sighed deeply, not as a relaxation exercise, but out of frustration. To her, hope seemed to be teetering on the brink of failure.

"Hang in there!" said Doug. "Remember. We live in Rhode Island, the smallest state. You can get anywhere in about forty minutes."

Before they knew what was happening, a dark sedan darted in front of them from the right side of the approaching intersection and stopped directly in their path. Gunfire erupted from the driver's side and back passenger windows smashing their windshield. Doug spun the steering wheel hard to the left almost avoiding it, but the front right quarter slammed the sedan, popping it's hood open.

Their car caromed off and continued on and Doug shouted, "You okay?"

"I think so!" she cried out.

He slammed on the brakes until the car came to a squealing stop at the edge of the road. The smell of burning rubber gagged them as they jumped out and stood looking back at the burning car two hundred feet away. He left the car running, because he didn't know if he could get it started again.

The sedan exploded sending the hood, trunk, and glass flying fifty feet into the air.

Marilynn shielded her eyes. "Do you think anyone got out?"

Doug wiped dampness off his brow. "I don't know," he answered flatly.

Breathing sporadically because of the smoke from the burning sedan, she asked, "How are you going to drive the car with a shattered windshield? You can't see out of it."

He didn't respond. Instead, she had to follow him around to the front of the car where he stood examining it. The windshield was broken in a mosaic pattern and the small cracks made it impossible to see through. He kicked the driver's side tire and punched the air yelling, "This sucks!"

"As true as that may be," she said, "having a hissy fit isn't going to help us."

After doing a double take, he said, "Maybe not, but it sure as hell made me feel better."

"Is it driveable?" she asked.

Besides the broken windshield, the right front side was caved in and the wheelwell was crushed towards the tire, threatening to puncture it.

"I don't know," he said, stooping down and pulling the crumpled metal away from the tire. "We'll find out soon enough." He walked back to the other side of the car and jumped into the driver's seat. Pushing it as far back as it would go, he set both of his feet against the inside of the windshield. Taking a deep breath he pulled his legs back to his chest and thrust his feet against the windshield. It buckled a little but didn't give. Taking aim again, he recoiled and rammed his legs a second time with the same result. Marilynn jumped in the passenger seat and got in position to do the same maneuver. They pulled their legs back into striking position.

"Ready?" said Doug.

She gave him a thumbs-up.

"NOW!" he shouted.

They drove their legs forward with as much force as possible and when their feet struck the window at the same time, the whole windshield pushed out onto the hood.

"HOO! HOO!" shouted Marilynn. Doug high-fived her.

Somewhere off in the near distance, the sounds of encroaching sirens wailed into the night. Doug jumped out and pulled the windshield off the car, throwing it to the shoulder of the road. Sliding back in, he floored the gas pedal and it picked up speed painstakingly slowly, as the engine gave everything it could. Air rushed into their faces through the new gap in front of them and out the back where the rear window used to be.

"We've lost a lot of time," he said, making a right-hand turn onto a darker and more obscure road. "But I know a short cut. We might still make it in time."

"What if we don't make it?" she asked.

"If we're late, I guess we can stand there and wave *bon voyage* as it pulls away. I don't know about you, but I can't swim that far."

She leaned her head back in her seat and sighed, this time from fatigue. They were both exhausted, and they rode in silence over back roads for the next fifteen minutes until the outline of a bridge, lit up by thousands of bulbs as if decorated for Christmas, popped into view.

Marilynn spoke first.

"You're going over the Point Street bridge. I recognize the shape."

"That'll bring us right out to the wharf where the ferry docks."

"How do you know that?"

"I've been to the Island a few times. I took my ex-wife there when we were dating."

"Was it romantic?" she asked, throwing a glance his way.

"Would have been with the right person," he answered, sending a look back.

Marilynn smiled inwardly. "You'd better slow down. A lot of people use the bridge's walkway to get across on foot."

The damaged breaks squealed, slowing the car to twenty-five. Up ahead, a handful of people, young and old, were walking back over the illuminated bridge. When car and bridge met, thumping tires on anti freeze grooves echoed loudly. Somber faces stared in at them as they edged their way slowly across.

"Look at these people," said Marilynn. "They look so desperate." Shooting Doug a look, she continued, "We need to find an antidote soon. We need to end this."

"We will, To-ens," he said soothingly. "We will."

She grabbed his arm and said, "Slow down! There's something up ahead."

They were halfway across the bridge, and he pressed the brake till the car crawled.

"If we go any slower, these people will beat us across," he said.

"I mean it. There's something up ahead on the right side."

He peered forward into a light mist that had come in off the ocean and saw it too.

"What the ...?" he said, as they came up on three people leaning against the bridge's protective side rail. The car squealed painfully like a poor animal caught in a bear trap, as it came to a stop.

"Lower your window," said Doug softly.

Several spotlights illuminated an area over a man and woman, about forty years of age, and a little girl of ten dressed in grungy clothing. Their eyes were hollow and their expressions lifeless and sweat glistened on their foreheads as they stood holding something wrapped in a blanket at the edge of the rusty orange railing.

Doug and Marilynn returned their glares, as if they had been challenged to a staring contest. Without warning, the man turned his back to them and said with a lack of emotion to the woman and child, "On one."

He counted slowly backwards and when the blanket was unfurled at one, they saw a dead boy of about four years. The three raised their arms, then shoved the boy over the edge. A large splash resonated upward and the suddenly disturbed murky water sent shock waves lapping against the sturdy wooden pillars that supported the bridge.

"Jesus! It's come to this?" said Marilynn shaking her head. "Let's go. The sooner we get there, the sooner we can find Professor Woodsen and put an end to this madness."

A horn honked behind their stolen car, prompting them to spin around for a look.

"Is it them?" she asked, anxiously looking back through the space of the missing rear window.

"I don't know," answered Doug. "Let's see what they do."

The car behind them inched closer till it almost touched bumpers. Doug held one foot hard on the brake and pressed the other foot on the accelerator, racing the engine. The tires spun in place. A stinky, rubber-smelling white smoke rose between the cars.

"What are you doing?"

"Hold on tight! I'm gonna try to outrun the bastards to the ferry!"

The car behind flashed its highbeams several times.

"Ready?" he asked.

Nodding once, she flashed a thumbs up.

In the rearview mirror Doug saw a head sticking out the passenger's side window. A teenager's shrill voice shouted, "Come on buddy! Move your ass out of the way!" The driver leaned on his horn and kept flashing his lights. Doug took his foot off the brake and the car lurched forward, spitting pebbles onto the tailgater's windshield. The Camry raced off the bridge and with Doug's strong effort, turned a short bend. A marina appeared about fifty feet ahead.

"There's the ferry!" shouted Marilynn.

Tied to large pylons painted orange around the top was an old wooden ferry called *The Misty Mae*. The draw gate was down and only two cars were parked inside and they looked expensive.

Doug drove up to a pay booth with a lowered stop arm. An elderly security guard sauntered out and stuck his face into Doug's rolled down window.

"Evenin' folks," said a sad voice. "You lookin' to go to the Island?"

"Yes, we are," answered Doug. "How much is it?"

The old man looked away and started to cry. With eyes diverted downward, a shaky and wrinkled hand swiped across his nose, suppressing a sniffle.

"I'm sorry, folks. I lost my wife yesterday morning," said the old man in a low voice. "It was the strangest thing, though."

"How's that?" asked Doug softly.

"She slipped getting out of bed and fell to the floor," replied the old man. "Not really hard, either. She barely made a noise when she landed. Several hours later she complained of being thirsty, and not much later than that she broke out into a nonstop sweat. I gave her bottle after bottle of water, but it just didn't seem to help. Last night, she lay next to me in bed, barely holding on. I poured water down her throat as fast as I could, but....."

"What was your wife's name?" asked Marilynn gently.

"Doris," he answered with downcast eyes. "Doris Marshall. I'm Dave Marshall."

"We're very sorry about Doris. She must have been a wonderful woman, and I can tell you loved her very much."

"That's very kind of you to say, ma'am," said the old man, his eyes never leaving the ground.

The mist had turned to a drizzle. Doug turned the wipers to intermittent.

"You shouldn't be working, Mr. Marshall – Dave," said Marilynn. "You should be at home resting."

"There's no one to go home to," he said, shaking his head. "No one to go home to."

The elderly man walked away dejectedly and stepped inside the booth where he struck a button, sending the stop arm up till it remained open. He waved them forward. From inside the booth the old man said, "You folks go on through. There's no charge for kindness tonight."

"Thanks," said Doug, stepping on the gas just enough

to move the car over the draw gate and onto the ferry. He pulled to the right, away from the other cars, and parked. Two short blasts of a horn from the old man's booth signaled the last car.

Two young men untied the ropes that tethered the ship to the pylons and flung them onto the deck of the ferry. Underneath them, a diesel engine roared to life. The ship shuddered, then lurched forward, moving methodically away from the wharf. Three shrill blasts of the ship's air horn meant they were really on their way across the ocean to the Island.

CHAPTER 18

11:07pm

Sitting on a bench on the starboard side of the boat, Doug stared longingly at the lump lying on his lap. He knew this was the first real sleep Marilynn had gotten in a long time. It had been a strange and harrowing couple of days on the run, and they both looked frazzled. But to him, she had never looked more beautiful. He stroked her hair gently several times and she stirred, but didn't wake.

A strange, breathless feeling gripped his queasy stomach. *Damn,* he thought. *"I haven't felt about a girl like this since I was in high school."* He sighed deeply, his breath pushing out a puff of smoky air. Layers of built-up anger and despondency seemed to be slowly peeling away, exposing his longing for a lasting, fulfilling, and loving relationship. She had that kind of effect on him. He thought about his relationship with his ex-wife and realized that he had never experienced feelings like this with her. And they'd been married eight years.

Surprisingly, he found his fingers lightly stroking her eyebrow, tracing its way down her cheek, and then finally settling on her full lips. This time she opened her eyes. He yanked his hand away and she smiled.

Sitting up and stretching her arms to the sky, she asked groggily, "Where are we?" Overhead, an airhorn blasted twice into a foggy night, until it dissipated into midnight darkness. The rain had stopped right after they'd put out to sea, and scattered stars randomly poked through a sky fighting to clear itself of dark, ominous clouds.

"We'll be docking in a short while," he answered softly.

"Did I sleep the whole way over?" she asked, looking up with half-closed eyes.

"I guess you were pretty tired."

"Did you get any rest?"

"There'll be plenty of time for that later. Besides, we should be on the island in about ten minutes."

She put her head on his shoulder, then reached down and slid her hand in his. "Tell me about Doug Talbot," she said, snuggling against his chest.

"Like what?" he asked.

"I don't know anything about you or your past, other than you work at a TV station, that you and your wife are divorced, and that you have Cassandra. I want to know more."

"There's not much else to tell, and the little there is, is boring!" he protested. "You tell me more about you first, and then I'll fill you in on the mundane trivialities of my life."

"Fine," she said, sitting up straight and unclenching her hand from his. She cleared her throat and breathed deeply. "I was born in Michigan thirty-one years ago in a small rural hospital. It was a complicated birth, so I won't bore you with the technical details and jargon, but suffice to say, my mother died soon after I came out."

Doug affectionately rubbed her back as she continued: "I was a healthy seven-pound, six ounce baby, who my dad, George Harwell, did a great job of raising by himself. He never remarried, so I never had any brothers or sisters. We lived pretty well, though, and I never wanted for anything. But I had to work for what I got, because my father was a strict, but fair, person."

She paused to catch her breath and thoughts. Soft laps of the endless jet-black ocean against the sides of the old wooden ferry, could be heard above the constant hum of her engine. Marilynn filled her lungs with salty air and went on: "I always worked hard in school and got great grades:

even way back in grammar school. I had to: my father was a professor at a big college and he wouldn't accept anything less than a 'B+'."

Doug manipulated her shoulders by applying slight, soothing, and affectionate pressure. Fully relaxed, Marilynn let out a deep sigh. Breathing the salty sea air deeply again she continued: "I breezed through high school. I actually skipped the second, fifth and tenth grades, because I was too advanced for them. I then entered medical school at an Ivy League college at the tender age of fifteen. It was the first time I struggled to get good grades and it took all of my effort, so dating was not an option till I graduated. Eventually, I made it through medical school and got my degree. On graduation day, my dad suffered a massive heart attack while sitting in the audience, and died right there." She paused, and Doug pulled her close against his chest. Her head dropped down to her own chest and he felt her body rise and drop with each labored breath. "Pretty funny, huh," she said sadly. "I get my medical degree and I can't even help my father."

He kissed her softly on her cheek. "Sometimes," he said, "things happen for a reason. They are beyond our control and no matter what we tried to do, or thought we should have done, it still would have worked out the same way. Some people call that destiny. Tell me more," he encouraged, squeezing her hands together in his.

She sat up and stroked his two-day-old stubble. "You're stalling."

"No, I'm not. I really want to know more."

She didn't believe him, but settled back in his arms and went on anyway. "There's not much more to tell. My residency was at Coventry General, where I worked my way up to top Trauma doctor for the past three years. I've never married, although I want a family with two or three kids."

"How come you never married?" he asked.

"I guess I didn't find the right one," she answered. She sighed and said downheartedly, "I don't know. Maybe I'm just too damn picky and should have settled on the first one to ask. Maybe the right person did come along, only I was too dumb to realize it because I was looking for the perfect one. *My dream guy*."

"I think you did the right thing," he said. "You should never just settle. Look at my marriage, that wasn't exactly a model one."

"Okay! I told you about me, now tell me all about you!" she said, mussing his hair.

"Like I said, there's not much to tell." He ran his hand over his head a couple of times in an effort to straighten his hair. "You already know every boring detail of my life."

"Bull!" she snapped. "I opened up my vault of personal information, now you have to do the same."

"Fine," he muttered. "Remember? I'm not good at this, but you know that already."

"Indulge me. Tell me about *your* past."

"I sure could use a beer right now!" he said.

"Is that part of your past, that you have a drinking problem?"

"No," he said, lightly tapping her on the nose with his index finger. Wiping his forehead dry, he protested, "You're making me nervous."

"Stop stalling, and start talking."

He shook his head and pouted. "I was born and raised here in Rhode Island," he started, his voice hinting of dread. "I went to school, got a job, got married, had a baby, got unmarried, and now I'm here."

Marilynn playfully slapped his forearm several times. "Do it right!" she demanded. "I'm serious. Tell me the right way."

"Okay! Okay! I'll do it your way." He paused momentarily to collect his thoughts then started again. "There were six kids in my family: three boys and three girls. I'm the oldest of the second three kids."

"Do you have any surviving family?" she interrupted.

"My mom and dad moved to Florida for their retirement. Pretty original, huh? The rest of us are scattered around New England and parts of New York and New Jersey. They're all married with their own families and lives, so Christmas, weddings, and funerals, are about the only time we get together. Are you sure you want to hear this?"

"I want to hear all of it, and I promise to stay awake no matter how boring it gets. But don't take it personally if I start to snore."

"Ha, Ha! Very funny," he said, scrunching up his nose. "You asked for it, so you're going to get it. Believe me, I'll make sure you stay awake. Anyway, I was a quiet, unassuming kid growing up. And unlike you, I was not very good in school. Actually, I hated it, and slept through most of it. However, I did like television. I was fascinated by it, even at a young age. When I was six, my mother would put me to bed and I'd sneak out into the kitchen and peek into the living room to watch along with the grownups. Of course, I'd always get caught, and would whine the same line every time. 'Why can the kids on the TV stay up, but I had to go to bed?' Mom would give the standard answer, *Because they were good kids that always did what their mother told them to do.*

"I played a lot of sports in high school and college, which left little time for studying. However, I did meet my first girl because of sports. Her name was Tiffany, and she was a cheerleader for the varsity high school basketball team. But that didn't last long, because she said I wasn't going in the right direction with my life. That was her way of saying that I wasn't good enough. Most of her family were doctors or lawyers and I didn't see myself smart enough to do that." He paused. "Are you sure you want to hear more?" he asked, hoping she would say no so he could weasel out of the rest.

"Yes, I want all of it," she said, relishing in the uneasiness he was feeling opening up for what she figured was the first time in his life.

"You are a glutton for punishment," he chuckled. "Anyway, I went to a small college on a basketball scholarship and met a girl who was in the drama study program. She was usually the lead in all the plays and was actually pretty good. After dating for a year, we talked about marriage and a family. But that didn't last too long, because she said I was too nice."

Several long, forlorn blasts of the foghorn pierced the never-ending pitch-black night. There were no echoes. Overhead, the sky had almost cleared itself of bursting rain clouds, and the moon was fighting to shine through a few scraggly clouds.

"I don't understand," she said, hugging herself from the cool night air. "What did she mean, too nice?"

"She said I didn't know how to fight. Imagine that! I'm telling her that I love her and that I want to get married and settle down and have a family, which I thought was what women want to hear, and she's complaining that I didn't know how to fight!"

"Calm down!" said Marilynn softly. "There's no need to get excited."

"I am calm," he said.

"No, you're not," she said, even softer. "Your tone and blood pressure are rising with every word."

"Don't tell me how I feel," he said.

She stroked his hand gently. "Please, Dougie, calm down and lower your voice," she said, in a tone that was overly sweet.

"Don't patronize me," he snapped, pulling his hand away.

She started laughing uncontrollably.

"What?" he asked, confused.

She stopped laughing and said, "You don't have a problem fighting."

"It's easy with you."

"What do you mean?" she asked, her voice serious.

"Because you say things that irritate me."

Her face flushed. "What!" she shouted.

He couldn't keep a straight face. This time he was laughing.

"You bum," she said, again mussing his hair. "So, how did you meet your wife?"

"I met Christine at a delicatessen near the station. I'd go over on my supper break and we'd talk and laugh. We became friends and started dating, and in six months we got married and had a beautiful little girl the following year. The rest is history, as they say."

"Did she ever tell why she left you?"

"Yeah! She said she needed to be young again. I had assumed wrongly that I had married an adult."

"She was going through an unstable mental state," said Marilynn. "Don't judge her too harshly."

"Is that your professional opinion, Doctor?"

"Yes. And it's my personal opinion. I've seen it too many times. And it's not reserved for just women. Many men cheat on their wives with younger women, just to make themselves feel younger, so they can try and cheat the inevitable - old age."

She sat up. "We've slowed way down."

Two short blasts from the foghorn and the shudder from the ship's underbelly as the engines were reversed meant that they had indeed arrived. Blurred by a light fog, the dock's bright floodlights gradually focused into view. The engines were cut and the ship drifted along the side of the dock, where several laborers stood patiently.

They sat silently as the ship glided to a stop, nestling against the dock like a kitten to it's mother. Several of the boat's crew threw lines out to the longshoremen, who secured the ferry to giant weather-worn gray pilings. The soft rhythmic laps against the side of the ferry, now under a moon swept sky was the perfect setting for a romantic interlude. Snuggled in each other's arms, thoughts of heartache and troubles were briefly forgotten. The anguish of the past couple of days ceased to exist, and they both wished they could stay like this forever as they embraced in a long, passionate, X-rated kiss. Several minutes later, it was interrupted by two long blasts of the foghorn, which was their signal it was time to get off.

"Back to reality," said Marilynn, getting to her feet. Refocused, they made their way to their car at the back of the boat, where they sat waiting for the others to leave.

"You know," said Doug, "the beaches and water sports are spectacular here in the summer. And there are souvenir shops with miniature lighthouses and sail boats, and a candy shop that in my opinion, has the best saltwater taffy in the world."

He slipped the gearshift into drive and drove down a short ramp and off the boat, after the second of the other two cars had pulled out. Tires crunched on dirt and stones, much like the crackling sound of a kid's bike rolling over dead bugs, as he steered the car across a sparsely-lit, unpaved road, looking for a place to leave the Camry.

"It's off season now," he said, guiding the car at a snail's pace, "but some day when things are normal, I'd like to bring you back to show you how beautiful it is here, and how much fun it can be."

"Maybe we could vacation here one day," she said. "I've never really been on one."

"Get out," he said, as he made for a small parking lot a short ways down on the opposite side of the dock.

"I'm serious," she said. "I've never been on a vacation."

He pulled the stolen car into a space reserved for visiting utility trucks in a lot that would comfortably fit three trucks or vans. Turning to her he said, "No, I mean it. Get out. We're here."

"Oh!" she said.

"I promise, I'll show you a great time, if we ever get back here."

"And I'm going to hold you to that promise."

"I'll take you on a walking tour, they're unbelievable. There are all kinds of protected endangered species of flowers, and the wildlife is incredible. The excitement in his voice and mannerisms rose as he continued: "You hike through the middle of the island, and it's nothing short of spectacular. At the end of your trek, which takes about an hour, you walk along a high precipice, where there's an impressive view looking out over the inlet, where all types of extravagant sailboats and yachts are anchored."

"It's a date," she said softly, placing her hand over his. Looking out the window, she said, "Is it okay to leave this here?"

With her hand still on his, he answered, "I don't know. Let's check it out."

They met at the back of the car, where Doug pointed out red taillights halfway up a tall wooded hill that led away from them. The car wound its way up a dirt road, weaving serpentine towards a hotel that sat high up, about a quarter of a mile away. If it had been the middle of summer, every room would be occupied and the building would have been lit brighter than Times Square on News Year's Eve, and nearly as active, but being the off season, only two windows were lit. When the car disappeared behind a cluster of pines and oaks, they walked a few feet over to a giant bulletin board that was illuminated by the soft glow of a florescent bulb, shining just enough light for them to read the list of ferryboat runs.

Doug felt his knees go weak. He leaned against the side of the bulletin board, for support. "According to this schedule, the next run won't arrive till noon tomorrow. No utility trucks can get here till then, so it should be safe to park here overnight."

"Now, all we have to do is find Professor Woodsen," she said, brushing hair back with both hands so it stayed tucked behind both ears.

"Let's do it," he said, taking her hand in his and heading down a long wooden boardwalk, where water splashed against breakers twenty feet below. Lightly swaying spotlights latched atop poles about every twenty feet, lit the walkway. The quick rest had given him a jolt of strength to go on.

Wooden planks squeaked and groaned as they stepped determinedly along the weather worn foot walk, even though they didn't know if it was the right direction.

There would be no street sign saying, *this way to the Professor's house.*

Marilynn stopped and stood partially under one of the lights. The left side of her face was dark, hiding the light purple bruise from the accident, and the other side was drenched in light. "Have you thought about how we're going to get there?"

"Block Island is small and there are few cars," said Doug. "See that bike shop up ahead?"

"What about it?"

"Most people rent bikes or mopeds to get around, if they don't care to bring their own."

"But it's closed. What are we supposed to do? Walk?"

"Don't worry. It's not that far. Remember, wherever we have to go, we'll eventually get there by walking. It's a small island. No matter which direction we start from, we'd eventually end up back here."

"What do we do if we can't find his house? Wait till morning and possibly risk the lives of more people?"

Doug squeezed her hand gently. Speaking softly, he said, "We'll find him."

"How do we know he's still alive?"

"We don't. But we won't know unless we try."

"After you," she said, waving him forward. "You're the guide."

They walked briskly away hand in hand, leaving the docks to the deep night and eventual changing tide. In no time they were off the boardwalk and had reached a small town with a general store, a bait and tackle shop, several restaurants, a Dunkin Donuts, and a couple of souvenir shops that were closed. Sitting on rocking chairs out in front of the bait and tackle store, bathed under fluorescent lights that hummed softly, were two white haired, dark-skinned old sailors, with weathered, lined faces.

"Good evening, gentlemen!" said Doug. "Do you know where Professor Woodsen lives?"

The sailor on the left pulled a wooden pipe from his mouth, puffed out a good sized wisp of smoke and said in a deep, crackly New England accent, "You want ta see the *Prof'* at this late time of night, do ya?"

"It's an urgent matter," said Marilynn.

"That's the trouble with young folk today," said the other crusty sailor to his friend, in much the same voice. Drawing several puffs on his pipe he continued, "They're always in a hurry. Everything has to be done yesterday. No patience. No patience a-tall."

Marilynn squeezed Doug's hand as they exchanged glances. Doug spoke again: "We really need to talk with him about a problem that we fear only he may be able to help us with."

"So what's so important that you can't wait till daylight?" asked the first sailor, his head tilted to one side and his face etched with curiosity, even through the deep facial cracks.

Marilynn stepped forward and leaned down till she was inches from their faces and said, "My name is Marilynn Harwell and I'm a doctor at Coventry General Hospital. I need the professor's help in saving a lot of people's lives."

"You don't say?" said the second sailor, rubbing his chin vigorously. "In that case, follow the beach for about three quarters of a mile and you'll see his house set back up on the dunes. You can't miss it."

"Thank you," she said, reaching out and shaking both men's hands in turn. "You don't know how much help you are to us, and your country."

They started briskly towards the pristine beach, with Marilynn struggling to keep up. Soft forgiving sand silenced their footsteps, and their course was straight and unobstructed, with only an occasional trash barrel off to the side, where another boardwalk set thirty feet back ran parallel to the beach.

After several minutes of walking, a faint cry from one of the old men came from behind. "Good luck saving those people."

Guided by a brilliant moon and serenaded by the rhythmic lapping of breaking waves on the smooth sandy beach, they reduced their pace to a brisk walk. The reflected brilliance of the moon over the ocean was like having a personal night light to guide them. Under ordinary circumstances, this would seem like just another couple out for a romantic stroll.

"You're limping," said Doug.

"It's been a while since the car crash. My leg is stiffening up from all these quick stop and goes."

"You've been running around all night with a bad leg and I didn't even know."

"I didn't want to make a fuss, because I knew you'd make a big deal about it," she said. "And it would've slowed us down."

Doug reached his arm around her shoulder and pulled her tight. She placed her head on his shoulder and he grinned as big as the Cheshire cat in *Alice in Wonderland*. Then for the umpteenth time he thought, "What a woman!"

The sands they now walked on had, only a week earlier, brimmed with Labor Day beach activities. There'd been a half dozen, two on two volleyball games, and plenty of frantic Frisbee throwers racing to pick up missed tosses. Sunbathers on blankets and book readers hidden under giant colorful umbrellas, had stretched from high up on a grassy knoll down to the water's edge. Surfers and kayakers had taken turns paddling out to a safe distance. The now silent beach had been loud with laughter, excitement, and lots of food, mainly consisting of steamed corn, baked lobster and crab, and greasy clam cakes.

"Breathe this salty air," said Marilynn inhaling deeply. "It's so refreshing."

"It tends to clear one's head and sinuses," said Doug.

"If we weren't on such a pressing mission," she said, "I'd lie down right here and fall asleep in your arms."

Doug rubbed her shoulder. "I'll be sure to remind you of that when things are better."

They walked arm in arm along the shore for a long distance, occasionally side-stepping dark green seaweed or smoothed-over driftwood, which the local antique dealers would use to make lamps and coffee tables. They hiked in silence. The soft cool sand gave way easily under their feet, leaving deep imprints of the soles of their shoes. Crickets cheeped intermittently as dry reeds tall enough to hide in, swayed gently in a slight breeze, giving the false impression of a light, falling rain. There were other random night sounds of the ocean and beach, which they didn't recognize. Although it was nighttime, there was still plenty of activity. It just wasn't humans providing it.

They had gone about half a mile when the shore turned outwards, around a small peninsula. They cautiously followed the coastline here, because overgrown plants abutted the seashore, forcing them to walk in shallow water until finally rounding the point and returning to a straight route again on land. They hadn't gone far when Doug suddenly stopped. Pulling his cell phone out he said, "Before we go any further, I need to call my friend Bill Murphy. He's the military contact that I told you about."

"Do you think he'll be awake, this late time of night?"

"He'll answer. He's waiting for this call."

"What'll he have for us?"

"One way to find out," he said, dialing. After several rings, someone on the other end picked up and a serious voice said, "Hello?"

"Murph, this is Talbot. What have you got?"

The night sounds continued, but the phone connection stayed silent for a long moment.

"Let's get together for drinks," came a response.

Marilynn saw a confused look on Doug's face. "What?" she mouthed.

He put a finger to his lips and said a silent "Shhhh" then asked into the phone, "Who is this?"

"It's Murph," said the voice on the other end.

To his ear it sounded like Murph, but for some reason he felt unsure. He waited a moment before asking, "If this is you, then tell me the funny thing you did as my best man the night of my wedding reception."

There was another pause, only longer. The voice on the other end finally said, "I was pretty drunk that night; it could have been any number of things. Unless being drunk is what you mean?"

"Bill Murphy, was never my best man!" Doug snapped. "Who the hell is this?"

"You and the doctor stay right where you are, Mr. Talbot. We know exactly where you're going. Someone is on the way to get you."

"And just who the hell is *someone*?"

"You'll find out soon enough," said the voice, dropping the impersonation.

"What are you people so afraid we'll find out?" He waited for an answer, but heard only clicking noises on the line. "You bastards are tracking this call, aren't you?"

There was no response.

"What did you do with Murphy?"

"He was relocated," said the voice that he couldn't put a face to.

"Relocated! Where?"

"Let's just say he won't have to worry about shining boots anymore."

"You sons of bitches!" he shouted, snapping the phone shut and tossing it out into the ocean where it fell with a soft splash.

"What's wrong?" asked Marilynn, grabbing his forearm.

"They killed him," he said, through clenched teeth.

She rubbed his back lovingly, but remained silent as Doug stared out at the water. After several minutes she said softly, "Come on. We have a job to do."

This time they didn't walk hand in hand. They moved along in silence, with her leading the way, and him following a step behind. His breathing labored like a car that convulses with a knocking engine and continues to run even though the ignition's been switched off. He wasn't doing a good job of hiding his aggravation.

They passed a makeshift barbecue made out of a circle of stones. The strong scent of vinegar and a tart, smoky aroma of barbecued chicken tormented their noses, reminding them of how hungry they were.

After many steps, they finally spotted a cabin cresting on a hill. It sat neatly nestled between tall dark trees, and lots of overgrown bushes that surrounded a large empty front yard. There was light in several windows, and a small floodlight lit the front porch. They quickened their pace in the sand and spoke no words. They were like stealth planes moving in on an unsuspecting target.

The house had a narrow front porch that ran the width of it. From where they approached, the railing that enclosed the porch was in need of major repair and appeared to be grinning a toothy Halloween pumpkin smile with many missing teeth, or in this case, wooden slats. The closer they got, the more obvious it became that the whole house was in disrepair, and probably hadn't been maintained in years. When they stepped onto the porch, their rubber soled shoes rattled an occasional loose wooden plank, echoing softly. They made sure not to touch the rickety railing.

Standing under a low wattage porch light, Doug pounded a wooden door, striking it rapid-fire.

Nothing stirred inside.

Marilynn shrugged. "Maybe no one's home."

He banged harder.

"What the hell do you want?" yelled a voice on the other side of the door.

CHAPTER 19

Sorry to bother you," said Marilynn, "but we're looking for Professor John Woodsen."

"Who the hell are you?" shouted a gruff old voice.

"My name is Doug Talbot and I'm here with Dr. Marilynn Harwell, of Coventry General Hospital."

"Go away!" the voice snapped, irritated now. "I don't need a doctor."

"We're not here for medical reasons," said Marilynn in an urgent voice. "We just want to ask a few questions."

The door creaked partially open and a round bespectacled face, crowned with a head full of pure white hair, poked halfway out.

"Are you Professor Woodsen?" asked Doug.

"Why?" asked a bobbing head.

"You don't know us . . . . "

"You're right!" interrupted the old man, slamming the door shut. "Now get off my property, or I'll call the island police!"

They both sighed deeply. Their long night appeared to be getting longer.

"Please, Professor Woodsen," she begged. "We're hoping you can help us by answering a few important questions. I promise, we'll go away if you don't know the answers."

The door popped open. An old man wearing a fancy black tux and an agitated face stood in the doorway. "Well?" he snapped.

"Well what?" said Doug.

"Don't just stand there looking stupid. Come inside."

Marilynn entered first. Doug followed right after, keeping his guard up for the first sign of trouble. The inside was in sharp contrast to the outside. It was well maintained with a wooden floor that sparkled and looked as if it had just been put in. A blazing fireplace had a mantle decorated with various deer and bird knick-knacks, and plates with landscapes overlooking the sea, giving the room a toasty, comfortable feeling. A gray cloth loveseat filled the right wall, and hanging above it was a steering wheel from a sailboat, with a picture of a ship's captain smoking a wood pipe tacked in the center. An antique dark-cherry china cabinet full of island trinkets from the town stores sat to the left of an old, worn leather chair and the fireplace. Lighting the room was a shiny polyurethaned lamp made out of three pieces of driftwood that intertwined like vines wrapped around a tree limb, which hung from the ceiling in the center of the room. What caught Doug's eye most however, was a round table covered with a white silk cloth and two place settings of food, adorned by two burning red candles and a glass vase of yellow roses as a centerpiece. Two chairs were pushed in to the table.

Doug's eyes drifted to the right, where a door opened into a small room. On a makeshift desk made of plywood, propped on four corners of stackable milk crates was an elaborate microwave satellite setup, complete with digital transmitter and receiver.

"I'm sorry to bother you and your company," said Marilynn.

The old man looked at them with swollen, bloodshot eyes. "I'm alone," he said.

"Pretty fancy clothes and supper for one person," said Doug.

The old man's narrow eyes zeroed in on Doug's. "If it *were* any of your business," he said sarcastically, "I'd probably tell you that, since we're all going to die from this deadly virus anyway, I thought I'd go out in style with a full stomach!"

Doug and Marilynn's eyebrows raised in tandem.

"Professor Woodsen, we need to know about the Noposam Project," said Marilynn. "Time's running out on a lot of innocent people. Can you help us?"

The old man took a few steps back and raised his voice. "I don't know what you're talking about! Haven't you been watching the news, young lady?" Waving his hands animatedly he continued, "Death is all around us – there's no way to stop it!"

"Are you saying there's no antidote?" asked Doug.

The old man's face turned scarlet. "What the hell are you talking about?"

"Please!" begged Marilynn. "Won't you help us?"

"What is this, the good cop – bad cop routine?" snapped the old man.

"Professor, in 1969 you discovered a way to use a crude micro chip to help mankind," she started. "Later, you were teamed with a group of elite scientists to work on Gov-69, *The Noposam Project*. What went wrong?"

The old man snatched a skillet off the stove and charged swinging. "Don't try to put that stigma on me!" he shouted. Swinging at their heads in short figure eights he said, "They modified the damn thing,"

Doug blocked the pan with a forearm and easily wrestled it away. The old man staggered over to the worn leather chair. He slumped and buried his head in his hands, and wept. Doug and Marilynn pulled wooden chairs from the table and sat facing him. "Is there something you'd like to share with us?" said Doug.

Raising his head he mumbled, "It wasn't supposed to happen this way."

Marilynn softened her voice. "How *was* it supposed to happen?"

The professor drew a deep breath through his nose and held it, then exhaled sharply out his mouth. "The only reason I went to the government was because they had the money to fund the research. They told me it would have great implications on the space program, which back then was in its infancy. Things were heating up between our program and Russia's, although I didn't get the connection for its use."

"You believed them?" asked Doug.

"Sure. Why wouldn't I? They supplied the finances to support the project and rounded up some of the best MIT technical engineers, then set us up with a fancy laboratory on a small minimum security installation in Virginia."

"Did you stay on the base?" asked Marilynn.

"At first we were allowed to come and go whenever we wanted. But the project moved forward with rapid results and they felt it best if we only left on weekends." He locked his hands behind his head. "After ten months of aggressive testing it got even harder to leave," he went on. "We were told that because we were so close to perfecting the chip, we'd have to stay at what was now, a heavily guarded facility, for what they deemed, safety and security reasons."

He stopped talking, and stared blankly at the large open-stone fireplace, with its crackling firewood.

Doug spoke first. "What was the government afraid of?"

The professor snapped out of his trance. "Huh? What's that?"

"What were they afraid of?" Doug repeated.

"They told me the chip had dangerous military implications and that they had evidence that other countries wanted it for its destructive potential. Specifically, Russia and a few middle eastern ones looking to make a name for themselves. Used the wrong way, the chip can also be a lethal weapon."

There was a deep silence. Everyone sat fixated on the white-hot glow of the logs, and the occasional tiny red-hot ember that popped out onto the wooden floor. Never at a loss for words, Doug again broke the silence. "What does Noposam stand for?"

The Professor struggled to get out of the leather chair until finally leaning heavily on his elbows, he pushed his rotund body up. He stretched skyward, then walked to the hearth where he stood with his backside to the fire. In his prime, he had been a pretty good physical specimen, even though he wasn't taller than Marilynn's height of five-foot seven. Standing in the radiance of the fire's colorful dancing sparklers, he still posed quite a figure at his advanced age.

"Young man, Noposam is the acronym for *No Pain Or Suffering Any More*. It was dubbed Government 1969 – or Gov-69, The Noposam Project."

Doug walked over and threw a three-foot log on the fire, launching mini Fourth of July sparklers of diverse hues up the chimney. Standing next to the professor and appreciating the warmth on his backside, he said, "I'm curious. How did you rationalize the microchip?"

"I told them the chip would be a humane way to stop pain and suffering in the world."

Doug looked at him with a questioning stare. "What do you mean?"

"Suppose a person was in a head-on car crash and lay suffering with unrecoverable injuries. The chip would activate by sending an electrical impulse to the brain telling it to shut down the body's functions."

"In essence, it would put that person quietly to sleep?" said Marilynn.

"Simply put, yes. They would go to sleep and never wake up again. No more pain or suffering."

Doug asked, "What was the government's attitude?"

"They had big plans for it," said the professor, his eyes large as half dollars.

Doug waited for him to compose himself, then asked the sixty-four thousand-dollar question: "Like what?"

"They changed the chip!" he snapped.

"You mentioned that earlier," said Marilynn. "How?"

"By altering it."

Doug looked at Marilynn and then at the professor. "What the hell did they do to it?"

"I don't know. I was taken off the project in 73' and was

no longer privy to the experiments or any of its data. I heard rumors over the years of what they were doing, but it was never substantiated."

"Do you think that's the reason the chip is going haywire?" said Doug.

"I can't verify that, but if I was a betting man, I'd say it has a lot to do with it. There was a rumor floating around even back then, that one of the plans for the chip was to help American soldiers in Vietnam. Lots of young men were dying in a gruesome war the country didn't even want us to be in, so the government thought the chip could serve as a quick fix."

"What kind of fix?" asked Doug and Marilynn in tandem.

"Supposedly, the chip could keep soldiers from dying."

"How?" said Marilynn.

"I don't know how they modified the chip, but its purpose was to send impulses to the brain telling it not to shut down under extreme stress."

"Did it work?" said Doug.

"Think about it," said the professor. "How could it stop someone who'd been ripped apart by a bullet from dying? By telling the brain not to shut down? That's an impossible task." He paused to catch his breath. "A lot of innocent kids died in that war," he continued, "because they were used as guinea pigs." He sniffled several times, fighting back tears. "It was all a front for what they really wanted it for: a new type of weapon. Around that time, they were also dabbling in chemical warfare, I believe it was called Agent Orange, of which they knew little of the side effects. They only cared if it was effective in killing."

"But how could the chip kill people?" asked Doug, stepping away from the fireplace.

"That's an easy one," said Marilynn. "We're seeing examples of it right now. People dying who shouldn't be."

"That's right, Doctor. Somehow, they found a way to make the chip work to their advantage. But something must have gone wrong and it got into the private sector by mistake. Now, we're in trouble, without a way to stop it!"

The two guests slipped into a slight depression. Despair was not the kind of response they were expecting from this man. They had hoped he would have a solution to the problem.

"I'm confused," said Doug, wiping a bead of water off his forehead. "Why is the chip suddenly going haywire, now?"

"That's a good question, young man, to which I don't have an answer. The only educated guess I can make is that the body's electrical impulses send a false reading, causing the chip to send an unwarranted signal to the brain."

"It's as if it has a short in it?" said Marilynn.

"That's right. Don't forget, we don't know how many people have died over the years who were adversely affected by it. It's only recently that it's been so prevalent because of all the unexplained deaths."

He looked to Doug and then at Marilynn. "Think of how many times you've heard about someone just suddenly dropping dead out of the blue." Marilynn knew that to be true. She had seen it often over her ten years as a doctor.

"I think I understand," said Doug. "A lot of times death notices have no explanation other than passed away unexpectedly at home or the hospital."

After a short pause the professor said, "I haven't been totally truthful with you."

"How so?" said Marilynn.

"You must have heard all the hoopla there's been over microchips they're putting in dogs and cats for tracking them, in the event they get lost."

"I have," said Doug. Marilynn nodded.

"There are also many other applications for these chips, but in people. I got wind of it a while back, through some of my former students, who have been working on the reclamation of the NOPOSAM Project. It's now called E.C.C.P. - Embedded Control Chip Project."

"I'm afraid to ask," said Doug. "But what the hell is the E.C.C. Project?"

"Basically, they took my chip and found a way to make it kill randomly. It was designed to activate at the slightest sign of trauma."

"That explains a lot," said Marilynn.

"All I ever wanted was to help the terminally ill, and anyone suffering slow and painful deaths. And it worked great the first couple of years on a select group. We helped the suffering to a peaceful ending. People who would have been tormented for months, maybe even years."

"Kind of a pre Dr. Kervorkian, wouldn't you say, Professor?" said Doug in an edgy tone.

The professor's eyes were trained on the floor. "My intent was compassion," he answered in a low voice.

"Don't you think that maybe you should have left life and death in the hands of the real professional – say, God, instead of trying to play him?" asked Doug.

Marilynn shifted uneasily. She too was interested in his answer.

Agitated, the professor snapped, "Our intentions were for the betterment of mankind!" He drew another deep breath, and thought for a moment. "We only helped people on the verge of dying. We wanted to terminate pain and suffering, not precious lives."

"Did you ever stop to think that maybe some miracle drug or operation might be found to cure those illnesses or diseases, and that you would deprive them of that opportunity?"

"Of course that crossed my mind. But you're delusional if you think pharmaceutical companies work in the best interest of the sick, and that they want everyone cured. Think of the millions, and quite possibly billions of dollars they'd lose, if suddenly there was no need for all the products on the market that supposedly help people with diseases and illnesses." His voice rose as he continued: "It's like the oil industry! There are alternative ways to run our cars and heat our homes that have been invented, but they've been either quashed or bought up, otherwise, that multibillion dollar stronghold they have over us would suddenly cease to exist. A lot of wealthy and influential people would find themselves in a useless industry. Call it conspiracies, if you want." The professor sat down in the leather chair and went silent.

"Jesus," said Doug. "This is all so *Twilight Zone*."

The professor looked up. "Technology's putting us in astonishing situations, with unique problems we've never encountered before," he said. "Trust me Mr. Talbot, there are a lot more things going on behind closed doors that are scarier than this."

"Like what?" said Doug.

"How about nanotechnology."

"That's right," said Marilynn. "I Googled it once and got over three and a half million hits. Mostly start-up companies trying to break into one of the hottest technologies to come along in a while, although I was surprised by the number of well known businesses as well."

"There are many applications for nanotechnology," said the professor, "but one intriguing one is in the medical field. Microscopic robotic devices, which can be injected into the body to locate and attack a cancer area, till it was no longer there."

"Damn," said Doug. "How small are they?"

"To put it into perspective, the size of one device would be 1000 times smaller than the diameter of a human hair."

"Sounds like it would be more beneficial than your chip," said Doug.

"Sure, it sounds effective. But what happens if it doesn't stop at the cancer and keeps eating away at the patient's insides?"

"I guess they'd be eaten alive," said Doug.

The professor looked at the floor for a brief moment. Glancing up he said, "They're also working on *Inclination Projection,* which is a type of mind control. That's where a group of people with psychic power, project their will on, say, a national leader, in order to skew his way of thinking."

Doug sat biting his nails. "Anything else?"

"Weather?" said the professor. "Think about all the times you've seen extreme weather conditions mysteriously hit an area."

"Holy shit!" said Doug. "They can control the weather?"

"You know those jet exhaust trails you see for long periods of time in the sky?"

"Their called contrails, aren't they?"

"When they aren't used for military purposes to control climate change, they are. When you see them linger for long periods, say many hours, they're chemtrails, which are loaded with chemicals that can globally affect the weather."

"Are these chemicals harmful to people?" asked Marilynn.

"They've been known to cause headaches, ringing in the ears, and bowel and respiratory problems, among others."

Doug said, "Any other clandestine operations you'd care to share?"

"They've devised a short lived virus that can be located in any specific area inside an enemy country. The virus could eradicate a part of it, or parts of it, then itself die out, and no one else would be harmed."

"Pinpoint, strategical targeting," said Doug.

The professor cleared his throat. "You must remember the Philadelphia Experiment?"

The room became silent. "One weird problem at a time," said Marilynn, shifting uneasily in her seat. "Let's get back to ours. When did your chip go active?"

"We got the okay to test it out in seventy-one, two years after we were brought together at Stockton."

"Were you still part of the project when it was first administered to the public?"

The professor got up and went back to the fireplace

and with his back to them, leaned on it's mantle. "At that time I was," he answered.

Doug slipped into the vacated leather chair. "There's something I'd like to know," he said.

"What?" asked the Professor, turning to face to them.

"How was it given out?"

"That was the easy part," he said, turning around to face them. "Early on, all vaccinations or shots were pre-loaded with a chip. Putting them in babies was even easier. Later, it was installed in flu shots and before you knew it, almost everyone in the United States had one in them."

"How do you know that?" asked Doug.

"They constructed a giant underground database, right under the base. It's a quarter mile down, and only a select few have access to it. I heard through the grapevine that men that go down to work, never come back up, and eventually die there. Washington's not even aware of it."

"You mean the White House doesn't know it exists?" asked Marilynn.

"That's the scuttlebutt," answered the professor. "Anyway, once the project was up to date, it was just a matter of giving it to newborns, then maintaining the files."

"Must be one hell of a file," said Marilynn, softly.

"And I guess the results of it prove it really *was* for the betterment of mankind, huh?" said Doug.

Woodsen turned his back to them and with a sweep of his arm pulled several glass knickknacks off the mantle, sending them smashing across the floor. He started pacing back and forth like a caged cat. Finally he stopped and raised his hands high and in a composed voice said, "What's going on is not my fault and it certainly doesn't represent my original concept."

"Whose fault is it?" asked Doug.

"That's not hard to figure out," answered the professor. "Keep in mind that everything changed when the government brought in new engineers to replace my team, then the project suddenly became classified and I was kicked out. This was all courtesy of one person who offered me a million dollars for the design plans, and to keep me silent."

Doug shook his head. "So you sold everybody out, then retired here?"

"Not because I wanted to!" snapped Woodsen.

"So who's the mystery man?" asked Marilynn.

"Captain Uxbridge of the SIA, came to my house one night and spelled out in no uncertain terms that I should think seriously about taking the money. He said it would be in my best interest to accept the deal."

"Uxbridge," said Doug. "There's that name again."

"You know him?"

"Oh, we've come across his name once or twice," said Marilynn. "Except, now he's a General."

The professor sat on a wooden chair to the left of the fireplace. The side handles were loose and the varnish had long since worn away, but he looked comfortable as he crossed his arms and legs. After releasing a loud hmmm, he said, "That's interesting." He shifted in his chair and said, "I tried reasoning. I told him I didn't want the money, because my goal was to ease pain and suffering."

Marilynn rose from her chair and stood beside Woodsen's. "What was his reaction?"

"He said foreign countries wanted the chip for evil purposes and that they would stop at nothing to get the plans, and that he couldn't spare protection to safeguard my wife and me."

"He couldn't or wouldn't?" said Doug, cocking his head to one side.

Putting his forehead in the palm of his hand, the professor answered, "I suspect it was the latter."

Marilynn asked, "How did he take your refusal?"

"He said that the government could legally confiscate all rights to the project if it wanted without my permission, because it had become a threat to national security, and I'd get nothing."

"So he had you over a barrel," said Doug.

"I refused his offer and said that I would take this to my

state senators. He became extremely agitated and swore all the way to his car, but before he got in he shouted back, *'Your stubbornness could end up costing you and your wife your lives!'* I was pretty shook up after that."

"I hope you reported him," said Marilynn.

"How could I? We were stuck out in the middle of nowhere in what had now become a heavily secured military base, with no phone, and no way to communicate with the outside world. They *were* the authorities. Besides, even if there was someone to tell, they surely would have believed him over me. They tend to protect their own."

Doug stood next to Marilynn and asked, "What happened after that?"

"I received a message on military stationery two days later from my wife. She wrote that after coming back from shopping, she found our family dog hanging from a tree in the back yard."

Marilynn said, "The bastards made their point."

"It got worse. A week later, I received another note in handwriting I didn't recognize that my wife was driving home after a night out with her lady friends, when the brakes gave out. Her car slid off the road and rolled several times down an embankment before righting itself. A friend told me later that the service station, which fixed the car, said the brake lines had been tampered with."

"Was she okay?" asked Marilynn.

"She survived, but she had to go in for extensive emergency surgery."

"I'm confused," said Doug. "Why didn't the chip put your wife to sleep?"

"Ahhh," said the professor. "I never exposed her to it back when the project was in its infancy. Unfortunately, she received it in a shot the day of her surgery. I wasn't there to oversee her procedure."

Marilynn placed her hand gently on his arm. "I know it's painful, but we need to know everything."

The professor sat with his eyes closed, wringing his hands. A trickle of water from his eyes, slipped silently down his cheeks. When he'd collected himself, he opened blood-shot eyes and said, "Uxbridge showed up at the lab with some of his goons the next day, shoved a document in front of me, and told me to sign over the rights to the chip. He can be persuasive. He said, that by not signing, I was condemning my wife to a terrible death, and it would be my fault, because they couldn't provide her protection."

Marilynn took the professor's hands in hers. "You realize none of this is your fault?" His head dropped to his chest and he said nothing. He seemed to have aged many years before their eyes in just the short time.

Doug stood and said, stretching, "How did you end up here?"

The old man lifted his head slowly. "Once I signed off on the project, I wasn't of any use to them anymore. They told me they would set me up anywhere I wanted to go, so I talked it over with my wife. She was homesick and wanted to come back to Rhode Island. The government compromised and put us on Block Island, where we could ferry back and forth to the mainland. I got a job with EDC, an experimental company, and later a teaching position at MIT, before retiring for good in ninety-two.

"How do you communicate?"

"I don't know if you noticed, young man, but I have a direct satellite uplink to anywhere in the world. I've only used it twice, but they say that it has the capability of tapping into any live satellite feed around the globe, and putting my face on millions of television sets."

"That would be the ultimate TV reality show," laughed Doug.

Marilynn softened her voice. "Where's your wife, Professor?"

The professor's head sank back to his chest and there was a long, uneasy moment. His eyes became extremely moist. He was shaking when he spoke. "She was knitting a scarf for me when the needle slipped and the sharp point jabbed her thumb. It only bled for a short time. She didn't even need a bandage, but she put one on anyway."

Sorrowful, bloodshot eyes looked up at them. "She really loved it here, you know. She enjoyed the serenity and natural beauty of Block Island." Rubbing tears away with the palms of his hands, he said, "Ruth, especially enjoyed the tourist season. She had a modest souvenir shop, not just to keep her busy, but so she could meet and talk to as many people as possible, before the winter off season. She always undercharged whatever she sold."

His shoulders sagged and he slumped. "Several hours later she began experiencing the symptoms – you know them - sweating from the forehead and unquenchable thirst. I checked her shoulder and to my horror discovered the chip embedded there. I sat with her all evening, praying and hoping that it would malfunction. But some time during the night I fell asleep and when I woke, I found she had passed. The chip had done what it was designed to do." He paused for a moment, then, pointing his arm towards the back door, continued, "I buried her in the back yard this morning, because she loved it here. We were supposed to celebrate our fiftieth anniversary today."

Motioning with her head towards the table, Marilynn asked, "Is that what this is all for?"

He didn't answer. Something loud had snapped outside.

CHAPTER 20

Day Two
12:07am

The front door shuddered from three heavy blows. Turning to the professor, Doug said, "Who the hell can that be this time of night?"

The professor shrugged.

Marilynn went to the front window and parted the imitation green satin curtain back enough to peek through. She had to squint, because two powerful Army floodlights were placed on either side of the front yard, aimed towards the cabin and lighting up the whole place.

"This isn't good," she said in a low voice. "The Army's out there."

"How many?" asked Doug.

She turned from the window. "Maybe a dozen, but I don't think they're regular Army."

"What do you mean?" said Doug.

"They're dressed in black uniforms, with the letters SIA on the sleeves."

"They're Uxbridge's special forces," said the professor.

The three exchanged worried looks.

Doug spoke. "You can't let them know we're here."

"I think it's a little too late for that," said the professor.

"Woodsen!" bellowed a deep voice from outside.

Marilynn shielded her eyes as she peeked out again.

"There's a tough looking guy in front, Professor," she whispered.

The professor didn't react. He just stroked his chin.

"Woodsen! It's General Uxbridge!"

Doug and the professor joined Marilynn at the window. The professor opened it and shouted through the screen, "So, they've gone and made you a general?"

"That's right," said Uxbridge. "The country recognizes greatness."

"You know the old saying, Uxbridge?"

"What's that?"

The old man winked at Marilynn and Doug. "Crap rises to the top."

Everyone smiled nervously.

"The expression is *cream rises to the top*," said the general, pulling his gun from its holster. "Still have to do things the hard way, don't you? Have you forgotten how persuasive I can be?"

Staring out, the professor saw the imposing man's features perfectly under the floodlights. Although many years had passed, Uxbridge looked exactly the way he remembered him only with salt and pepper hair and quite a few extra pounds. "What the hell are you talking about?" he said.

"I guess senility's distorted your thinking, professor. Don't you remember the trouble your wife experienced the last time you were defiant?"

The professor's wrinkled, freckled hands became tightly clenched fists. "I'm not a violent man, Uxbridge, but if I had a gun right now, you'd be dead."

"I'm surprised at you, Professor. Whatever happened to peaceful endings?"

"Those are reserved for human beings, Uxbridge, of which you're not one!"

"Stop," said the general, with a cynical laugh. "You're hurting my feelings."

"What do you want, Uxbridge?"

"You're harboring a couple of people of extreme interest to the United States government."

Doug pulled Marilynn close.

"Please," Marilynn whispered. "Don't give us up."

Yelling through the open window, the professor said, "There's no one here but me, Uxbridge."

The general gritted his teeth. "I know they're in there."

"You've finally lost it, Uxbridge."

"Enough games. You can come out peacefully or we can do it the hard way. Which is it going to be? You and your new friends have all of sixty seconds to make up your minds before we come in."

The professor turned to Doug and said, "Maybe we should do as he says. I don't want anyone to get hurt. I told you how evil he is."

Marilynn's mouth went dry and with a struggle she forced out, "What do you think he wants?"

The professor stepped to the middle of the room and Marilynn and Doug followed. "I should think they only want to talk with us about the chip back on the mainland," he said. "It can't be any more than that."

No one spoke for several moments. A clock on the wall above the fireplace mantle, decorated with a different species of bird at every hour, shrieked the mournful cry of a blue jay, temporarily grabbing everyone's focus.

"What's it going to be?" shouted Uxbridge.

"There's only one thing to do," said the professor. Stepping back in front of the window, he yelled, "We're coming out, Uxbridge! Tell your assassins to hold their fire."

The general yelled the command.

Turning to his visitors the professor said, "I'm an old man, Mr. Talbot. Would you be so kind as to lead the way? Don't forget, it's me he has a vendetta against."

Shaking his head, Doug said, "I have to be honest. The Doc and I aren't happy."

"I don't trust him," said the professor. "The man's a maniac."

Reluctantly, Doug gripped the doorknob. "Actually, it's us he's after. You don't need to go out there."

The professor did a double take. "What do you mean?"

"They've been hunting us ever since we discovered the chip and its real purpose," said Marilynn. "They know that we'll expose their biological warfare tactic for what it really is, a cover-up."

The professor thought deeply, then said, "That may be true, but he and I have a history."

* * *

Outside, Major Edwards stood at the general's side. Behind them, ten combat-ready soldiers were positioned in a semi-circle in the front yard, their rifles aimed at the cabin. These same men had been chosen by the SIA only months earlier from a potential group of hundreds, because they qualified as expert marksmen, and because they would be loyal.

The major said, "Talbot, Harwell, and Woodsen. Not a bad day's work."

General Uxbridge leaned close and spoke low so only Edwards could hear. "After we're done with the two decoys, Woodsen's mine."

"General, do you think it's wise to take care of that business here, in front of witnesses?"

The general's eyes grew wide and his face became ugly.

"I've waited a long time for this day, and no one is going to stand in my fucking way!" he barked, not caring if anyone heard. "The son-of-a-bitch has haunted my life long enough; now it's time for him to pay with his life."

"Just trying to help," said Edwards, shying several feet away.

"When I need your help I'll ask for it!" snapped the general. "Otherwise, keep your pathetic opinions to yourself."

Everyone stared at the major, waiting for him to answer back, but nothing came out.

"You've been a pain in my ass ever since I brought you into this collusion. I was wrong about you, Major. I actually thought you'd be an asset."

Major Edwards bit his lip. You never won when the general was in a foul mood.

Still fuming, Uxbridge bellowed toward the cabin, "That's it, Woodsen! Get out here, or we start shooting!"

"We're coming!" yelled Doug, from behind the closed door.

Uxbridge turned to the strategically placed marksmen dressed in gear better suited for big game hunting and said viciously, "None of them leaves here alive!"

The door creaked open as Doug stepped slowly over the threshold with his hands held high. Ten scoped rifles followed him. Marilynn looked to the professor. He looked tired and drained, but smiled and nodded at the door. "Don't worry, young lady. Everything will work itself out."

She stepped through the doorway with arms raised in surrender. Her shadow stretched well behind her and far into the cabin from the force of the bright floodlights. She took her place next to Doug on the narrow porch. After several moments the general yelled, "Join us, Professor!"

The door slammed shut.

"Son-of-a-bitch!" snarled Uxbridge. "You're testing me."

"Do what you have to do, Uxbridge," yelled the professor through the door, "and I'll do what I have to do."

The general flashed a sinister grin and mumbled, "On my terms." Turning to Doug and the doctor he barked, "Put your hands behind your head and walk to me!"

Doug looked back over his shoulder and caught a glimpse of the professor peeking through the corner of the window, but the curtain closed quickly.

"I gave you an order, Talbot," said the general, looking down the sight of his gun.

"I'm not one of your minions, Uxbridge."

"It would be in your best interest if you did what you were told," said Major Edwards, in a lighter voice.

"We're coming!" shouted Doug. He put his hands down

in defiance and Marilynn did the same. Taking her hand in his, he led her across the front porch. "I'm sorry I failed you, To-ens," he whispered. As they started down the front steps, she whispered, "I'm sorry I got you involved."

They walked deliberately across the short yard to Uxbridge until Doug stood face to face with him. Both men measured about the same height - six foot three - but the general outweighed Doug by at least - fifty pounds. They eyed each other, stubbornly waiting for the other to flinch. The general stepped back.

Major Edwards posted two guards next to Marilynn and two next to Doug.

"You think you're pretty funny, Talbot," said Uxbridge. Doug never saw the general's handgun coming as it struck the side of his face, and blacked out temporarily as he hit the ground.

Marilynn screamed and tried to reach down to him, but the guards held her back. She turned to Uxbridge with wide eyes and said in an even tone, "We have a disc filled with information from the SIA database, and we've given it to a friend who's going to the news media if we don't show up by a specified time."

"You mean this?" said Uxbridge, producing a disc from inside his khaki jacket. A twisted smile worked its way slowly across his face. "We found it in the car you left parked back at the dock." He threw it to the ground and stomped on it with his boot till it cracked. "Pretty ingenious, hiding it inside a tampon box," he sneered.

Marilynn softened her voice. "You're sick, General, but I can get you help. I have a lot of influence at Coventry General."

"Is that diagnosis free, Doctor?"

"Why won't you leave us alone? We only want to help the sick and dying."

"Not that crap again?" he snarled. The general's eyes were mere slits and his face was devilish. Marilynn shivered. She knew he would never listen to reason.

"You're wasting my time," said Uxbridge, snapping his

fingers. The two soldiers assigned to Doug suddenly yanked his arms behind his back and dragged him across the yard in the direction of the cabin. Marilynn tried to follow, but her guards held her back. He resisted, but the armed men tightened their grip. "What the hell are you doing?" he said, as the three scuffled across the yard. "You'll find out soon enough," said the soldier on the left as he twisted Doug's arm up toward the back of his head. Doug grimaced.

When they reached the cabin, the soldiers shoved him backward against the wooden building, slamming his already sore head into weather-stripped clapboard. He wanted to fight back, but he was weak from the blows he'd sustained. Grabbing the back of his head, he was barely able to stand.

"Stay put!" snapped the bully who had twisted his arm. The two soldiers stepped ten feet to either side, out of the way. Free now, Doug tried to walk back toward the general, but could only stagger short steps.

The general grabbed Marilynn and held his gun to her side.

"Get back to the wall, Talbot, or I drop her."

Doug stopped, and stood swaying like a sapling in a stiff breeze. Rage surged through his body.

"I mean it," said Uxbridge, shoving the gun under the doctor's chin.

* * *

Back inside the cabin, Professor Woodsen switched on the satellite transmitter. Nothing happened. He waited a few seconds, thinking maybe it needed to warm up. But then he realized it was digital, and didn't need to warm up like the old ones with tubes. His overly liver-spotted hand pressed the ON button. Again nothing happened. He stepped to the side of the makeshift desk with its intricate satellite set-up and gingerly pulled it away from the wall, then stepped behind and removed the cover from the transmitter. He gasped. There was nothing inside it. His shaking hand removed the cover off the receiver, revealing it also had no working parts - no guts at all. Someone had removed the entire insides of the satellite transmitter and receiver, without his ever knowing it.

He tried to think back to the last time he'd used it, and realized it was the blizzard of last winter. He and Ruth had been stranded for a week, until help in the form of three army privates had reached them. They had seemed nice enough at the time, laughing and joking, while plowing out the front yard, and even shoveling off the porch. They ended up spending the night, telling stories and drinking hot toddies in front of the fireplace till everyone was a little tipsy and nodded off to sleep, before heading back to the mainland at early daylight.

Staring hard at the desk, the professor understood. It had been under the cloak of night, when the gutting had taken place. He walked back to the window on unsteady feet, and grabbed hold of the window frame for support. What was he going to say to Uxbridge now? he wondered.

CHAPTER 21

Marilynn tried to swallow, but the gun under her chin made it difficult. Finally, she forced the saliva down. No one moved. No one spoke.

No one dared.

The roar of crashing waves carried up the beach by a changing tide broke the silence. Off in the distance, a mournful foghorn blasted several times, warning approaching ships nearing Block Island Sound of hidden rocks and sandbars. Staring with sharpshooter eyes down narrow scopes and watching the standoff that was unfolding, restless soldiers shifted weight off one leg to the other, or their rifles from a tired shoulder to a fresh one. They were tensed, but poised to perform anything asked of them.

Doug stood calculating his options. It would be one thing to risk his own life in a bold attempt, but he didn't want to compromise Marilynn's.

The air was thick, almost stifling.

Suddenly, there was a flash and an explosion. Doug fell to the ground and grabbed his arm. Close by, an owl, disturbed, fled its hunting perch. The salty September air had a sharp edge of coolness as Doug inhaled short gasps. In contrast to the therapeutic air he and Marilynn had earlier breathed back on the beach, its sole purpose now was to help him to regain his feet.

General Uxbridge turned to his right and barked, "Who shot?"

The soldier at the end of the line, not more than twenty

years old and built like a linebacker, took two steps forward. "I did, Sir. My hand slipped."

Another shot rang out and the soldier was dead before he hit the ground. "Back against the wall, or I shoot your girlfriend next!" snapped Uxbridge.

Doug retraced his steps as best he could walking backward, never losing eye contact with the general. Finally, he stood with his back to the cabin. The two soldiers on either side of him, walked over to the dead soldier's body and dragged it unceremoniously out of the way, then flung it to the ground, displaying no sign of pity. They rejoined the other soldiers, who stood with blank faces.

Uxbridge pointed to the firing squad. The soldiers formed a tight line to his left. Major Edwards stood to his right.

"You bastard!" yelled Marilynn, struggling to free herself from her bodyguards.

"Sticks and stones break bones, Doctor." She swallowed hard as tears flowed down her face. "Would you like to join him? I would be more than happy to accommodate."

She looked back at Doug. The only reason he remained vertical was because the cabin was holding him up. He was in a bad way, slumped and holding his head with his wounded arm. She locked eyes with the general and said, "Let me go to him."

"You heard her. She wants to die with her boyfriend."

Her bodyguards rushed her aggressively to his side, then returned to take their places on a now nine-strong firing line. She put her arms around Doug's waist in an effort to support him, and felt his shivering body against hers. The gunshot had been to the forearm, and the bleeding was minimal. It was the blow to his head that worried her. Her instinct told her the force of it probably gave him a concussion, and she feared that he would go into shock. Her main concern, however, was the trickle of sweat that rolled off his forehead.

"How do you feel?" she asked softly.

"Besides the headache, gunshot and firing squad, not too bad."

"Are you thirsty?" she asked, believing she already knew the answer.

"No more than usual," he said, rubbing his head to take the sting and sweat away. "Though I could use a beer."

She stared hard at him. Was he making jokes to distract her from the symptoms? Did it matter, given their imminent execution?

"Guess we're never going to find that antidote," he murmured.

"Looks like a *Hallmark* moment," said the general sarcastically. "What a shame that you'll never get to marry your *Dream Guy*, Dr. Harwell."

"If I ever get out of this, Uxbridge, you're a dead man!" shouted Doug.

"Enough bullshit," snapped the general. "Get ready to die!" The firing squad raised their rifles. They awaited his command. "If it makes you feel any better, Dr. Harwell, I won't even fire my gun. I'll leave it to the experts."

"You'd probably miss," Doug quipped.

"Firing squad!" boomed the general. "On my mark, shoot till you hear the order to stop!"

Stepping in front of the general, Major Edwards said, "Sir, I implore you. Don't do this."

"Have you lost your nerve, Edwards?" snapped Uxbridge.

"There are too many witnesses," said Edwards, lowering his voice. "Besides, there must be another way. Maybe we can make them disappear like you did the first time with the professor. There must be some obscure part of the country we can relocate them to."

Uxbridge raised his gun to nose level of the major. "Step aside, Major Edwards, or you'll be breathing through a big gap in your face."

The major didn't move.

Uxbridge fired at his feet. A shocked Edwards quickly sidestepped two giant steps and the general followed his right hand man with searing eyes. Waving his pistol, he screamed, "I don't give a shit if anyone here knows that I'm killing these people!" Through clenched teeth he went on, "My main concern is getting my money for the chip's design. So keep your mouth shut, Edwards, or you'll join them. I'm not going to let you screw it up!"

The major swallowed hard, but said nothing.

Uxbridge said to the prisoners, "Any last words?"

Doug embraced Marilynn. "I'm really glad I got to know you, To-ens," he whispered in her ear.

"There's no one else in the world I'd rather be with, Marilynn said through tears." Their lips met in a hungry kiss.

Uxbridge smiled with smug satisfaction. Killing them was going to feel so good, he thought.

After their kiss, they shut their eyes and hugged hard to the count of "Five!"

"Four!" continued Uxbridge.

"Three!

"Two!

"One!"

There was a loud crack and a quick flash of blinding light. And then quiet. Doug opened his eyes and strained to see through a white wall of light. His ears rang as he peered harder into the bright haze. While his pupils adjusted, he began picking out faint silhouettes of willowy trees, overgrown bushes, and people pointing skinny sticks in his direction. So this is that light at the end of the tunnel they talk about, he thought. But what was that shouting?

"What's happening?" asked Marilynn, very much alive beside him.

"I don't know," he answered, turning towards the yelling.

"You think I'm going to back down, Woodsen?" bellowed Uxbridge.

"You don't have any choice!" yelled the professor, from inside the cabin. "Mr. Talbot! Are you

and Dr. Harwell all right?"

"You okay?" he asked her.

"I'm fine," she said. "It's you I'm worried about."

"I'm not that bad, " he reassured her.

"We're okay, Professor!" shouted Marilynn.

Doug scanned the front yard with semi-adjusted eyes and realized what the cracking noise and bright flash of light were. Four powerful spotlights located high up on poles in the four corners of the yard illuminated an area of about a hundred yards.

"What's going on?" he yelled for anyone to answer.

"The professor thinks he's stopped me!" answered Uxbridge, with a trace of laughter in his voice.

"I have," responded the professor, sticking his head partially out the now opened screen. "The spotlights up on those poles have wide-angle lens cameras attached, and powerful external microphones that can pick up a conversation as far as a hundred feet away. Right now, a live shot of my backyard is being uplinked to every satellite in space, and is being shown on every cable television and satellite receiver around the world. I'm pretty sure the White House has TV's."

Doug chuckled, "I knew this would be the ultimate reality show!"

Suddenly, the two army floodlights snapped off, leaving all the characters in this precarious game visible to each other.

"If you have them over a barrel, Professor," shouted Marilynn, "then why are they still aiming guns at us?"

The front door of the cabin groaned slowly open on rusty hinges – much like the groans of a poltergeist's nightly haunt. The tuxedo-clad Professor stepped out onto the front steps. Traces of saliva appeared in the corners of the general's mouth at the sight of Woodsen, and the grip on his gun was so tight his hand began to shake. It took all his effort to keep from charging the elderly man on the porch.

The professor puffed out his chest and spoke firmly. "You just tried to kill innocent people on live television and admitted to the country that you're selling it out, Uxbridge. Give yourself up. It's all over."

"Everything I've ever done was for the safety and security of the country!" shouted the general.

"How many innocent people died because of the government's bad microchips?" said Marilynn, "and how many more will die because of your cover-up and phony vaccinations?"

"If a few insignificant people have to die to achieve national safety, then that's a sacrifice I'm willing to take."

"Sacrifice *you're* willing to take!" she cried. "Who the hell made you God? What about the rights of all the innocent people you've sold out to get *your* money?"

The general's eyes glowed red with blood vessels ready to explode. "Do you honestly believe that anyone gives a shit about some retard that was sacrificed because we needed to buy time until we found the real terrorists and a cure for the virus? And do you -"

"*Imaginary* virus," she corrected.

"Don't interrupt me," sneered Uxbridge. She wanted to say something, but the words stuck in her throat. Seeing her hesitate, Uxbridge said, "Do you really think anyone cares how threats are handled?"

Marilynn gathered her wits and chose her words carefully. "People care. Especially when *innocent* people die. The country wants justice, but at the right price. You never took the time to ask."

"The only thing the public wants is for each and every crisis to be handled quickly!" said Uxbridge. "They don't give a rat's ass how we do it. If there's a threat of a building being blown up or someone's poisoning our food supplies, or plotting to assassinate the president, then they want us to do whatever it takes to stop it!"

"You're crazy with power, Uxbridge," said Doug. "You justify killing in that warped mind of yours, by saying it's for the good of the country, when it's the thrill of playing God that excites you."

The general fired a shot that struck inches to the right of Doug's head, exploding splinters of wood off the side of the cabin.

"Knock it off, Uxbridge!" yelled the professor. "Keep in mind this little scenario is being played out on live television. I'm sure the White House will have a different point of view than yours. Face it. Your career is over. *Now put that gun down!*"

The general eyed Talbot and Harwell with disdain, then focused his animosity on the professor. He eased his sidearm down until it rested against his thigh, then stood frozen and expressionless, like a figure in a wax museum. The eyes of nine soldiers were fixated on him, wondering how this spectacle would play out. Without warning, he let loose a short thunderous laugh, then reached behind himself and fired a shot that took out the back left spotlight. He spun around quickly to face the opposite side and shot the back right light out, leaving both rear corners of the yard in darkness. Only the two on poles to either side of the cabin remained lit.

But he wasn't finished, this time firing and hitting the right spotlight, leaving the spot on the pole to the left of the house as the only light source.

"Like I said, Professor, I like to play the hard way. Major Edwards, get me the professor and the others."

The younger officer commanded several soldiers to retrieve Marilynn and Doug, then went up onto the porch to get the professor. When they were all standing in front of the general, the soldiers returned to take their places on the line and Edwards stayed several feet off to the right. The general studied them up and down for several long moments, then swung around and slammed his weapon against the back of Woodsen's neck, dropping the elderly man to his knees. Three soldiers stepped between Marilynn and Doug, blocking them.

"Such a paradox, Professor. No chip in *your* shoulder for a peaceful ending."

The professor tried to respond but couldn't catch his breath.

Uxbridge leaned down so his face was next to the professors. His breath was hot and smelled of stale cigars.

"Do you understand how the SIA works now, Professor? We like to kill. That's what we do best. No - peaceful - endings!"

The professor took several deep breaths from his knees and asked simply, "If you like to kill with conventional weapons, then why do you need the chip?"

Meanwhile, Marilynn had slipped back unseen until she was standing under the pole with the only working light, where a camera and microphone pointed down. Doug stayed put, so as not to draw attention.

"Hey!" said Uxbridge. "I didn't say the government didn't want to go high tech."

Looking directly at the camera, Marilynn spoke solemnly, but loudly. "General Uxbridge is a sadistic man, who uses his power to manipulate life the way *he* wants it! I know of two beautiful people who were murdered in the name of America's safety."

Uxbridge motioned two marksmen to go and get her. They stepped forward until they were a couple of feet from her, and stood aiming their rifles at her heart. They could have just as easily taken her out from a hundred yards.

"Tell them to back off, Uxbridge!" yelled Doug. "Remember! This is live TV."

The marksmen looked to Uxbridge for help. His face was scarlet. Through clenched teeth, he snarled, "Stand down." The soldiers reluctantly lowered their rifles, but stayed their ground in case of a change of mind.

Doug went to Marilynn's side and wrapped an arm around her shoulder. "Go get'em," he said. She flashed a nervous smile, then looked up at the camera again. "They were murdered because they knew there was no terrorist attack. It was a cover up by the SIA."

She paused

"Please, General, let it go," said Major Edwards. "It's over. Let's do the right thing and stop this. Enough people have died."

Uxbridge raised his gun and dropped the major with a single shot.

Marilynn swayed. Her knees buckled and she was about to slide to the ground when Doug caught her. He whispered something in her ear, and she gathered enough strength to continue while in his clutches. "My friend Jennie Sprague was brutally murdered, but before she died she saved a copy of the SIA database to her Website, Yogagirl.com. If you go there, you'll learn the truth about the conspiracy."

Suddenly, Uxbridge was upon her, shoving her to the ground. Doug tried to pull him off, but several soldiers wrestled him over to the side.

"Leave them alone!" shouted the professor, still on his knees.

"Get up, Woodsen!" yelled Uxbridge, "or do you want to die groveling on the ground?"

The professor staggered to his feet. Two soldiers took him by either arm and rushed him to the general.

"Reform the line!" he snapped.

The marksmen formed a line twenty feet back from the general and his prisoners. Standing in shadows, just out of reach of the last spotlight and masked by their dark uniforms, it almost seemed as if they weren't there.

"Are all of you cold-hearted killers too?" said Marilynn. "Haven't you a conscience, or are you hell bent on murdering innocent people, just like Uxbridge?"

"They're trained to follow orders, Dr. Harwell," boasted the general with wide eyes. He had left them and had retreated next to his men, who stood emotionless and unchanged, with rifles aimed at their intended targets. They were idle robots, waiting for someone to push their *On* buttons. He knew they wouldn't deviate unless he told them.

"Listen to me," she pleaded. "Killing innocent people is not what you pledged when you entered the service. Protecting them is what you signed on for, not following the orders of someone with his own agenda."

The soldiers stood ready. Guns at eye level, captives in sight, eerily silent.

"They are true soldiers," said the general calmly, an

abrupt change from the enraged madman. "They do as they're told. You see. I always win."

Doug pulled Marilynn into his arms. Tears flowed freely down her cheeks. The tension was as dense as the thickest fog that had ever rolled over the Island.

"On my mark!" yelled Uxbridge.

In a desperate appeal, Doug pleaded to the marksmen, "I beg you – you can stop this. You know it's wrong!"

"Shut up!" shouted Uxbridge.

"Listen to me," he continued, "the doctor and I know the real truth about the sudden deaths. It's not a biological attack like they say. If we die, the secret dies with us, so does any chance to find an antidote."

"Save your breath, Talbot," snapped Uxbridge, "for that last gasp before you die."

With nothing to lose, Doug turned to the firing squad. "Suppose we're right. Don't you want to give your families a chance to survive?"

The general was as taut as an elastic band wound to the breaking point. The night air had cooled considerably and steam fumed from his nostrils like a panting horse after a long run on a cool day. Pure evil flowed through the veins of this monster.

Doug and Marilynn remained embraced and the professor stood next to them, slightly bent at the waist. Uxbridge threw back his head and in a moment of delirium that would have made the most sadistic murderer on death row proud, uttered one word: "Die!"

A shot rang out, then another. Then stillness after the cracking thunders.

A sudden burst of wind came up, sweeping across the yard as if sent to wipe away the foul smells of anger and hatred. Everyone breathed deeply as one. It was a tension breaker that would have made Jennie proud.

Major Edwards sat leaning on his elbow, his gun smoldering. General Uxbridge lay gasping, blood seeping through the backside of his government-issued jacket. The professor edged closer till he stood above his wounded adversary. Doug and Marilynn went to the major. Helping him to his feet, Doug asked, "How you doing?"

"I lucked out," he said, getting his balance, as a dark wet spot formed on his upper shoulder area. "The bullet struck to the left of my heart. It's not like the general to miss like that."

Leaning on Doug's shoulder for support, the major walked over and joined the professor. "Put your guns down," he instructed the shooters. "There'll be no more killing today." They lowered their rifles and gathered randomly with the others.

"What? No chip, General?" said the professor.

"You think it's over?" said Uxbridge, his voice raspy.

"Oh, it's over," answered the professor. "Die knowing that everything you believe in dies with you."

Uxbridge leaned on his elbow and tried to stand, but after struggling, he slipped to the ground. "There'll be others," he murmured. "This is bigger than you realize. It's bigger than even the president knows."

"It's something you fabricated a long time ago," said Doug.

The professor touched Doug's forearm. "You're wasting your time, Mr. Talbot. You need a conscience to realize the difference between right and wrong."

The once-rugged general looked frail and ashen as strength drained from his body. He gathered what little energy he had left and lifted his head, then proudly uttered in a clear voice, "Told you I like to do it the hard way."

"Violent endings, general," saluted the professor.

"Sergeant Bates!" yelled Major Edwards. A tall, slender soldier stepped forward.

"Yes, Sir!"

"Sergeant, bring a flashlight for these folks."

The sergeant saluted and went to a large metal case that sat just on the outskirts of the front yard. He returned carrying a silver flashlight and handed it to Doug.

"It's a fifty thousand candle power flashlight," said the

major, "for you to find your way back to our transport ship. Just follow the beach back to the dock."

"Thank you," said Marilynn. "Before we go, we'd like to tie up a few things here."

"Do what you have to do," said Major Edwards, "but don't take too long. I'd like to get underway while the waters are fairly calm."

"I'll make sure of it," said Doug. Looking down at the general, who still had breath in him, he said, "Do you think he'll make it back alive?"

The major shrugged and instantly regretted it when a sharp pain shot up his shoulder. "He's in a bad way," he said wincing. "I really don't know. We'll try our best, though. He and I have a lot of explaining to do to some important people." He saluted with his good arm, then turned to the sergeant and said, "Let's get the general back to the ship and get ready to leave. It's time we go back and try to make things right." Turning back to Doug, Marilynn, and the professor he said, "Please don't judge the SIA by Uxbridge and me. Not everyone is bad." He turned and walked away, eager not to hear a response.

It took three soldiers to hoist the general. Two of the other men broke out more of the powerful flashlights so they could find their way back. Marilynn, Doug and the professor watched the soldiers walk down the dune lugging the semi-conscious general to a point, where they would follow the shoreline back to dockside. After they had disappeared from sight, Marilynn turned to the professor and asked gently, "Are you okay?"

"Nothing a long sleep won't cure," he said in a tired voice.

"That was pure genius, Professor," said Doug. "Putting us on live television for everyone to see. It doesn't get any smarter than that."

"I don't deserve any credit, young man. I was only bluffing."

"I don't understand," said Marilynn. "You told us you could put your face on every satellite."

"That's right; I could at one time. But when I went to turn the system on, I found it had been tampered with, so I decided to try and fake it."

"That's a hell of a gamble you took!" said Doug. "It's a good thing *they* didn't know that!"

"Desperate times call for desperate measures, Mr. Talbot."

Grabbing hold of the professor's forearm, Marilynn said, "Let's get you packed up so you can come back with us."

The professor shook his head slowly. After a pause he said sadly, "I've lived here with Ruth for the better part of forty years. There are too many memories. I can't leave her here by herself. You kids go back and see about that antidote. I know you'll find one."

"I'm going to call whenever I can," said Marilynn. "And Doug and I will come visit every week. That's not just a promise. It's a guarantee."

"That's nice of you, Dr. Harwell, but I'll be fine. Besides, I suspect you have other more pressing issues to tend to than checking up on an old man."

"Nonetheless, Professor, I intend to do just that."

"Trust me when I say this," laughed Doug, "she's very stubborn and thick headed. If she says she's going to check up on you, she will."

"Very well," said the professor, pumping Doug's hand. When he tried to shake Marilynn's, she pulled him into a tight hug.

"Go find that antidote," he said, turning away and heading back to the cabin. At the doorway he turned and yelled back, "Remember me as someone who tried to do good," then disappeared inside.

"I'm really worried about him," said Marilynn, glancing back towards the cabin. "He's pretty unstable right now with the death of his wife, and the knowledge that his Noposam project is the crux of the nation's dilemma."

"We can't make him come back with us," said Doug.

"I know, but my gut tells me something's not right."

Suddenly, a single gunshot sounded inside the cabin.

They raced for the front door and burst in. They found the professor slumped on the table, victim of a self inflicted wound.

"I should have recognized the signs!" cried Marilynn. "He couldn't see life without his wife, so he planned this Last Supper. Damn it!"

Doug looked at the professor's slumped body. His face turned ashen and his shoulders slumped. It wasn't a pretty sight and he wasn't used to seeing that type of death first hand. Especially, when it was a person he'd just been speaking with. He gathered his emotions and said in a soft tone, "You kind of had a lot on your mind when you got here. You can't blame yourself for every death that happens."

"That's what I'm trained for, to prevent death whenever I can. *This - was - preventable*!"

"Maybe for the short term. He was determined, and would have eventually found a way. By his own volition, he wanted to be by her side. You couldn't watch him every minute."

"One more time, death gets the better of me," she said, burying her face deep in his chest.

"So let's go back and find an antidote and put a stop to this," he said firmly. "Let's get the better of death."

"But we're back to square one again," she said, pulling away and turning her back to him. "We're no better off than we were yesterday when we first started!"

He placed both hands tenderly on her shoulders from behind and she flinched. "That never stopped us before," he said soothingly. "If anything, it should make us more determined."

"Fine!" she mumbled.

They laid the professor on a neatly made bed in a back bedroom, making sure to prop his head so the blood didn't run over his body, then left the cabin feeling dejected at leaving him behind. Doug switched on the flashlight, and a powerful beam pushed out thirty yards ahead. They walked slowly down the hill to the beach, and spoke of how some unknown stranger would come for the professor in the morning, and would take him away from the island and Ruth. They quickened their pace, walking briskly and silently along the shoreline, heading back to find the transport ship. When she wasn't looking, Doug swiped his forehead clean of moisture.

CHAPTER 22

12:44am

Lindsey Palmer stood at Cassandra's side; tears flowed freely from her bloodshot eyes. Father Donnavan, from St. Mary's Church up the street, was also at the sick girl's bedside, administering last rites. It was quick and sloppy. He had many others to administer to at the hospital and his mind wasn't functioning as acutely as usual. His hand had rubbed away sweat from his brow many times before he had finished the ritual.

He drew a fatigued breath as he turned to face her. "Bless you child. Go in peace." Lindsey wasn't Catholic, but she still crossed herself. The priest, bent shoulders sagging from his heavy burden, walked out of the room, trying to suppress a nasty cough, while swiping beads of moisture from his forehead. He would be dead, like many others that day, before he finished the next one.

12:51am

"Damn!" said Doug, as they came into view of the dock.

"What's the matter?"

"I wanted to call the hospital. We haven't checked on Cassandra since we were at the restaurant."

"Your phone's in the ocean."

"I know. What can we do?"

Marilynn glanced up the shoreline. "Locate Major Edwards. He'll know where to find one."

Doug grabbed Marilynn by the hand and started dragging her towards the wharf.

"Hey!" she cried. "I have a sore leg, remember?"

"Sorry, I forgot. Do the best you can," he said, slowing his pace to one she found manageable.

They did slightly better than two people in a three-legged race as they walked along the boardwalk and passed the two elderly fishermen, who still sat rocking and smoking their pipes.

"How'd you do, Doc? Did you find the Prof okay?"

Keeping pace with Doug, Marilynn glanced back over her shoulder and shouted back, "Yes, thank you!"

Doug spotted the major up ahead and called out, "Major! I need to ask a favor."

The officer was giving orders to a group of soldiers, who he dismissed with a wave of his hand as Doug and Marilynn approached. "What can I do for you, Mr. Talbot?"

"I need to borrow a cell phone." said Doug. "We need to call the hospital to check on my sick daughter."

"She wasn't doing well when we last saw her," threw in Marilynn.

The major reached into a side pocket of his khaki jacket and pulled out a small flip phone. "Just so happens I have one," he said, handing it over.

"Thanks," said Marilynn. "We won't need it very long."

All at once a helicopter started its engine. Startled, they glanced to their right. It was the first time they'd both taken notice of it.

"Take your time!" shouted the major, over the roar of the chopper.

Marilynn snatched the phone from Doug. "Let me call!" she shouted over the uproar. "I'll call my back door number!" She punched in the secret seven digits and it rang immediately.

"West Three, Beakerman."

"Nance, it's Dr. Harwell."

"Hey! What's going on? You sound like you're in the middle of an airport."

"We're on Block Island!"

"Block Island! What the heck are you doing there? Don't you know that you and that cameraman's pictures have been plastered on the news all day?"

"I'm on my way back to the hospital with him right now. We'll clear everything up when we get there." She covered her open ear with her free hand and raised her voice to be heard over the roar of the helicopter. "The reason I'm calling is to check on Cassandra Talbot! Do you have any information on her?"

"Sorry, Doctor. They gave her last rites. I don't think she has much time."

"Oh no!" said Marilynn.

Doug grabbed her wrist. "What?" he shouted.

The noise of the helicopter was deafening and its wind swept up swirls of sand. She put a hand up to shield her eyes and looked at Doug with pity. "I'm sorry," she said.

Doug began pacing. "I need to get to her!" he said, fighting back tears.

Major Edwards reappeared from behind them. "How we doing?" he asked over the roar.

"Not good, Major! I've got to get back to Coventry General Hospital as quick as I can! My daughter's dying."

"If you and the doctor jump on our high speed boat, we'll get you there in about twenty minutes."

Marilynn grabbed the major's arm and nodded towards the helicopter. "Wouldn't that be faster?" she asked.

"It sure would, Ma'am."

CHAPTER 23

12:57am

A soldier reached over and pulled Dr. Harwell's seatbelt tight across her chest and lap, securing it with a snap. She smiled. He motioned Doug to do the same, then stepped away and slid the helicopter door closed. Another soldier sat across from them. On his head was a silver helmet with a tinted visor that was pulled up. "Hold on, folks," he said over the engine noise and whirling blades. "Our pilot, Captain Whitaker, will be flying us over the ocean and it'll get a little rough at times when we hit air pockets. The turbulence won't last long, though." He turned and shot the captain a thumbs up.

Doug and Marilynn glanced at each other as the Army Bell series Iraquois helicopter, also known as the Huey II, began to lift gently off the ground. Doug slipped his hand in hers. "We'll be fine!" he said. Marilynn smiled, but her mouth was straight, and her face muscles twitched.

Red and blue lights on the dependable helicopter, built to transport troops with plenty of speed in adverse conditions, pulsed and strobed from its underbelly, lighting the dark ground beneath them. The copter's nose dipped as it lifted gently off the ground. Looking through the windshield, which was equipped with night vision, they could see soldiers loading floodlights onto a mid-sized transport ship. Suddenly the helicopter righted and rose rapidly to a manageable altitude, leaving the large boat quickly behind. The man across from them, a stocky, but not fat, seasoned looking soldier called out, "My name is corporal Shelton. Our estimated time to the hospital is three minutes."

Marilynn mouthed the words "Not bad," to Doug.

He nodded and made a mental note of how pale her face looked and how tightly her hand gripped his. The helicopter shuddered and dipped several feet, then leveled off.

"Just an air pocket folks!" shouted the corporal. "Nothing to worry about! Captain Whitaker's a great pilot."

Doug could see Marilynn was having difficulty breathing as she inhaled short, quick breaths and exhaled quick bursts. Their eyes locked and Doug knew from her facial expression that she was stressed.

"We used to call helicopters eggbeaters when I was a kid," he said, trying to make her smile. But she closed her eyes and went silent, locked in thoughts only she would ever know. When she finally opened her eyes she said, "How are you doing?"

"Got a hell of a headache. Other than that I'm okay. Why?"

"I'm concerned."

"You're worried about the blow to my head," he said.

She drew a deep breath and sighed heavily. "You'd better be telling me the truth."

"What do you mean?"

"Everyone who suffered trauma, even the slightest, ended up dying. Yet you suffered several, with no ill effects, and never even had the symptoms. Why haven't you died?"

He shrugged. "I'm tough, I guess."

"And why has Cassandra hung on for so long?" she asked.

He stared hard at her, wondering how could she ask a question like that. He suddenly became anxious, and decided to be honest. "I've had the symptoms on and off since the situation at your house."

"What do you mean, on and off?"

"They seemed to settle down right after I left the station, but are getting worse again, with every passing minute."

"We'll be over land soon," interrupted the corporal. He glanced at Marilynn. "Your wife isn't doing too well, is she?"

"*My wife*'s afraid of flying," said Doug.

Marilynn squeezed his hand tighter and smiled. "The answer has to be something you did at the station," she said, with closed eyes.

"The only thing I did was use the degauser," he said.

"What's that?"

"It's a machine that de-magnifies video tape. That's what screwed up my watch."

"What do you mean?"

"My watch got too close to it, and it drained the battery."

"You said the symptoms got better after you left the station, right?"

"Yeah, so what?"

The helicopter rose and dipped quickly, then groaned as a shudder pulsed through the ship and their bodies. Marilynn gulped hard. After catching her breath she said, "I can't believe it can be this easy."

"What can't?"

"The degauser got too close to the chip in your shoulder and must have caused a short, making it malfunction. That's why you felt good on and off. And that also explains Cassandra."

"We're over land," broke in the corporal. "We should have the hospital in view in just a few moments!"

"Finish your explanation," said Doug.

"Ever since yesterday, I've been trying to figure it out, and you just gave me the clue."

"How?" he asked, wide eyed.

"Remember the trouble Cassandra had with the MRI?"

Doug tilted his head like an inquisitive puppy.

"An MRI could have de-magnetized the chip in her, too."

"But she never completed that MRI."

"That's right. So the chip was only partially de-magnetized. That's why she's been hanging on for so long. But time's running out. We need to get there soon."

* * *

At 12:53, exactly five minutes after their flight off the island began, corporal Shelton said, "We're here." The giant red letters of Coventry General Hospital sat majestically atop an eight-story building in full view. The helicopter spasmed another quick shudder as it began a gradual descent. The tiny red and white strobe lights darted over the ground and grew below them as they got closer.

Corporal Shelton said, "I called ahead and notified the hospital that you were coming."

"Thanks," said Doug.

"Not a problem, but Captain Whitaker has alerted me that we're going to have to land you a safe distance from there, because they don't have a heliport."

"Not a problem," said Doug.

The helicopter rose slightly, banked and circled back. The beating of the blades was more pronounced as it bounced off tall city buildings. Leaning forward in his seat the corporal added, "He spotted an empty parking lot a short ways back, which would be a good place to set us down."

Within seconds they were descending. Their drop slowed as a large empty parking lot belonging to some obscure closed business opened up below them. The pilot skillfully maneuvered the helicopter in two soft circles searching for the right spot, then gently set it on the ground. The engine wound slowly down to idle speed and the beating blades followed in kind, tweeting and whistling.

"The hospital's about six hundred feet from here!" said

the corporal. Doug and Marilynn undid their seatbelts and slid out.

Standing on firm pavement, Marilynn's face immediately filled with color. "Thanks for the lift!" she shouted to the corporal. He saluted, then the blades began turning fiercely and the engine whined and grew louder. Their hair blew out of control from the instant wind tunnel they were standing in.

"Come on!" shouted Doug grabbing her hand. "Let's get out of here!"

Bending low, they hurried off hand-in-hand, until they were at a safe distance. They turned back in time to see the helicopter heading up into the pitch of night. The strobing lights were dwindling dots high in the sky, as the copter raced off to its final destination.

Standing hand clasped, Marilynn said emphatically, "It's time to finish this!"

The hospital wasn't far away and it didn't take long to get there as they hugged the sides of empty office buildings, walking in protective shadows. Several minutes later they were within earshot, peeking from behind a tractor-trailer.

Doug said in a low voice, "Let me scout ahead first."

Marilynn nodded, and he slipped away. She watched him maneuver his way behind a large double oak tree some twenty yards up ahead. He was so secretive that it was doubtful anyone could have seen him, even if they had been watching for him.

He stared towards the well-lit front parking lot. It was packed with cars. A few were even parked up near the front of the hospital where there was a small rotary for dropping off. Three rescue trucks were lined up on one side of the entrance and two ambulances on the other. He saw no sign of movement, so he motioned Marilynn with a wave of his hand and she made her way just as silently to his side.

Putting a finger to his lips, he whispered, "I didn't see anyone. I think it's safe, but keep in mind, it's important that we walk in as if we belong here."

"But we do belong here," said Marilynn softly. "Did you forget I'm on staff here and that your daughter's a patient?"

"You know what I mean," he said in a hushed tone. "If someone sees us sneaking, that'll rouse suspicion."

Marilynn pursed her lips. They were working her territory now.

"Follow me," she said, taking the lead. They stepped out from behind the tree and walked confidently towards the front entrance. They were halfway there when they froze in their tracks. Footsteps and voices sounded close.

"Seems like it's coming from around the corner of the building," said Doug.

They remained frozen, like statues in the kids' game Red Light, waiting patiently to see the faces that went with the voices. Marilynn slipped next to Doug. Their bodies touched and she felt the same tension in him as she felt. He recoiled like a wild cat in the jungle that's about to pounce on unsuspecting prey.

Though not intelligible, the muffled voices came closer. Marilynn forced a noticeable swallow as two dark shadows preceded whoever was about to round the corner. Hands and feet came first, then the rest of the bodies followed, but it was nothing more than a young couple walking arm in arm. All at once they stopped and kissed.

"Let's go," said Doug softly. "It's a couple of lovebirds. Lead the way."

They reached the front in no time, just as the couple disappeared around another corner. Doug was still edgy.

"What's wrong?" Marilynn asked.

"Seems a little odd."

"What does?"

"Two lovers out for a walk, late at night in front of a hospital."

"What're you saying?"

"I don't know. Maybe I'm overreacting and it's probably nothing, but what better way to sweep the perimeter of the hospital while looking out for us?"

"You think it's a set-up?"

He shrugged. "Let's go find my daughter."

"I have an idea," she said, heading off towards one of the rescue trucks.

Confused but intrigued, he followed her to the back of the parked truck. She yanked open one of the double doors and stepped confidently on the bumper at the same time motioning him to stay put, then went inside. He seized the opportunity to walk around to the hospital side of the vehicle. He saw no one, so he continued his surveillance the rest of the way around till he was at the back of the truck again. Marilynn stood wearing a white lab coat and a stethoscope around her neck.

"Take this," she said, handing him a wheelchair.

"Coast is still clear," he said softly, placing it on the ground.

Marilynn grabbed a couple of blankets and jumped down. "Get in," she said. Doug immediately understood and sat in the chair. She placed a blanket over his lap and draped another around his shoulders. "Pull the blanket across your face and hunch forward," she told him.

He pulled both ends to his face, crossing one over the other so it was concealed. Marilynn leaned her face close to his. Rubbing his back affectionately, she whispered, "To quote you, it's *show time*."

From under the covers she heard a muffled, "Be careful. You're not wearing a disguise."

"Don't worry about me," she said in a low voice. "I'll just be a doctor pushing a patient in a wheelchair."

Holding the left handle with one hand, she released a hand brake with the other, then started pushing him up the front cement walkway. As she approached the hospital's entrance, she could see through the sliding doors to the front desk. A nurse she didn't know was on the phone behind the nurse's station. To her right, another nurse she wasn't familiar with stood talking to an older couple. Just normal activity.

When Marilynn and the wheelchair were close enough,

the pneumatic doors slid open with a whoosh sound. She rolled her covered patient in. After passing through a short vestibule she steered the chair right, aiming straight towards the elevators. Leaning down, she whispered, "So far, so good."

When they arrived at the elevators she stopped and pushed the UP button. The light for the fourth floor lit, then the third floor. A tap on her shoulder caught her off guard and she jumped.

"Sorry if I scared you, Doctor," said a female voice from behind. "Can I help you with your patient?"

When Marilynn spun her head back, she saw a nurse taller than herself with broad shoulders and short dark hair, reaching out. "No thanks," she said, holding the handles firmly. "I'm a good friend of the family and I told them I'd bring their father back to his room on the third floor." Turning back towards the elevators, she saw the light for floor one lit.

The nurse came around to face her, blocking her path. "I don't mind," she smiled. "I'm going up to the nurses lounge for my break."

Instantly, Marilynn processed the offer through her brain, almost as fast as a computer doing a simple mathematical equation. What better way to get into the room unnoticed than to have a nurse wheel Doug in? It would be perfect cover.

"Okay," she said, relinquishing control. "But I want to do something nice for you. Let me pay for your coffee break."

"It's a deal," said the nurse. Two metal doors whooshed open to the sound of a chiming bell and the nurse rolled Doug into the elevator saying, "My name is Elizabeth Dougherty, but everyone calls me Liz."

"Nice to meet you Liz," said Marilynn, pressing the button for the third floor. "I've never seen you before - are you new here?"

"I'm from Providence Hospital. We received your call yesterday morning asking for help, so after it slowed down there, I came over with a few others to lend a hand."

"Trust me, Liz, we really appreciate it. It's been hectic and crazy for the past couple of days, on top of already being short staffed because of layoffs."

"Not a problem. It's actually a nice change from working the same old boring job every day back at PH."

"I once felt like that too," said Marilynn, with a chuckle.

Underneath the blankets, Doug smiled broadly as he thought, "Way to work it To-ens."

The elevator shuddered to a stop and the doors opened as a loud bell dinged overhead. Nurse Dougherty rolled Doug out into the hallway and said, "Where to, Doctor?"

"Three ten," she answered. Before following, she glanced back towards the nurses' station, which stood about thirty feet behind them and was brimming with activity. None of the nurses looked familiar. Must be that extra Providence help, she thought. After a few moments, she shrugged and headed up the corridor. As she jogged to catch up, she wondered why all the nurses had the same kind of short haircut. When she overtook Liz and Doug, they were waiting outside room 310.

"I was trying to talk to your patient, Doctor, but he mumbled through the covers and I couldn't understand him."

"He's had a long couple of days and is pretty tired."

"Trust me," said Liz. "I know the feeling."

"I can take him from here," said Marilynn, handing the nurse a dollar bill and taking hold of the wheelchair. "I'm not sure if this will get you a cup of coffee. It's the only bill I have."

"I can't take your last dollar, Doctor, but thanks anyway."

Marilynn took the bill back and said, "Have a good night, Liz, and thanks for the helpful hand. I know you nurses from Providence Hospital have sacrificed a lot by coming to help out. The entire staff of Coventry General thanks you."

The nurse smiled. "Like I said, it was a pleasure." She

then headed off down the corridor, in the opposite direction of the nurses' lounge. Marilynn, confused, watched the woman turn the corner. Doug was getting anxious and shook the wheels to get her attention. "Okay, I get it. Let's go see your daughter."

"Good," said a muffled voice from under the blankets. "I can't breathe in here anymore."

Reaching out her left arm, she held the door open and pushed Doug's chair inside. He yanked the covers off and staggered to his feet, inhaling deep breaths. "Air," he said. "Sweet, ever-loving air."

But Dr. Harwell took no notice. She was already at Cassandra's bedside.

* * *

Standing at another nurse's station, nurse Elizabeth Dougherty stood speaking into a cell phone. "Yes, sir," she said. "They're both in room three ten." After listening for a moment she spoke again. "I didn't get a look at his face, Lieutenant Betters, but I'm certain that's Mr. Talbot in the wheelchair. We're just waiting for your order to move in."

CHAPTER 24

Room 310
1:11am

"My God!" gasped Doug. He wasn't prepared for what he saw. Cassandra was hooked up to several IV drips and an oxygen mask covered her face supplying her lungs with pure air. Wire leads were attached to her ankles and hands, which connected to an electro-cardiograph machine that was printing a steady paper readout of her heartbeat.

Marilynn felt for a pulse. "It's weak," she said. "Look at her color, she's white as a ghost. I'm not going to lie. We may be too late."

Doug stared in disbelief. "Do we have time to give her an MRI to demagnetize the chip the rest of the way?" he asked. His face looked as though he had just gone twelve rounds with the heavyweight boxing champ.

"There isn't enough time. I have to try and save her by other means."

"What can I do?"

"Bring that cart in the corner over to her bed, I may need something from it." She didn't have the heart to tell him it was the defibrillator that she'd need.

Doug staggered towards the cart. When he got there he was so weak that he had to brace himself up by holding onto the side handle. Unaware, Marilynn grabbed the phone off the wall and did an all-page: "Code ninety-nine to West 310," she said in a firm but anxious tone. "I repeat: code ninety-nine to West three ten."

She raced back to Cassandra's bedside. Pulling aside the covers, she took the girl's thin wrist in hers to check for a pulse. "Very weak, but still there!" she called out. Yanking off the oxygen mask, she lowered her ear close to the girl's mouth, listening and feeling for breathing. It too was weak.

"Anything ... else... I," said Doug, collapsing to the floor.

Marilynn slipped the oxygen mask back onto Cassandra's face, then knelt beside him. He didn't look good. His dark, two-day old stubble made his pale face stand out even more, and he was sweating freely from the forehead. The deadly signs.

"Damn it, Doug! Why didn't you tell me the chip was affecting you this much?"

With half-closed eyes, he answered the doctor in a faltering voice, "Wanted... you... to help...Cassandra first."

She got to her feet and grabbed a scalpel off the cart. Squatting beside him, she pierced a hole shoulder high in his shirt. With both hands she ripped the sleeve in a circle till it came free, revealing his bare shoulder and arm. An ache crossed her stomach harder than the tree that she crashed Jennie's car into. The faint beginning of a red mark appeared on his shoulder. The microchip was doing its job.

Placing the scalpel against his skin, she said, "Don't move! I'm cutting it out."

Doug nodded. Despite his low pain tolerance, this was one he wouldn't mind. Besides, he didn't have the strength to stop her. She flicked her wrist clipping away a thin layer of epidermis and the chip. Doug's face started taking on color.

"How do you feel?" she asked.

"Better already," he said. "Do you think that's all we have to do?"

She stared at him with a blank face and said softly, "I don't know."

"Can we do the same thing for Cassandra?" he asked.

"She may be too far along."

"I want to help."

"There's nothing you can do. I've called for a team to assist me and a lot of decisions and complex procedures will happen fast, so I'll need all the space and quiet I can get."

He looked withered and strained. She hugged him hard and whispered, "Hang in there, sweetheart. I'll do all I can."

It had been minutes since she'd called the code, when the door suddenly burst inward. "It's about time you -" but she never finished her sentence. Surrounding them were nurse Dougherty, a second nurse, and three soldiers with guns.

"What the fuck is this?" shouted Doug. A gun pushed sharply into his side.

No one answered. The soldiers and nurses stayed in their intimidating stances, waiting for further orders. They didn't have to wait long before heavy booted footsteps walked towards the doorway and continued into the room. A large muscular man stepped to Doug's side.

"How's your groin?" laughed Doug, recognizing him as one of the thugs that had grabbed him back at the station. A roundhouse right sent Doug to the floor in a heap.

"Enough!" shouted a deep voice, belonging to Lieutenant Betters. He had entered the room unnoticed. Dr. Harwell recognized him. He was one of the idiots who'd tried to run her off the road.

"This is a hospital!" she yelled. "There's no place for that kind of behavior!"

"Respectfully, Doctor, it is," snapped Lieutenant Betters. "By orders of the United States government, you and Mr. Talbot are under arrest for treason."

"Bullshit!" shouted Doug, who had regained his feet. "We've straightened everything out with Major Edwards of the SIA. He cleared us of any wrongdoing."

Betters screwed up his eyes. "I don't take orders from a nobody named Major Edwards. I answer to General Uxbridge!"

"The general's kind of been relieved of duty," said Dr. Harwell, still leaning over Cassandra.

"Now *that's* bullshit!" snapped Betters. "We've had no such communications."

"Don't be stupid!" barked Doug. "Call the SIA, they'll verify our story."

The muscular goon raised his arm in preparation of re-striking Talbot, but Betters blocked it.

"Later," he whispered in the man's ear. "You'll get another chance."

Turning towards Talbot and Dr. Harwell he said, "I'm not wasting any more time on you two, so I'll only say this once. It would be to your benefit to come quietly."

Doug snapped, "That's the second time we've heard that today!"

"I'm running out of patience," said Betters.

"I'm trying to save this little girl's life!" shouted Marilynn. "I don't care what your damn orders are. I need to do my job."

Everyone stared at the lieutenant, waiting for his next move, but he said nothing.

"Are you so coldhearted you'd let an innocent little girl die?" she asked.

The lieutenant didn't flinch.

"For God's sake, Betters, that's my daughter lying there!" said Doug, his voice on the edge of breaking. "Let the doctor save her and I'll do whatever it is you want!"

No one spoke or moved. An unsettling quiet swept across the crowded hospital room, sucking the air out of it. Only the steady beeping of the monitors and the pumping of oxygen broke the agonizing stillness. With every passing moment, the sounds crescendoed until they seemed to blast off the four walls. The soldiers and nurses remained ready, tension and tightness straining their unmoving arms and legs. It was an ache that might provoke someone into making a mistake.

"These nurses are trained in emergency medical procedures," said Betters. "They can take over for you."

"They are *not* doctors!" snapped Marilynn. "*I am*! Right now, I'm the only one in this room who has any chance of saving this child's life!"

Betters stayed silent, contemplating his decision. He needed to choose his words wisely and wasn't about to rush.

"I can't wait any longer," Marilynn said, pulling back the bedcovers, her mouth set in grim determination. Betters said nothing.

"Give me a scalpel!" she barked to Doug. The cart was full of them. He reached down and hesitated.

"Which one?"

"Pick one," she said brusquely, while pulling Cassandra's shirtsleeve back to reveal the girl's right shoulder. A small mark appeared above her vaccination, much bigger and a darker red than Doug's.

He chose the closest knife and handed it to her. Seeing the discoloration, he said, "I thought you only saw that on dead people."

Marilynn placed the scalpel on Cassandra's shoulder, just under the blemish. Applying slight pressure, she flicked up and out, slicing out a small portion of skin and the chip. Looking at Talbot, she said straight-faced, "That's right."

Suddenly there was a piercing monotone pitch. The electrocardiograph machine had stopped. Marilynn glanced at the readout and then at the monitor – it had flat-lined.

She felt for a pulse. Nothing.

She yanked off the oxygen mask and lowered her head above the girl's mouth. Feeling no breathing she said, "I need to do CPR." Moving with precision, she placed her left hand under Cassandra's neck, then her right hand on the girl's forehead, pushing it back so her chin pointed straight up. She pinched the girl's nose closed, took a deep breath and covered the girl's mouth, giving four quick, gentle breaths. Cassandra's chest heaved with each push of air.

She listened – there was nothing.

Her eyes were wide when she looked to Doug. "Get a

watch and start timing. Call out the minutes so I can hear them. We only have about four."

"Give me yours," said Talbot, grabbing Betters' arm.

Betters pulled the twist-o-flex from his wrist and handed it over.

"Are either of you OR nurses?" Marilynn shouted towards Dougherty.

The woman looked to Betters for help.

"Well, are you?"

Betters nodded approval.

"We're both trained in OR and ER," replied Liz, stepping forward. "What can I do?"

"I need you to assist," said Marilynn.

The second nurse came over and asked what she could do.

"Check the electrocardiograph machine and make sure it's functioning properly," Marilynn ordered.

The woman, an army nurse in hospital disguise, restrapped the leads to the girl's wrists and ankles, and checked the monitor to see if it was operative.

"One minute!" shouted Doug.

Marilynn ripped open Cassandra's hospital johnny and placed her middle and index fingers on the lower edge of the girl's rib cage, then began tracing the ribs up to the notch where it met the breastbone. She put the heel of her other hand next to the fingers, right on the breastbone, and quickly removed the two fingers. Keeping her elbows locked she pushed down several inches and counted, "One and two and three." She did fifteen of these compressions in approximately ten seconds.

Nurse Liz checked for a pulse and breathing. "Nothing!" she shouted.

Marilynn lifted Cassandra's head and repeated the four quick breaths of mouth-to-mouth, then jumped back into position to do compressions. "One and two and three!" Fifteen compressions in ten seconds, then let the nurse check for any response. She could feel her own heart racing inside her chest.

Once again, the nurse known as Liz put her ear next to Cassandra's mouth, listening and feeling for signs of life. Frustrated, she reached across the girl's neck and felt the carotid. Her face looked pained as she shook her head.

"Two minutes!" shouted an anxious voice.

Most of the soldiers had crowded close to bedside.

"Stand back!" yelled Marilynn.

The monitor continued its piercing death pitch.

She drew a deep breath, then repeated the four quick breaths and fifteen compressions. Nurse Liz leaned down a third time. Marilynn didn't need a shake of the head to know that it wasn't working. She looked at the cardiograph machine. It was still flatlined.

"Come on Cassandra, breathe!" she shouted, repeating the breaths and compressions.

Nurse Liz did her best to find a pulse, but again came up empty.

Turning to the unnamed nurse, Marilynn yelled, "Give me one milligram of Epinephrine."

"I'm not an anesthesiologist, Doctor," said Liz, "but could that be too strong a dose for a child?"

"Three minutes!"

Marilynn sighed loudly and deeply. "You're right, Elizabeth. I'm used to dealing with adults in these situations. Make it only half a milligram."

The nurse handed her the syringe of adrenaline. Marilynn shoved the needle directly into the child's heart, pushing the plunger and liquid straight in. She was hoping the adrenaline would stimulate it.

Unrelenting, she repeated the CPR all over again. She was expending a lot of energy and it was physically taking a toll on her. Her arms were leaden and her compressions had less energy behind them. The monitor remained unchanged.

"Get the defibrillator ready!" she commanded.

Sweat flowed down her face. Time was running out and she had to do something drastic, or risk losing any chance of reviving the girl. Glancing at Doug, she saw a lost and troubled face. He stood off to the side, hands together as if in prayer. She wanted to go over and put her arms around him and tell him everything would be okay. But she had work to do.

Switching focus to nurse Dougherty, she snapped, "Set it to three hundred joules."

The nurse turned the machine on and set the dial to the requested setting. Marilynn knew by the woman's movements the past couple of minutes that she was skilled.

Handing the paddles over, she said, "All set, Doctor."

"Four minutes!" shouted Doug, his voice cracking.

"Clear!" she yelled.

After everyone backed away, she hit the button to activate the paddles, which were pressed firmly against the girl's bare chest. Cassandra's body convulsed upward like a tossed rag doll and settled back on the bed as limply as one. The electrocardiograph's needle jumped several times, then flatlined again. The readout paper had a couple of squiggly lines, then went blank. The tone continued.

"Four hundred joules!" shouted Marilynn.

Nurse Liz set the new voltage.

"Clear!"

This time the jolt lifted Cassandra high off the bed, as if she were possessed by a demon in a bad horror movie.

"I think we've got something!" shouted the nameless nurse. "There's a reading, very weak, but it's there." The cardiograph needle was jumping and registering a rhythm that was growing stronger with every heartbeat.

Nurse Liz felt Cassandra's carotid and quickly a smile broke through the tension in her face. "It's there and it's getting stronger!" she shouted.

The room erupted into loud cheers.

Doug stepped to Cassandra's side and whispered through tears, "Daddy's here, honey. Can you hear me? Can you open your eyes?" He caught his breath, then said, "Hey! Remember what I said this morning? You're not getting out of doing your homework that easily. Come on, honey. I'm right here." He knew he was rambling, but he didn't care. Joy surged through his body and tears ran down his face. He took her hands in his right hand and lightly stroked them with his other hand. Cassandra stirred, drew a deep breath, and slowly opened tired eyelids.

"I heard you the first time, Daddy," Cassandra whispered, with the slightest trace of a smile.

Doug laughed loudly, suddenly releasing all the pent up anguish that had built up inside. Putting his arms around her, he pulled her tight against him. Marilynn also cried tears of joy, a strange contrast from the tears she almost suffered. Nurse Dougherty moved over and put her hand on her shoulder. "Nice job, Doctor," she said warmly. The other nurse stood beside her too, nodding in agreement.

"Thank you, both," said Marilynn with a smile that stretched her face. "You were a big help. I'll make sure your superiors are informed."

"Yes, a very nice job, Doctor," mocked Betters. Everyone had forgotten about him. "I believe we have a little bit of unsettled business. Now if you and Mr. Talbot would be so kind as to accompany us."

Lowering his head to Cassandra, Doug said softly, "Honey, I have to go away for a little while, but I promise I'll be back as soon as I can."

All at once the door burst open and more soldiers with guns rushed in with Major Edwards leading the way. The room was suddenly overcrowded with military.

"Are we glad to see you!" said Marilynn.

"We have everything under control," said Lieutenant Betters. "We've contained the prisoners and don't need any assistance."

But the new soldiers remained with their guns pointed at Betters and *his* men. The major, his right arm in a sling, stepped forward until he was standing next to Betters. "These people are no longer under suspicion, Lieutenant. You and your soldiers need to stand down your weapons, and are to come with me back to the base for questioning."

"What sort of questioning!" said Betters in a raised voice. "We're only following orders."

"Those orders were rescinded over an hour ago," said the major, "when base command notified you. You knew full well what was going on."

"My orders come from a higher source," snapped Betters. "I don't answer to the likes of you!"

The major's eyebrows raised and his eyes grew wide. "Those of you under the lieutenant's command, place your weapons on the floor and stand down!" he commanded sternly.

Marilynn slid over next to Doug and he held her tight around the waist, while holding Cassandra's hand. The lieutenant's soldiers and nurses immediately did as they were told and metal weapons clanked as they hit the floor.

"If you would do the same, Lieutenant," commanded the major.

Betters quickly pointed the gun at his *own* head. Two soldiers stepped forward and placed their weapons against his sides.

"It's over!" said Edwards.

Betters sneered.

"Uxbridge doesn't care what happens to you or anyone else," said Doug. "He only cares about his own ass." He squeezed Marilynn and Cassandra tighter. The odd laugh that escaped Betters sent a chill up everyone's spine and the wild expression on his face, betrayed the struggle in his mind.

The room was tense and would have been dead silent if not for breathing. Betters' neurotic eyes surveyed the room, taking in everyone and everything. The long, uncertain moment ended when the gun slipped from his hand and rattled onto the floor.

There was a collective sigh.

"Take all of them to the van," said the major to his men.

The room emptied quickly. Only Major Edwards remained behind.

Facing Doug and Marilynn, he said, "The President and

the United States government apologize for the inconvenience you have encountered the past several days. Measures will be taken to prosecute those responsible. On a personal note, Mr. Talbot, I'm delighted to see that your daughter is doing well."

"Thanks to you, major," said Doug pumping his hand, "we got here in time. I'll be forever grateful."

"From what I saw," said Edwards, "it wasn't a moment too soon."

"That begs the question," said Doug, "How'd you know to come here?"

The major drew a deep breath. "On my trip back to the mainland, I received a message that Betters hadn't returned several calls to command center. This was his last known position, so when our transport reached land, I headed straight here."

Marilynn said, "Major, we discovered an antidote. We'll need help getting it out to the public?"

"Washington knows all about the effects of magnetism on the chip, Doctor. Most of your movements the past few days were known to the SIA. Our Washington scientists had figured it out yesterday and have devised a simple way of deactivating the chip. They're already administering it."

"So we really didn't find the antidote?" said Doug.

"Sure you did, Mr. Talbot. It was only through your efforts and the doctor's that we even knew there was a problem in the first place." Turing to Cassandra he said, "You should be very proud of your mom and dad, little girl."

Marilynn smiled.

Cassandra laughed and said, "Oh, I am!"

Saluting smartly, the major spun on his heels and left.

Doug pulled Marilynn into his arms and they embraced in a deep and passionate kiss.

Cassandra laughed even louder.

EPILOGUE

Cassandra Talbot raced excitedly around the playground, laughing and playing with a few of her friends on swings and slides. Her mom and dad, Doug and Marilynn Talbot, sat reading the daily *Rhode Island Gazette*. The front page was adorned with a half-page picture of the couple receiving an award from the president at the White House. The caption read: Local heroes receive the *Distinguished Citizen Award* from President Newman.

They read the story together out loud: "Douglas M. Talbot and Marilynn To-ens Talbot received the Distinguished Citizen Award in a brief ceremony at the White House yesterday."

Marilynn playfully tapped Doug on the shoulder. "You told them my middle name is *To-ens!*" she shouted.

"You don't have a real middle name, so I thought that could be your adopted one."

"Are you crazy!" she yelled, but she couldn't stay serious and soon broke out into laughter. "Actually it's kind of cute, and it does have a lot of sentimental meaning. I guess I'll keep it. My question to you, though, is what does the 'M' stand for in *your* name?"

"None of your business, that's what!"

"Come on! I let you pick out one for me, the least you can do is tell me yours."

"It doesn't stand for anything!"

"Is it Michael? I like that name."

"No!"

"How about Mark? Mark's a great name."

"No! Don't ask me again!"

"Is it Mitchell? That's a sexy name."

"If I tell you, do you promise not to laugh?"

"I'm a distinguished doctor. I think I'm beyond anything as childish as laughing at your middle name. So what is it?"

"Marion!"

"I'm sorry, did you say Marion?"

"Yeah! Remember your promise!"

She held in a smirk for as long as she could, then finally exploded into an uncontrollable fit of laughter.

"You promised!" said Doug, tickling her under the ribs.

Marilynn fell back on to thick green grass, and rolled side to side as he tickled her harder.

"Okay! Okay! I give," she relented after a few minutes of torture.

Catching her breath, she looked up at him and calmly said, "I'm curious. Why did your parents decide to name you Marion?"

"My father wanted a boy with the name Douglas. My mother wanted a girl with the name Marion, so they compromised and called me Douglas Marion Talbot."

"Well, I for one am glad they had a boy," said Marilynn, pulling him down to her and embracing him in a long, passionate kiss.

Coventry General Hospital
Later that morning

Lindsey Palmer pulled into the employee's parking lot of Coventry General Hospital for her first shift working daytime. As she got out of her car, she grabbed a couple of magazines off the passenger seat, just in case it was a slow, boring day.

PEACEFUL ENDINGS

National Television
Prime time
Five days later

President Donald Newman stepped in front of a microphone and adjusted it to mouth level in preparation of speaking live before a national television audience on all the major networks. His straight back shoulders and erect posture fostered the impression that his news would be good. As he glanced down at his notes, his captive audience knew that he was pondering the right moment to speak.

Finally, he stared straight into the cameras with focused eyes and resolute face, a ploy he used when making a point he wanted accepted at face value, or when trying to put a spin on things so they sounded better or worse than warranted. He knew how to play the game: tell the people what they want to hear, and avoid bothering them with superfluous facts. That's how you get seventy-five percent of the popular vote.

He cleared his throat.

"Ladies and Gentlemen of the United States, I want you to bear with me for just a moment." The president glanced down again, adding another strategically placed pause. His face was wrought with anguish. It was the look that anyone would have when faced with divulging painful news to a friend.

"I want to speak to you tonight as an ordinary person, not as your president." He waved a bunch of papers he held in his right hand. "I was sitting in the Oval office going over a speech my press secretary, Robert Baker, wrote for me to read to you tonight. It really is a very fine speech. But as I sat there skimming through it, I realized you deserve more than a well thought out rationalization from my press secretary." The president flung the papers into the air and they scattered over the floor. Looking at the strewn mess, he remarked, "I used to get in trouble for leaving my bedroom like this when I was a kid." The room broke into strained laughter. He really knew how to work it.

"The country and the world," he continued, his voice rising a notch, "want to know, and quite frankly deserve to know, what initiated the events of the past few days." He hesitated a long moment again, and only the clicking and whirring of cameras broke the silence in the media room. Pointing towards the television cameras he continued, "As I said, I want to talk with you person-to person, not as the president of the United States."

Staring into the plethora of media he said, "There were important reasons so many of you voted for me in the last election: my integrity and honesty, to name a couple. My ability to get the job done was another." He put his hand to his mouth and cleared his throat: "We recently went through a grim time in our nation's history. People with the best intentions back in our parents' generation, and for many of us our grandparents' era, tried to do something humane and beneficial for future generations. They wanted to stop needless pain and suffering. I don't know about you, but I think that was very admirable on their part."

The president paused momentarily to catch his breath. "Unfortunately, there were a few people who tried to use it for the wrong reasons. They took something that, although morally wrong, was meant to do good, and changed its intended purpose. Their callous alteration caused a serious defect and a national epidemic to our generation and our lifetime." He lowered his head for a moment, then looked up. "We lost a lot of innocent and extremely special people from our lives," he said, choking on his words. His eyes teared and he said softly, "I, too, felt loses dear to me."

Stiffening, he looked toward the cameras as if he were talking directly to each person watching and said, in a voice that rose louder with each word, "But you also voted for me, because I won't stand for shenanigans." Slamming his fist on the podium he shouted, "When I see wrong done to the American people, I'm - going - to - take - action!"

He shifted his weight to the other side and went on. "I placed my faith in some important people within the Government structure: these people failed me and in essence they failed you. Those people have some serious explaining to do before a grand jury. It will take time to figure out all the guilty parties, because there are many people who are to blame. But rest assured, those people will be identified and dealt with severely."

The president drew a deep breath, then sighed. "I wish I could say something that would make everyone's lives better. I wish there was some special presidential wand that I could wave to reverse bad things that happen. But there isn't, and I can't. And it saddens me that I can't do more than what I'm doing. If I could only be *Superman* and swoop in and make it all right!" He hesitated briefly, then continued, "As president, there are powers that I do have, and I hope that you have faith in me to do the right thing once again. Good night and God Bless."

He turned and walked slowly away, while an FBI agent started picking up the mess of papers. No one could see they were blank.

Six months later
9:30am
B.J. Stockton Military Base, Virginia

A military doctor goes into a walk-in refrigerator and picks up a bottle marked Gov 09, Experimental Bullet Repellent – version three. He sticks a needle in and draws two cc's of a cloudy solution, then returns to a small medical room, where a soldier sits patiently on an examination table.

He dabs the man's shoulder with a cotton swab moist with alcohol, then jabs the needle in.

"This flu shot should keep you safe," he says.

The soldier jumps down and thanks him, then leaves the room.

A side door opens and a large muscular man with salt and pepper hair walks in.

"What do you think about this batch, Matt?" he asks in a deep voice.

"I think we're getting close, General Uxbridge. They're not dying so quickly now."

LOOK FOR MICHAEL K. TUCKER'S
NEXT TECHNOTHRILLER

HISTORY MAN

Coming in early 2010

Trauma specialist, Dr. Marilynn Harwell Talbot, is summoned by the SIA to B.J. Stockton Military Base, Virginia, to help an amnesia patient. She eventually finds out that he is one of several time travelers who go through time collecting snippets of history for students in the future.

The United States government is extremely interested in learning how to travel back in time. It would be a valuable device in helping to correct previous military mistakes, and a way to put handpicked people in positions of power. A foreign government also learns of History Man, and plots to get their hands on the man who can teach them how to alter history in order to change the face of the world, by achieving power, money, and dominance.

After gaining History Man's trust, Marilynn decides to sneak him off the base and back to her home in Rhode Island, so she can help him get back to his own time. Avoiding the SIA and the foreign faction at every turn, adds to the dilemma of getting the traveler back to his own time before his window to return closes, or else his existence will have never happened.

* * *

"What's your name?"

He didn't respond.

"I'm Dr. Marilynn Harwell Talbot. "So who are you?"

There was a long silent pause. Finally the patient looked up with sad deep blue eyes and said, "Day."

"First or last name?"

"Last!"

"Do you have a first?"

"Sunni, with an 'I'."

"You're kidding? Your full name is Sunni Day?"

He looked at her with contempt.

"How'd that happen?"

"My family was a product of the sixties."

"The nineteen sixties *were* a crazy time."

"My sixties, not yours."

"What do you mean?"

"Twenty-one sixties, not nineteen sixties.

"That'd make you over two hundred years old."

"I'm thirty-one."

"Explain."

"I'm from the twenty-second century.

"You've watched too many *Star Trek* movies."

"What are they?"

"Captain Kirk - Mister Spock?"

He stared blankly.

After an awkward silence he said, "Go ahead, laugh at my name. Everyone does."

"I won't. I kind of have a problem my with my own."

"What do you mean?"

"My name is Marilynn, with two 'N's."

"Why is that a problem?"

"Most people omit the second 'N'"

"Ahhh! That's important to you?"

She shrugged. "My husband's nickname for me is To-ens – meaning two 'N's."

There was another long pause.

"My best friends last name is Hed. His first name is Dick."

Both laughed till it hurt.

"Tell me about the twenty-second century."

"Don't mock me."

"I'm not. I really want to know."

"It's not much different than now. Just a lot less pain and suffering."

"How'd you get to this time?"

"A space-time portal in the fifth dimension."

"I loved their music."

"Huh"

"You're too young to remember. That was the name of a singing group in the sixties and seventies."

Sunni shrugged.

"Why are you here?"

"That can be answered several ways."

"Give me several reasons."

He kicked the ground with his shoe a few times and cleared his throat.

"I'm what's call a *History Man*."

"What's a History Man?"

"Do you want me to explain or are you going to keep interrupting?"

"Sorry!"

"There's at least one thing your time and mine have in common."

"What's that?"

"Women still interrupt."

"Careful! Doesn't matter what time you're from. Women have been liberated for a quite a while and you're treading on serious water, mister!"

"Now, I'm sorry."

"Accepted. Go on."

"I travel around through time collecting visuals and documenting major history events for our schools."

"What happened to all the history books?"

"Books are outdated. They're no longer used. We save on the environment. And neither is what you call video and film. Over time they've either worn away or have been trashed or lost. They became obsolete. I think you can still find them in museums, though."

"Your job is to document major history events to be used in schools?"

"Yes."

"Why?"

"It was felt that if kids could see the actual event as it unfolded, they would understand it better. Maybe even have an educated opinion about it."

"Name one you've seen."

"Titanic."

"You witnessed the sinking of the Titanic?"

"I was there the night it happened."

"Right where?"

"I was on the bow when it hit the iceberg."

"If you knew it was going to happen, then why didn't you warn someone?"

"I collect history. I don't change it."

"A lot of innocent people died that night. You should've done something."

"Think about it. Taking evasive actions could make it worse."

"Saving lives isn't a good thing?"

"That's not the point."

"What is the point?"

"Altering history could have an adverse affect."

Marilynn was puzzled.

Sunni drew a breath then said, "Think about the people that died that night. Suppose there were several that, if they had survived would have gone on to be serial killers, or others that went on to become politicians that got bills passed that changed life drastically from what we know today."

"I still don't get your point."

"If all the people that were destined to die that night had survived, then many other lives outside their life span, would have been affected in some way. They may have ended in a tragic death before their scheduled time."

He stood and stretched, grunting and moaning like a giant bear from a winter's snooze.

"For every change you make in time," he continued, "there is an adverse affect on some other innocent person or persons lives. It's a ripple affect. You can't change or alter destiny."

"Not every change has to end badly."

"You're saying it's okay to play God and choose who dies and who doesn't?"

Marilynn snapped to with a jolt. "I understand," she said. "I've dealt with that kind of mentality before."

"So you believe me?"

"This *is* pretty far fetched."

"For your time and place in history it is. But I come from the future where life is dramatically different than yours and this is commonplace."

"Like I said, this is farfetched to me."

"What do you think the people of 1700's Salem would think if you went there and told them about airplanes?"

"They'd think I was crazy."

"Probably want to burn you at the stake."

"I see your point."

"So you believe me?"

"I'll keep an open mind."

Printed in the United States
123824LV00010B/55/P

9 781432 727390